NO QUARTER!

Musketry crackled, lead balls slapping the schooner's deck. British marines were seen on the enemy stern and quarter galleries, their red coats bright against the broken timbers, making targets of themselves in reply to the deadly broadsides . . .

"Brave men, Captain," Clowes murmured, standing near Gideon Markham, sword in his hand. A man nearby spun to the deck as a musketball clipped his shoulder.

"I do not want them admired, I want them dead," Gideon said.

THE YANKEE

Volume II in the Action-Packed Saga
PRIVATEERS AND GENTLEMEN

**THE
PRIVATEERS AND GENTLEMEN
SERIES**

The Privateer: Volume I
The Yankee: Volume II

PRIVATEERS AND GENTLEMEN

THE YANKEE

Jon Williams

A DELL BOOK

Published by
Dell Publishing Co., Inc.
1 Dag Hammarskjold Plaza
New York, New York 10017

Dell ® TM 681510, Dell Publishing Co., Inc.

ISBN: 0-440-19779-1

Printed in the United States of America
First printing—May 1981

HISTORICAL NOTE:

For dramatic purposes I have compressed into one day the three-day siege and attack of Fort Bowyer (12–15 September, 1814), in which Major William Lawrence and 130 men held off 130 marines and 600 Indians, supported by a squadron of five British warships, inflicting a loss of 232 casualties, including the sloop of war *Hermes* (20), suffering only eight casualties in return. The actual battle for the fort occurred much as described here. The engagement at the Passe Maronne, and the ships and men involved, is fictional; in all probability the water was too shallow to support the action herein described.

THE YANKEE

1

EMBAYED

When he saw the enemy squadron drop from the wind, their studding sails blossoming as they raced to get a clear look at what some alert lookout had seen, Captain Gideon Markham, of Portsmouth, New Hampshire, knew that his privateer was probably doomed. The British squadron consisted of a seventy-four of the line, a frigate, and a sloop of war, with over a hundred guns altogether and perhaps a thousand men; while the *General Sullivan* was a New England schooner with thirteen guns and a crew of sixty, embayed by an offshore wind in a Cuban inlet, and moored alongside two captured British prizes—Gideon would have abandoned his schooner and his prizes there and then, but it was low tide and the British would not be able to get their vessels over the bar until after dark; the two-decker wouldn't be able to get over in any case. Gideon controlled the frustration and rage he'd felt when he'd first seen those studding sails sheeting home. He had time. Cutting himself a plug of tobacco, Gideon Markham chewed meditatively and studied the enemy through his glass. If he were that enemy captain, he thought, he'd give the lookout a guinea.

Unquestionably they were British. Never mind that they were in Spanish—and therefore neutral—waters; so was *General Sullivan,* and on an illegal mission to boot. If the British attacked in neutral waters, Gideon could scarcely appeal to any Spanish court. The Spaniards, though neutral in the fight between Britain and the American commonwealth, were nevertheless allied with the British against the French armies that had invaded Spain; the Spanish found it politically expedient to overlook the occasional British irregularity.

Anger flashed through Gideon, and he fought to control

it. *Helpless.* He had been helpless too often in his lifetime. *He hath enclosed my ways with hewn stone, he hath made my paths crooked* . . . Gideon fought down his despair. All travail had its purpose. He spat his tobacco over the lee rail and turned to his first officer.

"Ye will go ashore, Mr. Harris," he said. "Find the fastest horse ye may and ride to Rio Lagartos. Ye will carry to Don Esteban a letter. I will give ye that letter in five minutes. Be ready."

"Aye aye, Captain," said Alexander Harris. He was in his shirt-sleeves and in no condition to pay a visit. He ran his fingers through his shock of wheat-blond hair and turned hastily to pick out a boat's crew. Gideon returned to his glass and his observations of the enemy. Behind him he heard Harris run down the aft scuttle for a quick wash and change of clothes.

The British frigate was in the lead, a fine, fast-lined ship, her yellowed canvas taut as it bellied out with the following wind, her studding sail booms spread wide like the claws of a pouncing eagle. As fast as the frigate looked, Gideon knew his own *General Sullivan* could show the enemy a clean pair of heels in any wind—but he was anchored in a Cuban bay, trapped. *He was unto me as a bear lying in wait and as a lion in secret places. He hath made me desolate.* Gideon grit his teeth as the despairing verses welled up from his mind. *The Lord will not cast off forever,* he reminded himself firmly. From the frigate's fore shrouds he caught a wink of light, twice repeated. Gideon's lips twitched in the beginnings of an ironic smile: the British were studying him as intently as he investigated them. He swept his glass to the shore, to where the sandbar met the palms of the forest's edge.

"*Mr. Willard!*" he called.

George Willard's eyes were an intense, absorbed black; his dark hair was worn in the old style, unfashionably long and caught in a queue behind. The second officer was a Gay Head Indian from Martha's Vineyard, one of the small, able tribe of American natives brought up from the cradle to sail upon the breast of the sea. More white than Indian, and more sailor than either, George Willard had been at sea from the age of six, his profession chosen for him by generations of island ancestors, as had been his Christian name and his Congregational religion.

"I want ye to go aboard *Linnet*—I understand the prize has two long twelves?"

"Aye, Captain."

"Move them to yonder point and set up a battery; take ye powder and shot. Ye may have the pinnace. Take care to see that the battery may be hidden from the enemy."

"Aye aye, Captain."

"Have it done by tonight."

Willard's slight hesitation before his "aye aye" did not go unnoticed. Gideon pounced upon that hesitation like a lion in wait.

"I do not give orders lightly; I expect that battery built by nightfall," he said. "Ye may have ten men. Ye will stay with the guns; if the enemy crosses the bar, fire on them. Ye will kill as many Englishmen as ye can."

"Aye aye, Captain," George Willard assented. He turned to gather his men. Gideon did not spare the battery another thought, for he knew that *he* could have set up the battery before nightfall—therefore Willard could, or would be answerable. Gideon did not consider his orders subject to question or himself obligated to explain the reasoning behind them. He picked up his telescope once more and turned it on the enemy: the frigate was drawing nearer, less than two miles offshore. He could see the white commission pendant sailing out from her mainpeak with the red St. George's cross. *British.* As if there were any doubt.

Forward of *General Sullivan's* mainmast Gideon could dimly hear Browne, the bosun, commencing an anecdote in his high-pitched Briton's voice, the general theme of which was the dull-wittedness of Englishmen in general and naval officers in particular. Browne, a candlemaker from Bristol, had been pressed into the Royal Navy and had fought at Copenhagen and Trafalgar; but he now maintained, as frequently and as loudly as he was allowed, that after the death of Nelson there was no man left in the British fleet who could command his allegiance. One night in Plymouth he'd slipped over the side and swam to an American ship. Now he fought his former countrymen and would probably be hanged if caught. As far as Gideon could tell, Browne wasn't much bothered by either fact. He had volunteered to be a privateer; there was no compulsion in the American service. He was an American seaman now and carried his citizenship papers to prove it.

Gideon considered cutting himself another plug of tobacco, but resolved to resist the inclination as long as he could. The British frigate was flying signals; Gideon could not make them out, but the ship-sloop was repeating them, and the seventy-four answering. There were hours yet before any hard decisions would have to be made.

He returned his telescope to the rack and walked to the quarterdeck scuttle, descended the companionway, and walked the short, narrow corridor to his little cabin. The place was small and tidy, the furniture partly built by the ship's carpenter—there were no paintings or costly rugs, and the service was pewter rather than silver. Gideon placed his beaver hat on the little table, reached his sword down from its peg, and laid it next to the hat. Standing at his desk, he wrote a note for Harris to carry ashore and sent it up via his steward. Then he knelt stiffly by the bunk, clasped his hands, bent his head, and began to pray.

2

AT PRAYER

As he bent over his bed, the privateer's form was echoed by the shaving mirror on the wall, and it reflected him in shades of brown: his face had been burned very brown by the sun and showed every one of its thirty-four hard-fought years; his clothes were a deep brown, and though neat, were modest to the point of plainness. His hair was brown, lightened a bit by the sun and cut in the modern vogue, short and combed forward over the temples; long side-whiskers advanced down either jawline and were also in the time's dashing fashion, but on Gideon they looked more severe than gallant.

It was August of 1813; he had commanded *General Sullivan* for more than a year. The year had seen disaster for the young America on land—one entire army surrendered along with the entire Northwest, and other armies beaten or driven back in humiliated defeat. Only on the sea had the United States been able to inflict a surprising series of defeats on British arms: *Constitution* had defeated and sunk both *Guerriere* and *Java*, *Wasp* had captured *Frolic*, *Hornet* had sunk *Peacock*, and the frigate *United States*, on which Gideon's cousin Favian Markham served as lieutenant, had not only captured *Macedonian* but brought the British frigate home to an American port. The victories had stunned Europe and heartened a bitter and divided America, but they would not win the war. Gideon Markham knew what would.

As a good New England Federalist and an admirer of Congressman Josiah Quincy of Massachusetts, Gideon looked upon the war with suspicion. He would rather have fought the French—assuming the United States was to fight anybody at all—for the French had disregarded the rights

of neutrals as callously as had the British, and Gideon
would rather have had the strength of the mightiest navy in
the world on the side of America instead of against it. But
war had been declared against George III rather than Bonaparte, and therefore Gideon felt it must be the will of God
that England fight the United States. And as it was the will
of the Lord, Gideon had become a privateer.

Privateering was a Markham family tradition, for Gideon's father, uncles, and grandfather had all in their own
time been privateers. Privateering was by now the only
profession for a New England seaman that could hope to
show a profit. With luck Gideon might be able both to do
the Lord's work and bring himself out of the endless condition of debt into which the disastrous Non-Intercourse Acts
had plunged him.

For almost an entire year *General Sullivan* and other
American privateers had virtually wiped out the British
West Indian trade; they had laid naval seige to Jamaica,
and the British had utterly failed to produce a ship capable
of catching the swift, big-sparred American clippers. British reinforcements had made the pickings in the vicinity of
Jamaica a good deal less easy—even if they couldn't catch
the privateers, they could recapture the prizes—and so
General Sullivan had been forced to sail farther abroad in
search of prey. But Gideon knew that privateering was the
only hope America had of winning the war. The United
States had a long, irregular seacoast, hard to blockade efficiently; England's trade was spread thinly and was often
unprotected by the Royal Navy cruisers, which were con-
centrated off Europe's coast. England was a merchant nation, and her trade was vulnerable; if enough ships were
taken, if Consols dropped thirty points and forced the resignation of the government, if enough cargoes were auctioned off in American ports, and if the insurance under-
writers were afraid to guarantee cargoes except at twenty
or thirty percent, then England would be willing to make
peace.

And Captain Gideon Markham, privateer and deacon,
was prepared to squeeze the British as hard as he could
and make himself the richer thereby. Two weeks before the
British squadron had appeared off Cuba, Gideon had cap-

tured three prizes at once off Anguilla, filled with drygoods and plantation equipment destined for Jamaica. Gideon had filled *General Sullivan*'s hold with the goods from the smallest vessel and set it free along with his prisoners; the other two craft he took in company.

The British presence made it risky to take captures back to an American port, and Gideon thought he'd had a better idea. He knew a Spanish planter in Cuba, one who owed him a favor from before the war. Don Esteban de Velasco y Anaquito had riches enough and influence enough to dispose of Gideon's captured cargoes, and at good prices in a Cuba desperate for European goods. Velasco's principal plantation, Rio Lagartos, was also situated comfortably near the mouth of a river where the cargoes might be easily landed. Gideon would not dare to enter any Spanish port; the Spanish authorities had been seizing and condemning any American privateer entering their jurisdiction, and although the seizures were illegal, the American government, hard-pressed by the British, had no hope of enforcing any demands.

A small, *private* arrangement was what Gideon had proposed: *General Sullivan* and her two prizes had been taken over the bar and anchored in the center of the little bay where they could be guarded and kept safe. Gideon had gone ashore by boat. Don Esteban had been friendly and interested but had been in no hurry. They had haggled for two days, ever nearing agreement. Now, the morning of the third day, a British squadron had appeared.

This called for assistance from God Almighty; and so Gideon prayed.

It was Gideon's opinion that the Lord rarely allowed his children to be beset by difficulties but that he also created opportunities to be exploited. That belief had been sorely tried during the Embargo, but Gideon had managed to maintain it; and now Gideon attempted, through urgent and systematic prayer, to discover any such opportunities the Lord may have left within his reach.

He had no doubt that the British would attack. The situation was obvious: an American-built schooner armed as a privateer, with two captures, found anchored quietly in Spanish waters, protected by a bar and low tide. The Spaniards were in England's debt—Wellington's army was even now attempting to drive the French off Spanish soil. The Spanish authorities would not interfere.

The tide was not great here, two or three feet at its highest, but it would not be as safe for the British vessels to venture over the bar until the tide was in their favor. Gideon would not face attack until after nightfall. But when it came, would the attack be delivered by boats, or by the ships of war themselves?

Lord, let me see thy path clearly, Gideon prayed, but somewhere in the back of his mind was the thought, *What would Malachi do?* Malachi Markham, his uncle, was the most spectacularly successful privateer of his family, and perhaps of his generation; Gideon had been raised on legends of Malachi's genius and conquests, and a copy of Malachi's biography by his former first officer, John Maddox, lay in Gideon's sea chest next to his prayer book and bible.

"The greatest natural sailor I have ever seen," Josiah Markham, Gideon's father and Malachi's brother, had said; and from Josiah that was no mean praise. The praise had been echoed by Malachi's former brother-in-arms, many of whom Gideon had known around Portsmouth in his youth: Captain Andrew Keith, John Maddox, the blaspheming and free-living Finch Martin—all agreed on Malachi's skill, charm, and brilliance. Malachi had gone barefoot and bearded in an age when merchants affected gentility; he had fought a duel, and in battle recklessly exposing himself to danger; he was impious, profane, and indiscreet; he could judge the wind within half a point and steer his privateer by the seat of his pants; and his love for an English noblewoman was a family legend. Josiah and Malachi had cruised together for years. They had destroyed the British frigate *Melampe* and captured a stunning bag of prize ships, including a thirty-gun Indiaman; but Malachi alone was responsible for his stunning victory over the British fifty-gun man-of-war *Bristol*, the only such ship taken in open sea battle by the American forces during the entire war—bigger, in fact, than any of the large English frigates America had captured during the current struggle.

Gideon had absorbed the family legends eagerly and had

sought out stories of the uncle he had never known. Malachi's portrait, "drawn from life," had sat on his desk, and his daydreams pictured himself as Malachi's loyal lieutenant, standing by him on his quarterdeck as the grapeshot whirred. Josiah had tried to protect his son from the more extreme elements of Malachi's example, pointing out that though Malachi's bravery and talent were to be admired, much of what he'd accomplished had gone to waste due to a lack of attention to his duties to God and to Christian civilization, as well as to a lack of steadiness which only a true, unpolluted moral sense could provide.

Josiah need not have worried; Gideon was safe. His natural tendencies were conservative, and his moral sense unimpaired. Gideon had established a reputation as a "bluelight" captain, meaning not only a practicing Christian, but a preaching one. *But what would Malachi have done?* Embayed on a Spanish shore with an English squadron just over the bar? No doubt Malachi would have done something desperate and daring, bringing off his prizes while humiliating the British at the same time; but Malachi's nephew could find no such means.

Gideon explained his dilemma to God: the bar, the British, the narrow, deep river, the two unloaded prizes anchored in the bay. Fearing his appeal lacked clarity, Gideon explained the situation again; and this time he began to see a ray of promise. Perhaps he could not save *General Sullivan*, perhaps he could not save his captured goods, but he could fight and kill Englishmen as his God intended.

He could not help thinking as he rose from his knees and strapped on his sword that Malachi would have approved his decision.

3

1794: JOSIAH IN TIMES OF PEACE

Josiah Markham's visage was fierce and worn, all softness and compromise carved away, a forecast of what his son's face became after time and grief and the eternal coursing runnels of salt spray furrowed his young, yielding face. From Josiah's temples the white strands reached out to encroach upon the domain of youthful brown; the white hairs were caught up into his sailor's queue behind, and the tail of hair hanging outside his shabby coat was streaked with white—white, not gray, for Josiah's hair disdained the compromise, intermediate color, and turned straight into patriarchal white. Josiah made his crew drill twice each week with Revolutionary pikes, spearing imaginary Englishmen off the bulwarks and tossing them back into their spectral boats. The hands laughed uneasily and privately wondered if the unbent man in the battered clothes was not a little mad. For it was 1794, and America was at peace with the world.

Gideon, aged fifteen and already a topman, knew this; but he performed his drill with the rest of the crew, unquestioning in public, enjoying the change from the eternal manufacture of rope-yarn or the tarring of the rigging, which he, an agile youngster, was forever asked to perform. Gideon handled the pike expertly; it balanced well in his two hands. The grain of the wooden stock was worn smooth from years of handling; the wicked steel point, newly brightened by the ship's grindstone, gleamed in the tropical sun. Interlaced near the point were the letters GR—the pike, like so much other Markham property, was taken in battle from the British. Gideon's heart swelled as his father, the captain, complimented his dexterity, but he wondered if the drill was not a little absurd.

The war had ended a little too soon for Josiah; it left him with scores yet to settle. Those years of war that had established the American republic had been victorious years for Josiah: he had never lost a ship nor failed to bring home a prize. But he had seen too much and lost too much to ever forget what he had seen and lost, and what nation was responsible. The Revolutionary cannon had been taken out of the ship years before and replaced with cargo. Josiah made the men drill with their pikes, excluding no one; the entire crew, twenty-two seamen, a cook, a steward, five boys, and the mate, each was required to know the drill.

Josiah knew how effective those pikes could be, those seven-foot spears, superannuated on land. The middle finger of Josiah's left hand was severed just above the knuckle, leaving behind an inch-long scarred stub. The rest was torn off when an English privateer's canister swept his schooner's decks in 1781. Josiah bound the bleeding stump in a handkerchief, ran his bowsprit into the enemy's mizzen shrouds, and called for boarders. With pikes the British had been driven from their decks, driven or left behind in the scuppers cut open like fish, their lives bleeding over the sides and into the waiting sea. Josiah knew that his life might depend on those pikes and on whether his crew knew enough to use them. Josiah had no illusions that he lived in a peaceful world . . .

After drill Gideon returned the pike to the rack circling the mainmast and reported to his father. Josiah and his son descended to the captain's cabin, and there they spent an hour in meditation, prayer, and reading Scripture. Afterward Gideon was sent forward to have supper with the rest of the foremast hands. Gideon was a common seaman, assigned to the larboard watch and to the maintop, treated no differently from any other hand so assigned except for that one hour each day. At supper Gideon squatted with the others, opened his jackknife, and ate his beef from the common pot. The gravy stained the keen blade, and Gideon licked it clean, feeling the sharp edge against his tongue.

The exprivateer ship *Cossack*, its crew drilled in handling the ship and in the use of antique pikes, entered the port of Jérémie, in Haiti, past an anchored British sixty-four. The ship of the line sat squat and powerful, its ports opened to the cooling breeze, at the harbor's entrance; although England and France were at war, the ship had been invited to the port by the local planters, hoping to cow the island's slaves away from their muskets and machetés, away from their red massacres and the leadership of their black prophets, and back to the sugar harvest and the life of happy toil that had made the planters rich. There was yellow fever aboard the man-of-war; British tars were dying at the rate of a dozen each day. *Cossack*'s crew could see the bodies committed to the deep, sliding each morning over the standing part of the foresheet, each wrapped in canvas with an iron shot to anchor it to the sea's bottom. The slaves saw the deaths as well; they watched the planters' imported strength declining and counted the days until the English would be no more. Their machetés were hidden away but kept sharp, sharp as *Cossack*'s pikes, as Josiah's eagle eyes. Josiah paced the quarterdeck, grim-faced, watching the man-of-war, his eyes straying anxiously to his son, unloading cargo, and to the gleaming edges of the old pikes standing ready in the racks.

He saw men with cutlasses filling one of the two-decker's launches. Accompanying them was a man with a cocked hat. Josiah snatched a glass from the rack and trained it on the boat. And when he saw the launch heading for the exprivateer, he knew that his war with the British was not over . . .

The pikes were taken from the racks. The crew—twenty-two seamen, a cook, a steward, five boys, and the mate—crouched hidden below *Cossack*'s bulwarks. Gideon, the haft of the pike cool and familiar in his practiced hands, remembered that *Cossack* was his uncle Malachi's first ship, that some of the planks still bore the marks of British grapeshot, and that behind the sheltering bulwarks where he now crouched the twelve-pound cannon once roared brimstone and iron.

The man next to Gideon was chattering with fear, his lance-tip trembling. Gideon was surprised to find himself cool, strangely analytical: he charted the rise in his own heartbeat and, to comfort the man beside him, put out a hand and clasped his shoulder.

The British officer affected an offhand drawl, as if there were a hot potato in his mouth. He introduced himself, standing in his boat, as Lieutenant Lord Rowland, and asked that the ship's company be paraded so that he might search for deserters. Gideon knew that there were three such men aboard *Cossack*.

Only a fool would not have been terrified of Josiah's scowl. "By what authority do ye summon my ship's company?" the old privateer demanded. To Lieutenant Lord Rowland, that splendidly casual young man, Josiah must have looked like a witless bumpkin, standing alone and ramrod-straight in the entry port, dressed in shabby, much mended clothes, his broken straw hat flapping, his hand on his old Revolutionary sword.

"By the authority of His Britannic Majesty," Rowland drawled, condescending to banter with the old Yankee gentleman, conscious, perhaps, of what an amusing story this could make in the wardroom.

"The authority of His Britannic Majesty ends where that flag flies!" Josiah roared, his outthrust arm pointing at the Stars and Stripes. "Clear off! Ye have no authority on my deck, mister!"

Lord Rowland shrugged offhandedly, suddenly tired of the Yankee scarecrow, of waiting for Josiah to give him the opportunity for a telling witticism. Perhaps he was also conscious of the fact that he was the agent of a cynical, ancient, Old World tyranny, that banter was pointless in the face of his orders, which were to take off ten men whether they could be proved to be British deserters or not, that he and his ship were in harbor to support the vicious economic system represented by the decaying Haitian planters and, incidentally, to keep the Yankees and their preposterous republic from gaining trade and enrichment from the rebellion of slaves. In the face of those imposing facts, what need was there for dialogue?

"Look here, my good man, His Britannic Majesty's authority goes wherever his navy takes it, and today it's being taken aboard your ship," he drawled at last. "Step aside before you hurt yourself, old man," said Lieutenant Lord Rowland.

From where Gideon crouched by the bulwarks he could see Josiah's profile cutting the sky like a knife. Gideon watched in amazement: couldn't the Englishman see the magnificence of that uncompromised, triumphant scowl, that desperate anger, the readiness of that fierce pride? To cross Josiah would bring lightnings down, would char Lord Rowland's body to ashes and shrivel his wailing soul.

But Lieutenant Lord Rowland could only see a ragged old Yankee whose refusal to acknowledge the inevitable was becoming tedious.

"Confound you, Brother Jonathan!" Rowland said as Josiah refused to make way. Rowland nodded to his bosun's mate, and the British seamen began to climb *Cossack*'s oaken walls.

"Boarders!" Josiah bellowed, clearing his sword from its scabbard. *"Boaaarders!"*

The pikemen rose from hiding. There was a swift, vicious melee; four heartbeats and it was over. Gideon's first well-practiced lunge, coming up from the deck as he rose, directed without conscious thought toward the center of the nearest striped jersey, threw the bosun's mate back into the boat. The air resounded with a bone-concussing, squelching thud, and Gideon found the man next to him reeling back, his brains open by a cutlass. The cutlass came up for another blow, but in that instant Gideon shortened his pike and brought it up under the British seaman's right arm. The well-honed edge pierced the man as if he were a bag of suet, but the lunge brought Gideon in under the cutlass and he knew that he could be killed unless he got out of the way. He was already moving forward; rather than throw himself backward he continued his forward movement, diving inside the arc of the cutlass, grappling his dying victim. Gideon hugged the British tar until the man's lungs filled with arterial blood, until the muscles slackened and the eyes rolled up. It was not until the sailor had turned from person to thing that Gideon finally heard the cutlass ring on the deck. Surprised by his own coolness, Gideon cleared his pike from the corpse as he'd been taught and awaited the next enemy—but the fight was over.

Lieutenant Lord Rowland, his left eye dangling on his cheek by a bloody thread, was thrown whimpering from *Cossack*'s deck and into his boat, and the press gang, counting its dead, backed water and made its escape, too breathless to curse their luck. Josiah picked up Rowland's unbloodied sword from where it lay on the deck, his craggy face beaming fiery joy; he added it to the rack of captured weapons above his mantel in Portsmouth.

Gideon was sent aloft to unfurl the main topsail. A bower anchor and thirty yards of cable were left behind on the harbor bottom. Josiah, wiping Lord Rowland's blood from his coat with a handkerchief, defiantly steered *Cossack* within fifty yards of the sixty-four-gun ship, within easy shot of those gaping ports and their practiced guns. But the man-of-war had not yet learned that it had lost five men killed and eight wounded, pierced with privateer pikes; they saw Rowland's boat bobbing in the Yankee ship's wake and wondered what interesting story Rowland would tell when he returned. The British officers watched Josiah without interest and did not see the sprinkles of red on *Cossack*'s proud planks.

Later Gideon cleaned his pike before returning it to the rack. The lungs' rich blood running down the shining edge reminded him of the way gravy ran down his jackknife at supper, and he tasted keen metal in his mouth. For the first time he felt sickened.

The next day the only American casualty, the man who had knelt next to Gideon and trembled with fear, died of brain fever. Josiah, following the immortal custom of the sea, auctioned off the dead man's belongings. Gideon bought a spare shirt. The pike drills continued, twice each week, for all Josiah's remaining voyages, until his hair went all white and he retired from the sea. For Josiah another score had been settled, another piece of his youth avenged, another arm of the octopus that was Britain had been severed.

For Josiah there would be no end: he was too old to forgive or forget and knew it. He prayed often for forgiveness for the fact that he could not bring himself to stop hating, and he prayed for his son Gideon, that the young man would not in his lifetime be compelled to hate so thoroughly, or to feel such triumph at the humiliation of an enemy.

4

HIGH TIDE

When Gideon returned to the deck, he carried nails and a hammer. He turned to see the English squadron, the three ships hove-to beyond the bar, a mile away.

"Clear for action!" he roared. "Stand by yer guns, New England! Drummer, beat the long roll!" And as the bay echoed with the rattle of the drum and the deck rumbled to the sound of bare, running feet, Gideon stepped to the flag locker and brought out the largest national ensign the schooner carried. Walking to the main shrouds, he put the hammer in his pocket and stuffed the flag into his waistband. Gideon ascended slowly to the tops. Reaching through the shrouds, he nailed to the mainmast the national ensign with its fifteen stars and fifteen stripes.

Returning slowly to the deck, he saw the men's eyes on him as they stood at their station. He had just made a gesture that could not be misinterpreted: that flag would never come down in surrender. "Clear away one of the larboard six-pounders and fire it to windward," he ordered, his brown eyes as fierce as an eagle's, and returned to the flag locker. He fixed the flagstaff to its socket on the taffrail and raised another, smaller Stars and Stripes over the quarterdeck; at the forepeak he raised a white banner lettered in black, FREE TRADE AND SAILORS' RIGHTS; at the mainpeak he raised a blue flag with fifteen stars circling an eagle and the argent legend CATCH ME WHO CAN.

With the men at their quarters the boy with his drum began subtly to change the rhythm of his beating, tapping out a familiar cue; the privateers, flushed with bravado after Gideon's audaciousness, began to stamp their feet to the rhythm, and a high, sweet tenor sang out:

Our schooner is a privateer,
For the Indies she is bound;
And the pier it is all garnishéd
With bonnie lasses round.
Captain Markham gives the order
To sail the ocean wide,
To seek the British lion bold,
And seize from him a prize.

The stamping seamen joined in on the chorus; Gideon
wondered as he stood by the flag halliards if their roar of
defiance could be heard among the ships of the British
squadron.

So stand up, my lads,
Let your hearts never fear!
For is there man among you
Wouldn't be a privateer?

The English send their men-o'-war;
They think to hunt us down.
But never shall they find us, boys,
The Yankees of renown!
We've taken brigs off Nevis sands,
And sloops off Kingston Bay;
We'll take all ships of English oak,
And swiftly sail away.

So stand up, my lads,
Let your hearts never fear!
For is there man among you,
Wouldn't be a privateer?

Gideon clasped his hands behind him and walked back
to the quarterdeck, his eyes still anxiously turned to seaward; he jumped as the gun went off forward, the bang
accentuating the final stamp of the second chorus. He
picked up his glass and trained it on the enemy. The drum
rattled at his elbow.

Here's a health to Captain Markham!
The Yankee privateer!

For with such men to lead us, boys,
We have no cause to fear.
Our guns are made of iron, boys;
Our yards are made of pine;
Our Captain of New Hampshire oak;
Our flag above us shines!

So stand up, my lads,
Let your hearts never fear!
For there's no man among you
Wouldn't be a privateer!

That stamping on the final chorus must have carried for miles, even to windward. The drummer was changing his rhythm again, picking up another tempo. "Secure that drum, boy, and take yer station," Gideon growled; he resisted the rattling interruptions of his thought. The boy finished with an impudent flourish and ran forward to his position by the number one starboard gun.

The British frigate was hove-to just off the bar, its quarterdeck black with men in cocked hats. Through his glass Gideon could see that the sound of the gun, if not the hands' outrageous bellowing, had caused a stir on the enemy ship; their own flags rose into the breeze, and as Gideon whiffed the scent of powder, he smiled grimly at the reaction his gesture might have created. A gun fired to windward was the traditional challenge to combat: Gideon had dared the British to attack. He could picture a dignified Knight of the Bath snapping to his subordinates about "demmed Yankee impudence" and "Brother Jonathan growing too big for his britches." Gideon hoped he had made them angry.

He turned his glass to the prize brig *Linnet* and saw George Willard lowering the last gun truck into the pinnace, which already cradled the menacing iron tubes of the prize's twelve-pounders. The Lord alone knew what the merchant brig was doing with such ordnance. He had planned to install them on his own gundeck; but if there was to be a fight now, he'd prefer to have his crews using guns they knew.

"Boat comin' from shore, Cap'n," reported Browne, the bosun. "That's our Mr. Harris aboard."

Gideon turned his telescope on the boat, seeing Harris's blond head, the four tarred hats of the crew, and a bright yellow top hat that could only belong to Don Esteban de Velasco.

"Get ye ready to pipe our guest aboard, Mr. Browne," Gideon said.

Velasco was a short, almost tiny man, so delicately built he gave the impression of fragility; he dressed at the height of Spanish fashion in yellow striped nankeen trousers, a bright green coat over a quilted piqué waistcoat, a black satin cravat worn over another cravat of white linen and fixed with a diamond stud. His top hat elevated his stature past Gideon's chin. As he doffed his hat and bowed, he revealed elegant spit curls arranged just so on his temples and forehead. His eyes were bright and intelligent, his face eager. Gideon guessed that he and Velasco were about the same age.

"Honored, sir," Velasco said, his English flavored more with the Thames than with the Hudson.

"Honored, Don Esteban," said Gideon. His attention was momentarily diverted from his guests.

"Avast, there! Don't spread the boarding nets!" he roared over Velasco's shoulder. "We want those to be a surprise!"

Don Esteban looked about him with eagerness. "So this is the deck of a Yankee man-of-war!" he smiled. "I have been on a British ship-sloop—it was the *Nymphe*, eighteen guns, that captured us ten years ago. Your vessel compares favorably for its size."

Gideon refrained from mentioning that another comparison might be made merely by looking seaward at the British squadron.

"Thankee, Don Esteban," he said. "Perhaps ye would oblige me by stepping below to my cabin for refreshment."

"Delighted, sir," said Velasco.

As they stepped down the scuttle, Gideon wished fervently that he could speak at least a little Spanish; but beyond a few dockyard words he knew none. He had inherited his father's inability to remember foreign sounds. His uncle Malachi, he never ceased to remind himself, had been granted a gift for languages and had spoken several fluently.

They entered Gideon's little cabin, and Velasco took a seat.

"We are a temperance ship, so I cannot offer you wine," Gideon said. "Perhaps you would care for some chocolate or coffee?"

"Chocolate would be splendid, thank you."

Gideon called for his steward and ordered chocolate and cheese, and the bargaining began. The desperate nature of the situation was known both to Velasco and to Gideon: both would lose if the British took *General Sullivan* and her prizes. Nevertheless their bargaining was leisurely, for neither wanted to give the impression of haste. Their haggling was interrupted once by Harris to report that the British sloop had lowered a boat and was taking soundings off the bar. Gideon ordered that the long twelve-pounder amidship be cleared and fired on the boat; the rest of his bargaining session with Velasco was punctuated every minute or so by the regular roar of *General Sullivan*'s long tom until after twenty minutes Harris came below to inform them that the enemy launch had been demolished.

"Convey my congratulations to Tate," Gideon said. "He is ten dollars the richer."

Shortly thereafter Velasco presented Gideon with a bill of exchange for fifteen thousand dollars—Cuba was desperate for European goods, in short supply due to the war—and then returned to shore to arrange for the unloading of the prizes. On deck to see his guest off Gideon saw that the British had sent another boat to pick up survivors from the first and bring them back to their ship.

Watching the boat with interested eyes and clutching a smoldering linstock in his hand was Thomas Tate, the tall, broad-shouldered black man who captained *General Sullivan*'s long gun.

Gideon knew that any tall hand named Thomas was going to be called "Long Tom" by his shipmates, just as any literate seaman would be called "Professor," for sailors dote on obvious nicknames—the coincidence that Tate also captained the schooner's long gun only heightened the hands' pleasure at the appropriateness of their conventional sobriquet. Long Tom Tate had learned his gunnery in a hard school: he, as well as Bosun Browne, had been at the battle of Copenhagen, but while Browne served as second loader aboard Nelson's *Elephant*, Tate had commanded a Danish gun aboard the *Elephanten*, supporting the Trekroner battery. They had probably first met while squinting at one another over the hot barrels of cannon, and now they battled the British together—it was not uncommon to see such men serving together on American privateers.

"Tate, I'm pleased with ye," Gideon said.

"Thankee, Captain," Tate said. "Them British, damn 'em, me and this gun bugger 'em to blazes."

"Er—watch yer language, Tate," Gideon glared. The big fifteen-stripe flag snapped overhead.

"Mr. Willard's ashore with the twelve-pounders," Harris reported. "He's got the barrels ashore and is setting up a tripod and a tackle to hoist 'em on their carriages."

"Thankee, Mr. Harris," said Gideon. "I will be obliged to ye and Browne if ye'd sail those prizes to the mouth of the river, then warp 'em up to the landing. Take as many men as you need."

The first officer and the bosun filled a boat with men and pulled off to the prizes. Gideon paced the deck, watching the British rescue boat recede toward the frigate, and rewarded his labors with a plug of tobacco.

The prizes raised their anchors and coasted gently down to the mouth of the river, where hawsers were made fast to trees by the landing and the captures were warped upstream by men working at the capstans. Later in the afternoon the work details returned, and *General Sullivan*, watched every second by British telescopes, raised its anchors and coasted to the mouth of the river, where the privateer was anchored across the current, bow and stern.

Gideon was amazed at the number of drays already lined at the landing, ready for the prize cargo. Velasco was a man of power in the countryside, and appeared to have mobilized every slave and peasant for a hundred miles. The landing was choked with drays, with the shouting of impatient Cubans and the braying of their mules. Velasco, riding a handsome, shining stallion whose shoulders stood higher than his own, rode through the confusion, brandishing a whip and trying to impose some kind of order. Flat-bottomed boats came down the river, manned by slaves under a driver; men ashore began building a large raft. Gideon sent forty men to the prize vessels to break open the hatches, and begin to transfer goods. It was almost noon. The tide still ebbed. The first drays began to be loaded to take the goods inland away from the vengeance of the British.

General Sullivan was slightly under a hundred feet long from her taffrail to the tip of her jib boom, and the river was at least a hundred feet wider at its broad mouth. Gideon contemplated these facts as he watched the enemy squadron as the river lowered with the tide. There was no hope of the privateer schooner's being able to prevent British boats from getting past her toward the prize ships; that was why the cargo had to be moved inland. But they would have to face *General Sullivan*'s fire, and they would probably choose to take the schooner first. He looked at the bank. The high-tide mark was plain to see, ringing a few of the palm trees at the water's edge. He cut himself a new quid of tobacco as he contemplated the possibilities occasioned by those marks. . . .

"Ahoy, Captain!" It was Velasco, climbing the schooner's entry port, crossing the deck to where Gideon greeted him.

"We need only three hours more," Velasco said, looking significantly at the sun—reddening, the sun's lower edge was already touching the lush Cuban hills, and above the opposite horizon a gibbous moon was rising, signalling the turn of the tide.

"Very good, Don Esteban," Gideon said. "May I impose upon you to the extent of your keeping for me a few possessions ashore at yer plantation? Things that may be useful if we find ourselves cast adrift in Cuba."

"But of course."

There were several thousand dollars in gold and silver kept in Gideon's cabin under lock and key, the money used to pay for the privateer's incidental expenses. Gideon did not want the money taken by an enemy: they could keep his crew fed here.

"Thank you, sir," Gideon said. "As soon as it grows a bit darker, I'll need twenty of my men back and one of my boats."

"Do you mean to fight them?"

Gideon spat the last of his tobacco over the side and wiped his mouth with a handkerchief.

"Aye," he said.

"These Englishmen, they are good," said Velasco. "I spent almost a year as a prisoner in one of their ships and another three months ashore in Portsmouth waiting for a cartel." He squinted at the three enemy hove-to off the bar. "They are good men, very efficient," he said. "You do not need to fight them; you and your crew are welcome at Rio Lagartos as long as you wish to stay."

"I thank ye, Don Esteban. We'll fight first."

Velasco was earnest. "In the name of mercy!" he said. "You have sixty men, they have—how many?"

"Perhaps a thousand."

"You will all be killed or taken!"

"That is as the Lord God wills," said Gideon. His voice rang clearly over the water. "He has given us this war, and he has given me an opportunity to strike the enemy a blow they will not soon forget. I must not waste it. Whether we win or lose this fight, the glory will belong to the Almighty either way."

Velasco spread his hands in frustration. "Our God has never asked us to commit suicide!" he exclaimed.

"It will not be suicide, Don Esteban," Gideon said calmly, watching the sun lower on the green horizon. "I'll show ye. It is time."

He reached for a speaking trumpet and summoned Harris and twenty men, then began to give the list of orders he'd been preparing all afternoon. He turned to Velasco to explain.

"We will put out two kedge anchors off our stern, one upstream, one down," he said. "That way we can slip one anchor cable while hauling on the other and swing *General Sullivan*'s stern either direction, so that the British boats will not be able to hide from our guns. Each anchor cable will be fixed to a spring so that if one of the kedge anchors is cut away, we still may be able to pivot on the cables remaining to us. Mr. Harris will break out our best bower—that is our heaviest anchor, normally kept inboard so that it won't be lost in a collision or some other accident—and we'll fix a cable to it and prepare it for dropping in case the enemy cuts all three cables and tries to tow us out."

"Very clever, but I think it will only delay matters, no?" asked Velasco.

"Boarding nets will be draped over our decks," Gideon went on. "They will cover the entire vessel, hanging loosely so that any Englishman trying to climb aboard will be caught like a fly in the web of a spider."

"Ah—I know these nets, the British used them," said Velasco. "But you will still be outnumbered perhaps ten to one. That is a seventy-four-gun ship off the bar, Captain Markham!"

"Battles are decided not by men, but by God," said Gideon. "My preparations are only to make me worthier in his eyes. Samson was vouchsafed to slay a thousand men at Ramathlehi and armed only with the jawbone of an ass; my namesake destroyed the Midianites at Moreh with only one hundred men—if the spirit of the Lord is with us tonight, we will be victorious, and if he is against us, a thousand guns and ten thousand men will make no difference."

"My friend, do not tempt Providence to your destruction," Velasco urged, taking the right tack at last. "He may look upon this defense as arrogant pride on your part."

"I pray not, Don Esteban," said Gideon calmly. "Drape that net loosely there!"

"Captain—" Velasco began.

"I'm sorry, sir—I must see to some business just now," Gideon said, fending him off for the moment. He left Velasco standing on the quarterdeck, watching as he drew the first officer aside and gave him a quiet series of orders, pointing first to one bank of the river, then to the other. Harris nodded, took two men, and went below, returning with the end of a three-and-one-half-inch cable normally used as a sheet for the schooner's big mainsail. Working efficiently, a line of men brought the entire cable up from below and coiled it neatly in Harris's boat. Harris and a dozen men lowered themselves into the boat and rowed to the shore just at the lip of the river.

"Now ye'll see why I am sanguine, Don Esteban," Gideon said. They watched as one end of the cables was fixed to a palm growing at the water's edge some inches above the high-water mark; then Harris rowed across the river mouth, playing out the cable behind him until he came to the other bank, where his dozen men drew it taut and belayed it to two trees.

"Yon cable is stretched six or nine inches above the water, Don Esteban," Gideon said. "It will stop the boats dead for the time it takes to cut it. During that time"—he gestured to the larboard battery facing the river's mouth—"these guns will be firing. Before the light fades altogether, they will be aimed carefully on the cable. They will not miss."

"Brilliant! Glorious!" Velasco was excited by the prospect of the planned massacre. He swept off his hat and dabbed with a handkerchief at the perspiration on his brow. "You are inspired, Captain!" he said.

"All credit is the Lord's," said Gideon simply, but he found himself smiling at the praise. Carefully he extinguished the smile.

Harris returned to report his tasks finished.

"Very good," Gideon said. "Call the men back from the prizes. We'll sight our guns on the cable and then give the hands their supper."

He watched the British through his glass in the waning light, dark shadows floating on the gray of the sea, anchored now for the night. They would have Americans in their crews, men pressed into service. Gideon prayed the enemy captain would not force the Americans to fight for him tonight.

"Captain Markham?" asked Velasco.

"Don Esteban," Gideon replied. "May I be of assistance to ye?"

"Your plan with the cable is brilliant, Captain," the Spaniard said hesitantly. "But do you think it is consistent with the laws of civilized warfare to trap the enemy so? Could a gentleman do such a thing?"

When Adam delved, and Eve span, who was then the gentleman? Gideon thought, the words of the old rhyme coming to him unbidden. But it would not do as an answer.

"I believe it is," he said. "If I am wrong, the Lord will judge." *If the Lord,* he thought, *cares about such notions as gentlemen possess.*

"In that case I have a request to make," said Velasco. "I would like to spend the night on your vessel. Your hold is filled with my cargo, and I should look after it." He smiled as Gideon stared. "Also," he said, "I would not want it said that Spanish bravery is inferior to Yankee impudence."

Gideon laughed. His laughter was a rare thing, and the men nearby looked up with curiosity. "Ye're welcome, Don Esteban," he said. "We're honored."

"The honor is mine, sir," said the Spaniard. "You understand that I cannot fight with you; my nation is neutral. But I will render whatever service you may require short of using a weapon."

"Please stand by me, then," Gideon said. "I can use ye as a messenger."

"Thank you, Captain. I would like to write a letter to my wife and send it ashore if I may."

"Certainly. Please use my cabin," Gideon offered. The planter accepted with thanks. When he returned to the deck, Gideon had a boat ready for his message to the shore, and had his chest of ready money in it to be taken by two of Velasco's loyal henchmen to his plantation.

The western sky deepened to black, and only the moon showed the rest of the privateer's crew returning in their black boats. *General Sullivan* had six guns each broadside ranging in size from short sixes to short twelves, most of them having been taken from prizes. The guns were loaded with grape and cannister, and the crews hauled on the tackles to run them out, the gun captains adjusting the quoins to lay the barrels directly on the almost invisible cable stretching across the river's mouth. Long Tom Tate loaded his long twelve-pounder carefully and swung it on its pivot to bear on the cable. Supper was served, and the galley fires doused. The sea breeze fluttered the privateer's flags one last time and died. Water chuckled beneath the

schooner's stern as the incoming tide rippled the surface of
the river, but the carefully placed anchors held the privateer steady in the river. Muskets were loaded and placed
carefully within reach of the crew. Browne was placed in
charge of the fo'c'sle; Gideon commanded the quarterdeck;
Alexander Harris took charge of the gun crew's amidships.
General Sullivan's three swivel guns were emplaced, one
forward, one astern, one amidships facing inland in case
the enemy got behind them. Gideon put on a heavy coat to
help protect him from British blades and stowed a pistol in
each pocket.

The nightbirds called as the privateers stood silently by
their guns, each man and gun, each rail and line of rigging,
outlined in faint silver by the moon. Ten o'clock passed.
Somewhere forward a seaman was snoring softly. Gideon
bent his head and prayed that the Lord had vouchsafed
him to do the right thing. The birds and the laughing river
mocked his prayers. Velasco, standing nearby, cleared his
throat loudly.

Suddenly twin explosions shattered the night's peace,
rocking the still air, shocking the nightbirds into silence.
The British were crossing the bar, and George Willard's
battery of two guns was spangling the water over the bar
with iron shot.

Willard's battery thundered on, firing swiftly, invisibly,
on the unseen enemy. Gideon could sense the uneasiness of
his crew, the nervous shifting of weapons in their hands. In
the moonlight Gideon could barely make out the taut, dark
line above the water, the cable stretched to catch the enemy. The privateers must wait in the dark for their moment, Gideon reminded himself, even if the enemy were
ten thousand. It was impossible to retreat now.

The last shots from Willard's battery died away, and
Gideon was suddenly aware of how loudly his own breathing rasped within his chest, and how overwhelming was the
crazed thudding of his heart. For a moment he felt panic,
not at the situation, dangerous though it was, but at the
sudden revelation of his own fear. . . . The regular crash
of the guns had kept his mind occupied, provided a rhythm
to his prayers and a companion in the darkness, but now
he was alone and in shadow and afraid. He gulped air,

mentally grappling with his terror, trying to wrest control of his body back from the spectral demons that had taken it; he was forsaken in the darkness, companionless . . .

Nearby there was the unexpected *clink* of a cutlass blade against a gun breech.

"Silence there!" Gideon shouted, his voice echoing on the river, startling himself with his own vehemence. A whispered voice passed an apology. Gideon felt the sudden, crazed urge to grin at his own overreaction; the brief metallic sound had reminded him that he was not alone with his fear, and his command was almost a shriek of relief. Mastering the spasm of fear and joy, Gideon forced his face to return to its normal forbidding lines and clasped his disciplined hands behind his back. And when he turned his eyes to the mouth of the river, suddenly it was full of black, silent boats, creeping upstream with the tide. . . .

His heart turned over when he saw them, and then quite suddenly he was thinking clearly, swiftly, his mind racing as coolly as if it were a machine made of ice. His fears had a name and a shape, and they were before him where he could strike them down. *"Each man shake his neighbor, make sure he's awake!"* Gideon whispered, and the order was passed forward.

Gideon picked out the boats in their formation, ten of them altogether, black shapes on the moonswept river. They were in two lines abreast, five boats per line. They were big boats, cutters. Cutters . . . each could hold up to forty men. In another few seconds his fifty could be dealing with four hundred. He reached for his speaking trumpet, missing it in the dark and knocking it over with a clang. Voices, not knowing it was their captain who had made the noise, *shushed* him in the dark. Furious at himself for his clumsiness, Gideon bent over and picked up the trumpet. He put it to his mouth, and his voice echoed over the face of the river.

"Stay clear or I will fire into you!" he boomed. "We are in Spanish waters, and we may not fight here!"

"Tell that to your damned battery!" roared out a voice from the boats. The voice was followed by jeers and hoots. The British seamen bent to their oars and sped the boats along.

"Stay clear or ye shall all be fired upon!" Gideon shouted, annoyed for having provided the British with an excuse for attack. The boats were picking up speed, racing over the hissing waters, eager silhouettes leaning forward hungrily in their bows. . . .

Along the larboard bulwark Gideon could see the red pinpricks of light as the gun captains blew their slow matches into brightness. Gideon let the speaking trumpet clatter to the deck. . . .

And then the lead boat struck the cable, a man in the bows going overboard with a splash, the boat slowing sideway in a confusion of flailing oars and alarmed shouts. Another boat struck beside it, hanging in the current, a swivel gun in its bows going off with a bang. Gideon heard grapeshot whirring overhead, sounding like a million angry bees.

And then the larboard broadside lit up the night, yellow tongues of flame lapping the waters twenty feet or more from the gun barrels. Gideon blinked, his night vision ruined, hearing screams from the river resounding above the triumphant growl of the privateers. *"Madre!"* Velasco breathed in awe; a boat swivel banged out, and Gideon felt the thud as shot struck the schooner's hull. Musket fire began to crack from *General Sullivan*'s quarterdeck.

"No muskets! No muskets!" Gideon shouted. "Wait till they're closer!"

As his eyes gradually accustomed themselves to the darkness, he saw that one boat had been shattered, its stern canted up in the air; two others were swinging broadside to the current and drifting helplessly with the tide, a few oars waving wildly. Other boats were up against the cable—at least four of them—their bows full of milling men.

General Sullivan's broadside roared out again, flailing the water. Through the smoke Gideon could hear British screams, and then the black form of a boat parted the gunsmoke and rowed madly for the privateer's bows. Another boat appeared, and then a third: the cable had been cut, or the schooner's own broadside had cut it.

"Boarders!" Gideon bellowed. *"Boaaaarders!"*

The bow swivel spat at the first boat. The second thudded up against *General Sullivan*'s main chains, and at once the privateers rushed to meet it, pikes thrusting down, mus-

kets and pistols snapping. Gideon held back from the
stampede—hadn't anyone seen that third boat? He
watched it anxiously. It hesitated for a moment, then sped
cunningly under the stern. Gideon heard the scrape of a
boathook.

Suddenly he realized that he was entirely alone on the
quarterdeck; every man with him had run to deal with the
first two boats—only Velasco, conspicuous in his yellow
hat, stood close by.

Gideon groped on the deck for a weapon and encountered the broad muzzle of a musketoon. He imagined he
could hear whispered orders from the boat beneath the
stern. Gideon's back dazzled him with pain as he snatched
up the heavy musketoon and ran to the taffrail. He balanced the bell-mouthed musket on the rail, tipped it up so
that it pointed down into the boat, and fired.

Pain shot through him again as the discharge of half a
dozen musket balls and a handful of nails, wire, buttons,
and other metal scrap threw Gideon backward onto the
deck. Gasping for air, Gideon felt hands helping him to his
feet and found they were Velasco's. Pistol balls whistled
and hummed past the stern as the British in the boat fired
randomly up into the darkness.

"Thankee," Gideon breathed. "For God's sake get five
men here!"

Velasco vanished into the darkness and smoke. Gideon
drew his pistols and ran to the rail, seeing the boat below
swinging wildly in the current as the British tried to control it, hampered by dead and wounded men lying on their
oars. An officer's voice barked a desperate series of orders.
Gideon fired his pistols down into the boat, seeing flashes
and hearing reports as the enemy fired back; then the boat
was swept away by the tide, the officer still bawling commands, the cutter cartwheeling as its crew tried to get it
under way.

"Here we are, Captain!" Velasco had arrived with five
men and in the nick of time: another boat was approaching through the dark. It swept up to the stern, the privateers' banging muskets answered by wild pistol shots from
the cutter. Black forms swarmed up the side but were
beaten back by pistols and clubbed muskets, and the boat

pushed off and rowed farther upstream, swinging around the privateer to board from the starboard side. Velasco was sent running to tell First Officer Harris he was about to be taken from behind, and Harris met the British with a swivel gun fired at point-blank range and rattling musketry. The boat, out of control, was drawn against the privateer's side by the current, and every man in the cutter slain with pikes. Gideon looked wildly around for an enemy and found none. The few boats still in sight were withdrawing. The privateers ran to the great guns and sent grapeshot after them until the enemy boats vanished in darkness.

The silence that followed was shocking in its depth. Gideon could hear distinctly the gurgle of the tide as it rocked the schooner, the rasping of ramrods in musket barrels, the thudding of the boat full of corpses as it bumped against the privateer's side. There was no cheering. Everyone knew that the British would be back.

"Mr. Harris! Mr. Browne!" Gideon called. The first officer and bosun came aft, carrying their weapons; Browne's sword arm bled freely onto the deck. The bosun clutched his wound and apologized for marking the clean deck.

"Never mind, Mr. Browne, just get the wounded tended to directly," Gideon said. "Can ye man yer station?"

"Aye," Browne said with a savage grin. "I'd rather swing a cutlass left-handed than swing at Plymouth Howe, if you get my meaning."

"Do we have any others hurt?"

"Some scratches like mine," Browne said. "We can all still fight."

"Jem Hamilton has a cut over one eye. That's all," Harris added.

Gideon breathed relief; the first British attack had been beaten off without the loss of a man! He felt like capering madly in celebration. Instead he said as calmly as he could, "The Spirit of God was with us. Let us give thanks and make ready." He felt in his pockets for his pistols and looked carefully over the deck, but they were gone—he must have hurled them into the enemy boat without remembering it.

The nightbirds, their astonishment fading, began once

again to cry aloud. Gideon waited patiently in the shadow of the mainmast, hearing his own sweat pattering on his coat.

The British came again just before midnight. There were six boats this time, firing small carronades or swivel guns from their bows as soon as they came into range, *General Sullivan*'s broadside thundering in return, raising from the quicksilver river avalanches of spray.

Three cheers chorused from the enemy as the boats shot alongside the privateer, but there were only five: the sixth had been sunk or decimated by grape. Two boats grappled to either side of the stern as crackling, blinding volleys of pistol and musket fire cracked down at them and the great musketoon roared, but this time the British were not turned back. Wraithlike figures climbed the ship's side, claws clutching at the rail. Cutlasses slashed madly at the boarding nets, their wielders uttering harsh, inarticulate cries, like fierce nightbirds sweeping down on their prey. Thrusting pikes and whistling swords threw them back to their boats. Gideon battled in that clattering maelstrom of steel, slashing with his keen hanger, feeling deadly fingers plucking at his coat and sleeve. An officer in a cocked hat hauled himself over the rail, his teeth shining in the moonlight, an animal grin; as he swung a knee up and over, Gideon lunged at this insubstantial form and suddenly it was gone, vanished utterly. Gideon wondered if it was some illusion, until he felt warm arterial blood dripping from his sword onto his hand.

The British dropped back into their boats then, baffled, and rowed to the starboard side and tried again. Once more Gideon sent his men to drive them off, the pikes reaching down to the British in the dark. It was then that Gideon saw through dissipating smoke and the enveloping darkness that a British boat was trying to cut the larboard stern anchor cable.

He looked around him desperately. The muskets and pistols had all been fired, and the pikes could not reach to where the enemy boat hovered on the river five yards out. He ran to the rail, peering out, seeing axes flashing on the enemy cutter, the cable vibrating; as he thrust his neck out beyond the bulwarks, he could see another boat clinging tenaciously to the fore cable. Something would have to be done quickly.

Panting, Gideon ran to the waist of the schooner where the long tom rested on its pivot. Men were snatched from the bulwarks, the capstan was manned, and Tom Tate and two of his men swiftly loaded the twelve-pounder with grape.

"Heave, boys! Put yer backs into it!" Gideon shouted and threw his weight on a capstan bar, his shoes digging into the deck for traction. The capstan lurched, pawls clattering, as the starboard stern cable was hauled in while the larboard cable was slacked. The schooner's stern swung upstream, and the British boat suddenly swung confusedly as the cable they were trying to cut was slacked and disappeared below the surface of the water. Tate blew on his slow match, his eyes glittering redly in reflection. The long gun roared, blowing the British boat and its axemen to smithereens. For an instant, in the gun's mighty flash, Gideon saw a frozen, yellow moment of the battle, the privateers with their knightly weapons, lances and swords, defending their bulwarks as if the schooner were a castle, while the wounded sprawled on the bloody planks and the host below tried to scale the ramparts against a wall of steel and furious humanity.

Tate's voice rang out as the twelve-pounder was reloaded. The fore cable was slacked, and Gideon bent his back to the capstan. *General Sullivan* pivoted sluggishly on its springs, the bow lurching upstream, the enemy boat exposed. The flame from the long tom scorched the deck as it was depressed to bear on the British boat, and the grapeshot swept through the enemy like a hurricane through chaff. The boat spun away out of control.

With the crash of the long tom came the cessation of other noise; the rasp and clatter of steel on steel died suddenly away, replaced by the shouts of British officers as they ordered their men to the oars. "Man the great guns!" Gideon bellowed. "Load with grape!"

The broadside guns pursued the enemy, grapeshot skipping after the British boats. The silence that followed did not last long: from the darkness came the distant thumping of George Willard's twelve-pounders—and suddenly the privateers were cheering, waving hats and cutlasses, screaming their triumph and relief. The British were heading back out to sea over the bar; they'd had enough. Gideon felt a grin twitching at his lips as he loosened his sweat-heavy neckcloth and gasped for air.

"My felicitations, Captain Markham," Velasco offered, taking off his hat respectfully. "I had not thought it possible."

"Thankee, Don Esteban," Gideon said, still gasping for breath. "The author of this victory was Almighty God; the congratulations are His." His face grew troubled. "I fear that earlier this evening during the first attack, when we were in danger of being boarded, I spoke the Lord's name in vain when I told ye to bring men."

"I am sure he will not hold it against you," said Velasco with a smile.

"I pray he will not," said Gideon. "Mr. Browne! Mr. Harris!"

Browne and Harris reported two men killed and seven privateers wounded, none of the latter seriously. Browne's head was bandaged, and the bandage stained red; he'd taken another wound. The dark stains on his cutlass blade showed that he'd dealt out ruin as well as received it.

The two dead Americans were laid on the planks abaft the foremast, and the wounded who could not be attended on deck were sent below, where a carpenter's mate acted as surgeon. With Willard's guns still booming regularly in the background Gideon gathered his crew around the bodies and took off his beaver hat.

"Off hats!" Harris snapped, and Browne blew his pipe. Gideon clasped his hands and bowed his head.

"We implore Thee, Lord, for Thy mercy on behalf of these men who have fallen today," he said, his voice echoing from the river and the rustling palms, "and we implore Thy grace as well on our enemies, whom we have slain in obedience to Thy will. And thirdly we implore Thy benefit upon the wounded that their pains may be eased and their wounds healed. And this we ask in the name of Thy blessed son, Amen."

"Hats on!" Harris shouted, and suddenly there was

much work to do—pistols, muskets, and cannon were re-loaded, boarding pikes stacked neatly in their racks, the capstan manned, and the schooner placed over its three anchors again.

"I noticed, Captain, that you asked God for mercy on the slain," Velasco said, still at Gideon's elbow. "But not for mercy upon yourselves, who have performed all this killing."

"The killing was done in obedience to Divine Providence," Gideon said confidently. "We do not need to ask his mercy on us; we merely did his will."

"You seem to know your God's mind very well," said Velasco.

Gideon looked at him sternly. Velasco coughed politely into a fist.

"I submit my thoughts to His when I can," Gideon said. Velasco saw the gleam of utter self-assurance in his eyes and shivered in spite of the heat. He had seen that gleam only once before, in the eyes of a fanatic hedge-priest who had preached slave revolt and who, after stirring a group of slaves into attacking their masters, had been executed. Velasco had been a spectator, hypnotized by the conviction in the priest's lunatic eyes, until the firing squad had closed his eyes forever. For a moment Velasco had felt that such a man could turn the world upside down simply through his own fierce determination, and because a man so lacking compromise was as strong as fifty.

In Gideon's eyes Velasco saw conviction and anger and absolute confidence; there was nothing weak there, nothing human. He shivered again.

"Shall we send the starboard watch to their hammocks, Captain?" It was Mr. Harris.

"Nay, Mr. Harris," Gideon said. Now that fanatic gleam was gone, and Gideon's face was soft again. He peered over the water toward the sea. The tide was running out now, taking bodies and shattered boats with it.

"The enemy may return," Gideon said. "The crew will lie rough tonight."

"Rough it, sir? Very well."

Gideon awarded himself a plug of tobacco, feeling the harsh juices bite his welcoming tongue. He clasped his hands triumphantly behind his back and stood quietly on the quarterdeck, inhaling the sweet, warm airs of Cuba. The moon was setting behind the trees, and the schooner's flags flapped darkly in the heavy, sluggish land breeze. The only light on the schooner was provided by the slow matches winking redly in their tubs.

An hour passed. The crew, those not on watch, snored on the deck. *General Sullivan* tugged at its cables, testing its careful mooring, as tide and current united in an attempt to sweep the schooner out to sea. Standing quietly at the rail, Gideon found himself looking up and losing himself in the dazzling eternity of stars.

He heard Velasco's quick step beside him and turned to the Spaniard.

"You're not asleep, Don Esteban?" he asked.

"I cannot."

"Nor can I, Don Esteban," Gideon said. He spat tobacco juices over the rail to clear his mouth for conversation.

"I am astonished at the neatness of your vessel," Velasco marveled, gesturing with his cane to *General Sullivan*'s orderly, flush deck. "I have been on many Spanish ships, merchantmen and men-of-war both, and never have I seen such order. Even after a battle your deck is clear, the weapons are loaded and laid neatly by—even your crewmen, laid out on the deck, are sleeping in rows! On a Spanish ship all would be in confusion, ropes and guns and men lying everywhere."

"Orderly habits are the habits of the successful sailor," Gideon said. "The Yankee sailor is a successful one."

"The English as well," Velasco said. "They are orderly; the *Nymphe* was an orderly ship. They observed a rule of silence as well."

"That makes for a sullen crew, I believe," Gideon said. "Besides, if one of my crew sees a sail or notices that we're about to run into land, I want him to sing out without fear of reprimand."

"That is sensible."

There was a flash of lightning inland from the Cuban hills. Seconds later distant thunder rolled down to them, a reminder of the entire world at war.

"Forgive me, Don Esteban, if I offend," Gideon said, "but I cannot in good conscience fail to speak my mind. It is my considered opinion, and one that I do not hold lightly, that the success of Yankee and British commerce must be traced to the Protestant religion."

"Indeed?" said Velasco. Gideon felt warmly uncomfortable under Velasco's polite gaze, but he cleared his throat and continued earnestly.

"It is the Roman Catholic practice of interceding for their flock with God which is chiefly to blame," he said. "It encourages people to get into all manner of irregular habits, knowing that they have a priest to absolve them afterward of the consequences. A Protestant, who must keep his conscience clear at all times and who has no priest to intercede with the Lord, but must each face the consequences of his own acts himself, will develop regular habits, leading to industry and neatness and to their consequence, prosperity."

"Very interesting," said Velasco. "I must ask Father Reies's opinion—after you leave, of course. I should warn you also that if you should be forced to stay in Cuba any longer, to please reserve your opinions—ashore here you could get into dire trouble if you voice such utterances."

"But surely ye can understand my point?" Gideon asked, his hesitance waning under the force of his faith. "Take the matter of feast days, now—thirty or forty calendar days in which ye papists are not obliged to work. I have often seen Roman Catholic ships wasting the days in harbor, their crews singing and indulging in liquor, celebrating some saint's day, while Yankee ships loaded their cargoes and sailed home to make their profits. A man of education and sense like yourself can surely see the commercial advantages of Protestantism—not to mention the benefit it does to the immortal soul."

"I shall have to consider the matter," Velasco said tactfully.

"Perhaps ye may wish to look at some tracts? If ye would care to step below—"

"Do you think the British will come again?" Velasco asked quickly.

"Eh?"

Gideon cast a searching glance out to sea. "The British aren't used to failure," he said. "The moon will set soon, and they may have another try. The tide is against them, but the tide is very small here. Mr. Willard will warn us if they come again."

"Mr. Willard's battery is vulnerable to land attack, no?" Velasco asked. "He may not be able to give warning."

"Aye, that's so," said Gideon. He considered briefly, his eyes worried, and then walked to the rail and peered anxiously into the darkness. At last he called for Harris.

"Man a boat and bring that cable up," Gideon said. "Splice it and lay it across the river again."

"Aye aye, Captain." Harris looked at Gideon curiously. "Do ye think they'll come again?" he asked.

"What I think is not yer concern, Mr. Harris."

"Indeed not, sir. I'll do it directly."

The cable was untied from the trees on one side of the river, brought across to the other side, spliced, and set again. Gideon called to his steward to make coffee for himself and Velasco.

Shortly after two rain clouds swept down from the Cuban hills, and for half an hour the privateers ran busily on the wet decks, setting up awnings to catch the rainwater and pour it into the fresh water tubs. Some of the crew asked permission to block the scuppers in order to create a little lake the length of the schooner and be able to do laundry in fresh water. Gideon, rain dripping off his beaver hat, reluctantly forbade the exercise: if the British came again, he didn't want his men slipping about in a two-inch soapy lake.

The rain subsided, and the sky cleared quickly. The rainwater began to steam from the decks. Bats fluttered low between the masts, snatching insects, avoiding the jungle of halliards and stays. Gideon tightened his neckcloth against the chill. Upstream the mist began forming, slipping slowly down the river with the night breeze, enfolding the privateer schooner in its moist cloak. Gideon cut himself more tobacco and began to chew anxiously. The schooner rocked as the increased flow of water from the rainfall nudged its bilges.

From below there was a sudden shriek. Standing in the

mist, Gideon felt his hackles rise. Another scream rent the night. Somewhere below a wounded crewman had just awakened to the fact that he lacked an arm. The third scream was muffled, as if the carpenter's mate who served as the privateer's surgeon was trying to silence the man. In the sudden comparative silence Gideon could hear one of the crewmen near him muttering a prayer in some incomprehensible gutteral tongue, German, perhaps, or Danish— the language the man had spoken as a boy and in which he'd learned his prayers. From below there was another wail, a single, sobbing shriek that trailed gradually away and left the privateers awake and stung with horror.

General Sullivan seemed to hover in the gentle mist, wisps floating over the bulwarks, creeping among the crew. The flags hung sodden on the masts. In the shifting, claustrophobic world of clinging vapor all movement, all noise seemed unnaturally loud, and the echo of the crewman's cries seemed to last forever. Gideon paced, his heels thudding loudly, his head craned anxiously toward the mouth of the river. The mist had obscured the cable stretched across the waters, and he might not be able to see a British attack in time. He would have to hope that he could hear it. He wondered if he should call hands to their stations: there would be more noise, more interference, but their reaction to any attack would be quicker.

The wounded crewman shrieked again and Gideon shivered. The wails echoed skyward. He decided to call his men to their stations. That screaming had wakened the crew anyway. It was best to give them something to do rather than have to listen to it.

Gideon turned to give the order, but suddenly the shore was alive with yellow fires, and the air with humming. Bullets cut white wood from the mainmast near him. Gideon threw himself to the deck, his tall hat tumbling off his head as he shouted for all hands. Muskets on the riverbank continued to flame.

There was a rush on deck for the muskets, and the roaring voices of Harris and Browne as they tried to establish order among their men. Barefoot privateers ran to the quarterdeck, firing a hasty volley over the taffrail. Bullets buzzed overhead, cracking against the bulwarks. With an astonishing roar the number three larboard gun leaped inward on its tackles, belching fire into the night.

"Avast, there!" Gideon bellowed, jumping to his feet. "Avast firing the great guns!" He glared fiercely at the crew of the gun and ran to the rail to look out into the night—there was no sign of boats. Two men sheepishly began to reload the six-pounder.

Another volley spat forth from the shore. Gideon ducked behind the rail, feeling the wood leap as balls struck it. Privateer muskets barked in reply. Gideon's heart froze as he realized that the British were methodically sweeping the quarterdeck with their volleys, trying to kill the captain and the other officers. Kicking his scabbard out of the way, Gideon crawled to where Velasco, trying to look unperturbed, was sheltering by the mainmast.

"I have been keeping your hat for you, Captain," Velasco said, handing it to him. "A gentleman should look to his attire in these situations."

Gideon jammed the hat on his head and ducked involuntarily as a bullet whined between them. "Marines!" he gasped. "They must have landed during the squall."

"Your man Willard must have been made a prisoner," Velasco said. "Ah well, these *Indios* are expendable, no?"

"Be silent and let me think!" Gideon roared. Velasco fell obligingly silent as the hissing bullets continued to cut the air. Gideon knew that things could not continue this way for long with British volleys regularly sweeping over the decks. The privateer muskets were firing blindly into the darkness or at the flashes of the British muskets, but the British had a large target, the dark stern of the schooner outlined against the mist. Soon the British boats would come again.

The stern swivel gun went off with a defiant bellow. Gideon lunged across the deck and seized a man by the shoulder.

"You!" he shouted. "And you there and you! Ready the capstan!"

Crouching as the bullets whimpered overhead, Gideon hurried more men into place, stationing them at the capstan while all was made ready below. "Now!" Gideon shouted. "Heave, all!" He threw himself against a capstan bar, feeling a hot stab of pain in his back. The capstan spun as the man bent to their labor, swinging *General Sullivan*'s stern upstream as the kedge anchor was hauled in. "Vast heaving!" Gideon gasped. "'Man the great guns!"

General Sullivan's broadside of six guns, charged with grape and canister, roared out at the invisible enemy, revealing in the great yellow flashes the shadowy forms of the enemy marines in their tall shakoes among the palm trees. Musketry crackled out defiantly in answer to the cannon, but the great guns lashed out again and again, flailing the shore with grapeshot until the British were extinguished. The kedge anchor was slacked off, and *General Sullivan*'s stern swung downstream again, broadside to the current once more.

Shouts of warning rang over the deck: the boats were coming again! The hot cannon spat into the mist, and British grapeshot from the boats' bow guns wailed overhead and thudded into Yankee timbers. The cable stretched across the river stopped them only for a brief moment. Soon the schooner was surrounded by shouting men in boats, and the mist rang with the clash of steel.

Gideon fought with his men at the rail, slashing at the enemy, parrying their pikes and swords. Screaming, demonic faces appeared at the rail, men with scarves wrapped around their heads, who shouted, swung their cutlasses, and died beneath American iron. Some of the British seemed to have been detailed to run up the shrouds, and soon there was musketry from the schooner's own tops, firing down into privateer backs. Gasping for breath during a brief respite from battle, Gideon shouted that the wounded should take up muskets and deal with the threat from above.

General Sullivan lurched, and then its bows began to swing downstream. The bow anchor cable had been cut. There was a rumble overhead as the fore topsail was loosed and filled with the breeze: the British were going to try to take the schooner out to meet the squadron whether the privateers wished it or not.

Gideon sliced at a blackened visage that appeared above the rail, and the face opened from chin to eyebrow as the Briton was hacked down. The boarders tumbled back into their boats, gathering themselves for another leap. Gasping for breath, Gideon jumped back from the rail, seeing, as he had before, another boat working madly to cut the stern cable. He would have to man the capstan again, slack that cable, haul in on the other so that his men could get a good shot at the boat . . . but suddenly commands rang out from the boats, and there was another rush of men over the stern, dark figures swarming through the sagging, tattered boarding nets. Gideon, his privateers at his back, ran to meet them, his sword meeting metal or cutting flesh or blindly slashing at the air until the enemy were thrown back into their boats or left dead on the decks.

"Captain! Captain!" A hand tugged at Gideon's elbow, and he spun with his sword raised, ready to hack the man down, until at the last instant, he realized it was Velasco.

"Browne and Harris are dead!" Velasco shouted. "They've captured the front part of your ship!"

At that moment there was a lurch, and a British cheer—the stern cable had parted. Gideon leaned wearily on Velasco's shoulder, his mind whirling. The schooner was drifting downstream. All three cables must have been cut. He could hear desperate fighting forward, screams and the clash of steel. The British had been driven off the quarterdeck: there were three boats nearby filled mainly with dead and wounded. If only he weren't so tired . . .

Suddenly he reeled, then stood erect, feeling energy coursing through him. His eyes flashed in the mist and the gunsmoke. *"Forrard!"* he heard himself roar. *"Forrard, all ye men of Israel!"* As if flung by a giant hand, Gideon led his men across *General Sullivan*'s deck, the Yankee seamen bellowing as they ran for their enemy.

"Let death seize upon them, and let them go down quick into hell!" Gideon shouted as he felt his sword bite. He saw Long Tom Tate, a boarding axe in one hand and a cutlass in the other, swinging both weapons madly as he fought his way among a pack of enemy. There was a man in a cocked hat on the privateer fo'c'sle, and Gideon flung himself at the man, his first desperate stroke glancing off the enemy sword. *"Wickedness is in their dwellings, and among them."* Gideon's sword rang as he lunged again, was parried again. The enemy officer was wearing

epaulettes, one on each shoulder. Gideon could smell his sweat, his fear. *"As for me, I will call upon God; and the Lord will save me."* Through the melee Gideon caught a glimpse of a yellow top hat—Velasco, a noncombatant no longer, dangerous laughter rippling past his lips, beating down an enemy seaman with his cane.

A British epaulette took Gideon's next cut and turned it, then Gideon stumbled backward as he tried to throw himself out of the way of the officer's return blow. The stroke missed by an inch and carried well past. *"Evening and morning and at noon will I pray and cry aloud: and he shall hear my voice."* Gideon lunged again as the officer's sword struck the deck. He saw terror in the Englishman's eyes as his enemy realized there was no way to parry the next blow. He tried to throw himself backward but took the blade full in the chest and fell to the deck with a sob. Gideon spared him no more time; he stepped over his victim and ran on, and when he next bothered to look, the man was dead.

The privateers swept the decks from one end to the other, Gideon roaring aloud his devotions as he struck at his enemies. The British were driven back into their boats or killed where they stood. Gideon, his strength evaporating as suddenly as it had filled him, leaned against the fore shrouds and gulped in air, oblivious to all but the overtaxed beating of his heart.

"He hath delivered my soul in peace from the battle that was against me: for there were many with me," he whispered and closed his eyes in weariness. The sudden sound of surf reminded him that they were under way and heading to sea. Gideon sprang up and almost fell, his foot sliding on a patch of blood; he glanced wildly and saw the best bower, readied earlier that evening, still poised at the cathead.

"Drop the anchor!" he shouted wildly. *"Cut it! Cut!"* Tate, the tall black gunner, leaped to the bulwark and swung his axe. A pike thrust at him from below; he parried it and swung again. The cable holding the anchor to the cathead parted, and from below there was a shriek and a rending crash as, on its way to the river bottom, the best bower shattered a British boat.

General Sullivan jerked and swung in the current, the fore topsail going aback as the schooner pointed upstream. The river around them was littered with British boats, some few under control, the rest content to drift. Weary privateers reloaded their muskets and fired, driving off those few enemy still trying to draw near.

"Quarter! Quarter!" It was an English seaman, trapped at the foretop, his friends either killed or jumped for their lives to the river below. Another man was found hiding at the main masthead, wrapped in the FREE TRADE AND SAILORS RIGHTS banner; the two prisoners were sent below and put in irons. The east began to pale with the oncoming dawn.

As the privateers began to sort through the jetsam of battle, assembling weapons, counting the dead, and comforting the wounded, Gideon sat wearily on a gun carriage, trying to catch his breath. Glancing down, he saw a yellow top hat at his feet. With a weary grin he picked it up from the deck and walked to where its owner stood on the quarter-deck.

"Your hat, Don Esteban," he said. "A gentleman should be careful of his attire in these situations."

"Thank you, Captain," said the Spaniard. He placed the hat carefully on his head and turned to silhouette his profile against the approaching dawn.

"It will be good to see the sun again after such a night, Captain," he said. "I hope I was able to be of some little service to you."

"I thank God you were here, sir," said Gideon, and the Spaniard smiled.

Dawn brought the return of George Willard and his ten men. They had been attacked by enemy marines during the squall and had tried to fire their guns as a warning, but the powder was damp and they'd had to run before a gun was fired. They'd managed to escape in their boat, however, and had hidden in the trees all night. Willard and his men were positive they'd sunk a boat during the retreat of the first British assault.

General Sullivan swung at its cable at the very mouth of the river, in plain sight of the enemy squadron: the three

ships were lying within half a mile of the bar, signalling
continuously to one another, boats plying back and forth.
The privateer's flags flew conspicuously in the brisk ocean
breeze. Eight Americans were dead, including Alexander
Harris, the first officer, slain by an enemy pike as he stood
on the bulwarks. Nineteen were wounded seriously enough
to require attention, including Browne the bosun—who
hadn't been killed, as Velasco had mistakenly reported in
the heat of the fighting, but had been wounded twice more
and then struck in the forehead with a spent pistol ball that
had knocked him senseless until the end of the battle. Gideon sent the wounded men ashore, where they would be
tended by a Spanish surgeon Velasco had sent for. The two
British prisoners were paroled. The surviviors ate a cold
breakfast.

General Sullivan's hatches were opened, and the weary
crew was set to work unloading the schooner's cargo,
transferring it to Velasco's boats and rafts, where it would
be rowed upstream to the waiting drays. The bay's white
beaches were littered with dead men, and boats that rocked
in the surf without a live man's hand to guide them.
Sharks' fins efficiently cut the water.

Gideon went to his cabin to change his shirt, stock, and
coat, all splashed with blood; he stayed for half an hour on
his knees, his prayers so confused—a mixture of thanks, imploring mercy for the dead and injured and awestruck gratitude for the divine wind that seemed to have taken possession of him in the last of the fight—that in the end he
struggled to his feet and vowed to give proper thanks later.

On deck again he watched the enemy through his glass.
They were a beautiful sight, those taut men-of-war—even
anchored, the frigate seemed alive, tossing its proud head
at the waves; the seventy-four-gun ship of the line, presenting its gilded quartergalleries, showed itself a bluff, proud,
commanding warrior, perhaps a veteran of Abukir Bay or
Trafalgar, confident in its own power and majesty. Yet
they had been beaten the night before, humiliated by the
sixty men of a thirteen-gun privateer schooner. Fifty corpses
decorated the bay. English wounded would be screaming
their lives away in the red-painted cockpits. The officer
with the epaulettes, killed by Gideon during that mad, in-

spired fight at the fo'c'sle, had been a post-captain and had probably commanded the frigate. The British would be aching for revenge, and the sight of the schooner's taunting flag, CATCH ME WHO CAN, would be an infuriating reminder of their unqualified defeat.

But the British could not blockade the schooner forever; sooner or later they would be forced to leave. Gideon could afford to be patient. The British might yet be tempted into a rash gesture.

"Another two hours, Captain Markham," said Velasco, "and you will be unloaded. Will you try to run past them tonight?"

"The tide is coming in again," Gideon said. "It will put another twelve inches of water over the bar—at least twelve. Look ye—there are boats putting off from the seventy-four. Those are tarred hats those men are wearing. Sailors. I think they're reinforcing the sloop of war so she can come at us."

"This morning?" Velasco asked in alarm. "May I use your glass?"

"Certainly, Don Esteban."

The Spaniard adjusted the telescope to his eye. *"Hijo de la flauta!"* he exclaimed. "There must be a hundred men in those boats. Can you fight her, that sloop?"

Gideon shook his head. "Not if she's handled well," he said. "I could outrun her on the open sea, but embayed on a lee shore, she'll destroy us. She's armed principally with carronades—thirty-two pounders—and they'll wreck us at close range. I could fight them at a distance, but not close in in this little bay."

Velasco looked up with concern. "What can you do, my friend?" he asked.

"I shall pray," Gideon said. "I shall pray that there is not enough water over the bar, and I shall pray that Long Tom's gun is accurate today."

"I will add my prayers to yours, Captain," said the Spaniard and returned the telescope to Gideon. "And I will tell my men to hurry."

"Haste may well be necessary, Don Esteban."

Gideon returned his telescope to the rack and called for Tate.

"Man yer gun, Long Tom," Gideon told him. "If ye have not enough, pick more men—the best. I'm relying on yer marksmanship to keep the British from crossing the bar."

"Aye aye, Cap'n," Tate said. He peered expertly out to sea at the stretch of brown water over the bar, seen clearly against the ocean's sparkling blue.

"The range be long, Cap'n."

"Do yer best, Tate."

Tate arranged his shot carefully on the ready racks, choosing the roundest, most perfect iron balls to be fired first for the straightest possible flight. Shortly before high tide the sloop of war hove its anchor short and ran up the White Ensign. Faintly the sound of three cheers came down the wind. The sloop weighed its anchor and sheeted home its jib, spanker, and fore-topsail, and came cautiously down the wind.

"Do your fastest, lads!" Browne shouted, standing at the loading port, his five wounds bandaged. "No lookin' over your shoulder, just do your work, and quickly!"

Tom Tate's gun, elevated prodigiously high, spat flame and iron. Gideon peered seaward to spot the fall of shot. He failed to see it, but he heard one of Tate's men shout, "Two hundred yards short!"

"Fine, fine," came Tate's voice; apparently he was pleased. The gun was loaded again, and again it barked. This time Gideon saw it splash twenty yards before the ship-sloop's plunging bowsprit.

"Swab her out careful, Hijinks," Tate said, "and this time we hit her."

Gideon saw no shot fall, nor did any of the crewmen. The crew of the long tom cheered, confident they'd hit the enemy, but Gideon was far from sanguine. The range was just short of a mile; it was absurd to expect a hit at that range.

"We make widows today, boys," Tate laughed and carefully drove the quoin a little farther past the breech, lowering the twelve-pounder's muzzle. The shot that followed was a clear hit, pockmarking the enemy ship's fore-topsail. Again there was a cheer. There was no obvious fall of shot for the next attempt or the next. Gideon looked at Tate in amazement: could he hit the enemy so consistently at this range?

"I seen Nelson over my gun at Copenhagen, but the ball not fly straight," Tate remarked conversationally, and again his gun roared. White splinters flew from the enemy rail, shining brightly in the sun.

The ship-sloop tried to cross the center of the bar where the water was probably deepest, but the British warship slid quietly onto the sand and stuck fast. Even Gideon raised his voice in a cheer, waving his hat, while the privateers went mad in celebration.

Again and again the long tom crashed out, striking the enemy with almost every shot. The sloop tried to kedge off, to no effect. They tried firing their broadside to jar the ship off. The frigate came in to tow them off the bar, but the wind was dead against the work, and the tow seemed only to jam the British more firmly onto the sand. The enemy stayed hung on the bar for over an hour, until their foretopmast was shot away and their main yard hung in its slings. Through his glass Gideon could see water being pumped over the side as the British started their water casks, trying to lighten ship.

"We're whippin' up the last load, Cap'n," Browne reported. Gideon blinked for a moment at the report and then remembered they were putting off cargo—he'd been so intent on the battering *General Sullivan* was giving the enemy that he'd forgotten their purpose in being here.

"Very good, Browne," he said. "I'll thank ye and Mr. Willard to report to me afterward."

Tate's long gun roared again, spitting another iron round at the enemy. Gideon felt triumph surging through him—he'd weigh anchor and fight them, raking them at pistol-shot range as they lay helpless on the bar unable to reply.

He put the glass to his eye once more and saw two broadside carronades being heaved off the ship-sloop's bows. Gideon's eyes blazed fire. An eighteen-gun sloop shot to pieces on a Caribbean bar by a New Hampshire privateer! Even in Federalist New England they'd ring the bells in celebration for that! Tate's twelve-pounder thundered once more.

As the gunsmoke was blown slowly away, revealing the

enemy, Gideon's heart sank. Through his glass he could see clearly that they were afloat and crossing the bar under the main topgallant. For a moment Gideon felt fury at being cheated out of his victory. *Why*, he demanded in despair, *must all my joys be so qualified? Why must every happiness be attenuated with such misery and loss?*

Slowly he mastered his despondency. The Lord was testing His servant, he told himself, there was opportunity in this. He must search through his anger and hopelessness and find it.

The last bundle of dry goods was dropped into a waiting boat, and slaves turned the flat-bottomed scow around and paddled it upstream. "Man the guns!" Gideon shouted. "Two roundshot and a round of grape!"

The crew cheered as they ran to their stations, confident they would engage the enemy, ready to follow their captain against the battered sloop of war.

Their expectations were in vain. The guns were loaded, run out, and primed. "Ye have five minutes to bring yer belongings to the boats!" Gideon shouted, his face masking his anguish. Gideon brought up his two sea chests, his privateering commission, and his spyglass, and had them all carefully put into a boat. The crew, all except Tate's gunners, carrying their belongings wrapped up in scarves or hammocks, filed quickly down into the waiting boats.

"Don Esteban!" Gideon called, seeing the Spaniard standing quietly by the taffrail. " 'Tis time for ye to leave!"

"I believe I shall wait, Captain," Velasco said. His smile was nothing short of impudent. "If you will not object to my company, I would prefer to see the end."

"Very well, Don Esteban!" Gideon answered, feeling a kind of mad recklessness rising inside him. "We'll kill a few more Englishmen before the end!"

Tate's twelve-pounder roared out another challenge. Gideon reached into a weapons tub and picked out two tomahawks.

The enemy sloop was five hundred yards off and approaching rapidly. A puff of smoke appeared over its fo' c'sle, followed seconds later by a moaning shot that passed over *General Sullivan* and crashed among the trees on the riverbank.

"Follow me, Don Esteban!" Gideon called, and he and the Spaniard trotted forward along the deck to the fore scuttle. Descending the companionway, they passed through the berth deck to the carpenter's storeroom and the forward storeroom. From the carpenter's stores they removed all the odd bits of lumber and piled them on the berth deck, then took barrels of tar from the storeroom and rolled them out, tomahawking them open onto the pile of lumber. There was a crash from above as one of the sloop's chasers smashed home into the schooner's timbers.

"Follow me!" Gideon repeated and led Velasco up onto the deck.

Tate and his gun crew, sweat streaking their gunpowder-coated faces and bodies, were working their gun with demonic fury, the twelve-pounder barking every thirty seconds. The enemy were three hundred yards off, their chasers cracking out in systematic reply.

There was not much time. Gideon snatched a slow match from a ready tub and dashed down the aft scuttle, Velasco following. In his little cabin Gideon emptied his desk drawers into a pile on the floor and threw his bedding over the mound of papers. "Smash the windows!" he shouted, and Velasco began the shattering with his tomahawk. The sound of breaking glass mixed with the tortured noise of rending wood as Gideon smashed up his desk drawers for kindling and added them to the pile.

When all was done, Gideon lit the brass lamp and took it down from the chain that swung from the cabin beams; he gestured Velasco aside and smashed the lamp with his tomahawk, flaming oil spitting down onto the papers and the bedding, the slivers of New England pine, and the rainbow-edged shards of glass.

And then they were running again, up the companionway, through the scuttle, and forward, Gideon snatching a lantern from the bulkhead near his cabin and lighting it with his slow match as he ran. The enemy sloop seemed huge, a little over a cable length away, its starboard broadside sliding menacingly out of its ports. Within seconds it would be crossing *General Sullivan*'s stern.

"One more shot, then into the boat!" Gideon shouted as he ran past Tate, and the black man nodded. Down the forward scuttle Gideon smashed the lantern into the pile of lumber and tar. It caught fire instantly, the flames shooting upward toward the beams. Gideon ran back to the deck.

The long tom rocked back on its swivel once more, and then the gun crew ran for the boat warped alongside. The sloop loomed like a huge shadow off the stern. Its sails stole the wind. Gideon snatched an axe from a weapons tub and ran for the boat.

Velasco waited at the entry port. "After you, Captain," he urged politely with a bow.

"Nay, after you, Don Esteban," Gideon said.

"Sir, I insist."

"The captain must leave last of a—" The enemy's first starboard carronade fired, the schooner rocking as the raking shot crashed massively into her stern. The air around Gideon and Velasco shrieked with musketballs as canister swept the deck, and suddenly both men were airborne, crashing simultaneously into the boat's stern sheets as Thomas Tate shouted, "Fend off! Out oars!"

"Stop at the . . . the anchor cable," Gideon gasped, breathless. The axe haft had caught him a painful blow on the hip as he'd landed. Canister shrieked and moaned around them as the enemy sloop crossed the schooner's stern at fifty yards' range, the thirty-two-pound shot smashing the length of the privateer, threatening to tear it asunder. Gideon heard the hearty thunk of musketballs cracking into the boat's stern. Blessedly the gunsmoke poured over the boat and hid it from its enemies.

The last carronade roared. There was a sudden, anxious silence, broken only by the sound of British anchors dropping to the bottom of the bay and by the high-pitched commands of British officers.

"*Stop yer vents!*"

Gideon stood in the stern sheets as the boat approached the anchor cable, picking up the axe, hefting it to his shoulder. Tate maneuvered the boat expertly, bringing the fifteen-inch cable over the stern sheets. Gideon coughed in the thick smoke.

"Better let me do that, Captain," Tate said, standing, his long, muscled arms reaching for the axe.

"*Sponge out!*"

"I'll do it myself, blast ye!" Gideon roared, sweat pouring down his forehead. He blinked, almost blind. "If my *General Sullivan* is to be destroyed, I'll do the job!"

He brought the axe down onto the cable. It vibrated to his steady blows.

"Reload!"

Gideon coughed again in the smoke, and then, as he labored, he realized that the choking smoke was not all from the British cannon but from the fires he'd set aboard his privateer. The smoke stung his eyes, and he blinked away tears.

An enemy carronade barked out. Gideon could hear the progress of the enemy shot, bashing its way through bulkheads, fetching up with a crash against the timbers of the schooner's bows. The next carronade sent sparks showering into the air, dark ashes landing on the boat's crew like some sinister snow.

With a crack the anchor cable parted. "Bring us ashore, Long Tom," Gideon said wearily as he threw the axe into the water. He sat down in the stern sheets. The black man nodded and sang out the necessary commands. Gideon sat facing forward in the boat as the crew stroked for shore, refusing to look back.

The rest of the boat's crew, facing sternward as they pulled at the oars, saw *General Sullivan* begin to drift with the river current, stern first through the shroud of gun-smoke that wrapped the schooner at its death and obscured it from the waiting sloop of war. Fire spit from its hatches as the schooner thudded gently against the sloop's tumble-home; and the privateer's guns, primed and run out, began to fire randomly as the flames reached powder. The British ran madly to slip their cables and get away; they had been handled roughly by Tate's long gun and had lost their fore-topmast, which kept them from working into the wind and making their escape. Brave men, risking immolation, fended the schooner off with pikes. The sloop broke free, its main topgallant afire; bucket brigades running frantically up the shrouds. The sail was cut free, and the fires doused. *General Sullivan*'s guns continued to fire randomly through the haze of smoke. She was half a mile from shore when the magazines blew her open to the sea. She settled on an even keel and sank in shallow water. The masts, their defiant flags still waving, remained above the waves.

Gideon Markham saw none of it. He could not bring himself to watch, through the tears he could no longer hide, the destruction of the only home and the only joy he'd known since he'd laid down the schooner three years before.

5

AT THE GRAVESIDE: GIDEON

The afternoon of the battle Gideon presided wearily over the funerals of Harris, the first officer, and the other men who had died. The graves had been dug hastily, and there was no canvas for coffins. The dead men were laid to rest in sacking.

Alexander Harris's heart had been pierced with a pike; his face lay untouched, slack in the tropical heat, expressionless, but still recognizable as Harris. Gideon found himself wondering, as he read from the burial service, whether or not he was reading over the grave of a friend.

He shook his head—there had been no friendship here. For over a year Gideon and Harris had sailed together; they lived and worked alongside one another, fought the same enemy, battled the same storms, and faced the same death with its chances of mutilation or disfigurement. Harris had been a burly man, a seaman born, with a temper the hands had been careful not to provoke. Gideon knew that he'd drunk in secret, that somewhere on board he'd had a cache of brandy. Once each week Gideon had invited Harris to dine with him, but they'd spoken of professional matters, whether the standing rigging should be tarred down, where the next cruising ground should be, how much the latest prize would bring in New Orleans. Gideon did not know if Harris's parents were still alive somewhere in New England—in his papers, burned with *General Sullivan*, there would have been a record of that. Gideon didn't know if Harris had a sweetheart somewhere, whether he was a Federalist or Republican or if he believed in the Life Eternal. He knew that Harris had obeyed orders well, that he could be trusted with a job. That was all. Now Harris was dead, and Gideon wondered how he could have lived so intimately with the man for such a length of time, and ultimately know so little. Gideon, the man who longed to *know*.

Harris's slack face gave away no secrets. Gideon found the dead man's expressionless face irritating. The dead should be wiser than the living, they should speak eloquently of the beyond. *Doth not wisdom cry? and understanding put forth her voice?* The words rolled cynically from Gideon's mind, and he suppressed them. He believed in God, and His Son, and the eternal life to come. He told himself fervently that he believed, that one day the answer would come. But Harris spoke not, and wisdom cried not. As hard as Gideon listened, he could not hear the voice of his God.

6

RIO LAGARTOS

"An interesting sort of barbarian," said Velasco, handing his wife a glass of claret. Olivia accepted the glass without speaking. They sat on the veranda of Rio Lagartos, their principal plantation, watching the burial service being conducted in the white cemetery down below. It was consecrated ground, and when Father Reies found out there might have been Protestants buried there, there might be trouble; but Velasco was a civilized man and saw no reason why white men should be buried in the colored cemetary merely on account of some three-century-old doctrinal dispute.

"He chews tobacco and speaks of God as if the Almighty had him to dinner once a week," Velasco said. "We shall have to go over the plantation very carefully after he leaves, and burn all the Protestant tracts. He is bound to leave a few. I don't want Father Reies to find them."

He delicately smoothed out a wrinkle in the trousers of his pale blue suit. Velasco had returned to Rio Lagartos in dreadful disarray, with tar and gunsmoke streaking his green and yellow outfit, and his collar stock torn by a bullet he hadn't even noticed. He found the pale blue restful. He reached out and took his wife's hand.

"I hope those dreadful sailors don't stay long," said Olivia. She peered out over the veranda toward the sea and toward the long black plume of smoke that rose from the green horizon.

"Those ships are still burning," she said.

"Yes. I put the Spanish flag over them and tried to tell the British they were my property, but they were not appeased. The prizes were in shallow water, and the flames will not quench. They will burn for some time."

"You should not take such risks, my love," said Olivia.

Velasco affected a lazy, feline shrug. "It was nothing, my dear. A little skirmish in the night."

The party at the graveside dispersed, the majority organized under George Willard to build temporary lodging for themselves. Gideon Markham, carrying his bible, walked across the long plantation lawn to the veranda. His brown coat was still stained with gunpowder and ash. Velasco introduced him to his wife. Olivia did not speak English, and Gideon could not speak her tongue. Velasco interpreted the necessary formalities.

"We would offer you wine, Captain, but I remember you do not drink," Velasco said. "Perhaps we could offer you lemonade?"

"Wine would be excellent, Don Esteban," said Gideon. "I do not drink spirits on my vessel; it would be bad for discipline. But ashore there is no reason for abstinence."

"Have some claret, sir. It is the best we can get in these difficult days."

"Thankee, Don Esteban."

They drank quietly in the shade of the great porch. Señora Velasco could not entirely keep her eyes from wandering over Gideon, observing the dark blood under his fingernails, the little wounds in his clothing from enemy lead and iron. The sea breeze, soft this far inland, cooled the veranda.

"Don Esteban, I must find my way to a ship," Gideon said. "I must travel to Mobile to meet my other privateer."

"Then you must go to Havana," said Velasco. "Even there you may have trouble finding a ship to go to Mobile, since your, ah, countrymen have seized the place. You will probably find a ship bound for Pensacola and can make your way from there. I will give you a horse if you wish."

"Thankee, but it would be faster to go by sea. Mr. Willard saved a boat and hid it carefully; other boats are upstream past the landing. If the British don't find them all, we'll be able to outfit a boat and be in Havana in two or three days."

"Much faster than the land route, indeed," said Velasco cautiously. He sipped his wine. He thought he knew where this conversation was going to lead.

"Don Esteban, I cannot take my men with me," Gideon said. "That many Americans in San Juan would attract attention. They would almost certainly be arrested—the Spanish authorities have imprisoned any American privateers they could find, even those that were in distress. As a single American gentleman I may be able to get by, but my men—never."

Velasco carefully brushed a silken lapel. "How may I assist you, my friend?" he asked.

Gideon coughed uncomfortably. "They need a place to stay for two or three months," Gideon said. "I would of course pay for their food and for any other articles they may need. They're all skilled—if ye needed a building put up or a grove cleared, they could be put to use."

"I could be in serious trouble were it found out," Velasco said. "The British will certainly complain to the authorities in Havana, who will send men to make inquiries for your crew."

"Don Esteban, I trust you are not without influence," Gideon said as tactfully as he could. "My men could live by the landing. No one goes down there, and it's on your land. You would know of any searches. Willard could enforce strict discipline; they wouldn't be found wandering about."

Velasco sipped his wine. He could use the labors of fifty white men for the autumn months. He had licensed a sugar press a year before, but hadn't found the skilled labor to build it—slaves were useless in such matters. A new stable had to go up, since the last had been burnt by a trouble-making slave. The privateer's boats had been so much more efficient than the flat-bottomed craft hammered together by the slaves that it would be nice to have a few. As for any search conducted by the local forces, Velasco was himself the local magistrate, and the head of the local garrison was known to be very approachable in these matters, and to be so extraordinarily lazy and inefficient that any search he conducted would easily be diverted. Besides, he could tell the man that he had with his own eyes seen the privateers sailing away in their little boats and that they hadn't returned.

"You may tell your men that they may stay, Captain,"

he said. "They will keep out of sight on Sundays—that's when the priest comes. He was here earlier today but has gone."

"Today?" Gideon said. "Today is the Sabbath?"

"It is Sunday, the third Sunday in August."

"Thunderation!" Gideon gasped. "I'd forgotten!"

"You had other things on your mind, Captain."

Gideon seemed quite agitated. "I should not have forgotten," he muttered. "The Sabbath is holy, and I should have kept it." He stood. "Thank you for the wine, Don Esteban, and the chance to meet your beautiful wife," he said. "I thank you on behalf of my men. I will tell them the good news, and then we'll have a little service. The two of ye will be most welcome."

"A Sunday service after a funeral?" asked Velasco, puzzled. "Have you not already—?"

"Not in the proper spirit," said Gideon firmly. "The men are used to special Sunday services. I must choose a text. Good day to you, sir. Señora."

Velasco rose hastily. "Good day, Captain," he said. "Supper is at eight if you would care to join us."

"I would be honored, Don Esteban. Tonight, then."

Velasco sat down as he watched the receding form of the Yankee captain. "An interesting sort of barbarian," he said to his wife again, and took her hand.

7

ABOARD PRINSESSA

The ship *Prinsessa* had once been Swedish but now flew
Spanish colors; she carried dry goods to Mobile, and her
mate kicked and cursed the crew. Her American captain,
named Addams, was one of those driven from his country
during the embargoes to find work where he could. Gideon
seemed to remember hearing an unsavory story about a
Captain Addams from Marble Head, but he could not remember the details.

There were twenty other passengers, most of them heading for New Orleans, where many owned land or had
places of business. No Spanish ship would head directly to
New Orleans for fear of Baratarian pirates; to sail to Mobile was risky enough. Gideon shared a little cabin with his
sole companion, Grimes, his steward and suspected cousin.

His legendary uncle Malachi had apparently left a few
indiscreet bastards in Caribbean ports; it had been a family
anxiety that one of them would arrive one day to claim an
inheritance. But the worry had waned over the years—at
least until Grimes, with his smooth mulatto features, fine
manners, and utter ignorance of the sea, had walked
aboard *General Sullivan* two years before when Gideon
was making his first Caribbean voyage after the disaster of
the embargoes. Grimes had been able to offer no evidence,
and his handsome, impassive face certainly bore no family
likeness, but the claim that he'd been fathered on a freed-
woman named Sarah by an American captain named
Markham struck Gideon as far too likely for comfort. The
family orphan was adopted as a servant and proved to be a
good one: somewhere in his forty years he'd learned discretion, excellent manners, and acceptable cooking.

Wallace Grimes spoke Spanish, Dutch, Portuguese,

French, and other Caribbean languages—he seemed to have inherited Malachi's gift for tongues—and had been taken to Havana as interpreter. The ride in *General Sullivan's* old pinnace had taken two days, and then Gideon had spent three days hiding in a dark, stifling Havana pensione while Grimes went out in search of transportation to Mobile or at least Pensacola, the only major Gulf port still in Spanish hands.

Transportation on a Spanish ship to Mobile was hard to come by, for Mobile had been seized earlier in the year by James Wilkinson, American general and former Burr conspirator, ending a long quarrel over whether West Florida was part of the Louisiana Purchase or not. The seizure had been made on the grounds that if the Americans didn't take the place, the British soon would in order to use the harbor as a base for an attack on New Orleans. Wilkinson had been supported by the American government, but Spanish resentment over the loss of the finest port on the Gulf easily explained Cuba's less-than-courteous treatment of American privateers found sailing within their jurisdiction, and fully justified Gideon's caution.

Nevertheless *Prinsessa*, a Spanish ship, was bound for Mobile. It carried dry goods that would command high prices there no matter whose flag was flying over the fort at the bay's entrance. It was luck, and extraordinarily good luck, that *Prinsessa* came into port to water, take on passengers, and receive instructions from the ship's owners just a day after Gideon Markham had sailed past Havana's elaborate fortifications and anchored the little pinnace in the harbor.

His fellow passengers struck Gideon as a trivial collection of people, thirteen men and six women, most of them Spanish gentry, chattering away at the breakfast table in their musical, frivolous-sounding language. Gideon said a quiet grace over his meal and tried to suppress his irritation when the others who bothered to say their grace also crossed themselves—a custom he didn't enjoy seeing. A few polite Spanish questions addressed to him were met by his annoyed apologies in English. One of the lady passengers, whose head was wrapped in a fashionable lace veil that hung dramatically over one shoulder, seemed to consider him particularly amusing. He'd eaten quickly, gulped his final cup of breakfast coffee, and excused himself. On deck for a walk he'd almost taken his habitual place on the weather quarterdeck, but he was warned off at the last minute by a glare from the mate. The weather quarterdeck was another captain's privilege. Gideon's privilege and his quarterdeck had gone down with *General Sullivan,* and the reminder of his loss sent a bitter spike of anguish into his heart. *As it happeneth to the fool, so it happeneth even to me,* he thought, *and why was I then more wise?*

Blind to the glorious summer day, to the sparkle of the foam, and to the weird buzzing leaps of the flying fish that surrounded the vessel, Gideon paced out the watch. The new watch was driven on deck with blows and curses and sent aloft to set the studding sails. The captain, an odd, bent man in black, came on deck to escort some of the passengers.

The passengers clustered by the rail to watch the flying fish, and the captain took his place on the weather quarterdeck, spitting Spanish curses at the crew as they struggled to set the studding sails in the brisk breeze. Gideon cocked an eye at the mainmast. The studding sails were being set clumsily, it was true, but the combined oaths of the captain and the mate were doing little but confusing the situation. What the crew needed was practice, not curses. And perhaps a mate who was willing to go aloft and show them the work rather than swaggering on the foredeck and swearing.

In due course the studding sails were set aloft on their booms, and *Prinsessa* sped rapidly through the water, the great canvas sails billowing full, the clipper prow slicing through the green waves. Gideon spared himself a moment of grudging admiration. *Prinsessa* was yare, whether she was badly served or no. The Swedish designers must have taken a few pointers from the Yankee ships that passed through the Baltic every year—or had, before Tom Jefferson had forbade it and the war ruined the trade.

"Captain Markham?" It was *Prinsessa*'s captain, a rough old brute by his looks.

"Aye," said Gideon.

"Gideon Markham of the New Hampshire Markhams?" Captain Addams persisted. He was a tall man, but bent, almost twisted, like a tree planted on an exposed cliff and bowed by the winds. He was dressed in a battered black coat and an old Quaker-brimmed hat, his white hair straggling out from underneath.

"I am he," said Gideon. "Captain Addams, is it not?"

"Aye, that's me," Addams said, clasping Gideon's hand firmly. "Peter Addams of Marble Head."

Gideon almost shrank away from the smell of rum. It was three hours to noon, and the man had been drinking already.

" 'Tis good to see a New England man after all these years," Addams declared. "I've been living among these garlic-eating dagoes ever since Mad Tom Jefferson made it impossible for a seaman to earn a living where he was bred and born. I believe I know yer brother, Obadiah. I was once interviewed for the post of the master of the *Abigail*, but I suppose it didn't work out."

"*Abigail?* That was my first command," said Gideon. "I'd come back from the Mediterranean unexpectedly and was given the schooner."

"Aye, I see," said Addams. His grin was friendly, but there was bitterness in his eyes.

"I suppose that's what families are for," he said.

Gideon remembered *Abigail* well, the little two-masted schooner, over twenty years old but still as seaworthy as the day she was launched. He'd loved every plank and line of her, even the cranks and crotchets, the unexpected leaks and the way she hesitated slightly before answering the helm. He'd been newly married then. After each voyage, to Baltimore or Halifax or the Mediterranean, Betsy had welcomed him home to the warm house of New Hampshire granite he'd built for her. It was those lost years of happiness to which his bitter imagination returned again and again, preventing the scars from healing; to those years before the Embargo when he had sung daily to his God of blessedness and gratitude. Before the Embargo wrecked it all.

"The *Abigail*," he said, remembering. "She was broken up six years ago, during the Embargo. She was worth more as scrap."

"Aye, the Embargo," said Addams bitterly. "I was beg-

ging for my bread for two months before I got the chance
to ship out on a dago ship, some old Portuguese hooker
with a British master. I know men that died of starvation
rather than beg."

"Women, too," Gideon said, seeing in his mind the little
room, the single candle, the cold ashes and bloody handkerchiefs . . .

"Damn Tom Jefferson to hell!" Addams spat. He turned
suddenly on his heel and roared an order to the mate, who
in turn seized one of the sailors who had been standing too
closely to one of the lady passengers; the mate threw the
man against the mainmast fife rail and thrashed him with a
colt until he fell to the deck and cried for mercy. The passengers watched impassively. Captain Addams turned back
to Gideon.

"It's scum I've got for a crew, Captain Markham," he
said. "None of 'em know a rat's ass about discipline, and
none of 'em want to know. They'd be playing their guitars
and singing their sad, sad songs all day if I didn't watch
'em. If they weren't stealing the passengers' watches and
jewels, that is. Did ye see how them stuns'ls were set? By
Christ, if I only had New England men!"

"Yer men are untaught, Captain," Gideon said. "If they
were shown patiently what they were expected to do—"

"Patience, hell!" Addams swore. "They think it's weakness if I'm not always hazing 'em to do better. Threats and
blows are all they understand."

"I wish ye would moderate yer language in the presence
of ladies, Captain," Gideon said with an uneasy eye toward
the passengers. Addams laughed.

"Moderate!" he said. "They can't speak English! Besides, they've probably heard far worse in their time.
There're a few stories I could tell ye—perhaps we could step
below for a spell and yarn over some Jamaican rum?"

"Er—I'm temperance, Captain," Gideon said. "But I
thankee for yer offer."

"Ye're welcome any time ye wish," Addams said. He
scratched his chin and began to ramble on about his adventures, apparently needing no further stimulus of Jamaican rum to do so. Gideon let the battered, twisted figure
talk, wandering on about his adventures and ill-luck, while

he looked out to the far horizon and wrapped himself in his own black meditations. Gradually it began to dawn upon Gideon that Addams, in his plodding, discursive way, was trying to ask for a job.

Gideon was then obliged to explain how the Markham family business was no longer dependent entirely upon shipping, and how his elder brother, Obadiah, and his brilliant cousin, Lafayette (who had persuaded his father and uncle to turn over primary control of the business on January 1, 1800, to mark the new century with the footprints of the new generation), had turned the family business toward small manufacturing, timber harvesting, and land speculation. After the Embargoes the shipping part of the business had been neglected and almost sold altogether; the Markham family, once known as merchants and shipowners, had become landbound capitalists, and the only reason a few ships still carried the Markham name on their books was that Gideon would not countenance another trade. There were no jobs to give, at least until after the war when the shipping business might be expected to increase.

Addams shouldered his disappointment and left the poop, presumably for his overdue appointment with Jamaican rum; Gideon saw him speak to the mate before going below. With a weary, uncomprehending shrug the mate turned to bawl a series of orders to the crew, and the hands turned out to hose and wash the deck. Gideon frowned. On his own vessel the task would have been done before breakfast.

The passengers came up the poop ladder or went below as seawater began to gush over the maindeck. With the sudden crowding on the poop Gideon was unable to continue his pacing; he stood at the lee rail, watching *Prinsessa*'s wake widen as it passed from beneath the ship's graceful stern.

"Beg pardon, sir. You are an American, are you not?"

It was one of the lady passengers, the woman with the dramatic veil that fluttered out a good three feet in the wind; she spoke English with a surprising Dixie accent.

"I am, ma'am," he said, a bit taken aback at her forwardness. "I'm from New Hampshire."

"I am from South Carolina," she said. "I apologize for my directness, but there doesn't seem to be anyone on this ship who could introduce us. It's good to talk to a fellow American!"

"I'm pleased, ma'am," said Gideon. She was about thirty and tall, with broad, almost masculine shoulders. She wore the white, European gown with a short blue spencer jacket to keep off a chill, that is if a chill could be found in the Caribbean in August. Her face was pleasant, expressive, almost pretty—but for Gideon's taste there was too much boldness in her eyes.

"I am Captain Markham," said Gideon.

"Maria-Anna Johnson de Marquez Suarez," she said and dropped a curtsey.

"Señora Marquez," Gideon said and bowed.

"Are you a sea captain? Or do you hold a commission in the militia?"

"I am a privateer, Señora," Gideon said. She looked at him with curiosity; he felt obliged, for no reason he could understand, to offer further explanations.

"The Lord willed that I should lose my ship," he said. "I'm preparing to meet another vessel in Mobile, of which I shall have the command."

"I'm sorry for your first ship, sir."

"The Almighty would have it so. We are not to question His purposes."

"Amen," she said, a touch too lightly.

There was a long silence. The flying fish whirred about the ship, scattering droplets of water that gleamed in the sun.

"There's my maidservant, talking to a sailor again," Señora Marquez said, pointing out a pretty, dark-haired girl with disheveled hair standing next to one of the hands who was engaged in scrubbing the planks.

"I cannot teach that girl discretion!" Señora Marquez frowned. "She's only fourteen, and she's mad about sailors. I can't seem to keep her away. It can only do her harm at that age."

"It's good that ye're concerned," said Gideon.

"Campaspe!" she called. The girl heard and ran to her side. Señora Marquez spoke to her fiercely in Spanish; the girl nodded, answered in a respectful tone, and then turned to go below. But as her mistress turned back to Gideon, he saw the girl turn and flash him a dazzling, impudent smile, cast at him from behind her mistress's back. The girl went below, tossing her head.

"My adopted cousins, the Spaniards, fear privateers from America," Señora Marquez was saying. "Those that fly the Cartagenian flag. They are called pirates by the Spanish."

"Those would be the Baratarians, Señora," Gideon said, recovering from that audacious, astounding, and entirely shameless smile. "They are ruled by two men named Lafitte. I have met one of them, Pierre, in New Orleans. Your Spanish friends are right; they're pirates. I am a lawful privateer, and I take only British prizes."

"I'm sure I did not think otherwise, Captain Markham. Is it profitable, this trade of yours?"

"It is profitable or not as the Lord wills," Gideon said.

"And as luck and talent may provide, I'm sure," she said with a smile.

Gideon had been subjected to one easy smile already; he did not entirely approve of women who smiled so easily. His answer was deliberately grave.

"Luck and talent come from above, Señora Marquez."

"To be sure, Captain." The mate bawled out an order from forward. There was a rush to trim the sails.

"Does your wife await you in Mobile, Captain?" she asked. "Or in some other port?"

Gideon's eyes did not leave the sea.

"My wife and son are with God," he said.

"I am sorry, Captain. I'm sorry as well for my tactlessness."

The mizzen yards creaked as they were trimmed to the wind, which had backed a point since sunrise. Gideon turned to the woman beside him, a kind of impatient distaste rising like bile in his throat. He had almost welcomed the gap of language that had separated him from the others aboard *Prinsessa*; now that the gap had been bridged, he wanted nothing but to return to his own solitude.

"Perhaps ye should go below, ma'am," he said. "They are about to wash the deck here."

"Thank you, Captain. You are kind."

He watched her go as he cut himself a plug of tobacco, her lace veil fluttering out behind her as she walked down the poop ladder, surefooted in her slippers. The muslin gown was thin and showed her form, but he could find no reaction within him, neither lust nor disapproval, nothing but the yearning to set foot on his own deck again, with the invisible line of the quarterdeck to separate him from the rest of mankind.

8

SAVANNAH

Gideon had never forgotten that little bare room with its straw bed, the cold ashes in the grate, the bloody cloths used as handkerchiefs, the candle lit only when company came because once the candle was spent there was no money to buy another . . . The little room in Savannah, where Gideon Markham had condemned Betsy to die.

In January 1808 the schooner *Abigail,* with a cargo of English goods, made its final voyage to New Hampshire. Before Gideon was able to say a proper hello to his wife and son, Obadiah and Jeremiah, his brothers, wheeled their carriage to his door. The Embargo Act had been passed, and the shipping business had collapsed. Decisions had been taken in Gideon's absence: rather than enter the vicious competition for what remained of the coastal trade, the Markham vessels were to be laid up until times were better. There was no longer a place at sea even for a brother to be kept employed. A place had been made for Gideon at a family-owned lumber camp in Vermont—he was to be manager. They hoped he understood.

Betsy was pale and overworked; it was manifestly unfair to force her to Vermont, although she wanted to go. She had been a servant for Gideon's rich cousin Lafayette when she married him, but Gideon could have had the hand of a cousin of the Crowninshields. Betsy felt slighted by the other Markhams and their ever-so-suitable wives.

But after prayer Gideon decided to accept the job. Betsy would have to remain in the house at Portsmouth, taking care of little Jos. Jos, it was thought, would probably be a strapping young lad: his muscles seemed highly developed, almost abnormally so.

Husband and wife consoled one another with the

thought that they would actually be closer to one another
than during most of Gideon's voyages. Gideon headed inland to Vermont just before the first snow fell.

The lumber camp worked efficiently for the first few
months; Gideon found himself enjoying the crisp winter air
even though it lacked the tang of salt. He worked hard,
and hundreds of trees lined the banks of the stream, waiting for the thaw to carry them to the mills. The pay at the
camp, however, was in arrear, and Gideon anxiously paid
the men out of his own pocket. Letters were sent to Obadiah and Lafayette, imploring aid. The spring broke the
rivers free, and the logs were rafted to Markham mills.
There they waited until the rot took them.

Most of the orders had been cancelled. The shipbuilding
interests had been the chief support of the lumber trade;
shipbuilding was wiped out, and the demand for lumber
had fallen. It was no longer profitable to cut new timber or
to ship it. It seemed to Gideon that such a thing should
have been foreseen; but he paid his men, again out of his
own funds, and dismissed them. He returned to Portsmouth in a Piscataqua gundalow and discovered that Jeremiah had been sent by the family to Washington to urge
repeal of the Embargo.

Obadiah and Lafayette could not cover Gideon's losses;
Lafayette had even sold his carriage. They offered to make
Gideon the manager of a mill—not a lumber mill this time,
but a corn mill. New England may no longer be able to
build ships, they said, but it will still need bread.

But Betsy was alarmingly thin and pale, and the doctors
had their own news. Gideon's wife was consumptive, and
the condition was worsening. They recommended a vaca-
tion in a southern climate. They had also examined Jos,
who, despite his overdeveloped muscles, was having difficulty learning to walk, but they had concluded that he was
simply slow.

Gideon's father offered him money, but he refused; he
knew that Josiah was having difficulty covering David's
debts at Yale. The snug New England house was sold, and
Gideon purchased passage for his family on a coasting
schooner. Savannah was as far south as he found himself
willing to go; he did not want Betsy ill in a strange coun-

try. But Savannah was not entirely a healthy place: yellow
fever and malaria lurked on the town's outskirts, and pesti-
lential African fevers were occasionally brought by the incoming slave ships. The blackbirders, carrying ebony men
and women who wore strange tattoos and scars and who
bared their filed teeth at auction, were the only craft moving in and out of harbor. Savannah's port was choked with
ships that rotted slowly at anchor, while cargoes spoiled in
the warehouses. The merchants were beseiged with captains desperate for any kind of work. Gideon, without
friends or kin in town, watched his funds dwindle.

Their first home in Savannah was a comfortable four
rooms: two bedrooms, one for the child, a kitchen, and a
parlor. The street was eminently respectable, and perfect
strangers tipped their hats to Betsy in the streets. The summery South was good for Betsy; her health improved, but
that of Jos did not. Age two, he was covered with bruises
from trying to walk; the doctors fitted his legs with iron
braces. Gideon, his funds sinking, was forced to work for a
few weeks as an overseer on a rice plantation, but the misery of the slaves was overwhelming, and the work dis-
gusted him. He wondered, as he rode his horse and unwill-
ingly brandished his whip, whether his cousin Favian, a
naval lieutenant, could find him a place as a warrant or
petty officer in the young American navy.

The Embargo Act was replaced by the Non-Intercourse
Act—trade was reopened except with France and England.
A few ships were put in commission, ready to leave Savannah. Gideon begged hat in hand for work and found himself desperate enough to embrace a scheme by two merchants as desperate as he.

A brig, the *Two Sisters*, was fitted out, loaded with
cargo of turpentine, and equipped with manifests declaring
its object to be Palermo in Sicily, a part of the Kingdom of
the Two Sicilies and not interdicted by the Non-
Intercourse Act. Instead *Two Sisters* would try to run the
British blockade into French-occupied Naples, or Leghorn
if possible, where the turpentine could be sold for a better
price.

Gideon agreed to his backers' desperate scheme. Most of
his pay as captain of the venture was to be given to Betsy;

it was assumed that she and Jos would be able to live comfortably, if not elegantly, until Gideon's return. Gideon enrolled a crew and set sail for the embattled Mediterranean. Betsy collected the first of his pay on schedule.

Her second home in Savannah was of two rooms, a bedroom and a sitting room, rented from a respectable widow. She was determined to live frugally, since much of Gideon's pay went for doctors' fees. The Georgia physicians concluded that Jos, just three years of age, had acquired a degenerative muscle disease; his overdeveloped muscles had shrunken to pitiful bands, and soon he would be unable to walk even with his braces. At some indefinite point in the future he would probably find himself unable even to crawl. Betsy's prayers grew more fervent, and with the coming of autumn her cheeks again grew pale.

Off Algeciras *Two Sisters* encountered a British frigate. Under its overwhelming broadside five of Gideon's crew, including a Cherokee Indian who could not by any stretch of the imagination be called a subject of George III, were declared to be British nationals and pressed aboard the frigate. Gideon was left with two men and three boys as crew and wondered whether he could somehow have resisted.

In Savannah debts of honor were called due, and *Two Sisters*'s owners were bankrupted. Betsy's payments ceased. She wrote to Josiah Markham in Portsmouth, but Josiah was ill, and it was Obadiah who answered. Some little money was sent. As the doctors had predicted, Jos was no longer able to walk.

Betsy's third home was rented from an Irish widow: the single room contained a large feather bed and a chest of drawers, and the curtain separating her from her landlady could not keep out the latter's songs that were howled at the ceiling while she took snuff and added dollops of whiskey to her tea. Betsy wrote to Josiah again, but Josiah was away with Obadiah, and the letter was answered snippishly by Obadiah's wife. The family was not made of money, the good woman reminded Betsy, but a little money was condescendingly enclosed. Betsy vowed never to beg from the Markham family again. It was a promise she was not to keep.

Gideon discovered problems in Naples. Napoleon's customs service seemed to think that Gideon's cargo had been transshipped in Palermo—*Two Sisters*'s false papers may have suggested the idea—which under the Berlin and Milan decrees would make the brig and cargo liable for confiscation as a trader with the enemy. *Two Sisters* was searched twice, soldiers in green uniforms poking into the hold with bayonets. Gideon's agents made discreet inquiries, hoping to settle the matter in the usual way. The third time the soldiers came Gideon was arrested and charged with the attempted bribery of a customs official. Apparently the agent had been careless, and someone hadn't got his proper cut.

The trial was secret, short, and farcical. The American consul was never informed. The proceedings were conducted in Italian, which Gideon could not understand. He was sentenced to life in the galleys. *Two Sisters* and its cargo were impounded.

Although the sentence was life in the galleys, there were no more galleys; they had all been destroyed in the wars. Gideon shared a subterranean, lightless room with a hatchet murderer, a halfwit accused of rape, and a Turkish homosexual. After three months lying on the wet stone, listening to the murderer ramble endlessly about his crimes, his bloody revenge on the neighboring family he thought had slighted him, Gideon was brought from the prison and sent aboard the Venetian warship *Carolina*. Though his eyes were dazzled by the sun he hadn't seen for over ninety days, his face possessed a fierce, secret joy. From the cell there was no possible escape, but pressing Gideon Markham aboard a ship was almost as good as handing him the keys to the prison door. . . .

Betsy's fourth home was on a street populated by freed slaves and drunken, vicious white trash, the only whites degenerate enough, in local opinion, to have blacks for neighbors. Betsy worked, when well, as a seamstress or a governess for other people's children, tasks the locals called "nigger work," work no self-respecting white would perform. But increasingly Betsy was too ill to work, and she discovered that Jos required constant tending. The South-

ern winter was surprisingly bitter. At night she slept with a
pet cat cradled on her chest to help keep her warm.

The *Carolina*, named not after a province in America
but after a sister of Bonaparte, slipped through the Straits
of Messina and into the Ionian Sea. Her captain heard
from a passing Venetian xebec that there was a British brig
in the vicinity, bound for Corinth. The information was to
prove correct, and the capture was made.

Gideon, in his two months aboard the warship, had been
promoted from ordinary to able seaman, and made a loader
on the starboard broadside. He was learning Italian slowly,
and only his ignorance of the language kept him from further promotion. He and five others, in the charge of a
drunken lieutenant, were put aboard the British merchantman with orders to take her up the Dalmatian coast.

Gideon prepared his escape carefully. He had sold his
daily wine ration for what he could get and had a pouch of
silver. Volunteering to stand watch that night, he bribed
his fellow watchman to turn his back as he lashed together
the oars and masts of one of the prize's boats and leaped
with the improvised raft over the side. The Bay of Corinth
was still and narrow. By morning Gideon was washed up,
like Odysseus, on the stony Greek shore.

He found dubious work in a fishing village; his fellow
crewmen, explaining themselves in shattered English and
broken Italian, claimed to battle for Greek liberty, but
Gideon smelled piracy in the wind. Dubious, he boarded
the tartane fitting out on the beach and made himself valuable in teaching the crewmen the elements of pike drill.

The Greek tartane's first victim was a Turkish felucca
found off Crete. The Turkish sailors failed to see the tartane until the two vessels were almost alongside. The tartane had no carriage guns, so the felucca was carried in a
rush of boarders. The Turks fled below decks but were
eventually persuaded to surrender. The Greeks celebrated
this blow for liberty with wine, and their mood turned vicious.

The surviving Turks were put to the sword. Two women
found aboard were cheerfully raped, then decapitated. Gideon watched, as the corpses were cut open to discover
whether they had swallowed money or jewelry, fighting not

to show outrage or anger, knowing that in this mood his fellow pirates would as soon kill him as the Turks. The bloody scraps of the massacre were tossed overboard, and the felucca was cleaned, painted a new color above the waterline, and sailed into Iraklion. There the cargo and vessel were sold. After receiving his share of the loot Gideon stepped ashore, turning his back on the pirates. If he had not needed it so desperately, he would have flung the money into the sea.

That night while the Greek crew made free with their money and their tongues, boasting of their prowess to the Cretan whores, Gideon bought passage to Malta on a Sicilian felucca. By the time he left Iraklion the pirates' heads were decorating the walls of the castle: they had grown too drunk and spoken too much.

At Malta a ship for Charleston was found, and Gideon worked his way to America as a seaman, taking the place of a man pressed by the British. From Charleston a coastal schooner was taken to Savannah.

It was then that Gideon first heard of his backers' bankruptcy and discovered that his wife, a year before, had left her second address. Anxiety gnawed at him as he walked the streets of Savannah from address to seamier address, hunting the vision that waited for him in the end, that single room with its single candle and Betsy dying.

Betsy and Jos were moved to Savannah's finest hotel, and their bills paid by the last of Gideon's loot and his seaman's pay. Betsy had swallowed her pride and written again to Josiah from her fourth Savannah home, that single dirt room. Gideon's father, recovering from the broken hip and recurrent pneumonia that had troubled him for over a year, had awakened suddenly to Betsy's danger. His bill of exchange for five hundred dollars arrived the day following Betsy's death.

It seemed the Markham family was prosperous once more. Jeremiah, the family propagandist in Washington, had received advance warning of the repeal of certain of the Non-Intercourse Acts, and Markham ships were equipped on the sly to be the first out of harbor. The profits were enormous, but Gideon, of course, had missed them.

Jos, thinned to a stick figure, finally, mercifully, died a month after his mother. Gideon, unable to find a Congregational minister in Savannah, himself committed the boy to the earth, the little coffin lying in clay next to Betsy's.

Gideon raised the gravestones on what would ever to him be a hated land, the American and alien South, in the soil of which lay the last of his happiness. His unreasoning curse lay on Savannah, and as he set forth again for New England, he resolved never again to make his home anywhere but in the cabin of a Yankee ship.

9

GAMBLING FOR HIGH STAKES

After breakfast Captain Addams asked the ladies to stay below, and the gentleman passengers to come on deck. While Gideon and the other passengers stood on the poop, Addams and the mate assembled their crew with the usual accompaniment of shouts and threats. One man, a thin, shifty individual, was singled out from the rest by the mate and led by two unwilling crewmen to the main shrouds. Under the mate's supervision the man was stripped to the waist, spread-eagled, and seized up against the shrouds. His ribs and plaintive scapulae stood out on his thin frame. Seizing him up was an act that Gideon for all his years at sea had never seen performed on a merchant vessel.

Merciful heavens! Gideon thought. *He's to be flogged!*

But another of the crew—a tall, dignified man, aged forty or so, obviously a practiced seaman—came forward to speak to the mate. His tone was reasonable, but the mate turned red and roared, and Captain Addams shouted down from the poop. The sailors' spokesman was stripped and seized up beside his companion.

Enough, Gideon thought. He hastily made his way to the side of Captain Addams. "Beg pardon, Captain," he said hastily, "but why's the man to be flogged?"

Addams turned an angry, bloodshot eye on Gideon. "I'll have no interference from a passenger, Captain Markham!" he snarled. "This is *my ship!*"

"Aye, ye are within yer rights, Captain Addams," Gideon said as smoothly as he could, "but perhaps these men have—"

Addams face twisted with fury. He reeked of rum. "I will have no more of yer jaw!" he shouted. "Or these men neither! I will have no more insolence nor answering back nor surliness on this ship. Not from passengers and certainly not from my crew! Now, *good day to ye,* Captain Markham!"

Gideon drew himself erect. "As ye wish, Captain," he said and walked away. He condemned himself for his clumsiness; challenging Addams when the man was well within his rights was altogether the wrong approach. He should have been more subtle, should have angled carefully, as if driving a bargain on market day. He knew now he should have seemed to agree with Addams, offering to support ship's discipline, and then gradually turned Addams away from a flogging and toward more constructive means of punishment. Instead he had simply confirmed Addams in his stubborn arrogance. At the first sound of the whip Gideon turned to face the punishment and forced himself to watch. It would be his own penance for bungling his attempt at mercy.

The mate had made a proper cat-o'-nine-tails out of cord. The first man, the man whose ribs stood out so prominently in his thin flesh, was given two dozen lashes. The victim's breath was knocked out of him with each blow and he could not scream. At the end his ribs shone white through the bloody muscle and flesh. He was left to moan against the shrouds while the mate refreshed himself with a cup of water. Clearing the scraps of skin and blood from the cords, the mate gave the second man, the spokesman, three dozen. Presumably he gave the extra dozen because he was tired and his blows were not falling as savagely as they had at first. Somewhere the victim found breath enough to scream.

The crewmen were told to cut down the bloody, striped victims. When they obeyed, the first sufferer was found to be dead. The pain had stopped his heart.

Captain Addams grew red and bellowed out an order. The men balked. The mate waved his bloody cat at them and reluctantly they picked up their dead comrade and threw him overboard for the sharks. Addams leered triumphantly from the weather quarterdeck.

The last grotesque exercise of power made Gideon's heart swell with hot fury. Tight-lipped, he went below to his cabin and brought out his seaman's bible. He walked to

the entry port amidships and took off his hat. He opened
the bible to the burial service at sea.

"What are ye doin', Markham?" came the voice of Addams from the poop deck. Gideon began to read the burial
service in as steady a voice as he could manage; he did not
realize that his voice boomed out, its volume matching the
dimensions of his anger. He could sense the crew gathering
around him.

"They don't understand a word, Captain!" Addams
taunted. "Speak Spanish, if ye know it!"

Gideon continued to read. The crewmen stood in a half-
circle around him, respectfully silent; even if they could
not understand the words, Gideon's action and sentiment
were clear.

Gideon finished the service and bent his head to offer a
prayer. His mind was curiously bare of speech; he had
acted out of instinct and anger, without conscious thought,
and now that the time had come for prayer, he was aware
only of his own fury. He did not know what had caused
the flogging: it might have been that the man had deserved
to be punished, but the act of flinging the body overboard
without benefit of proper sea burial was the act of a vicious, dangerous man and no fit captain. "*Receive, Lord,
this poor man, and let his soul dwell with Thee in para-
dise,*" he forced himself to offer, and then repeated it twice
because he could think of nothing to add.

He closed the book and put on his hat. As he walked
past the silent crew toward the companionway that led to
the passengers' saloon, he could feel on him the defiant
glare of Addams. As Gideon approached the companionway, Addams jumped into motion. Panting hard, he came
running down the poop ladder, barring Gideon's path.

"I will not have ye interfering with my crew, sir!" Addams shouted, his voice outraged, high-pitched.

"I did not interfere, Captain," Gideon said, trying to
keep his anger under control.

"Do ye not call that interference, sir?" Addams demanded. "That reading from yer book kept the men from
their work, and it softened the lesson I was trying to give
'em. If there is any more such interference, I will have *you*
seized up, sir, mark my words!"

Gideon's anger exploded as he heard Addams' threat. "I performed an office demanded by God and by common humanity!" he raged. Addams shrank back from Gideon's indomitable glare, fear and defiance mingled in his face, his eyes flickering to the mate for support. "If ye were a proper captain instead of a drunken sojer, ye would have cared thus for yer men and performed as I did," Gideon cried, "whether they are the dregs of the Spanish Main or proper saints come down from heaven! And before I let ye or *that man*," he said, his chin jerking at the mate, "—lay a hand on me, I'll cut it off at the wrist, God help me!" He threw back the flap of his coat to reveal the hilt of his sword. Addams stared at him, speechless.

Trembling with rage, Gideon brushed past Addams and went down the companionway, his thundering footsteps beating counterpoint to his outraged heart. With Gideon's back turned Addams at last found his tongue.

"Drunken sojer, am I?" Addams sneered. "Drunken sojer or not, I am the captain of this ship, and I will have no interference, d'ye here me? Ye dast not interfere again!"

"Good morning, Captain. What—"

Afraid to give voice to his anger, Gideon brushed past Señora Marquez with a barely civil nod and walked through the saloon to his cabin. He sat on the bed, warring with himself, trying to master his fury. He let the bible fall open to a place at random and began to read. His anger faded slowly, but his agitation did not.

Gideon closed the book and opened his chest. The case of pistols was heavy in his hands. He cleaned the four pistols and charged them with powder. The pistol balls rolled smooth and cool in his palm. He dropped a bullet down each barrel and rammed down a wad to keep the charge and bullet secure. He put a pistol in each coat pocket and put the other pair away.

After the watches had changed and he could be sure Addams had gone below to his rum and bitter memories, Gideon went abovedecks. The bloodstains still spattered the decks: today the planks would not be washed. The mate was defiant, the crew quiet. He could see the crewmen exchanging secret glances. Every so often one of the watch would disappear down the fo's'cle hatch and appear again a quarter of an hour or so later. The pistols felt heavy in Gideon's pockets. He wondered where the ship's arms chest was kept.

Grimes came up from below to call him for dinner at the next change of watch. Taking the steward into his cabin, Gideon gave Grimes the second pair of pistols and a long sailor's dirk. Grimes nodded solemnly, without being told knew what they were for. Servants and men who serve before the mast have many things in common.

Gideon stayed on deck during the mate's watch, while Grimes remained abovedecks when Addams walked the poop. Addams and the mate seemed subdued. Their orders were given without the usual kicks and curses, as if they, too, seemed to have realized that the rules of the game had been changed by the morning's outrage and were perhaps evolving swiftly beyond their own control. The crew accepted the change with sullen triumph; they seemed to know that power was ebbing from the quarterdeck to the fo'c'sle. Gideon knew it too. He watched them all, knowing that the small pebble dislodged that morning had turned inexorably, inevitably, into a landslide. He was sickened by what he knew was going to happen.

There were usually two stages in a mutiny. The first mutineers were usually few in number, bold with desperation or anger or driven beyond endurance. They performed the first overt acts of rebellion, the murder of the captain or the mate, the seizure of the wheel and the arms chests; they would mouth the first proclamations.

The second stage was the worst. Those of the crew who had held back during the first hours would become bolder after the officers' authority had been destroyed; they would realize that they had yet to prove themselves in the eyes of the ringleaders. It was usually this second group, greedy for recognition and out of control, who perpetrated the inevitable atrocities of a mutiny: the murder of the passengers, the killing of any officers not yet dealt with, the inquisitions among the crew to ferret out any who might still owe the old allegiance. Just a few years before the British frigate *Hermione* had mutinied in these very waters, and the mutiny had followed the classic two-stage pattern. First the captain and a few of his officers had been killed by the ringleaders, and the ship seized. Then the rest of the crew had rebelled, and every violence, every insult offered them during their years of service had suddenly demanded revenge. The remaining officers were murdered, including the young midshipmen; the bosun was killed so that a mutineer could rape his wife; a man dying of yellow fever was taken from his bed and hurled alive into the sea.

Gideon knew that if the mutiny followed the classic pattern, the first attack by the ringleaders might be repulsed, the mutineers beaten by a show of force. The rest of the crew then might not join them. They could be battened down in the fo'c'sle and held there until the ship made port.

Cutting himself a chaw of tobacco, Gideon gazed anxiously sternward. Cuba lay there, five hundred miles away. To the eastward was the coast of Florida, its western coasts almost uninhabited by white men, the lair of unknown and possibly hostile Indians. Dead ahead, another five hundred miles, was New Orleans or Mobile. In between lay the blue waters of the Gulf of Mexico, where any sail sighted might be a pirate or belong to a British squadron—perhaps the same British squadron that had destroyed *General Sullivan* in Spanish waters.

It was a bad place to deal with a mutiny.

Gideon prayed that he was wrong, but the pistols hung in his pockets like lead weights to remind him that soon he must make a choice. And he was enough of a Yankee captain to know what his choice would be.

At night the studding sails and the royals were taken in—the usual precaution against sudden squalls—and most of the crew retired to the fo'c'sle. Gideon could see that occasionally one of them would peer out of the hatch, searching the quarterdeck for officers or passengers. Waiting for a moment or an inspiration.

The watch changed. Addams and Wallace Grimes came on deck; Gideon and the mate went below to their supper. Addams and Gideon passed one another in the dark corridor and did not speak.

In the saloon Gideon lingered over his supper, his appetite gone. On principle he forced himself to chew and swallow, for wasting food was sinful in a world of want. If only he had been more tactful with Addams that morning, if only the flogged seaman hadn't so unexpectedly died, or if Addams had managed to show compassion when he had . . . Gideon shook his head, clearing it of might-have-beens. The situation was complex beyond all reckoning, and he would have to deal with it as best he could. In some ideal, prelapsarian world, the Almighty might judge on intentions, on the simple willingness to do good; but in this flawed, tainted universe, Gideon thought, the Lord was perforce obliged to judge on results. Gideon had bungled that morning, and he must atone for that bungling.

"Would you join us, Captain?" It was Señora Marquez, speaking from the end of the long saloon table. She and two Spanish gentlemen were preparing to play cards.

"We are going to play *poque*," she said. "We would be honored if you'd join us."

Gideon stood and bowed. "I'm sorry, Señora," he said. "I do not gamble."

"Perhaps simply to learn, then?" she offered. "We would enjoy a fourth player."

"I am sorry, Señora," Gideon said. "I do not play cards at all."

"Then I am sorry as well, Captain."

Gideon sipped a cup of lemonade, listening intently to the regular sounds of the ship, the creaking timbers, the keening of the wind, the pacing of the captain over his head. Señora Marquez and her companions searched among the passengers and found another lady for a fourth. Five cards of each suit were extracted from the deck, the deuce through the six, and the rest put aside. The first *poque* hand was dealt. Gideon tensed as the pacing overhead stopped for the space of three heartbeats, then relaxed as the pacing began again. Señora Marquez's two pair lost to another player's three of a kind. The second hand was captured by the lady beginner with a sword flush.

Hands were called to trim the sails as the wind veered. The motion of the ship increased, the stern and its passenger saloon lurching in a peculiar corkscrewing motion.

Señora Marquez's maidservant Campaspe, watching the game while sewing in a corner, began to look slightly green. Gideon stood and walked to stand by the saloon door, his hands in his pockets.

The yards creaked as the sails were trimmed, bare feet thudding back to the fo'c'sle. The captain's footsteps echoed overhead. Not yet. Gideon returned to his place at the table. Two of the Spanish gentlemen were raising the stakes, the others having dropped out. Gideon looked at them irritatedly. It was bad enough that men were indulging in such folly; why were they allowing women to play alongside them?

There was a burst of loud Spanish from the gamesters: both had been bluffing, and two pair had beat out a pair of treys. The winner chuckled as he swept the stakes toward him. Gideon finished his lemonade and looked about the room for a spittoon. There was none. His craving for tobacco would have to be assuaged later. Señora Marquez expertly shuffled the twenty cards. The pacing overhead stopped again. Gideon strained his ears.

Money piled rapidly on the table as the stakes increased. Señora Marquez gazed serenely at the silver, and then the gold, accumulating in front of her. With a nervous blush the lady beginner dropped out. The captain overhead took three quick steps. One of the gentlemen was writing on a pad, adding his marker to the stakes. A voice bawled out unintelligibly as another frenzied round of betting commenced. Gideon stood, reaching for his pistols. There was thunder on the planking and a rush of footsteps in the corridor.

The saloon door was flung open by Grimes just as Señora Marquez laid down her straight flush in clubs, annihilating her opponents' flush and full hand.

"Fighting, Captain!" Grimes gasped.

"*Mutiny!*" Gideon roared, his shout stunning the passengers. He turned to Señora Marquez, frozen in the act of sweeping her winnings toward her. "Tell the gentlemen to bring their weapons, and quick!" he shouted and then ran through the door to the companionway.

The wheel was deserted by the helmsman, the ship running free. Gideon dashed up the poop ladder, cocking his pistols, hearing Grimes's feet thudding after him. Struggling figures blackened the poop, dim in the starlight. Capstan bars and marlinspikes whistled through the air. "Mercy! Jesus!" shrieked a voice.

"Avast, there!" Gideon barked. A man turned, his knife winking starlight. The yellow flash of the pistol froze the scene forever in Gideon's mind: Captain Addams, his face covered with blood, one ear hanging by a thread of skin, fighting desperately to hold off the attackers that were trying to club him and heave him overboard, and facing Gideon a man with a knife, his whipcord muscles shining in the yellow flash, his teeth bared . . .

The instant was over. A man fell moaning to the deck. Gideon dropped the smoking, empty pistol and shifted the other to his right hand. Beside him his dazzled eyes could just make out Grimes, standing grimly with a pistol in either hand.

The wounded man moaned again in the sudden silence. The pistol shot had stunned the mutineers; they hadn't expected armed resistance. Below his feet Gideon could hear the shouts of the gentleman passengers as they ran for their swords.

Captain Addams whimpered and fell slowly back against the taffrail. His knees buckled in slow motion and he slid to the deck.

"Hands up! To the maindeck! Slowly!" Gideon ordered. Grimes repeated the commands in his fluent Spanish. Dropping their improvised weapons, the mutineers shuffled carefully down the poop ladder. A Spanish gentleman, his small-sword cutting air in front of him, leaped up onto the deck, chattering out nervous questions, obviously prepared to fight or run. Grimes hissed out swift explanations.

The mutineers were herded forward to the fo'c'sle. A few sheepish crewmen, those who had stayed in the fo'c'sle without choosing sides, muttered out abashed explanations of their conduct, but were battened into the fo'c'sle with the rest. Gideon found lumber in the carpenter's stores and nailed the fo'c'sle shut.

"Captain Markham?" It was the voice of Señora Marquez. "These gentlemen wish to know if they can be of assistance." She was silhouetted in the hatchway, bending to peer down the companionway. She was bareheaded, her severe hairstyle—à la Chinoise, drawn back from the forehead and held with a comb behind—showing her ears outlined against the night sky.

Gideon drove in a final nail and turned to ascend the compaionway. To his surprise he saw that Señora Marquez was carrying a preposterously large pistol in both hands, one meant for a dragoon.

"Aye, they can help," he said, seeing the passengers clustered on the maindeck and poop, talking animatedly as they brandished swords and pistols.

"I would like them to choose watches," he said. "I would like a man—make that two men—to stand guard over this hatch at all times until the end of the voyage. We will also need two men to man the helm."

"I will tell them."

"Señora Marquez?"

"Yes?"

"Can ye ask them—as tactfully as ye may—not to wave loaded pistols about? The danger is over, and they may hurt one another."

She laughed. "I'll tell them," she said.

The guards were posted, and the two volunteer helmsmen were told to steer *Prinsessa* northwest until a more precise course could be worked out. Gideon stepped up onto the poop to find one of the passengers' manservants sitting on Captain Addams' head while Señora Marquez, with needle and thread, sewed on the captain's ear by the light of a lantern. Beside them lay the body of the man Gideon had shot. Gideon bent to examine the bloody, sprawling body and found the heartbeat extinct, the eyes rolled up. It was so easy, he thought, to kill a man, even a man one did not mean to kill. He bent his head to ask forgiveness, but the words would not come.

Instead he saw the big cavalry pistol lying by Señora Marquez. He reached out and picked it up, hefting it. He removed the priming pan cover and blew the powder out, rendering it safe. He looked up to see Señora Marquez watching him.

"Would ye really have used this, ma'am?" he asked.

Her answer was blunt. "Before I would let them touch

me, yes," she said. Her face turned toward Addams. "Captain Addams, that's the best I can do in this light. You'll be a mess, but I think you'll keep the ear."

The Spanish manservant, with a ghost of a smile, stood and allowed the captain to sit up. Addams wiped the congealing blood from his face and stared balefully at Gideon through bruised eyes.

"I suppose I should thank ye, Markham," he said.

"Rather thank the Almighty. It was His work."

Señora Marquez stood gracefully, picking up her pistol. "Nevertheless we must thank *you*, Captain Markham," she said, resting the heavy pistol barrel on her shoulder.

Who among the sons of the mighty can be likened unto the Lord? Gideon thought, but still the thanks pleased him.

"Captain Markham," she asked, "can we sail the ship with the men we have left? We have only you and Captain Addams and—what is the name of the mate?"

"Where *is* the mate?" Gideon asked out loud. He turned to Grimes. "Go below and find him."

"His name is Franco," Addams said.

"Can we manage the ship with two or three trained men?" Señora Marquez asked.

"If there's no storm, aye, we can," Gideon said. "The sails are set; they can be trimmed easily enough. We can use untrained men under the direction of those who know the job. We will make Mobile if the Lord wills it. Or close enough to send a boat in and ask for help."

"If there is anything I can do, Captain, please let me know," she said. "I can interpret your orders to these others or—or haul a rope if I have to," she said, a bit defiantly.

"If the other passengers are as willing, I don't doubt that we'll have a safe voyage," Gideon said. "Ye've been willing and useful, not like these others running about and waving weapons." He was a bit surprised to see her turn her head away as if concealing a blush.

"Beg pardon, Captain," said Grimes, appearing at Gideon's side. "Franco, the mate, has barricaded himself in his cabin and will not come out unless Captain Addams speaks to him." Grimes smiled. "He thinks I'm a mutineer, sir."

"Damn the brute!" Addams muttered. He staggered to his feet and went below. Moments later he emerged with the mate.

Franco had heard the scuffling and pistol shot and assumed the worst. He'd loaded his pistol, unsheathed his sword, barricaded the door to his cabin, and prepared to sell his life at as dear a price as possible.

Now, surly as ever, he came on deck, his pistol tucked into his waistband. With Señora Marquez interpreting they worked out a watch schedule: Addams, Gideon, and the mate would rotate watches, the passengers would rotate duties at the helm and the fo'c'sle guard, and everyone was to be prepared in case of an emergency.

In the meantime *Prinsessa* sailed on into the Gulf, leaving a trail of phospher in her wake, the steady winds filling her untended sails as she reached toward her destination.

Gideon relieved the mate at four in the morning. The sentries reported no disturbance from the fo'c'sle. Gideon climbed the poop deck and searched the horizon carefully for sign of a squall; there was none. He cast the log and estimated *Princessa*'s speed. The ex-Swede was making excellent progress.

He hauled in the log-line and coiled it in its proper place. The east was beginning to lighten. He wiped his hands on his coat and turned.

"Would you like some coffee, Captain?" asked Señora Marquez. She had come on deck, silent in her slippers, while he was busy with his calculations. He took the proffered mug with thanks.

"I'm surprised to see ye on deck, Señora," he said. "Will ye not catch a chill?"

"I'm not as fragile as all that," she said, touching her hair. She was still without a bonnet, her ears and high cheekbones, exposed by her drawn-back hair, gleaming whitely in the moonlight. In the soft night illumination she was almost pretty. She turned to face him, hesitated, then spoke.

"Do we—do we really have a chance of survival?" she asked. "I wouldn't tell anyone. I would just like to know."

"At our current rate of sailing, we should see Mobile in

two days," Gideon said. " 'Tis the season for sudden squalls and storms, so we'll have to be wary, but barring mischance we will see harbor safely."

"Good," she said calmly. "I would not like to die on the sea where I am not—where I am a foreigner. Perhaps it is vain of me, but if my life is to be risked, I would prefer to risk it myself in my own time, in my own way, rather than being forced to trust it to others—no matter how competent they may be."

"The Almighty foresees all our ends. We do not die in our time, but in His."

"That is no comfort."

He looked at her with some surprise. Gideon chided himself for his own lack of understanding and eloquence. If he could have explained his God better, she would have received comfort.

"Do you travel to Mobile to see your family?" he asked. "Your husband?"

"I am a widow, Captain Markham," she said. "My husband died six months ago."

"You are not in mourning."

"His death was not unexpected. We mourned together, he and I, while he was still alive. I stayed in mourning as long as I was at his house, but that was only two months. My stepson and I were not friends. He made it possible for me to leave."

"I'm sorry you were not made welcome in your grief," Gideon said.

"I was Don Carlos's third wife," she said. "We met in Charleston when he was the consul there. He had an estate in Spain, a house in Mobile, and half a province in Mexico. After our marriage we lived in Charleston until his period at the consulate ended, and then we lived in Mexico until his death."

"You were raised a Roman Catholic?" he asked. She glanced at him strangely; his tone had been a little sharp.

"No, I was not," she said. "I was raised an Anglican and converted when I was married." She saw his look and said quickly, "I was just sixteen and inclined to take such matters lightly. If you had ever seen the way Christianity was practiced in that segment of Charleston with which I was acquainted, you would have understood."

Gideon decidedly did not understand, but he wisely kept silent. He had been surprised at her offering her biography on such short acquaintance. It was indiscreet and presumed a certain familiarity which Gideon was not at all certain they possessed, but she had been raised in South Carolina and customs there were different. Women were raised to presume a kind of frivolous familiarity there, even with strangers. *Flirting,* it was called. Flirting was not a New England custom.

"And now ye travel to the house in Mobile?" he found himself asking.

"My stepson gave me the deed and a little traveling money. He was happy to see the last of me and supposed he could never use the house, not with the Americans in occupation. The place might not even exist. Do you suppose it was demolished in the fighting?"

"There was no fighting that I know of. The Spanish governor simply surrendered."

"Ah. We heard much about a gallant stand."

"I pray ye may find the house, ma'am."

"Thank you, Captain." Her eyes slid to his, and she smiled. "You must visit me. I know no one in Mobile."

"I shall be happy to call, ma'am." The ship yawed widely and Gideon glanced irritatedly at the amateur helmsman. "Will ye tell that man to steer northwest by north, Señora?" he asked. "He's being careless."

"Certainly, Captain." The helmsman accepted the correction cheerfully, and *Prinsessa*'s bows slid upwind to their correct heading. Gideon sipped his mug of coffee. The warm, acid liquid slid down his welcoming throat.

"You said you were a privateer, Captain," Señora Marquez asked. "Are you related to the privateer Markhams in the War for Independence?"

"Aye," Gideon said with surprise. "Ye've heard of us?"

"Every schoolchild has heard of Malachi Markham and the *Bristol*," she said. "You are his son?"

"Nay, I am his nephew. My father was a privateer as well."

"Then you come from good stock," she said. "You come by your trade naturally."

"I was born to the sea, aye," Gideon said. "I was first taken abroad by my father when I was eight."

"I never left Charleston until I was eighteen, and then I was a married woman," she said. "After that I saw Havana and then San Juan de Ulua. For the twelve years that followed I never set foot outside Don Carlos's Mexican district. Mobile will be a new place entirely."

"It's a good harbor. The town is small." He hesitated, then decided not to speak of the town any further. There was no need to begin her disappointment here, not when it could only add to the difficulties she already bore as a passenger on a mutinous vessel. Mobile was a frontier town, and a Spanish frontier town at that. The aristocracy lived in comfort in fine old dwellings tended by their slaves; but most of Mobile consisted of ragged shacks inhabited by half-wild poor whites and Indians, ignorant, dirty, and often savage. The aristocracy itself did not compare well with that of, for instance, nearby New Orleans, which carried a Creole culture and tradition that had grown over several centuries. The Mobile gentry seemed by comparison vulgar and mercenary; they carried with them the Spanish tradition of treating a colony as something to be exploited, as a source of money to be wrung from the land and from slaves rather than a place to be domesticated and civilized, like New England. Perhaps the difference, Gideon thought, was that New Orleans had made its money and was quietly intent on increasing it, whereas Mobile was still pirating its initial fortunes.

"Is the land fertile near Mobile?" asked Señora Marquez. "I believe I have enough money to buy land, and I might yet win more at *poque*."

"The land? Er—I don't know, ma'am. Perhaps ye could inquire from one of the other passengers."

"I shall do that. Thank you."

The rising sun began to break over the horizon, and they turned to face it, a single precious jewel that winked over the lip of the world, widening into a yellow, dazzling arc of light that whitened the wave-foam and stretched the ship's long shadow across its path. Gideon found himself smiling at the joy of it, the sight of the sun on the empty sea, an end to the night that might have brought them all sudden and brutal death. He was aware suddenly that Señora Marquez was smiling as well, perhaps welcoming the morning or perhaps to see him smile. Then he swiftly become self-conscious, and his smile faded; he drained the last of his coffee and she took the cup.

"I thank ye, Señora," he said. "I must go below and bring up the captain and the mate. I think we can set the royals."

Alone on the poop deck, her smile faded as well, but more slowly than his. Gideon caught echoes of it, tugging at the corners of her mouth, for as long as the sun kept its station in the sky.

10

DOUBLE OR NOTHING

That day *Prinsessa* sailed alone on the deserted Gulf, accompanied only by dolphins and a single petrel that rested for an hour on the maintop before being distracted by the dinner scraps thrown into the ship's wake. Meals had been a cause of discord among the passengers, since the gentlefolk felt it beneath their dignity to do any cooking and the ship's cook had been locked up with the rest of the crew. But the servants had been mobilized to cook what they could find from the stores.

Gideon and Addams had argued over whether the crew should be fed: Addams had expressed the opinion that the mutineers could starve as well as be hanged; but Gideon had been firm. He argued that most of the crew had been innocent of active mutiny and that perhaps there were those who were innocent of the knowledge of it as well. The innocent would be separated from the guilty by the authorities in Mobile, and in the meantime they should be fed. A small hole was cut in the fo's'cle door to allow water and ship's biscuit to enter. The crew would not eat well, but they would not starve nor die of thirst.

Gideon had a few hours' sleep in his cabin after breakfast and stood his afternoon watch in rotation with the others. Mounting the poop, he took out of habit the captain's privilege by the weather rail and found that the mate, who was on deck, did not dispute him. The wind backed again toward the end of his watch, and a little sail-trimming had to be done.

"No, no!" he shouted as he saw one of the passengers try to coil a line. The passenger, a merchant from Havana, stared at him in some confusion. His coil was even more confused than he, full of kinks, refusing to lie straight.

Gideon babbled at him in English, then attempted to seize the rope. The passenger resisted.

"Difficulties, Captain?" asked Señora Marquez, marching forward from the quarterdeck.

"Aye," Gideon said in relief. "Kindly explain to this gentleman that this is a left-handed cable-laid line—er, make that rope—and that he can't make a flat coil without giving the line a twist with each coil."

Señora Marquez turned to the passenger and favored him with a barrage of rapid-fire Spanish. The passenger nodded and understood. Gideon gave her his thanks and returned to the poop. It did not occur to him until later to wonder how she could have translated his nautical jargon.

She had been invaluable, running errands and translating orders for the benefit of the amateur crewmen. She had changed into a riding habit, more practical than her gown and jacket, but the double-breasted coat and top hat with its masculine style surprised Gideon. He was not used to women dressed in such vogue, and he was not entirely certain that he approved. But still he was not her husband or father, and she had been efficient and useful, so he said nothing.

That night Gideon went aloft with Addams to furl the royals and then down to his dinner. He did not think Addams had taken a drink all day. Señora Marquez was winning heavily at *poque*. He went to his cabin but could not sleep.

"I've taken that fool Gomez for fifteen hundred dollars," Señora Marquez told him early the next morning. As she had the night before, she'd appeared on deck with a cup of coffee just as Gideon had finished coiling the log-line. "Don Carlos, my husband, learned the game when he was governor of Mobile and taught me the elements. At home we used to play for hours."

Gideon sipped his coffee, amazed at the amount of her winnings. He had realized that she was talented, but not that she was so formidable.

"The problem with the game," she went on, "is that the odds keep changing with the number of players. Five cards are used for each player, you know, and the rest put away. I think if there were a version with all fifty-two cards so that the odds would stay the same from game to game, *poque* would be much improved."

"I would like to thank you, Señora, for the help you've given," Gideon said, shifting the subject. "You've helped us immeasurably."

"You're most welcome. I would do more if I knew how."

"I think the smooth way the ship is running is due to yer tact and helpfulness," he said plainly. "I can't make myself understood, and Addams and the mate are unpleasant company for anyone. It's to yer credit that we haven't had more mutinies than the one."

She turned her head away as if to conceal a blush; Gideon found it curious that a woman so independent and confident should still betray such a curious brand of vulnerability. Even on the night of the mutiny, kneeling next to a corpse and holding the needle with which she had sewn on Addams's ear, she had turned away from a compliment.

"How is it that a privateer sails to Mobile, Captain?" she asked, as if to cover her embarrassment. "Why do you not sail to New England?"

Gideon tasted his coffee and warmed his hands on the cup before replying. "The first prize I took," he said, "was on the tenth of July, 1812. That was less than three weeks after war was declared, less than two weeks after New Hampshire had heard we were at war. I outfitted *General Sullivan* with two six-pound cannon and put to sea. The prize was a British packet brig worth perhaps ten thousand dollars.

"The Boston Prize Court chose to return the packet to its original owners, with apologies for their inconvenience."

"Good God! Why?"

Gideon frowned at the blasphemy. "The British captain didn't know we were at war," he said. "It was not a fair capture."

"That is absurd, Captain!" She turned to face him, her features indignant.

"Aye," Gideon agreed. He sipped his coffee, remembering the anxious planning that had gone into his attack, the audacious schooner with its two little carriage guns against the well-armed post office packet. He remembered the first flush of pride and accomplishment as he sailed into Boston harbor, walking the quarterdeck of the schooner, glancing over his shoulder to see the Stars and Stripes flying over the brig's British ensign. He remembered also the collapse of his hopes, the feeling of awful futility that had crushed him when he was informed of the prize court's decision.

How could he explain to Señora Marquez that the new American republic was striking a pose, trying to prove itself as honorable and gallant as any European monarchy? Gideon did not appreciate such gestures, and he suspected that the English, after almost twenty years of fighting a bitter war with the French, would have thought the prize's return more senseless than chivalrous.

"I decided to sail well out of range of such official stupidity," Gideon said. Señora Marquez, the brim of her tall hat shadowing her face from the starlight, listened quietly as Gideon told of the arguments with his backers—mostly his brothers and cousins, he was forced to admit—that finally resulted in the acquisition of two more six-pounders and a long twelve to use a long tom, and the provisioning of *General Sullivan* for a journey to the Caribbean. A cutter, named *Rattler* and intended for use as a tender and scout, was fitted out to accompany Gideon and his schooner.

The backers had agreed to wait for their profits until they were forwarded from New Orleans. In return they had made it clear they expected the profits to be large.

There had followed a year of hard work, of haunting Jamaica's cays and beaches, of cutting out merchant ships from beneath batteries and cutting up convoys to share with other privateers. New Orleans had proved hospitable; their administration was far more oriented toward commerce than gallantry. If New Orleans winked at Lafitte's pirates, it would not raise any objection to the occasional, necessary irregularities of lawful privateers, particularly since the local prize court took ten percent off the top.

Gideon admitted that his prizes and cargoes fetched smaller prices in New Orleans, since the Crescent City itself exported many of the cargoes Gideon tried to sell; but this was more than compensated for by the fact that none of Gideon's prizes was ever retaken. If he had tried to sail his prizes to a port on the eastern seaboard, at least one in three would have been retaken by British cruisers. Even if he had taken them to a New England port—for New England was not yet blockaded—he would have had to sail past the blockaded Southern ports and would have lost cargoes.

Rattler had twice returned to New Hampshire, bringing to the Markham family the profits of Gideon's astonishingly successful cruises. *Rattler's* first return had been sufficient to pay off Gideon's debts, which had hung over his head like a Damoclean sword since the Embargo. His own profits, those left after his debts were annulled, had gone into laying down a new schooner.

"I'd planned that schooner before I ever left," Gideon told Señora Marquez, his eyes gleaming in the moonlight. "She'll be a tern schooner, clipper-built. I had old Joshua Stanhope draw up the plans before I ever left Portsmouth. He's a man I can trust to build her without slipping in rotten timber on the sly or weakening her with unsound knees.

"She'll be built as a privateer, large enough to hold a crew of a hundred and sixty. She'll have nine iron twelve-pounders on each broadside and a long eighteen amidships; she'll have room for powder, shot, and stores, and there will be a cargo hold to carry goods from captured prizes."

"This is the 'other privateer' you spoke of?" asked Señora Marquez. "The one you told me you were going to Mobile to meet?"

"Aye," Gideon said, suddenly self-conscious. Her interruption awakened him to the fact that he'd been droning on about his profession for at least an hour and gone into details which his audience of one could not possibly have understood—and that he'd received no encouragement at all except from the calm, deciding intelligence in Señora Marquez's shadowed eyes.

"Her keel should be tasting water now," he said, embarrassed at the way he'd been inflicting himself on her. "Two months back I sent *Rattler* with instructions for the new tern to meet *General Sullivan* in Mobile. It should be many weeks yet."

He fell silent. Just yesterday, he realized, he'd been mentally criticizing her for presuming an intimacy where none existed, and now he'd behaved with far greater abandon than she. She waited some seconds for him to go on and then spoke, her smile teasing.

"You haven't answered my original question, Captain." she said and laughed. "Why Mobile?"

Gideon was forced to smile himself at his allowing his conversation to wander so far afield.

"When our forces took Mobile, the town's regular source of supply dried up; the Spanish generally won't do business there anymore," he said. "There's a big market for finished goods, more than in New Orleans. Supplies had been low anyway because of the war in Spain. Mobile is not blockaded, and I can sell cargoes at higher prices. That's the reason."

"I see." She took the empty cup of coffee from him and held it in her hands. As she asked her next question she looked down into the cup as if she were embarrassed to ask or uneasy.

"Your first privateer, the *General Sullivan*," she said, "how did you lose her?"

Gideon suddenly found himself impatient with his own speech and annoyed with whatever impulse had urged him to speak so openly and for so long. He gave an abbreviated version of the schooner's loss, eliminating most of the details, the eerie sounds of the nightbirds, the undefined enemy shadows swarming over the rail, the unutterable minutiae of his own terror and inspiration.

He grew angry with himself as he spoke; it seemed as if he was cheapening the experience, making it seem as if men had died in a cheerful little scrap on the river. He ended the tale swiftly with the British sloop of war coming over the bar and *General Sullivan* being set afire to keep the enemy from possession.

"You said you knew Velasco from before the war and that he owed you a favor," Señora Marquez said. "If I'm not prying into secrets, how could you possibly know such a man and do him favors, when he's a Cuban planter and you've been at sea all your life?"

Gideon found himself relieved at her question. Plainly she had somehow divined—perhaps through his tone of voice—that he was annoyed or upset and had efficiently changed the subject.

"Off East Florida there's a place called Amelia Island," he said. "It's near the border with Georgia and is a great trading center. It's officially Spanish, but the Spanish exert no real control over the place, and for all intents and purposes the place is a free port—an important shipping center, thousands of ships stop there every year, and almost all of them are smugglers, trying to break the monopolistic trading practices of the world's empires.

"Don Esteban was there to buy some plantation equipment some ten years ago. Spain was at war with England, and his regular supplies had been cut off for some years. I was there for—well, for my own business—and we exchanged visits, as captains in strange ports do. He bought his equipment from an English smuggler and set sail the same day as I. A British cruiser hove in sight after we were two hours out from the port and sailed down on us.

"If the British had taken his ship, he would have been ruined. I went aboard his ship with an American flag and some papers that showed his vessel as an American. I pretended to be the captain of his ship, and my mate pretended to be the captain of my own. The British were satisfied with impressing two men from each ship and then let us on our way."

"You saved him from being ruined, and at some risk," said Señora Marquez, a little wonderingly.

" 'Twas no risk for me, ma'am," said Gideon. "I was an American and immune."

"May I ask why you did such a thing for a comparative stranger, and a foreigner at that?"

Gideon hesitated. "Christian charity, ma'am," he said. "We are obligated to offer aid without thought of recompense. Also, the Royal Navy is the common enemy of any seaman who thinks to call himself free. The Admiralty makes much of its fleet being democracy's wooden walls, but when an Englishman talks of *democracy* he speaks of the right to impress foreign nationals, to harass foreign shipping, and to cheat foreign traders of the right to trade freely across the wide ocean without fear of confiscation or tariff.

"And I was right to offer aid," he concluded, "for Don Esteban returned my charity, and is keeping my crew safe for the time it will take to bring the new schooner to Cuba and take them aboard."

"Yet Don Esteban could not prevent you from losing your first ship," she said.

"Aye. The Lord has taken *General Sullivan*. Perhaps I had grown too proud."

Señora Marquez touched her throat. "Does God punish pride on earth, do you think?" she asked. "I have been told the punishment comes after."

"The Almighty in His wisdom foresaw the schooner's destruction, comprehended it, and allowed it," Gideon said. "Nothing occurs that is not His will."

"And you believe that He allowed your ship to be destroyed in order that you, among all other men, be punished for your pride?" asked Señora Marquez. Her tone was not sharp, as it might have been, but genuinely curious. "Is it not a kind of pride," she asked, "to believe that God should single out your pride among all the arrogance on earth for punishment?"

Gideon looked at her with surprise, taken aback by her acuity. "I do not single myself out," he protested. "The Almighty foresees all our ends, not my own alone."

He felt the painful inadequacy of his answer, and he suspected the woman felt it as well. He knew himself to be no rhetorician; eloquence was not one of the traits that his God had seen fit to grace him with. He felt himself humbled by her question: *was* it pride to feel himself singled out for the loss of his privateer? Of course it had to be he. He had lost more than any other, and God would not have punished him so severely for another's sins. The alternative was to feel that *General Sullivan*'s loss was an accident, the result of a random disposition of forces, unforeseen by the Almighty and meaningless. . . . Given Gideon's unshakeable belief that the universe was contained in the mind of God and maintained by the Divine Will, the latter answer was clearly out of the question—a universe with a God could contain no meaningless acts.

There were questions, Gideon concluded, that were best not asked, and Señora Marquez's were among them. The flawed understanding of mortal men was not capable of comprehending the answer, containing as it did an apparent contradiction.

"If we see conundrums," Gideon said lamely, "it is only because our apprehension is clouded. We should pray for the grace of understanding."

But Señora Marquez had lost interest—she was staring, awed, at the great hemisphere of stars above them, the glittering band of the Milky Way cut by the yards and lines of the rigging. A strand of hair had come loose from her severe hair style and fluttered in the wind by her ear. The soft light of the stars hid the maturing lines of her face; for a moment, in the top hat and masculine coat, she seemed very young, a girl making a joke of dressing up as a man.

"In Mexico I would climb up onto the roof and watch the stars," she said. Her eyes came down from the heavens and grew dreamy. "At night a breeze would come up and bring in the desert perfume. Sometimes the hired men would be singing their songs. The songs were always sad and always lovely. Those were the best times. I could tell how far I'd come. Now I can't tell at all."

Her features hardened, and the illusion of youth was suddenly gone. "I was poor once," she said. "I won't be again." Her voice surprised Gideon with its edge of ruthlessness. She turned to him, suddenly aware of his watching her and smiled apologetically.

"I must beg your pardon, Captain," she said. "The sight of the night sky quite took away my senses—and my discretion, it seems."

"Think nothing of it, Señora." Gideon hesitated, then spoke further. "I have been poor myself. I know how the consciousness of one's own poverty can—can drive one's mind from those higher realms whence it ought to dwell."

He knew more about poverty than the pretty words implied, his treacherous memory reminded him. Against his will, he pictured Betsy lying white-faced on the sheets, staining them with the red of her final phthisis. And the little coffin that went into the red earth less than a month afterward.

Señora Marquez was smiling at his picturesque choice of phrase. "My father had no slaves," she said. "He had children instead. Being a Yankee, you have no idea how the lack of slaves changed status in the South. A white man who has no servants is not considered worth speaking to, not by gentlemen."

Gentleman, thought Gideon. That word again, with its implications of rank and caste, was infiltrating its Old World meanings into America through the South. *Gentleman*, used not in its New England sense, a complimentary designation for a free man and a citizen; but in its old sense, as a man of gentle birth, a man who, since he is not obliged to work for a living, thinks himself able to display finer feelings and more chivalrous instincts than the common herd—a man with a special sort of arrogance, thinking himself entitled to snub those who labor for a living.

Gideon shook his head. If the South continued to import such attitudes, there would be trouble ere long.

"My father kept an inn," Señora Marquez was saying. "Occasionally he was able to buy a nigger or two, but they died or had to be sold sooner or later. He had eleven children, and his sister's four children lived with us after my uncle died. We were not exactly poor—the inn was a respectable place—but a mouthful of food had to stretch far."

When she was sixteen the Spanish consulate in Charleston had been forced to undergo repairs. The Spaniards occupied the entire hotel and brought their own slaves with them. Señora Marquez's father was in ecstasy; he had come up in the world. And so had his middle daughter, who began to enjoy the courtly attention of the consul himself.

"I was sick of Charleston, sick of being poor, sick of an entire family who were as sick of me as I was of them," was how she put it. "Don Carlos was older, a gentleman, very kindly, very courtly. He needed someone young around him. He asked my father for my hand even before he asked me. My father jumped at the opportunity: there would be one less mouth to feed, and a wealthy son-in-law was more than he'd ever expected."

Gideon listened to this narration with half his attention, his alert seaman's instincts being drawn to the main topgallant, which was lifting rather more than it should. At a predictable instant the sail began to roar like thunder as the wind backed half a point. The helmsman cast Gideon a nervous glance.

"Beg pardon, Señora," he said and hastened to the wheel to bring *Prinsessa* a little off the wind. The roar ceased, and the topgallant's leading edge trembled slightly, as it should. Satisfied, Gideon returned to the poop.

"Perhaps, Captain, we can do a little business together," Señora Marquez said. Her face glowed in the early light of dawn. "You have prize money or will have it soon. My husband willed me a sum, and my stepson has given me a house and the income from it. Mobile has been taken by the American forces—do you think they will give West Florida back to Spain?"

"Nay, not unless the British win the war and force it."

"I agree. Those Spaniards who do not wish to live under American rule will be leaving—their property will be for sale, and at bargain prices. If we worked together, we could make our fortunes. To a poor widow they may sell at a more compassionate price than to a successful privateer—the Spaniards have a brand of gallantry toward women which can be used by those who know how. You could spend your time at sea, taking prizes, and I could be your agent on shore."

Good Heavens, thought Gideon. The proposition did not interest him; he was a seaman, and land speculation was for others, for specialists like his brothers. And if he could be coerced into buying land, he would think twice before involving himself with Señora Marquez, whose predatory, virtually unwomanly attitudes seemed quite alarming.

"Er—I am in debt, ma'am, for the new schooner," he said swiftly. "I can't spend my backers' profits buying up real estate."

"Why not?" she asked. "My father used to remark that if you owe a man a little money, then paying it back is your problem—but if you owe him a *lot* of money, paying it back is *his* problem, and not so much your own."

"I will not go back on a debt honorably incurred."

"Of course not—I'm not urging you to steal!" she said. "Just put your money where it will do some good in the meantime. Land and slaves will make a profit faster than any bank."

"I will not own slaves!" Gideon said, his eyes fiery. "I will not put a man in bondage. It is a practice abhorrent to God!"

Señora Marquez stopped short. Gideon sensed both mockery and appraisal in her eyes.

"I see that I have misjudged you, Captain," she said softly. "Take care that you do not make too much of a little virtue. Good night."

"Good morning, ma'am."

She turned and went below. Gideon stood still for a moment and then began to pace the weather poop. There was a satisfaction in being alone on a ship's quarterdeck, almost as if he were again his own master. Yet Señora Marquez had made him uneasy, although he knew he had nothing to reproach himself with, and that his principles were his own and proper. He cut himself tobacco and began to chew. He found himself a little relieved that she was gone.

Addams came on deck shortly after sunrise, and he and Gideon worked out their position.

"Mobile's north'ard of us," Addams said, working his position carefully. "We could see her by tonight if the wind was fair. We'll have to come about sometime today or else run into a string o' islands and reefs west of the Mississippi Delta—Chandler Islands, they're called."

Chandeleur, Gideon mentally corrected, knowing them well. He looked up to cast an expert eye over the rigging. "We could wear ship without great trouble," he said. "We don't need an expert crew for it, not like tacking."

"Aye," Addams said. Two days' beard was growing over his wounds, the dark scraggle deigning to hide the livid cuts.

"Shall we set the royals?" Gideon asked.

"Aye. It's time."

Gideon took a deep breath at the foot of the weather main shrouds, then steeled himself and began to climb, careful to keep his hands on the shrouds and not the ratlines, which on this carelessly tended merchant ship would tend to break. Addams followed. At the maintop he worked his way out on the futtock shrouds, hanging inverted over the boiling sea below, and then hauled himself into the topmast shrouds by main strength, assisted amply by fear. Until this voyage he hadn't been aloft in almost five years.

He remembered back to the time in his teens when he'd been a main topman, when he'd worked himself out along the yards every day and sometimes, to show his skill, disdained the footrope and ran barefoot along the yards themselves. He couldn't picture himself doing it, although he knew he had. Too much time had passed.

A ratline snapped under his foot, and he plunged down to the length of his arms, his musings cut alarmingly short. He could feel a wedge of pain entering his back, and he grit his teeth as his feet swung, seeking another foothold.

"A little to yer left, Markham," came Captain Addams' voice from just below. An eon passed before Gideon found a foothold, and an eternity before he was able to shift his weight on it and found that it held. He rested for a moment in the topmast shrouds, breathing hard, and then he steeled himself and finished the climb.

The main royal was unfurled and shaken loose, pushed off the yard to hang in its gear until Gideon and Addams could return to the deck and sheet it home. The masthead pendant snapped uncomfortably close to Gideon's ear. He looked over his shoulder at the horizon, at the harmless, fleecy clouds whose white touched the ocean's blue. His eye caught a flash of white that was not a cloud and held it.

"Sail ho, by Jerusalem!" he burst out. "Addams, look ye! To leeward and astern!"

Addams, who had worked his way back to the shrouds and was preparing to descend, shaded his eyes with his hand and peered at the distant dapple of white. "I hope she don't see us," he said. "I'll go down and fetch up a 'bring 'em near.' "

That white fleck on the horizon was like a colorless, ambiguous sheet of parchment capable of being shaded with almost any meaning: another merchant ship, whose captain could be expected to offer assistance in dealing with Addams's mutineers; a man-of-war or a privateer belonging to any of the belligerent powers, who would search the Spanish vessel and let it go; or, the worst and most likely possiblilty of all, the harmless-seeming speck on the world's watery edge could be a pirate, a member of the Lafitte colony or another, worse settlement, who would take the ship and cargo and murder every living thing aboard, man, woman, or mutineer.

Addams, his gaunt, scarred face set in a scowl, returned to the masthead with a telescope slung over his shoulder on its strap; he studied the horizon and then handed the glass to Gideon.

"Here. Take ye the glass and let me know what ye think."

Gideon took the telescope and put it to his eye. Years of practice compensated for *Prinsessa*'s pitch and roll, and the piece of chaff on the horizon came abruptly into focus: hull down, a brig, bearing east by south and flying no flag. But then as Gideon watched, the slit of blue between the masts widened, then narrowed again, and the yards were trimmed to the wind.

Gideon's heart sank. *Mine enemies chased me sore, like a bird, without cause*, he thought. The brig was hauling her wind to give chase.

Addams had seen it without the benefit of the telescope. "We'd better sheet home this royal," he said, his voice without hope.

Once down on the deck they slacked off the buntlines and leechlines and sheeted the sail, then, with the assistance of some of the passengers, manned the halliard and raised the royal yard until the sail's taut leading edge trembled as it cut the wind. The mate and the passengers trimmed the main yards to the wind while Gideon and Addams went aloft to unfurl the fore royal. The mizzen royal was set last of all. They were simple tasks, loosing the sail, letting it fall in its gear, sheeting home, walking away with the halliard and belaying it; yet Gideon found himself relishing the little burdens, the rustle and boom of the canvas, the feel of the hemp in his hands, the simple, plainvoiced commands. He saw everything with special acuity and performed the duties with a quiet, solemn joy, for he knew they would probably be his last.

Soon they would have to go about in order to avoid running into the Chandeleur Islands. Without a trained crew a big three-master like *Prinsessa* could not tack across the wind; they would have to wear right around. And when they wore, they would lose distance to leeward, and the brig would probably catch them. The chances were overwhelming that they would not survive such a capture. In these seas any pursuer was an enemy, and they were within less than a hundred miles of Barataria Bay, headquarters of the Lafitte colony. The Lafittes preyed on Spaniards exclusively, and their hatred was mortal. *Prinsessa* was a Spanish ship.

Addams and Gideon would try to fight, of course. *Prinsessa* had some rusty old four-pounders, and pistols and swords were at hand. The gallantry of such a fight would be matched only by its hopelessness.

Gideon, standing by the lee bulwark, looked around at the passengers. They had seen Addams go aloft with the glass; they had almost certainly guessed what was happening. Their faces were turned toward him, to Gideon, waiting for him to make a decision. Señora Marquez, still in her mannish coat and hat, spoke quietly to her maidservant, but even her eyes held plain expectation.

Gideon knew he had no comfort to give them. He turned his back on them to face the ocean and his pursuer.

"I think he's gaining a little," Addams reported from the poop, where he stood with his glass. "He'll gain at least five miles on us by nightfall if the wind holds."

Gideon looked gloomily to leeward. The brig was not yet visible from the deck, not with the naked eye. A flying fish broke suddenly from the water and buzzed briefly through the air before returning to the sea with a wet smack.

"Are we being chased by an enemy?" It was the quiet voice of Señora Marquez, approaching quietly to stand by his elbow.

"I believe so," said Gideon.

"I apologize for being short with you this morning," she said. "So long out of South Carolina I'd forgotten that Northerners do not understand about niggers."

Gideon did not reply. His mind worked dully on a plan for escape, revolving through the same insufferable patterns: tack or go aground—no possibility of tacking without a crew—wear and be caught by the cruiser behind. Before he quite realized it, he found himself explaining the predicament to the woman by his side.

"Are you certain we cannot tack?" she asked. "The passengers are willing."

The monotonous, inevitable cadence of orders echoing in his brain, dooming them, Gideon shook his head. "In order to tack the ship," he said, "we have to prepare carefully. Stays'ls halliards and sheets and the lee braces have to be faked out, and the leechlines, bunt-leechlines, buntlines, and lifts have to be taken off their pins on the lee side. Lee clewlines must be slacked. Then we drop off the wind a bit to pick up speed, the helm is put down, and men on the spanker sheets haul the spanker to windward. We've got to clew up the courses so they won't stop us dead in the water. The stays'ls are run down. Then we've got to haul the main yards and the mizzen yards around by the braces, slacking off on the lee side while hauling in on the weather side. The heads'l sheets will have to be run to leeward. The spanker sheets must be eased. The foreyards will have to be braced over and trimmed. Lastly the stays'ls and the courses are set again, and everything trimmed, belayed, and coiled."

Gideon gestured at the other passengers, at the willing landsman's faces. "How can they do it?" he demanded. "One thing done wrongly and we'll be in irons, head to the wind and dead in the water. They may be willing, but they can't pick up that much seamanship in a day. If I give a command, they won't know what it means!"

"And if we don't go to the other tack at all?"

"We'll probably go aground, ma'am. If we don't go aground, we'll have to run between the islands and be trapped against the Louisiana coast. If we're not taken by the enemy, we'll have to run into the swamps. The swamps will be less hospitable than most pirates, I assure you."

"And if we don't tack? If we—what did you call it—wear about?"

"With these amateurs we can wear easily enough, but we won't do it smartly, and we'll close the distance between us and that brig that's following, probably by some miles."

"Then what can we do, Captain?"

Her eyes were trusting. So were those of the other passengers who stood quietly on deck, awaiting his decisions, confident in his ability to save them again from the wretched consequences of being on *Prinsessa*.

"Pray," Gideon said, turning to her in bitterness. "Pray that Addams is wrong, and that we will not encounter the reefs and islands. Pray that the brig is a friend even though it's chasing us. Or pray that a storm will hide us from her or that the wind dies till nightfall."

Her gaze held his, at once evaluating and mocking, as it had the night before. "I shall leave the praying to your expertise, Captain," she said. "For myself I'll got to the saloon and play *pogue*."

She retired with some of the passengers. The others, perceiving that nothing was going to happen immediately, either wandered up onto the quarterdeck to look for the pursuer or went below to attempt breakfast. Gideon stayed by the bulwark, staring disconsolately into the sea, his mind working furiously, hopelessly, on the seemingly unsolvable problem. *Release the crew?* he wondered. The crew would have every motivation to sabotage the escape and join their pursuers, particularly if the brig was crewed by pirates. What mercy could Gideon expect from mutineers he had foiled? None.

Again his mind went over the impossibility of teaching the passengers seamanship. With his long years at sea he knew what chaos would result. He would shout an order— *"Off tacks and sheets!"* for example—which would then have to be translated, somehow, into Spanish and then performed. Contained in that single order were many others, for which, among seaman, the single order was a kind of shorthand: the course would be clewed up and the staysails run down. Clewing up the courses meant that the sheets and tacks had to be thrown off while the clewlines and buntlines were hauled; running down the staysail meant easing the halliards, taking care of the sheet to make certain the sail didn't slat about, while men on deck walked off with the downhaul.

Impossible.

Gideon was surprised to find himself hammering his

right fist into his left palm and wondered how long he'd been doing it. He clasped both hands behind his back and returned to the problem. *If only they understood the confounded terminology!* If only they could *dispose* of the seaman's specialized jargon: staysails, tacks, sheets, clewlines, clewgarnets, downhauls, lee and windward braces . . .

But each term was precise, describing to those educated in the ways of ships both the object and its uses; they could not be dispensed with. *Haul down on that rope over there! No, not that one, the one next to it!* Gideon shook his head. The things needed names, only the names were not understood by those who had to make use of them. Therefore they needed new names. But how could new names be any better than the old ones; how could they be learned any faster? *Haul down on Line A, slack off on Line B!* It was silly; there was nothing to mark the lines with, nothing to make the passengers remember.

For all the good his thinking had done, he might as well have been in the saloon with Señora Marquez, playing cards. . . .

He stiffened as the thunderbolt struck him. His brain worked frantically to find a flaw in the plan . . . the staysails could be taken care of ahead of time, and *Prinsessa* carried no cro'jack, so they could be left out of the equation. He and Addams could fake out the necessary lines beforehand, and some parts of the gear might be able to take care of themselves.

In the saloon the gamblers were thunderstruck when Gideon, wild-eyed, burst in and demanded, his hand outstretched, *"Praise the Lord! Give me the deck of cards!"*

11

TRUMP CARDS

Three hours later Gideon had made his preparations, and the waiting passengers stood at their newly assigned stations. Standing nervously by the wheel, he wiped sweat from his forehead and crammed his top hat down square on his head. Señora Marquez stood nearby, ready to translate the orders. Franco the mate stood well forward, near the windward monkey rail, while Addams stood on the poop, supervising the crews assigned to the main braces. He had required a lot of convincing, but Gideon's fervor and the lack of any real choice had finally brought his assent.

The passengers had been required to learn only two new words, "avast" and "belay." Nailed to each pinrail, fiferail, and monkey rail, marking each important line, sheet, or brace, was a pasteboard card taken from Señora Marquez's deck. Cups and wheels labeled the leeward, or larboard, side; swords and clubs labeled the windward, or starboard, side.

The deck was littered with line. Preparatory to the maneuver Gideon, Addams, and Franco had faked out or thrown off the pins all unimportant lines that were normally handled by crewmen while tacking but that would now have to look out for themselves. The pursuing brig had gained another mile. If they could keep the brig away until night, perhaps a change of course after sunset would lose them altogether.

"Land! Land ho!" The voice from the poop was that of Addams.

"Whereaway?" Gideon called.

"Dead ahead! Ten miles! I just noticed!"

Gideon ground his teeth in anxious annoyance, berating

himself for failing to set a proper lookout. Those islands should have been seen miles back.

Prinsessa would have to tack right away and trust that Gideon had been able to explain the procedure clearly enough and that the cards would do their job.

Time to begin.

"Let's get those stays'ls in, Captain Addams!" Gideon shouted. Addams took his station. Gideon picked two passengers to handle the downhauls of the mizzen topgallant staysail; then Addams tended the sheet, Gideon eased the halliard, and the two passengers walked aft with the downhaul, furling the staysail easily. The lines were belayed and then the mizzen topmast staysail was furled, followed by the main topgallant and topmast staysails. *Prinsessa* slowed perceptibly. Gideon cast a nervous glance over his shoulder at the brig, now visible from the deck. This was going to have to be done quickly.

Gideon returned to his place by the wheel. Señora Marquez, standing nearby, gave him a brief, encouraging smile.

"I knew we should do well if I left the praying to you, Captain," she said. "The rest of us would simply have confused the Almighty. *You* knew what to ask for."

"Take this speaking trumpet if ye please," Gideon said, impatient with her being frivolous at such a time. "The crew will be sure to hear ye."

"Thank you."

Gideon faced forward and took a deep breath, rehearsing in his mind the necessary commands modified by the cards. His brain swam with lines and braces, transformed now into numbers, court cards, and suits.

Ready about! he thought, silently giving the traditional command to himself.

"Get ready," he told Señora Marquez. "Any last questions?"

There were none.

Gideon took the spokes of the wheel from the quartermasters—Señora Marquez's maid Campaspe and another maidservant—and brought *Prinsessa* off the wind a bit, gathering momentum. He gulped air, trying to steady himself, hoping he hadn't forgotten anything. His mind reeling numbers, he sent an inchoate plea heavenward.

Helm's a-lee, he whispered to himself and threw the spokes of the wheel down. The bow began to swing.

"Ease the red knights!" he shouted. "Slack off the ace of clubs! Haul in the ace of cups!"

The Spanish deck had two knights per suit, one knight replacing the queen of the English deck: the inner, outer, and flying jib sheets were each marked with a knight.

Señora Marquez bellowed the order in Spanish translation. Gideon could see that the headsails were spilling wind. Franco stood by the monkey rail making certain the amateur crewmen weren't jamming their gear. Gideon glanced over his shoulder: the spanker had been hauled neatly to windward under Addams's direction. The bow was swinging into the wind. Gideon's practiced eye saw the edge of the maincourse beginning to lift.

Rise tacks and sheets.

"Throw off the nine of clubs and the nine of cups!" Gideon shouted. "Throw off the four of clubs and the four of cups!" The big sail began to slam back and forth, its controlling lines limp, the wind tearing at the canvas.

"Haul in on the five of clubs and the five of cups! Haul in on the six of clubs and the six of cups!" The leechlines and clewlines operated smoothly, controlling the sail, spilling what wind remained as the leeches were hauled up to the yard. "Haul in the seven of clubs and the seven of cups! Haul in the eight of clubs and the eight of cups!"

The course clewed up to the mast as easily as if seamen with twenty years' practice had been at the lines. Gideon watched, amazement turning to rampaging joy in his soul.

"Glory to God, belay!" he shouted, and Señora Marquez translated word for word.

"Amen!" echoed the passengers automatically. Canvas roared like a man-o'-war's battery as the mainsails all began to back. Now was the critical moment.

Mains'l haul!

"Ease off the ace, two, three, and four of wheels! Haul in the ace, two, three, and four of swords! Captain Addams, keep 'em together! Ease off the two, three, four, and king of cups! Haul in the two, three, four, and king of clubs!"

Canvas crashed as the ship lost way, the yards groaning

as they were hauled around to the other tack. Spray thundered over the bows as *Prinsessa* put its head to the wind. The passengers' inexperience began to show itself as the yards whirled around independently, cockbilled and awry as some passengers hauled at the braces more slowly or urgently than the others.

"Avast, three of swords!" Captain Addams was shouting, forgetting to speak Spanish. "I said *avast,* damn ye!" Losing his temper entirely, he charged into the men ranked at the main braces, fists lashing out.

"Steady, Captain Addams!" Gideon shouted in alarm. "Speak Spanish, and they'll understand!" The main topgallant yard crashed back against the stays. Gideon looked up at the sails in alarm—all intact, praise God, none torn by the wildly conflicting demands suddenly put on them.

"Señora, tell 'em all to 'vast hauling!" Gideon gasped frantically, feeling the ship lose way, beginning to pitch into each wave as forward motion was lost. The confusion at the braces increased as Addams knocked a man flat and tried to take over his line. Gideon felt a shriek of despair building in him: in another few seconds they'd be in irons, drifting hopelessly backward out of control.

The jib sheets would have to be set again, flat on their old tack to help bring the bow around; but it wasn't a maneuver the amateur crewmen had been told to expect, and Gideon could only hope they'd understand.

"Haul in on the red knights and belay!" he shouted in desperation. "Haul 'em in on the red side to larboard—I mean left!"

Dumbly the passengers obeyed. The jibs were set flat against the wind, and the bow began to swing. Offering mute thanks to the Almighty, Gideon dashed to the main braces to sort out the confusion. Addams had all the passengers back at their positions, except for the one he'd hit; that man stood nearby, resentfully holding his jaw.

"Slack off there, three of swords," Gideon said, addressing Addams. "Haul in a bit, three of wheels. Belay. Haul in a little more, ace of swords. Belay. Belay, all!"

The main yards were stacked more or less on top of one another, cockbilled at different angles but at least bracing the sails up into the wind that was beginning to gust in

over the larboard side. They'd done it! Gideon, his fist
pounding into his palm, returned to the wheel. He seized
the spokes and put the rudder amidships. The mainsails
rumbled and began to fill.

"Throw off the red knights, run them to the black
knights, and belay!" Gideon shouted. At last the men tending the headsail sheets received an order they expected,
and it was obeyed instantly.

"Ease the ace of cups! Haul in the ace of clubs!" The jib
sheets were run a-lee, the spanker eased.

Let go and haul!

"Throw off the king of swords and the king of wheels!
Throw off the ten of cups and the ten of clubs! Ease the
seven, eight, nine, and ten of coins; Haul in the seven,
eight, nine, and ten of swords."

The men at the fore braces had watched the chaos at the
main braces and profited by the example. The foreyards
swung smoothly and in line, the canvas thundering as it
filled.

"Belay!"

They'd done it! Prinsessa was on her new tack, the wind
coming over her larboard bow, riding each wave more and
more smoothly as the speed built.

The mainsail was set as smoothly as it had been doused.
Minor adjustments to the set of the sails were made; the
upper yards were properly fanned. Leechlines, buntlines,
and lifts were belayed and coiled properly. Then, reversing
the order in which they were run down, Gideon, Addams,
and the passengers reset the staysails.

Gideon could feel triumph filling him as he returned to
his place by the wheel, and as he looked aloft he felt an
idiot's grin tugging at the corners of his mouth. The great
taut sails swept arcs against the blue sky, each in its place,
each set perfectly to draw the ship up into the wind. Gideon lowered his eyes to the deck. The passengers were still
standing at their positions.

"I'll be obliged if ye tell the passengers to secure from
their stations," Gideon told Señora Marquez.

The passengers whooped in joy as they were told, the
men throwing hats into the air, two dancing along the
maindeck in impromptu hornpipes. There was a heedless

laugh beside him, and Gideon suddenly found himself embraced wholeheartedly, and entirely without modesty, by Campaspe, Señora Marquez's maidservant, who had flung her arms around his neck and kissed him vigorously on the ear. Gideon managed to firmly unlock her embrace and lower her to the deck, but he was surrounded by a dozen passengers, their eager Spanish faces surrounding him; his hands were shaken, his cheeks bussed, his ears filled with incomprehensible congratulations. Gideon tried to stammer out that the thanks were due to God alone, but he was overwhelmed by their fervor, and he allowed himself to be complimented for as long a time as they cared to do so.

The passengers, save those on guard duty and at the helm, went below to celebrate their deliverance, and Gideon found himself face to face with Captain Addams.

Addams scratched his whiskered chin and then thrust out a hand. Gideon took it.

"Damned if I thought it'd work, Markham," Addams said. "Ye can have a job aboard my ship any time ye wish."

"Thankee," said Gideon, surprised.

"I'll cast the log and see how many knots we're makin'," Addams said and sprang up the poop ladder. Gideon stood facing Señora Marquez.

"Congratulations, Captain," she said briefly. "You were brilliant. If I were an English admiral and had just seen what you did, I'd be bloody well terrified."

For some reason, of all the compliments he had received in the last few minutes hers was the only one that made him blush, and he had not blushed since he was a boy.

The pursuing brig sailed another twenty minutes before tacking, and lost much of what it had gained that day. Addams's computations showed *Prinsessa* making six knots close-hauled, as close to an ideal situation as possible, virtually guaranteeing that the brig would not catch them before nightfall.

Prinsessa tacked again between sunset and moonrise. The passengers went to their stations confidently and performed the operation as smoothly as any veteran tars. The pursuing brig was never seen again.

That night Campaspe was discovered in an amateurish attempt to set the mutineers at liberty; apparently she had conceived some sort of romantic affection for one of the crewmen. Señora Marquez irritatedly boxed her ears and confined her, weeping, to her cabin.

After midnight lights were seen dead ahead. Some hours later the passengers were called up, and most of the sails were clewed up. Gideon brought the *Prinsessa* close to shore and hove her to. He and Addams dropped the anchor.

Dawn revealed they were anchored beneath the guns of Fort Bowyer, guarding Mobile Bay. Addams hoisted an inverted Spanish flag as a distress signal, and soon Gunboat No. 163 of three guns, Lieutenant Blake, rowed out of Mobile Bay and came alongside.

The mutineers were brought up from the fo'c'sle and still blinking in the strong sunlight were herded into the gunboat. Blake, a smiling, sun-browned man of twenty-five, asked courteously if Addams would care to be towed to Mobile by the gunboat.

Addams, scratching his three days' beard, looked at Gideon. Their eyes met, and Addams smiled. "Thankee, but no," he said.

Under her own power and crewed by amateur hands, *Prinsessa* sailed past the sandspits guarding the bay's entrance, and that afternoon dropped anchor off the port of Mobile. A militia unit was drilling in plain sight of the ship, which surprised Gideon because it was not a Sunday; it was only after he'd had word from shore that he learned that the Creek nation had gone on the warpath against the American occupiers of West Florida, and had opened their campaign with a victory.

12

MOBILE

Gideon found Mobile to be a city of refugees, its popula-
tion almost doubled by the addition of rough men from
upcountry, men in buckskin or butternut, hardscrabble
farmers or small planters, Indians and half-breeds, living in
tents or dugouts on the fringes of the town. They carried
long knives in fringed sheaths, a musket or rifle in the
crook of one arm, and often as not a jug of whiskey in the
other. The women they'd brought with them—dressed in
homespun if they were white, buckskin and trade goods if
they were Indian—stayed quietly in their huts or tents, with
growing mounds of litter rising outside their doors.

The wealthier refugees were not so much in evidence.
Cushioned by slaves and gold, they lived their genteel lives
in accommodations that were not up to their usual manorial standards, but that were comfortable and respectable
enough. Mobile was a city used to transitions; in the past
few decades it had endured the rule of the English, French,
and Spanish, and although many of the town's old residents
were leaving for more congenial lands, those who remained
expressed optimism that the American occupation would
prove to be as transient as the rest. The men in fringed
buckskin—the companies of regulars and militia drilling in
the town plaza—were confident they would prove the
older residents wrong.

Gideon and Grimes had taken up residence at the house
of Lieutenant Blake, the sun-browned commander of Gunboat No. 163. After he had followed *Prinsessa*'s path from
Fort Bowyer to Mobile in order to deliver *Prinsessa*'s mutineers to the town gaol, he had proved to be an amiable
host. Blake was currently living aboard his gunboat, which
was now in dire need of repair thanks to an inadequately

supported sloop-topmast that had crashed overboard during a brief and surprising gale, carrying with it most of the running gear and a large section of gunwale. Apparently such accidents were common in Tom Jefferson's gunboats.

Archibald Bulloch Blake, who came from Augusta and had been named after the first president of Revolutionary Georgia, was a bachelor and a penniless naval lieutenant. The house he had loaned Gideon was not actually his own, but one he had been given use of by a cousin: Blake seemed to consider as "cousins" most of the aristocracy of Georgia, South Carolina, and other territories. He was a civilized, surprisingly humane man; even though a member of a rude, provincial service, raised on a tradition of grog and flogging, and assigned to a remote, woebegone station, Blake remained softspoken and genial. He spent his afternoon siestas ashore, smoking cigars and drinking whiskey with Gideon on the front veranda of what had been the Spanish governor's residence. With his feet up on the rail and his cocked hat in his lap he watched the drilling militia make regular fools of themselves on the drill field and spoke bewilderingly of Southern politics.

"The thing I can't understand, Captain Markham, is why the damn' Creeks went to war in the first place," Blake drawled as he and Gideon watched bellowing militia officers trying to shape their hopeless charges' drill. The American militia's chief function in the war thus far had been to disgrace themselves, having surrendered without a fight at Detroit, refused to cross the Niagara under Van Rensselaer, and in the brief Creek war having been routed at Burnt Corn Creek and massacred at Fort Mims.

"The Creeks were being left in peace, Captain Markham," Blake said. "The whites had built a road through their territory, and there were a few little disturbances on the frontier, easily settled by the police or by the Creeks themselves—but the Creeks weren't in any danger, and they weren't having their land taken away. Damnation!" Blake slapped a pair of gloves against his knee to express his bafflement. "The Creeks are farming Indians like the Cherokee, and like the Cherokee they keep nigger slaves. Why would they fight us?" Blake's bewilderment seemed genuine.

"Why, Captain Markham," he protested. "They were almost *white men*!"

"The whites entered this war without compelling reason," Gideon said. "I see no reason why red men should be any different."

Officers' shrieks echoed across the plaza as two columns of militia, apparently having confused left and right, collided with considerable force. Shakoes toppled from heads as the columns turned into merging, protesting mobs. Sergeants voiced profane dismay and entered the melee with fists. Two plumed Regular Army officers, observing from the shady veranda of the barracks, doubled over with laughter.

"Those men wouldn't stand for ten seconds against Billy Weatherford," Blake observed gloomily.

Gideon looked at the militia with growing disgust. These were the men from the South and West who had demanded war with Britain, claiming Canada could be conquered in a swift summer campaign, that the British army and navy could never intervene successfully. These militia were also the men who thus far in the war either had refused to fight, had surrendered, or had fled ignominiously from every battle. *He cometh in with vanity, and departeth in darkness,* Gideon thought sourly.

The Creek War, as far as Gideon could determine, was almost an accident; it had been created by a series of blunders and misunderstandings aggravated by tribal differences within the militant culture of the Creeks—all conflicts perhaps inevitable in the collision of frontier cultures, but ones that should have been resolved easily. Even now the Creeks themselves were bitterly divided; the Red Sticks faction, led by William Weatherford and Peter McQueen, had drawn perhaps three-fifths of the Creek Nation into war with the United States, while the other two-fifths, aided by the Chickasaw and Cherokee, whose lands had been plundered by Red Stick war parties, was busily mobilizing to fight the Red Sticks on behalf of the whites.

Even after the confused collision at Burnt Corn Creek, in which American militia attempted, with mixed success, to stop a British arms shipment to the Upper Creeks, all-out warfare could perhaps have been averted had not over five hundred whites, only two weeks before, been massacred at Fort Mims just forty miles north of Mobile on Tensaw Lake. The massacre, the details of which were unclear, had stunned the whites and precipitated an evacuation into Mobile. Army engineers were laying out fortifications and were trying to round up enough slaves to build them—West Florida whites were above such work—while the militia drilled daily, if not soberly, and the Creole inhabitants, preparing for the worst, began to hoard little Spanish flags to wave when Billy Weatherford captured the town, in hopes it might prevent them from being butchered and scalped.

"I've met Billy Weatherford," Blake said, watching the militia trying to sort out their companies. "He's the only Creek we have to worry about. He's worth fifty James Wilkinsons and Thomas Flournoys, the finest red man I ever met. He's got four thousand warriors, trained and equipped by the British, while Mobile has a few companies of regulars, some artillery left over from the French and Indian War, Gunboat One-Six-Three, and that bunch of bunglers out there on the drill field."

"If the Almighty intends to destroy Mobile, Mobile will be destroyed if it has ten thousand defending it," Gideon said.

Blake looked at him with an arched eyebrow. "Do you think, Captain Markham, that I ought to commence the search for ten virtuous men?"

Gideon frowned. Blake, with a sudden grin, tactfully changed the subject.

"It's been a damn' bad war for me, Captain Markham," he said. "I've been on the New Orleans station since it began, a thousand miles from any fighting at sea and in command of a gunboat that can't be taken out of Lake Borgne without beginning to ship water. When we sailed from Lake Borgne to Mobile, we almost swamped in the Mississippi Sound in a moderate wind—I'd hate to think what a gale would do to her."

Gideon shook his head, feeling a twang of cynicism invading his mind. Thomas Jefferson again. During his term of office the navy had been cut to the bone, and hundreds of useless gunboats built to defend America's inlets, bays, and harbors. Jefferson was responsible for the Embargoes that had wrecked America's commerce. Between those two acts he had probably made war inevitable: the Europeans, and the British in particular, had seen the United States as weak, cowardly, and helpless; their insults to the American flag increased, and the warnings of stiffening American resistance had been ignored.

"Tom Jefferson," Gideon said, his mind seething with hatred for the president who had destroyed his livelihood and all the happiness he had known. "I wonder if he is in the pay of the French? He's an Illuminatus, that much is known."

"Jefferson, an Illuminatus?" Blake asked. "I've heard that old story that he belongs to some Masonic conspiracy, and I don't believe it."

"The Reverend Jedediah Morse has made the claim, and Reverend Morse would not lie," Gideon said. "Besides, how d'ye explain—"

"The man is a Virginian and a planter," Blake said. "What does he know of the sea? He was ignorant, but he learned his lesson in Tripoli and built the navy up again."

"Stuff!" Gideon said. "Why are ye still in gunboats, then?"

Blake cleared his throat tactfully. "There's a place for gunboats, I'm sure. They'll provide harbor defense as well as anything—"

"Not if they're laid up half the time like yours!"

"They've been badly designed—by Jefferson's men, I'll admit—but the principle on which they're based is sound."

Gideon was astonished. Here was a navy man, one whose career had been hampered and life jeopardized by gunboats, prepared to defend the imbecile policy that had stranded him in an obscure port in command of a faulty vessel.

"If it weren't for the gunboats, Mr. Blake," Gideon said, "the navy would be strong enough to fight the British, and ye would be in a real ship, or perhaps commanding a schooner or brig of war."

Blake nodded, conceding the point. "My career would have been hampered in any case," he said. "I'm not one of Preble's boys, like your cousin Favian. All those who served in Tripoli look out for one another—not that I can blame them. They're good, all of them."

"The latest news is that my cousin was promoted master commandant and given the *Experiment*."

"The first piece of luck he's had in years," Blake said. "I've served with him, and he deserves better."

"Lafayette Markham, his brother, is a prominent New Hampshire Federalist. Jefferson and the Illuminati have been punishing the family by denying Favian promotion."

"I wouldn't take such an extreme view," Blake said. "Many good Republicans have been denied promotion as well—myself, for example."

"How can ye—how can—" Gideon spluttered, totally baffled by the idea of a Republican in the navy.

"I support Jefferson and the Republicans because they've been good for the country," Blake said calmly. "They've given us Louisiana . . ."

"Mountains, prairies, and swamps! We've got all the land we need, and besides Louisiana was taken unconstitutionally!"

"And they've given us the war with the British we need," Blake added.

"Which we're losing because of Jefferson's Embargo and his idiot naval policy!"

"But which will result in a strong navy," Blake said. "Washington realizes how well such a navy can benefit us now *Constitution* and *United States* have demonstrated it."

"A lot of good a stronger navy will do if there's no commerce for it to protect," Gideon pointed out. "And Louisiana and the West will do us no good at all if the British capture it—which they show every sign of doing!"

"Ah, well," Blake shrugged. "We're stronger in the end. We just need a little practice at fighting and we'll have Canada. After Napoleon drives the Russians out of the war, the British will be too hard-pressed to hold Canada and the Peninsula at the same time."

"But New England will take no more abuse, sir!" Gideon said, his temper flashing. "It's New England that's had to bear the wreck of American shipping, it's New England that the redcoats from Canada will invade because the

South and West wanted war." Gideon's fist crashed down on his knee for emphasis. "New England will not stand for it much longer!" he said fiercely. "If the rights of the New England states are abused much longer, there may be a second War of Independence, sir!"

Blake's reply was ominously cold. "Are you suggesting separation, sir?"

Gideon fought down his anger, which he knew had been released by whiskey. How could he explain New England's resentment of Republican policies, which seemed, even if they were well-intentioned, to be deliberate persecution? Explain this anger raised by the declaration of war, made by those whose lives and fortunes were in no danger, but in which New England could expect to find its coasts ravaged and its citizens taxed? He could not explain it now, not with Blake's cold glare fixed on him, as cold as the stare of a dueling pistol, which Gideon knew he might end up facing if he did not choose his words carefully.

"I am no separatist," he said. "But New England will not stand to see the Constitution so abused. There is the principle of States' Rights, and the Republicans do not abide by it."

"The South does not believe in States' Rights," Blake said sternly. "And never shall."

Only so long as the South controls Congress, Gideon thought cynically, but he knew better than to say it.

"I will fight the British as long as the war lasts," Gideon said. "I'm no friend of England, and no member of my family ever was. But to everything there is a season: a time to kill and a time to heal . . . If we were to fight England, we should have done it in its proper time, when we could win. The Republicans have refused to grant us a standing army or a strong navy, even though New England was willing to vote for both, saying that the military would tempt us to foreign adventures and entanglements; but now Madison and the other Republicans have forced us into a war for which neither they nor Jefferson have made adequate preparation.

"We shall be lucky," concluded Gideon, "not to lose the West, not to mention New England."

Blake, pacified, crossed his arms and leaned back in his chair. "We'll win it by and by," he said and then added wistfully, "I hope I'll be given a chance to prove myself before it's over."

"That chance exists," Gideon said. Blake looked at him questioningly.

"Ye can turn privateer," Gideon explained. "Privateering has always been this country's first defense against attack, and ye'll be hitting England where it hurts. The British will always find another thirty-eight-gun frigate should the navy capture one, and the navy can always be blockaded in harbor, but they can't stop all the privateers from escaping, and even with all the convoy escorts in the world they can't stop their commerce from being harried."

Blake laughed his easy Georgia laugh. "I appreciate your kindness, Captain Markham, but—"

"I make no offers!" Gideon said. "I can't set ye up in business, but I can give advice, and there is money aplenty in New Orleans that will find a fast hull for ye and a few guns. It's better, Mr. Blake, than rotting yer life away rowing yer gunboat from one pestilence-ridden swamp to another."

Blake smiled sadly. "To the navy I gave my oath," he said, "and I can not withdraw that oath when we are at war even if advantage lies that way."

" 'A good name is better than precious ointment,' " Gideon quoted, and the young lieutenant nodded. Blake smiled and stood, stretching his lanky legs, and put on his cocked hat.

"I'm afraid I must rejoin my gunboat," he said. "Number One-Six-Three is expecting a delegation of carpenters sometime after siesta, and I'll be expected to supervise their blundering."

"I'll walk with ye if I may," Gideon said, standing and donning his beaver hat. They walked the short distance to where the gunboat lay at anchor in the Choctaw Pass, the Georgian tall and erect in his blue uniform, the New Hampshireman of average height and garbed in brown, alike only in their profession of the sea and the sharpened swords they both wore at their sides. Their walk took them past Mobile's fashionable quarter where the big Spanish houses with their summery courtyards and liveried servants stood, and past one house in particular that stood with its windows open to the fresh breeze, with painters at work giving it a new coat. Lieutenant Blake looked up at the house from beneath his cocked hat.

"Have you seen Mrs. Marquez since your arrival?" he asked. "She is causing a stir in town, I believe. So much energy has not been seen in Mobile for decades."

"I have not seen her," Gideon said uncomfortably, stolidly avoiding glancing at the house. "Señora Marquez and I lived in a situation of enforced intimacy aboard *Prinsessa*, and if I were seen too often at her residence, the town might draw incorrect conclusions. I do not want to harm her chances or injure her socially."

Blake's expression was neutral. "Will you introduce me one day?" he asked. "I thought she was a handsome woman when I saw her."

"I would be happy to provide an introduction if one is needed. The two of ye met aboard *Prinsessa*."

"We did not speak," Blake said. "In a Spanish town especially the formalities ought to be observed."

Gideon felt himself irritated by Blake's chatter—he was speaking about Señora Marquez as if she were a horse. *Handsome.* Did he really think her that or was he being gallant? Gideon had thought she showed too much of the outdoors and a hard life; perhaps Blake, with his Georgia sporting background, preferred extraforaneous women. Gideon's own preferences were for women who were, well, *softer.*

Gideon waited until the gunboat's little jolly boat rowed to the bank for Blake, then shook hands with him and invited him to supper. "I feel strange, sir, inviting a man to supper at his own house," he said.

"Think of it as your house while you're here," Blake smiled courteously.

"Thankee. Ye're most kind. Eight o'clock?"

"Eight will be splendid."

They said their farewells, and Blake jumped into the boat's stern sheets. Gideon waved to the young lieutenant, then shifted his attention to the gunboat beyond.

No. 163 was dandy-rigged, like a topsail sloop but with

a tiny mast right aft that carried a lugsail to aid in fine
maneuvering. The dandy rig was an excellent choice for
the little craft, and it carried sweeps in case the wind fell, or
for battle. The little boat, somewhat less than fifty feet
long, was crewed by Blake, a midshipman, a steward,
twenty seamen, a corporal of marines, and four privates;
she was armed with three twenty-four-pound long guns firing right forward. She sat low in the water—the theoreti-
cians who had convinced Jefferson and the Congress to
build such craft claimed that the low freeboard made her
hard for an enemy to hit, but what the fourteen inches of
freeboard really meant was that she rolled so badly she
could not aim her guns, that she would swamp in any kind
of heavy sea, and in a gale would take every crewman with
her to the bottom. No. 163, and the other gunboats like
her, had been designed to guard harbors and inlets, but
frequently the navy had been so hard-pressed for ships that
the gunboats had been forced to sail abroad. Gideon knew
that during the war with Tripoli at least one of the gunboats had been lost in mid-Atlantic with all hands, and
another on its maiden voyage had fetched up in a Georgia
cornfield.

Blake, young and vigorous, was wasting his life in such
craft and perhaps would one day lose it. Gideon soured at
the thought. The government in Washington did not deserve such loyalty.

He turned and walked back to the town. He fell in behind a man in the street, a cobbler's assistant delivering
shoes who also carried a tomahawk thrust through his belt
and an antique shotgun slung over one shoulder. Prepared,
Gideon knew, for the sudden Indian attack. The details of
the Fort Mims massacre were sketchy, but rumor told of
careless guards, ignored warnings, and the eventual pouring in of Creeks through an opened gate to set fires that
burned the defenders alive or forced them into the open to
be murdered and scalped. The cobbler's assistant was prepared in case William Weatherford and four thousand red
men should appear without warning on Mobile's magnolia-
scented streets. Or perhaps, Gideon thought, his employer
had turned weapons dealer during the emergency, and had
sent his assistant to deliver a shotgun along with the shoes.

The cobbler's assistant turned to the right as he passed Señora Marquez's establishment, and Gideon found his glance lingering on the building. He had not seen Señora Marquez since she had departed *Prinsessa* a week before, and his reasons were not entirely those he had given Lieutenant Blake. She had been an intrusion into his life in many ways, attempting as one of two American passengers aboard the ship to share the solitary existence he lived and cherished. And yet against her intrusions he remembered her forthright action on the deck of the *Prinsessa*, the way she'd held her oversize pistol as if she were prepared to use it, the tactful way she had smoothed his path in his assumption of authority over the stricken ship, her confident manner in translating his commands to the passengers. It would be discourtesy to delay visiting her any longer.

Campaspe, the maidservant, opened the door to his knock and was in his arms in an instant. Gideon felt his ear wetly kissed.

"For heaven's sake, girl!" said a mild male voice. Gideon carefully detached Campaspe from his person and found himself facing a black man in livery, complete with antique powdered periwig.

"I don't know what we goin' to do with this child," the man said, taking Campaspe gently by the arm and steering her out of the foyer. Campaspe waved as she left, favoring Gideon with another of her dazzling, impudent smiles. "She don't seem to understand the formalities of the service, sir."

"I think she should be instructed. With emphasis, if necessary," Gideon said. "I am Captain Markham. I would like to see Señora Marquez if she's not occupied."

"I believe Miz Marquez be busy, Captain," said the butler. "Shall I take in your card?"

"I have no card," Gideon said, feeling his prickly temper begin to rise. There had been no such formality aboard *Prinsessa*, with the mutinous crew battened below and the unknown brig in pursuit.

"Please tell Señora Marquez that Captain Markham has called and will be back tomorrow," Gideon said, his urge for solitude growing. He found himself unwilling to face any more social niceties, any chats over tea about subjects no more controversial than the weather.

"Captain Markham!" called Señora Marquez, striding through the door, her face broadened by an unfeigned smile. She took his hand. "Campaspe told me you were here. I rushed down to meet you." She turned to the butler. "Alfred, should Captain Markham call in the future, please make him welcome. He saved my life aboard *Prinsessa,* and the very least we owe him is a seat in the parlor."

"Very good, ma'am," said Alfred and opened the parlor door. Señora Marquez took Gideon's arm and led him inside.

She wore the long white high-waisted gown that had been the fashion since the Directory, this time without a jacket to help conceal the fact that the gown was almost transparent, as was the simple shift beneath it. The gown's high waist made the most of her small, high, surprisingly youthful breasts, and the straight fall from the gown's waist to her ankles complimented the proportions of her broad-shouldered, slim-hipped, athletic body. Gideon, his arm pressed against her, was surprised to find within himself the stirrings of lust. He felt he should be shocked at himself—he'd thought such things were behind him—but somehow could not find words of reproach.

He seated her on a settee, and hitching his sword out of the way, sat in a chair on her right hand.

"You look well, ma'am," he said and was surprised to find her turning away, as she had twice before, from his compliment. The ear and the graceful curve of neck revealed by her taut hairstyle blushed a bright red. She took a deep breath and faced him.

"You have a most remarkable way with a compliment, Captain," she said.

"I'm afraid I don't understand."

"I am used to gallant compliments," she said, smiling, "flattering compliments, formal compliments, all manner of meaningless compliments—you give me none of these! Instead you look at me in the most sincere, steady way, and as if you were saying something perfectly matter-of-fact like 'Madison is a president' or 'the world is round,' you tell me I look well. How can I fail to blush before such uncompromising candor!"

"I don't know what to say, ma'am," said Gideon, baffled.

"You can stop *ma'am*ing me, I hope," she said. "My name is Maria-Anna, or Marie for short. And you will let me call you Gideon, I hope. That is what your friends call you, isn't it?"

Friends? thought Gideon. There were none left. Those of his boyhood had gone their ways, and he had made none professionally. The one true friend of his life, his Betsy, was gone. But *Gideon* was what his brothers and father called him; he had been *Captain Markham* to everyone else. There was no reason she should not call him by his first name, but he knew it would make him uncomfortable. Another presumption she had made, another barrier she had crossed without knowing it.

"Maria-Anna," he said, making himself form the syllables.

"It's not very harmonious, is it?" she said, a smile on her expressive face. "There were two maiden aunts to be appeased, and neither could be slighted—either one of them might have died and left the family money. As far as I know they're still alive. Living on spite if nothing else."

But it was obvious that whoever had named her had no ear at least. *Anna-Maria* would have been more usual and better-sounding.

"It's no less harmonious than *Gideon*, I think," he said.

"But *Gideon* is a strong name; no one would think of lying to a *Gideon*'s face. *Maria-Anna* is a meandering collection of syllables leading to a pointless, irresolute conclusion. A *Maria-Anna*, much more than a *Gideon*, would be thought a natural target for swindlers of all sorts."

"No more than anyone else, I'm sure," said Gideon.

"Oh, yes," she said knowingly. "I told you of my investment plans aboard *Prinsessa*, did I not? They have been much aggravated by sharp practice. The people evacuating the countryside have raised the demand for living quarters, and the hope that the Creeks or the British might capture

Mobile has meant that many of the Creoles who had planned to leave will be staying and not placing their houses on the market. I've not been able to put my *poque* winnings to good use, since buying houses in Mobile is no longer a good investment. When the crisis is over, you can be sure the prices will fall once more. All I've been able to do is buy some good niggers—they're cheap, at least, since there's no demand for their labor in the countryside with all the plantations evacuated. And as soon as my house is painted and refurnished, I'll rent it again, along with Alfred and the other servants. That will be a good living while it lasts."

"Buying land near the town, clearing it, and building new houses might do well if ye can afford it," Gideon said, drawn into the discussion in spite of himself. "There's a surfeit of labor here, although materials are dear, and you could find tenants right away."

She smiled brightly. "That's just what I'm doing, but in a modest way," she said. "Although I'm keeping most of my money, I'm considering buying land in the countryside. It's all been abandoned by the owners, who will be willing to sell it cheaply in order to feed their families for the length of the emergency."

Gideon shook his head. "It won't work, Señora—Maria-Anna," he said. "It would be impossible to know what ye're buying. Ye cannot go into the countryside to inspect the land without risking attack by the Creeks. It might be worthless—it might even be swampland!"

"That's true," she said. "But the land, I'm sure, could be inspected before the purchase by those who know how to move quietly in the countryside. There are plenty of such men in Mobile nowadays, don't you think?"

"Aye," Gideon said, dubious. "If ye could find someone willing to risk his scalp for your profit, and if they're trustworthy enough to know good land when they see it. But after the Fort Mims massacre I don't believe ye'd find men foolhardy enough to venture inland without an army of regulars to escort them."

"Ah, here's Alfred," Maria-Anna said as the butler entered the parlor with a tray. "Would you prefer tea, or coffee? Or perhaps something stronger?"

Gideon took coffee, and as he sipped he recognized the common Gulf addition of chicory. Maria-Anna added cream to her coffee.

"Have you seen Captain Addams?" she asked. "I haven't heard any reports of him."

"His men have all volunteered to serve in the regulars for the rest of the war, rather than be charged with mutiny," Gideon said. "There will be no trial. I ran into Addams on the street last week, and he was angry over it."

"Poor man," Maria-Anna said.

"He reaped only what he sowed," Gideon said. "The profession will be better off without him. No sailor will serve under him now. *Prinsessa* will stay in Mobile until it rots, or until it has a new captain."

"I'm surprised, Gideon," she said. "You are a captain yourself, and you acted to quell the mutiny—but you speak as if you sympathize with the rebels."

"That which is crooked cannot be made straight," said Gideon, remembering the twisted, rum-sodden man in the Quaker hat. "If I behaved toward my men as he did, I could expect nothing else. I'm happy there will be no hangings. I simply wish that Lieutenant Blake had been able to get a few of those men into the navy where they would be more useful in winning the war."

"It seemed in the last few days of the voyage as if Addams had reformed."

"Too late," Gideon said. "There is no future for him here. Those who expect obedience must take the responsibility of making certain their orders are not capricious." She looked at him with acute curiosity. "As a captain," he said, trying to explain himself further, "I expect my orders to be obeyed without question. My expectations require me to make certain my orders *cannot* be questioned, that they are correct. Those captains who misuse their authority in whimsical fashion only erode the authority of the good captains. They're the bane of the profession."

"Are there many such?"

Gideon looked uncomfortable. "Aye, there are," he said. He tried to explain. "In part it's the nature of the job. The master of a ship exists in isolation—his crew see him only when he gives orders or when he finds fault. He cannot be wrong; he cannot be familiar. It is a lonely profession. A man who cannot tolerate the loneliness may find himself ruling his ship through caprice."

"Are you accustomed to that loneliness, Gideon?"

The question took Gideon aback; but Maria-Anna, leaning forward on the settee, her expressive face showing solemn curiosity, was manifestly waiting for an answer. How could Gideon explain? That his solitude and isolation were chosen and cherished, that he never would have left the quarterdeck of *General Sullivan* even to step ashore if there had been some way to manage it? Maria-Anna's question, innocent as it sounded, pierced to the heart of his solitude, and even to answer it would be a betrayal of his own precious exile.

"It suits me," he said briefly.

Much to his relief she accepted his answer and leaned back to sip her coffee. Yet her dark eyes still showed lively curiosity.

"I am still intrigued by the idea of sending an expedition inland to look at the land for sale," she said. "The valuable land would be east of the Tensaw, the easternmost branch of the Alabama and Tombigbee, where excess produce could be rafted down to Mobile. Should the expedition go by boat? The Indians would have no boats, would they?"

"Perhaps they would not have sailboats, but they have canoes," Gideon said slowly. "A sailboat might outrun them with a good wind. But there is no way to hide a boat in the middle of the river; it would be slow sailing against the current, and the Creeks would discover it more easily than they would a few men moving carefully by land."

She offered Gideon another cup of coffee.

"Do you think the Red Sticks will still be out in force?" she asked. "They can't supply an army as whites do. Perhaps after Fort Mims they've had to scatter back to their farms in order to avoid starving. There has been no report of Creek activity since."

"Perhaps," said Gideon carefully, sipping his coffee. "I would not care to risk my life on that assumption. They might be organizing another large expedition, to Mobile or north to Tennessee."

"I'll make inquiries," Maria-Anna said. Gideon glanced

through the room, hoping to find a spittoon. There were none. Gideon's father Josiah had long denounced tobacco as a filthy and degrading habit, but Gideon had been more conventional than his father in many ways, and tobacco was one. It was difficult to keep a pipe alight on a ship, particularly in a gale with water slopping over the bulwarks and spray-drenched wind howling down one's neck. Tobacco chewing was a sailor's habit, and Gideon had accustomed himself expertly to it. But Maria-Anna, either more used to smoking or disapproving of chewing, had no spittoons. Gideon reluctantly postponed his pleasure.

"I would be obliged, Gideon, if you'd join me for supper," Maria-Anna said. "Perhaps we can continue our discussion."

"Thankee, but I can't," Gideon said. "I have another engagement. I'll be happy to see ye another time."

"I'll send you an invitation. Where may I reach you?"

"I am at Lieutenant Blake's," Gideon said, and gave her directions. He finished his coffee and stood. His sword clattered against a leg of the chair. "Please remain seated. I'll show myself out."

Maria-Anna stood anyway and took his arm to lead him out. "Perhaps we can dine Thursday next?" she asked. "That will be two days from now."

Gideon nodded. "I'd be pleased, Maria-Anna," he said. She led him to the door.

"What would you say if I told you," she said, a teasing smile on her face, "that I'm considering going upriver myself in a hired boat?"

"I'd say it was a mad thing to do!" Gideon said. "To risk your life so foolishly, and all for material gain!"

"Isn't that what privateers do?" she asked, dropping his arm as she ushered him out into bright sunlight. "Risk their lives day after day for profit?"

"There are other avenues open to ye," Gideon said soberly. "You may make your way in the world by many different roads. For me there is only one thing, and that is the sea; there is no other path." He groped for words, blinking in the sunlight. She stood in the doorway, her expression changing from one of private amusement to one of sober surprise.

"Maria-Anna, I think ye will do well," Gideon said. "For you there is no need for recklessness. It's a good start ye have."

She shook her head. "A good start in a provincial town," she said. "I've had better. I would like to be a lady again and not have to worry about ways and means. I think I'll succeed on the river. It will only be for a few days."

"I pray you will heed me and not go."

"Good afternoon, Gideon," she said. "I will consider your thoughts as well as your prayers." Gently she closed the door.

Gideon lingered at her door for a moment, considering the possibilities for stopping Maria-Anna from embarking on her mad quest. He could inform the military authorities; but they had no authority over a woman who was presumably a Spanish citizen—at most they would advise her not to go.

He cut a plug of tobacco as he stepped out into the street. He realized that in order to stop her he would have to marshal his best arguments against the expedition. Yet those arguments all boiled down to the single argument he had already advanced: it was a sin to risk life, not simply one's own but others, so unreasonably and in pursuit of profits. And yet how absurd that argument sounded coming from the mouth of a privateer. Surely he could argue that he had patriotic, even spiritual, reasons for his profession, but if profit were not a chief motive, he might as well have joined the navy.

He did not object to the basic idea of her plan. She was taking advantage of a crisis to buy land from the less fortunate; but she was doing it in a nation where land was cheap and abundant, where anyone who had bankrupted himself in some way could simply move west and start over. She was probably doing the refugees a favor by giving them cash to start over with.

Yet Maria-Anna's quest was not simply pecuniary: she wanted land as a way of increasing her social position; she wanted to become a *lady* again. He remembered her on *Prinsessa*'s quarterdeck, speaking of her father's poverty and how *gentlemen* felt obliged to snub him because he owned no slaves. Maria-Anna wished to raise herself above

her father's standing, to regain part of the status she had
once had as the wife of a Spanish landlord, the absolute
ruler of part of a Mexican province. To join the ranks of
those who had once slighted her father.

And to do that was wrong, and Gideon must prevent it.
As he hastened down the street to Blake's lodgings, he
racked his brain for a strategy he could discuss with Blake
to defeat Maria-Anna's scheme.

13

ON THE RIVER

Three days later, early Friday morning, Gideon walked with shouldered musket through the riverbank mud of the Choctaw Pass, the branch of the Alabama nearest Mobile. He let the heavy Brown Bess fall from his weary shoulder and faced the three persons in the boat.

"I've come to die with ye," he said. "Yer supplies are stowed badly. It would be better if the boat were farther down by the stern."

He directed the stowage of the boat's stores, ignoring Maria-Anna's eyes on him. Propping his musket in the stern sheets, he overhauled the running rigging and showed the two crewmen how to hoist the gaffsail and set the boat's jib. The canvas—worn, ancient canvas, lovingly repaired and patched—roared as it filled, and the twenty-foot boat tugged eagerly at its leash, as if yearning to follow the river's dark waters to the homeland of the Creeks. The anchor, a large rock, was jerked from the bottom, and the boat shook its sails once more and sprang to life, heading briefly downriver to cross the upper reaches of the bay and enter the Tensaw.

Gideon settled in the stern sheets, the tiller under his arm. His stowing of the boat had isolated him; food, ammunition, bad-weather clothing, and two jugs of whiskey were piled on either side of him and in front, separating him from the others in the boat. It was almost as if he were alone on a quarterdeck once more, the only place on earth he yearned to be.

"Thank you, Gideon," Maria-Anna said quietly, avoiding his eyes. Gideon said nothing, but cut himself tobacco to chew.

The supper the previous night had been a disaster for Gideon's cause. He had arrived with Blake to support him, both men primed with arguments, logical and moral, opposing the idea of Maria-Anna venturing up the Alabama. They had found her with her own allies, the two men she intended taking with her, and were horrified to discover that she had already bought a boat and intended to leave the next morning. Gideon had scented disaster: both of her crewmen, frontiersmen with hard hands and weaknesses for whiskey, admitted knowing nothing about boats, but seemed to feel there was not much to learn. Gideon and Blake had left Maria-Anna's early as other guests arrived for an evening game of *poque*, giving up their attempt to dissuade her. It had been a strange walk from Maria-Anna's house to the river, Gideon feeling strangely lightheaded, Blake pausing to light his cigar at a lamp—there had been a coin spun in the air, winking in the lamplight, landing in a kid glove, a walk to the river, a breeze that smelled of sweet gum and death. Gideon had gone in search of a man who would sell him a musket. He had left instructions for Grimes to wake him early and had slept well.

Maria-Anna's two companions sat in the bow of the boat, somberly watching the herons dotting the surface of the bay, the oystermen working with their tongs. One companion was Charles Jouhaux, a weatherbeaten Frenchman of forty in a black felt hat and battered clothes, a small planter made destitute by the war. His family, so far as he knew, had been killed at Fort Mims, and his slaves carried off; he had missed death only because he had been in Mobile on business. He spoke little, but Gideon knew he did not lightly estimate his danger: he was armed to the teeth with a musket, a shotgun, a brace of pistols, a tomahawk, and a big fighting knife the length of his forearm. He had come as a representative of several small planters, as destitute as himself—a *syndicate,* Maria-Anna had called them —all prepared to sell their land, their homes, and slaves as part of a single large scheme. Jouhaux in particular represented them because there was no one to mourn him if he were killed, but Gideon, who had seen a yearning in his eyes, knew why he had come—he wanted to find word of his family, either some sign that they had been spared, or certain knowledge that they lay in the earth.

The other man in the party was Sean MacDonald, a Cherokee Indian hired as a guide and scout. A small, quick man, he carried a long rifle almost as tall as himself, deadly at three hundred yards in the hands of an expert; he carried a tomahawk for close work. He seemed shy in company but smiled easily and giggled behind his hand at a joke; in the boat he was serious, polishing his rifle with a rabbit skin while watching the trees. He had expressed the previous night a quiet willingness to kill any representative of the Creek nation (whom he called *Ani-Gusa*) encountered on the journey. Gideon suspected that he, too, was on the boat for his own reasons; such deadly resolve could rarely be bought for money, and most often sprang from a tenacious and merciless memory.

The boat swept over the bay. Gideon told the others in detail to overhaul the jib sheets in order to keep them from jamming, while he saw himself to the gaffsail sheets. He gybed the boat, carefully moderating the gaffsail's swing, and they slid past the Spanish fort into the dark waters of the Tensaw. A water moccasin dropped from an overhanging branch into the water as they passed, a deadly usher indicating the path that led to the domain of the Creeks.

The boat was just under twenty feet long and very beamy; it drew eight inches of water beneath its almost flat bottom. It was a swift little vessel, skittering lightly along the water's surface, but without a keel it made a lot of leeway, and its heel was considerable. Four sweeps were stowed amidships in case the wind failed; the boat had been used to carry cargo to and from the plantations on the river. The mast was stepped into a tabernacle amidships and seemed fragile, supported only by four stays and four shrouds, but it somehow managed to carry a big gaffsail and a large jib and apparently had been doing so successfully for years. It was even armed: just abaft its ridiculous two-foot bowsprit was an ancient brass two-pounder swivel gun, green with verdigris; a waterproof barrel carried cartridges and a length of match. Gideon hoped it would not be needed.

The riverbank was shrouded in pine and Spanish moss,

alive with waterfowl but barren of mankind. The river ran at least three feet deep, but its course was tortured, and as they tacked or gybed beneath overhanging bluffs (the wind was uncertain, channeled by the pines and river canyons), there was always a choice of channels to take as they wound through marshy islands large and small. Gideon kept the gaffsail sheeted well in to guard against an involuntary gybe and carefully watched the surface of the river ahead, searching for snags or for cat's paws that would signal a fluke of wind crossing the current.

Maria-Anna sat quietly, almost motionlessly, amidships, dressed again in her riding habit and top hat, sweltering quietly in the sun. She had not spoken since the sails had been set, but watched the water birds expressionlessly and searched the bank with dull eyes. She had two pistols beside her in a case, the one that she'd brandished aboard *Prinsessa* and its mate. Gideon was surprised to realize they were not cavalry pistols as he had first thought, but heavy, long-barreled dueling pistols, probably rifled, still too heavy and awkward for Maria-Anna's small hands, but ideal for a big-handed male, and deadly in the grasp of someone who knew his business. Probably a legacy from her husband, Gideon thought.

When the sun was high overhead, Maria-Anna reached into the supplies and brought out their luncheon: hard biscuit and dried meat, with whiskey to wash it down. Jouhaux and MacDonald showed a tendency to keep the whiskey jug in circulation between them, but Gideon asked for a swallow, moistened his tongue, emphatically corked the jug, and placed it by his feet. The others looked at him sourly but did not object.

Here and there were clearings on the bank with cabins where settlers had ventured their hopes in attempts to establish themselves. All were empty now, doors hanging open like gaping idiots' mouths, nature asserting itself in the cornfields, fishing poles hanging over the dark water with draped lines that hadn't been checked in weeks. Alligators, slow, primeval inhabitants of this dark world, sunned themselves on the banks, their jaws open like the visors of ancient chivalry.

The sun was two hours above the western horizon and

the boat cruising in the river's main channel when a canoe quietly slid out from a tributary on the left bank a mere three hundred yards away, hung in the current for one astonished moment, and then spun swiftly toward them. Paddle blades flashed in the tropical sun, and as Gideon recovered from his surprise, he felt the hot sweat on the back of his neck turn icy cold.

"Load the swivel!" Gideon shouted—or perhaps from the way the command rang in the air they all shouted it at once. MacDonald and Jouhaux banged heads as they reached for the cartridges. High-pitched yelps and yipping cries rang from the canoe and echoed off the pines. MacDonald frantically puffed his tinderbox ablaze as he tried to light the swivel gun's slow match; Jouhaux shoved the cloth-wrapped cartridge down the gun's brass muzzle. Maria-Anna leaned out over the gunwale, trying to see around the boat's jib, her expression grim.

"Get yer head down!" Gideon shouted, his churning mind nettled at the distraction. "They might have marksmen aboard!" Maria-Anna obeyed, ducking below the gunwale to open the pistol case, her hands fumbling at the powder flask.

Gideon calculated swiftly: the boat was close-hauled, sailing on the larboard tack and almost in the center of the river; the canoe was coming swiftly down, moving into midstream from the left bank—or from starboard, from Gideon's perspective sailing upstream. If both boats continued their present course they would pass within fifty yards or so, each presenting their larboard side to the enemy. Presumably shots would then be exchanged, or the Red Sticks would run for them and try to board with knives and hatchets. Gideon shifted in the stern sheets as he tried to hitch his sword forward to where his hand could grasp the hilt when necessary, and found himself wishing fervently for boarding pikes.

He brought the boat a little nearer the wind, closing the distance between the two craft. The Red Sticks showed no response: perhaps they had no objection, perhaps they had a trick in mind. The canoe was probably faster in the short run, moving with the current, at least until the paddlers

tired—and it was far more maneuverable. With the paddlers on one side backing water and the others churning
their paddles forward, the canoe could spin swiftly and
without warning. But were the Red Sticks prepared for
such a maneuver, were they practiced at it? His white-
knuckled hand gripping the tiller, Gideon made up his
mind.

"I'm going to go about!" he shouted to the men at the
bow. Jouhaux was priming the swivel, the other holding
aloft the triumphantly burning slow match. "Overhaul yer
gear and stand by! We're going to cross their bows!" They
glanced back at him and nodded, their eyes bright. As an
afterthought Gideon added, "Aim low—the wind'll be
heeling the boat!" Again two frantic nods. Maria-Anna
crouched low, priming her pistols.

Carefully Gideon gauged the positions of the two craft.
Not yet. The maneuver he had chosen was simpleminded
to the point of idiocy, and he would never expect any competent sea captain to fall for it, or not to have a counterstrat-
agem prepared, but Gideon could only hope that the
Creeks had never studied naval tactics. Indian wails
whipped the air. Gideon glanced down and saw Maria-
Anna awkwardly balancing a loaded pistol in either hand.

"Give me a pistol—quickly!" he shouted. Maria-Anna's
eyes were dancing fires, her expression eager and breathless. The pistol felt weighty and cold in his hand.

"On my signal," he gasped, "I want ye to fire yer pistol
at 'em. I don't think we'll hit at this range, but I want 'em
to have something else to think about besides what we're
going to try to do." Maria-Anna nodded briefly, peering
above the gunwale to locate the enemy. Gideon followed
her gaze; they were still on the same course, uttering their
yipping cries. *Foolish,* Gideon thought, *they're going to
need their breath for paddling.*

Seconds to go. Gideon had a brief sensation of intense
color: blue sky, the white foam churned by the paddles, a
flash of silver from a Creek ornament . . . and then there
was a yellow flower blooming from the enemy bows and a
smack as a lead ball punched through the boat's mainsail,
then, as it sped away, the retrograde buzz of a tumbling

bullet. Gideon felt the breath catch in his throat. A ranging shot from the marksman in the bows. He restrained his impatience. Not yet. Not yet . . .

Now! "Sheets!" he shouted. Jouhaux frantically let the jib sheet run. Canvas crackled as it spilled wind, and Gideon threw the tiller hard over. The boat lurched as it swung into the wind and the current caught at it. The mainsail roared as the wind shook its leech.

"Shoot, Maria-Anna!" Gideon bellowed as he heard the enemy cries turn to whoops of perceived triumph—their shot must have hit the steersman, rendering their enemy helpless. Maria-Anna rested her pistol on the gunwale, steadied with both hands, squeezed the trigger. Gideon tasted gunsmoke on the wind. He frantically cocked the big pistol and thrust out his left hand—the right was on the tiller—and fired almost blindly. To his astonishment he saw a leaf-shaped piece of wood fly spinning through the air; either he had hit the paddle or the man who wielded it. He threw the pistol down.

MacDonald was furiously hauling in the jib sheet as the boat swung into the eye of the wind. Gideon ducked the swinging mainsail as it threatened to sweep off his hat; he could feel the boat beginning to pitch as the current caught the bows and began to swing them to larboard. For a moment all was motion: the mainsail swinging, spray kicking over the stem, MacDonald's hauling the sheet, enemy paddles flashing in the air.

The mainsail filled with the roar of an angry giant, and Gideon felt the rudder bite the sullen dark water. The current hissed beneath the boat as it heeled far over. "Ready now, aim low!" he shouted as Jouhaux leapt for the swivel gun. There were warning shouts from the Red Sticks and a melee of churning paddles; Gideon received an impression of widening white eyes in dark, brightly-painted faces as the enemy realized their danger. The canoe was at a distance of ten yards and bows-on; their T had been crossed.

MacDonald brought the match to the swivel gun's touch hole, and the boat lurched as the swivel spat smoke and scrap iron. The gunsmoke blinded Gideon to the damage the swivel had done; he kept the boat on course as Jouhaux and MacDonald leaped for their other weapons and added their own contributions to the smoke. Gideon looked over his shoulder as they went into a frenzy of reloading: the canoe was dead in the water with at least one figure lying lifeless in the bows, and the rest in milling confusion. Order was restored swiftly, the body fell or was hurled overboard, the paddles bit the water once more. MacDonald whooped as he lowered his reloaded long rifle, aimed carefully, fired. The bullet sang past Gideon's ear.

"The swivel!" he roared. "Reload the swivel!" Gideon wore the boat as the two men jumped for the swivel gun. On his new course the mainsail boom was almost touching water, the sail itself blocking Gideon's view of the enemy; he had to bring the craft into the wind again in order to see and waited for frustrating minutes as the swivel was reloaded and primed. The canoe had only three paddles going now, one on either side, and a third in the stern frantically alternating between starboard and larboard. They were running.

The loaders nodded. "Wear-oh!" Gideon shouted. The tiller tucked under one arm, Gideon tended the sheets as he gybed and brought the stern across the wind. The mainsail swung to starboard with a roar. With the wind and current behind it the little boat sped toward the canoe as the Red Sticks were trying frantically to make the shore. At thirty yards' range the swivel gun banged again as the boat crossed the canoe's stern, and then Gideon gybed once more and hauled his wind to the starboard tack, pursuing the canoe to shore.

The canoe grounded before the swivel was loaded again, and three Creeks leaped out, their blankets bright against the dark gloom of the forest, helping a fourth that seemed to be injured. MacDonald's long rifle cracked out again and the injured one spun and splashed facedown in the water. The Cherokee gave a whoop of triumph as the Red Sticks seized two muskets from the boat and fled.

The boat grounded just abaft the canoe, and with shouts of triumph Jouhaux and MacDonald drew their tomahawks and went leaping through the shallows in pursuit of the fleeing enemy. "*No!*" Gideon bellowed. "*Don't run off!*" They either didn't hear or ignored him, leaving him fuming in the stern sheets. He stumbled forward in the rocking boat and hurled the anchor overboard, letting the boat swing in the current as far as the shallows would allow.

"Blast those men!" Gideon said. He hadn't brought the sailboat inshore in order to chase the Red Sticks; he had gone in to smash their canoe so they couldn't easily warn their friends of a white party on the river. "They're outnumbered. And so are we." He seized an axe from the stores, leaped into the water, and splashed forward to the canoe.

"Is that man dead?" Maria-Anna asked. He glanced at the huddled figure, the bright cloth wrapping his head, turbanlike, the splayed leggings, the current of bright blood trailing away downstream, and didn't bother to reply.

He looked briefly over the canoe. It was a dugout, more awkward and heavier than the graceful Malecite birchbark canoes Gideon remembered from his time in Vermont, but also, unfortunately, much harder to sink. It was full of blankets, household tools, barrels of nails and flour; evidently the Red Sticks had been on a plundering tour of the abandoned white houses on the lower river. He threw the axe into the canoe and hauled it off the mud. It came easily. Splashing through the water, he drew the canoe to the stern of the sailboat and fixed it on a line; it would be easier to tow it away than to sink it. Then he splashed back to the Red Stick, searched the body, found a skinning knife, and took it back to the boat. He loaded the swivel gun again, blew the slow match into brightness, and waited.

"Damn those men," Maria-Anna said, her color high.

Jouhaux and MacDonald returned to the boat minutes later. Grinning, MacDonald splashed his way to the dead man, pulled the turban off, and expertly took his scalp, including the ears, while Jouhaux pushed the sailboat off the mud and jumped dripping into the bows.

"Couldn't find 'em," he said. "There was blood but it gave out. That's an island they're on, though—only a few miles long. We could search it."

MacDonald came back with his bloody trophy, looking longingly downstream where the first Indian casualty had been carried by the current. "I know this man," he said, brandishing the scalp. "*Ani-Gusa.* They called him Samson Scarface. His father was a Koasati, but his mother was a Muskogee. A bad man."

"Get in," Gideon growled. MacDonald legged into the boat and the anchor was raised. Maria-Anna sat furiously on a thwart, her mouth in a grim line. MacDonald and Jouhaux looked uneasily at one another and did not speak. In midstream Gideon threw the boat up into the wind and briskly ordered the anchor thrown overboard again. The towed canoe thudded into the stern. The flapping gaffsail and the jib were lowered.

"*Who gave you permission to leave the boat!*" Maria-Anna began, her voice cutting frozen through the humid air like a sword of ice.

"They was running, wasn't they?" Jouhaux demanded, blustering. "You didn't want 'em shootin' at us from the bushes!"

"There were three of them!" Gideon barked. "They could have turned on ye and killed ye while ye were running after 'em, or they could have doubled back, killed Señora Marquez and me, and taken both the boat and the canoe!"

"Scarface wasn't that smart," MacDonald said. "The others ain't that smart neither. Sampson wouldn't run with smart men."

"Ye didn't know it was Sampson when ye ran off," Gideon growled. "Didn't ye hear my shout?"

The two men looked at each other uneasily. "We—" MacDonald began.

"I can see by yer faces ye did!" Gideon proclaimed. "I see it!"

"I wanted to find one of the savages alive," said Jouhaux quietly. Gideon and Maria-Anna looked in shock at the man, at his merciless glowing eyes and his clenched jaw.

"I wanted to ask him about my family," Jouhaux said. He pointed to the big fighting knife at his waist. "*This* would have got it out of him. I would have had more than his scalp!"

The current gurgled beneath the boat's stem, filling the silence as Maria-Anna and Gideon absorbed the Frenchman's pitiless intent. Gideon felt sickened at this revelation

of the nature of frontier warfare. War at sea, even the privateering sort, was oddly genteel: one was expected to
treat one's opponents with honor and respect. The maneuvering itself was stately and slow, and combat, in which the
side with better foresight, tactics, and drill would prevail,
was almost always ended with a surrender, in which the
ship was given up to spare lives, and with the understanding that the prisoners would be well-treated. Frontier warfare, particularly here and now, was epochs apart: the Red
Sticks did not take prisoners because their religion valued
scalps over captives, and their white and Indian enemies
were almost as merciless. War had been reduced to its
most bitter and personal denominators—raids, ambushes,
massacres, and burnings, in which noncombatants were deliberately made the targets of assault and treated with ap-
palling pitilessness. Gideon knew little about Indian warfare, but he knew enough to understand that the
perpetrators of a massacre were rarely those that had to
pay for it: if an outrage occurred, the guilty would swiftly
vanish, and the avengers, white or Indian, would vent their
anger on the first available target; and the easiest targets of
either race were those who refrained from war and intended to live their lives in peace. These innocents would
then be massacred, and another outrage would demand another round of vengeance. And so the cycle would continue, bringing the survivors nothing but bitter memories,
burned homes, pillaged fields.

Gideon had no intention of bringing another cycle of
savagery to the woods and bayous of West Florida. Those
on the boat had defended themselves against attack; and
they had been lucky that only five Creeks had been involved and not a thousand.

"We should return to Mobile," Gideon said quietly.
"Three of them escaped. I don't blame ye," he said hastily
as MacDonald and Jouhaux looked up with fury. "It was
unavoidable. But they will alert the others that there is a
boat on the river and wait for us to come down. They may
have been scouting for a larger force. It was a mercy there
were only five. The next time we may not be quite so
lucky."

"*Merde!*" Jouhaux spat. "We have the boat, we have

their canoe. We can go where we want. Why should we run away?"

"Because we need to work together and because we are not doing so!" Gideon said. *"Confidence in an unfaithful man in time of trouble is like a broken tooth;* you ran off and left us all in danger—"

"Pah!" Jouhaux said with contempt.

"—and how are we to know ye will not do so again?" Gideon demanded. "If we were on land, I would put myself under a captain who knows how to fight on land. We are on a boat, and I have been in ships and boats all my life. I know their ways."

"You're a savvy enough sailor, Markham, but you don't know Indians," Jouhaux said.

"I'm a savvy enough sailor to know when we're in trouble on a river," Gideon answered. "If we lose one man, we can still run the boat well enough and have a chance at fighting. If we lose two, we can't maneuver and fight at the same time, and if we have to do both, we're all as good as dead. The margin is too small. We must turn back."

"I'm goin' up the river anyway," Jouhaux declared, his eyes still burning with grim frontier anger. "Even if I have to walk. And to hell with the rest of you." He folded his arms firmly, his face expressing grim resolution.

Suddenly Maria-Anna stood, the big dueling pistols balanced awkwardly in her hands. "You're forgetting, all of you, whose idea this trip is," she said. "You're forgetting who's in charge." She turned to Gideon. "You may have a hundred privateering ships at your beck and call, but you're forgetting this is my boat, not your own, and that you're a volunteer, not its captain!"

Gideon felt himself reddening. "Ye were all pleased to take my orders when the Creeks were in sight," he said.

"I'm sure we're all grateful," she said, her voice softening. "And I have more to thank you for than anyone. But that does not alter facts."

She turned to Jouhaux. "You're forgetting a few facts as well, mister. We're going up this river for *my* reasons, and if you intend to go for your own purposes, then as far as I'm concerned you're a passenger, not a guide, and I'll thank you to pay your passage right now!"

Jouhaux gaped at her, plainly baffled. MacDonald quietly hid his grin behind a bloody hand.

"You know I ain't got any money," Jouhaux said.

"And that's why you're on this boat, because you want to raise money by selling your land," Maria-Anna said, her tone merciless. "And no one will buy your land at the price I'll give unless they see it, so you must show it. And *that's* why you're here, not to hunt Red Sticks on an island."

Jouhaux's sullen glare was truculent, but no longer rebellious. Maria-Anna turned her back on him and faced Gideon. The brim of her hat cast shadows over her face, softening her features. "If you want to return, Captain Markham, you may take the canoe," she said. "I already owe you more than I can possibly repay, and I don't—I can't ask you to stay on the river if you think it would be unwise."

"For *social position*," said Gideon. He felt empty, all anger and resentment drained, his body a hollow vessel filled only with a despairing wind, at the mercy of its prevailing gusts. He spoke only as if to clarify things to himself, as if no longer interested in resistance. "Social position, so that you can be a lady," he said. "That is why we are going up the river."

"That is why *I* am going up the river," Maria-Anna said. Her face was not unkind, her voice low and tranquil. "So that I will have to take no more risks. So that I need marry no more old men no matter how loving. So that I will not end my days as a starveling in some dirt-floored shanty."

The wind gusted through the stays with a little scream as Gideon remembered the packing case, the single candle, the little bed with its breathless, desperate stick-figure; and Maria-Anna spoke on, saying that she could not ask him to remain, that he could take the canoe to Mobile without loss of honor or regard, that he had shown them how to maneuver the little boat, and that they would be all right.

"We'll do well enough," she said.

"Halliards," Gideon said. He could feel the wind carrying him on. *Let it,* he thought. "Halliards and jib sheets!"

The anchor was brought up, the gaffsail and jib set.

They tacked away from the island, their sails a fleck of confetti against the dark banks of the river. Maria-Anna, sober, a little apologetic, sat quietly on a thwart and put her pistols in their case. Later, wrapping herself as modestly as possible in a blanket, she used a chamber pot and threw the contents into the river.

14

JOUHAUX'S HOMECOMING

They spent the night on another island, surrounded by the moat of the river. Gideon had wanted to spend the night in the boat, anchored in midstream where any enemy could be seen approaching, but the others were tired of the cramped little craft and decided that an island would be safe enough. The boat was hidden in a reedy marsh, and while the others found a nearby hollow in which to camp, Gideon took his needle and palm out of his carpetbag and repaired the ancient mainsail. Gideon, fingering the sail-cloth assaulted by mildew, chafe, constant use, and the Red Stick bullet, knew that it would probably blow out at the first stiff gale and that he would have to be careful.

Supper was an extended version of the noon meal: dried meat, biscuits, and whiskey. The whiskey did not stop this time; Sean MacDonald grew merry, and Jouhaux clutched the tomahawk at his waist and brooded beneath the pines. MacDonald tapped the earth with the heel of his right hand, holding the jug of whiskey in his left, and chanted songs to himself; for a while he danced, shuffling in the dark, until he made too much noise and the others quieted him. Afterward, with Jouhaux on guard standing at the rim of the hollow, MacDonald grew talkative. He spoke of his grandfather, a Scotsman who fled the '45 rebellion and established himself as a trader in Georgia among the Cherokee. MacDonald's mother was half-Scots; his father an Okmulgee, a horse-breeder and a member of one of the tribes that the whites persisted in calling the Lower Creeks. MacDonald preferred to live with his mother's people. His brother married a Chickasaw, a woman later killed by Little Warrior's Creeks, in return for which MacDonald had taken his long rifle and joined the band of Chief McIntosh, a Creek friendly to American interests, who hunted down Little Warrior and killed him from ambush. Little Warrior's comrade, Tuskegee Warrior, was burnt alive in his house at Hickory Ground by MacDonald and his friends. His war over, MacDonald had said farewell to his brothers and migrated to Mobile, where he worked breaking horses until the outbreak of the Creek War, at which time he offered his services to the army as a scout. But they had only been interested in hiring him to break horses. Army horses were the worst, MacDonald maintained. Maria-Anna offered better work at better pay. He'd heard a Cherokee woman had been killed by the Red Sticks near Etowah, and that would bring the rest of the Cherokee nation into the war. He had never believed Tecumseh's prophets when they said that the red men could unite and drive the white men away. "Bad, stupid men," he said. "They'd get us all killed." MacDonald, said MacDonald, was a Christian; he'd been to a mission school and learned how to write Cherokee and English.

Gideon quietly said his prayers while MacDonald spoke and then rolled himself in blankets to keep the mosquitoes off. He lay on his back and felt the whiskey warming his insides. MacDonald's chatter was welcome: there were no silences that he, Gideon, felt obliged to fill. He listened absentmindedly, feuds between families and Indian leaders with their strange Scots names running together in his mind, mixing with the mosquitoes' whine and the hushed murmur of the wind in the trees. He sweated beneath the hot blankets. The air was tainted with the scent of honeysuckle, and it reminded him again of Savannah and the little room there and the woman who had been permitted to die without charity or thought. The single candle burned in his dreams, lowering and guttering, waning but never extinguishing, until MacDonald's hand on his shoulder told him that it was his watch. Still wrapped in the blanket, he stood with his Brown Bess until dawn.

MacDonald and Jouhaux were gruff but quiet in the morning. They'd had too much whiskey the night before. The river was peaceful and empty. Here and there a small farm or plantation stood amidst a silent clearing, the crops ripening and food only for birds.

At the juncture of the Alabama and Tombigbee some miles north of where the little sailboat tacked amid the dark channels, the rivers broke into bits, fragmenting into dozens of streams separated by shifting banks and islands, fed by nameless bayous, often flooding to create new channels, all emptying out into Mobile Bay just east of the town. The good land was to the east of the river on the higher ground, and there were found the principal white plantations and the ashy remnants of Fort Mims and its five hundred inhabitants. The easternmost branch of the multiple river was known as the Tensaw, and to the Tensaw Gideon now steered the boat.

Late in the afternoon they came to a small plantation owned by one of the syndicate, a man named Barger. Gideon stood uneasily, holding his musket, as he guarded the boat at the landing. MacDonald stood quiet guard in the fields, still as a scarecrow, while Jouhaux showed Maria-Anna the eighty acres of cleared land, the rude house of unfinished logs in which Barger and his family had lived, the big barn, the damp clay-walled dugouts in which the slaves had spent their nights. Even with the limited view from the landing Gideon could tell that the crops standing in the fields were abundant and rich. Maria-Anna returned to the boat with a satisfied smile on her face.

That night, camped on another island a short distance upstream, they supped on roasting ears plucked from the stalks. Tomorrow Maria-Anna would finish her business, Gideon calculated. That would be the second day after their meeting with the Red Sticks downstream. The next day the boat would commence its return journey, business completed and the current with them. Perhaps they could make Mobile in sixteen or eighteen hours of flat-out sailing, a safer course than staying on the river another night. That would be three days after they'd stranded the Red Sticks on the island; three days for the Red Sticks to search their island and find a hidden canoe or construct a raft or simply swim across the big river while hanging onto a log, escaping to one bank or another and alerting a war party that a boat of enemies had gone upriver. If there was a war party within twenty miles. If it had river transportation. If, if . . . Gideon felt stifled in the blanket. MacDonald again made merry with the whiskey, but Jouhaux refrained. The fire gleamed oddly in the Frenchman's eyes; he started at sounds, his hands clenched white-knuckled around the barrel of his musket. The next day he would see his home.

The next day they visited three more clearings, three more harvests lying in the sun, three more sets of lonely, desolate buildings, before they beached the boat at Jouhaux's landing. The plantation came right down to the bank of the Tensaw, and Gideon felt nervous about the landing: it was open, there was no place to hide the little craft. The plantation itself was out of sight of the river, half a mile inland past a stand of cedar trees.

Gideon handed the gaffsail, the jib was lowered, the anchor kicked overboard. Cicadas shrilled in the cedar grove, an aural presence so overwhelming that the disembarkation seemed by contrast to be made in silence. MacDonald, crouched low, slipped into the cover of the trees, a brown ghost, and then waved them ashore. Gideon slung his musket and assisted Maria-Anna, hampered by her skirts, from the boat; ashore she emptied water from her boots while the others stood guard. The cicadas were so deafening that they had almost to shout.

Maria-Anna was pleased by what she'd seen: the soil had been periodically enriched by the flooding of the river, neatly covering the land with deposits of the dark earth of the Black Belt upstream. The three plantations and one large farm she'd thus far seen were within ten miles of one another by boat. If put in production, the land would make its owners rich. There was Jouhaux's place to see and one other before her expedition could be pronounced a success and the boat turned homeward.

They walked through the cedars and into sunlight, moving cautiously—two of the houses they'd seen that morning had been looted, and the larger set casually afire, though the fire hadn't taken. Jouhaux's log plantation house with its split-cedar shingles stood coldly on an eminence, surveying acres of gently waving cash crops stretching from the cedar grove to the house and well beyond. A gently curved dirt road led to the plantation house; a big roofed barn, stables, and slave huts stood beyond, where they wouldn't spoil the view.

"She's on a hill, you see?" Jouhaux said. "She don't get flooded."

The plantation was obviously rich. Gideon and Maria-Anna looked with surprise at its owner, wearing his rude hat and dressed in battered clothes. A man with such a start, Gideon wondered, could not survive a few seasons of war? Jouhaux seemed to sense their questions. His answer was direct and without pretense.

"It's the cost of the niggers, you see," he said. "All the profits got to be used to buy more niggers to work more land. If you get a bad season, you sell some of the niggers or you live on credit. Now I ain't got no credit, and the niggers are dead or taken by the savages. I got to sell."

Maria-Anna nodded. "You'll get a fair price, Mr. Jouhaux," she said. Gideon looked up again at the plantation house; Jouhaux had just explained the great weakness of the slave economy, the reason why the ungodly institution was slowly dying out and would probably be extinct in another generation. The plantation owners' capital was all frozen in slaves, slaves who had to be fed, cared for, and who, worn out by the life of savagery and toil, would sooner or later die. There was no money left over for improvements, for turning the South's rivers into proper waterways, for building canals, for straightening the system of roads and tracks into proper modes of transportation. The South had forfeited to New England the initiative and success of commerce, because successful commerce requires large pools of capital, and the South had none. And so the jealous South, controlling Congress and the office of the president, had striven eagerly for its policies, for the Embargoes, and for the war, all of which were guaranteed to wreck New England's economy and allow the South to retain its backward ways, unthreatened.

With his long rifle cocked, MacDonald led the group up the road, past sixty acres of sugarcane—"An improved variety from Santo Domingo," Jouhaux explained proudly—past flowering hemp stalks eight feet tall, the air filled with the scent of their resin, past scrubby cotton stalks that

showed signs of being neglected even before the war had
forced the plantation's abandonment. "That's new West Indian cotton," Jouhaux said disgustedly. "They said it would
grow fine up here, but it rotted. No one'll ever grow cotton
in the South."

The sound of the cicadas retreated. They ascended the
low hill past the food crops for the family and the slaves'
corn and beans. From time to time Maria-Anna wandered off the path to feel, sniff, and taste the soil. Gideon was
surprised at her thoroughness: the plantation was so obviously rich there seemed no need for such exactitude. Gideon saw Jouhaux glancing up the hill, his hands clenching
and unclenching nervously as he saw his house, his face a
mask of longing.

Gideon turned to look back toward the boat. Perhaps he
should have stayed on guard at the river. They hadn't been
this far away from the boat before. Maria-Anna returned
from the rustling cornstalks.

"I'll get some roasting ears," MacDonald volunteered.
The Cherokee loped off into the rows of corn.

"It looks like the door's been busted in," Jouhaux said,
glancing anxiously at the house from beneath the brim of
his hat. The strain in his voice was apparent. Maria-Anna
looked up, surprised.

"I apologize, Mr. Jouhaux," she said. "I've been too
busy with the state of the land. Please go to your house.
I've been very selfish."

"Thankee, Miz Marquez." Taking a deep breath, his
face filled with a longing hope that both he and Gideon
knew was impossible, he began his walk toward the big
two-story log house. Gideon and Maria-Anna followed at
a slower pace. Gideon felt anxiety for the man; he could
not be entirely certain that despite Jouhaux's assurances
that his family had been evacuated to Fort Mims, he would
not find his wife and child tomahawked in their beds. What
then, Gideon wondered? There would be nothing to do but
to put them in the earth and say the proper prayers. But
what could replace in Jouhaux's heart that last bit of irra-
tional hope that he had so foolishly and so understandably
allowed to linger?

Jouhaux disappeared into his house fifty yards off.

A cicada flew buzzing from the corn and landed on Gideon's hand. The insect's feet gripped the flesh with a strength that surprised him; he raised the hand and blew to dislodge it. The flying insect, three inches long and as green as a sheaf of corn, refused to move. Gideon raised the barrel of the musket and brushed it off. The cicada shrieked, a scream so loud and sudden that Gideon almost dropped his musket; and as Gideon's heart pounded with sudden shock, the insect sped noisily away.

"I would like to thank you again privately, Gideon," Maria-Anna said, taking his arm. Trying to control his thundering, startled heart, Gideon allowed himself to be led from the path. "No, let's not follow so closely," she said. "We'll give the man a moment to be alone in his grief."

She led him diagonally across an unplowed field, the rows with which the field had once been sown eroding beneath their boots. It had been allowed to lie fallow, and Gideon wondered about it: grazing for nonexistent cattle, the beginnings of a front lawn for a planter with manorial pretensions? The corn rustled behind them. They walked across the field to a place near the stable.

Gideon felt her presence on his arm, an undeniably female warmth and weight that began, against his solitary will, to stir him, suffusing through him until he felt flushed and headstrong, an awkward youth.

"For whatever reason, you came," she said. "I thank you for it." *Thank the Almighty,* he felt he should say, but the words did not come. "Before this journey," she said, "I owed you more than I could possibly repay, and now I owe you much more. I owe you whatever success this venture may gain, and perhaps once again I owe you my life. Without you I would not feel as safe or as certain."

She raised her eyes to his, and in a rapt instant of recognition Gideon realized that he could take her in his arms and kiss her, and that she would allow it; and in that sudden flushed moment, with the hot September sun warming his shoulders and the corn rustling gently in the wind behind him, for the first time in years he wanted desperately to feel a woman in his arms. Crows cawed in the heavens and gyred wildly as they mounted above the hill, flying from MacDonald's presence among the corn. Cicadas shrilled in the distance. Somewhere a horse whickered, and Gideon's body grew cold. He remembered the scream of the insect, the sure grip of the cicada's feet on the back of his hand, that last longing look on Jouhaux's face as he began the hopeful, hopeless walk to his house.

"Don't . . . look . . . now," he said, spacing his words carefully, his heart beginning to thunder its terror, his mind flogging itself wildly in an effort to assemble the wayward pieces of a coherent plan. He would have to get between the house and the road, between the enemy and the escape route.

"We are going to turn and walk back," he said. "You will take my other arm. When I give the word, run for your life."

He saw shock and fear crossing her features, her high color draining away, leaving her dark eyes standing prominently and fearfully in her stricken face.

"What—where are they?" she whispered.

"In the house, I think. If they are, Jouhaux must be gone. We've got to walk toward the house, get between it and the road. Otherwise they'll cut us off from the boat."

Her face muscles tautened as she mastered her fear. She turned and determinedly put her arm through his. They walked, the old furrows crumbling under their boots. Maria-Anna forced a grin onto her face, its feigned tautness giving her the ghastly rictus of a corpse. *Almighty God help us,* Gideon thought. He felt his knees trembling as they fought the desperate, fatal compulsion to run like a madman for safety, not to walk toward the house, toward the windows where any number of Red Stick muskets might be tracking their path. *Give us strength . . .* If he hadn't heard the horse in its stable, they might have walked into the house, love-struck and careless, to be toma-hawked dead in the foyer.

"Do you see MacDonald?" Gideon whispered, covertly searching the stalks of corn into which the Cherokee had last vanished.

"No."

Twenty yards to go. *Help us . . .* Their goal would place them fifty yards from the house, right at the head of

the track leading to the boat. Dead if the Red Sticks were
any marksmen and impatient. Perhaps they wouldn't wait,
perhaps they would fire now and try to kill them as they
walked; or perhaps they would realize they could rush out
and cut off Gideon and Maria-Anna from the road and
that every second wasted allowed their prey to regain their
path of escape. Gideon sickened as he pictured an Indian
marksman in the cedar-shingled building, perhaps in an upper room, with his musket propped against the window sill,
the barrel sighted on Gideon's waistcoat or Maria-Anna's
linen cravat. Gideon remembered MacDonald expertly
wielding his knife, taking Sampson's scalp from his forehead
to his nape, and how the torn ears had dripped blood as they
were held aloft in MacDonald's triumphant hand.

Ten yards to go. *God help us* . . . Gideon forced himself to breath slowly, hoping to reduce the mad, wrenching
thump of his heart against his ribs. For some reason he
noticed the big plantation bell, its clapper swaying gently
in the wind, hung above the gaping front door. Maria-
Anna's arm trembled against him, or perhaps it was his
own arm that trembled. He clasped her hand, and the
trembling ceased.

"Ready . . ." he breathed, turning slightly toward the
house, giving the marksmen a broader target but perhaps
convincing them for an extra second that their targets were
not going to run for the road.

Help us!

"*Run!*" he shouted, and released her hand as he dropped
into a crouch, changing silhouettes. He ran forward for another five yards, hoping to draw their fire toward himself
rather than onto Maria-Anna, then abruptly changed direction and ran for the road as fast as his legs could carry
him.

There was the twitter of a mad bird and a report: the
musket ball had missed. A broad-headed war arrow
whirred between them, striking the road, its gleaming
barbs kicking dust. He almost stumbled over Maria-Anna's
top hat as it spilled from her head. There was another shot,
but the bullet didn't come close; he heard shrill cries behind them. Gideon chanced a look over his shoulder, saw a

yipping enemy, red shirt and deerskin leggings, pummeling down the road after him, tomahawk in hand . . . There was a sudden shot, and the Red Stick warrior collapsed like a rag doll, skidding in the dust of the lane. A triumphant cry came from the corn on Gideon's right: MacDonald giving covering fire with his long rifle. Maria-Anna, hampered by her heavy skirts and coat, was slowing, gasping for air. Gideon caught up with her and took her arm again, helping her race. Again Gideon heard pelting footsteps behind and he glanced back: it was Sean MacDonald, running in their footsteps, his face contorted as he tried to shout a message. "Going for horses!" the Cherokee gasped. "Horses!"

Gideon felt pain shoot through his chest; he had been a sailor on a small schooner and had no wind for running. If the Creeks were going for their horses, they'd easily be able to ride down their quarry in the lane. Maria-Anna's eyes were half-closed in concentration, her pallor a witness to her breathlessness. They ran past waving hempstalks, eight feet tall.

"Here!" Gideon breathed. "In here!" They ran in among the rows of hemp, stumbling through the fibrous, flowering stalks until they were out of sight of the road. MacDonald panted up behind them, gasping as he drew out his ramrod to reload his rifle. Gideon checked the priming of his musket and pistols. In the distance they could already hear the hooves of pursuing horses. Maria-Anna stripped off her heavy coat and cravat.

"I'll draw 'em off," MacDonald said. "You go through the fields to the boat. I'll circle around and join you. Light the slow match."

Gideon, breathless, nodded. MacDonald reinserted the ramrod in his gunstock, primed the lock, covered the priming carefully. With a terse nod he disappeared among the waving stalks.

"Can you give me a pistol?" Maria-Anna asked. "I left mine in the boat. They were too heavy." Gideon hesitated; a pistol was one third of his firepower and he hadn't seen Maria-Anna shoot.

"I know how to use it!" she whispered fiercely. "My

husband taught me!" He nodded and pressed a pistol into her outstretched hand. Her face was flushed, but she was breathing easier. Her eyes shone.

The hastening hoofbeats grew closer, slowed in confusion. Gideon decided it was time to attempt the boat.

"Follow me," he whispered. "Try not to disturb the hempstalks. They might wave and betray us."

Crouching they crept through the nodding stalks, pistols in their hands. Gideon's tortured lungs ached with every hammer of his heart.

There was a shot and a series of shouts and yipping cries: MacDonald's long rifle had gone to work. Hooves pounded, Creeks shouted in their own language. It sounded to Gideon as if there were a score of them. Gideon felt the sticky resin of the plants smearing the backs of his hands, his cheek. Behind him there was another shot, and a horse cried in pain.

They came to the end of the hemp plantation: between the hemp and the sugarcane was a short lane wide enough for two mules to pull a plow. Gideon gestured for Maria-Anna to wait, glanced swiftly to the left and right. Clear. He gestured again and they ran into the cover of the cane, fighting their way among the close-packed stalks. Gideon's sword-hilt caught on a shaft and he wrenched it free.

The ground rumbled nearby. Maria-Anna hissed for him to stop; alarmed, they knelt among the cane as horses' hooves shook the earth. The enemy were riding down the lane, brown forms on swift, beautiful horses, nodding feathers and bright turbans. The heavy form of a horse began crashing through the cane. Gideon's heart thundered as he realized it was very close. Maria-Anna cocked her pistol. Gideon put his hand over it.

"No. Too noisy."

There were other horses shouldering their way through the sugar stalks nearby. Gideon could hear the panting breath of a horse almost in his ear, the crackling protest of the cane as it bent or broke beneath the animal's weight. No hope they would not be seen. Gideon lowered his pistol and musket to the ground, drew sword, and leaped.

The Red Stick's reaction was fast; he dropped the bow in his left hand and swung with the tomahawk in his right.

Gideon's desperate stroke almost cut the man's arm in two, and the hatchet fell to the earth. The horse screamed and reared in panic at the man rising almost from beneath its feet; unbalanced and in shock, the Red Stick fell. Gideon pursued around the horse, still rearing and dangerous, anticipating with sickening clarity the impact of a flailing hoof. His next slash cut two fingers from the left hand raised to ward the stroke. The Creek scrambled backward, whimpering, his arms down and bleeding. It was horrible to kill a man so helpless. Gideon's third cut reached the man's throat, and the earth beneath his body grew dark. The horse, smelling blood, began to back away, its eyes dangerous; Maria-Anna lunged out from cover and seized the reins, quieting it. Gideon looked down at the dead man at his feet.

The dead Creek was dressed in red, a scarlet coat with buff facings and heavy bullion epaulettes, the coat of a British general officer given in friendship to an ally. The Red Stick even wore the officer's gorget at his throat, polished and shining brightly, unspotted with blood: the regiment's number was picked out on the gorget in Roman numerals. The Red Stick's face was streaked with paint and blood. A bright cloth, matching the color of the coat, wound around the man's head like a turban; downy feathers curled down over the ears, and a tall feather, dyed bright blue, was arranged to look as if it sprouted straight up from the man's scalp. There was a kind of skirt, leather leggings, moccasins, a knife. No firearms. Despite British friendship and the coat of a general there were no firearms, just a bow, tomahawk, knife.

The Red Stick had not cried out when he was butchered, perhaps because he was stunned, perhaps because his code forbade it. It was strange how little Gideon knew about these men, his enemies. Gideon knew he had little skill with the sword, unlike his uncles Malachi and Jehu, or his cousin Favian, who had faced men in duels. This had been a fight like the other on *General Sullivan*'s foredeck, a series of desperate, heedless cuts that had turned him and his enemy into something less than human, something to be cut at and slashed and trampled until one of Gideon's clumsy strokes finally had ended the fight. Bile in his

mouth, Gideon turned to where Maria-Anna stood cradling the horse's head, whispering softly to it, stroking it,
calming it. Gideon measured his stroke precisely and without a word put all his strength into a slash that cut the
artery throbbing in the horse's neck. With a sigh the horse
staggered, then fell heavily into the cane. Maria-Anna
stared in horror, first at the horse whose head she had been
cradling when Gideon struck, then at Gideon.

"Why did you do that?"

At least she'd had presence of mind enough to whisper.

"A riderless horse would have given us away." Gideon
wiped the sword clean on the blanket the Red Stick had
used as a saddle, then sheathed it.

"We could have ridden it out of here!" The whisper was
furious, intense.

"I can't ride very well. Not bareback anyway."

"But I can! I can!" Her eyes gleamed dangerously. She
wiped hemp resin from her cheek with the back of her
hand. "You didn't think to ask, did you? We could have
got away on that horse!"

"Two on one horse, bareback? They would have caught
us easily."

"Who said they would have seen us? Who said it?"

"How could they not have seen us?" Gideon demanded.

Her anger over the horse's death while the body of its
owner lay mutilated two paces away swam incomprehensi-
bly through Gideon's head. He picked up his musket and
pistol. "Let's go," he said. The other horses sounded farther off, toward the river. He felt his breath catch as he
remembered the boat, unguarded and helpless in shallow
water. A few planks stove in and they'd all be stranded.

Maria-Anna made no reply, but he sensed her intense
anger behind him as they made their way through the
cane. The enemy horses, riding randomly through the field,
came close again, and they crouched low. The hooves
passed, and they ran for the hope of the river.

The cane field ended suddenly, and breathless they
found themselves in the open. Gideon glanced wildly in all
directions: there was no one to be seen. The musket felt like
an awkward, alien lump in his hands. Maria-Anna was already running for the cedars. He followed.

It was darker, cooler, in the cedar grove. The scent of the trees was welcome and soothing; the needles and the sound of the cicadas muffled their pounding feet. Clear daylight shone on the water ahead. And then Maria-Anna, still in the lead, gestured violently and threw herself behind a tree. Gideon crouched low and slid up beside her. She gestured mutely ahead.

A horse stood fetlock-deep in the water, its neck arching gently to drink, its rider sitting in a leather saddle, arrow nocked on bow, gazing in triumph at the little boat that rode at anchor just yards away. The Red Stick turned to glance nervously at the cedar grove, and while he hugged the earth, Gideon saw the indecision on his face. He was watering the horse while making up his mind whether or not to loot the boat.

Gideon checked the priming on the old Brown Bess. Maria-Anna looked at him guardedly. Gideon knew that his own choices were limited; he could not afford to let the boat be looted, nor could he allow the Red Stick to return to his companions. "I don't think I can hit the man at this range, not for certain," he whispered. "I'm going to aim for the horse. If the horse throws the man, I'll rush him. You head for the boat."

She nodded, her recent anger gone in the face of their danger. Gideon braced the musket against the tree, cocked the lock, and sighted along the iron barrel. There were no sights, not so much as a bead. Even at thirty yards he could miss. He tried to calm his breathing, his thumping heart. The horse moved slightly, and he corrected. He knew he was not a marksman.

The snap of the lock and the firing of the primer caused the horse to jump, but the main powder charge went off without significant delay, and through the haze of gushing gunsmoke Gideon saw the horse crumple and fall into the shallows. Gideon lurched to his feet and ran, carrying the musket in his left hand, clawing his sword-hilt with his right. He had just announced his presence to every listener within miles.

The Creek rose to his feet, drawing his arrow back to his ear, the arrow foreshortening on the string. Gideon's sword sang clear of the scabbard. Behind he could hear Maria-

Anna's feet and the swish of her skirts. He ducked to one
side to shake the man's aim, picturing already the broad-
headed, barbed war arrow lying in his flesh, impossible to
remove. Another shot echoed from the cedars, and the arrow shot harmlessly high. The Creek whirled and fell, as
dead as his horse.

Gideon turned to see Maria-Anna kneeling with smoking pistol, both hands steadying her aim. "I told you I
could shoot," she said and rose.

And then there were cries behind them and the frenetic
drumming of horses; Gideon and Maria-Anna were both
running through the water, splashes rising white above
their feet. Gideon flung the musket and sword into the
boat and hauled himself in, then turned to help Maria-
Anna only to find her already rolling over the gunwale.
"Take the tiller!" Gideon gasped.

He threw off the gaskets. The topping lift warmed his
hands as he raised the gaff, the sail blossoming out with a
rumble, the boat swinging. A shot ringing from the shore
chipped paint from the boat's side, and then he heard the
heedless splashing of a pair of horses riding through the
shallows.

Gideon drew his pistol from his pocket, knowing there
was no time to get the anchor up. He lunged for the
swivel gun in the bows. Two Red Sticks, tomahawks flashing, were riding at him. The slow match hadn't been lit,
the swivel gun couldn't be used in any conventional way.
With a voiceless prayer Gideon put the barrel of his pistol
to the touch hole of the little brass gun and squeezed the
trigger. There was a bang and a fizzing snarl, and then a
crash as the swivel discharged, sweeping the Red Sticks,
their screaming horses, and their edged, dangerous hatchets into the swift and bloody waters. One horse rose, red
running from half a dozen wounds, and a rider staggered
to his feet, hurt badly, and stumbled to the shore. By then
Gideon had the anchor up, and the boat was under way.

"We'll wait for MacDonald," Maria-Anna said, the tiller
under her arm. It was not a request. Gideon nodded his
assent.

More Red Sticks appeared on the bank as the boat put
off into midstream; their volley of arrows fell short, and

two musket shots missed completely. Maria-Anna threw the boat up into the wind in midstream, and as the mainsail rattled and thundered, Gideon reloaded their weapons, blew fire into the tinderbox, lit the slow match. Maria-Anna primed the pistols in her case, emptied muddy water from her boots, and wrung out her skirts. Marksmen tried futilely to reach them from shore.

When the current carried them past the landing, they tacked gently upstream. If MacDonald chose to be rescued, they were willing to attempt it. The sun dropped slowly in the west. Gideon wondered if there were other Red Sticks nearby with canoes to whom a messenger could be sent. He wished he had a spyglass. Across the swift river the cicadas still called.

The shadows of the trees lengthened across the water. Gideon sat on a thwart amidships, letting Maria-Anna have the handling of the boat, his mind working dully as his heartbeat slowed in the late afternoon heat. Jouhaux, and possibly MacDonald, and any number of Red Sticks, were now dead as a result of Maria-Anna's territorial ambitions. He wondered if that fact had yet reached her, whether she was capable of remorse or guilt. She herself had killed, shot a Red Stick dead in the breast at twenty yards with a pistol inaccurate at ten. Maria-Anna Marquez-Suarez was a formidable and courageous woman; but Gideon wondered if she possessed a conscience or a moral nature. He watched her as she sat in the stern sheets, her hat gone, her cheek and brow smeared with hemp resin, her eyes active and alive as they searched the riverbank. Her face grew weary as her exertions caught up with her: short of fatigue her face was expressionless, and her eyes avoided his. If she felt regret, she could not open herself to let Gideon know.

Gideon's heart leaped as he heard a shot downstream. The puff of smoke was easily visible; MacDonald stood on the bank, half a mile away, waving.

The Red Sticks saw him as well: a futile shot was fired, and the whooping riders began to urge their horses downstream. Maria-Anna had the tiller over in seconds, and Gideon sprang to the jib halliard to raise the triangular headsail and increase the little boat's speed.

MacDonald had chosen well, Gideon thought. Downstream, so the boat would have the benefit of the current. The horses crashed through the brush, the Indians howling as the boat began to outdistance them. MacDonald quietly reloaded on the bank after he knew he'd been seen, and awaited his rescue.

The race was not even close: the Red Sticks were left well behind. As the boat approached, MacDonald waded out into the water, then began to swim sidestroke, his rifle and powder held high out of the water.

"Steer between him and the bank," Gideon called, spilling the wind from the jib, and Maria-Anna nodded. The actual maneuver was done neatly; MacDonald tossed his rifle, cartridges, and powder horn to Gideon, then hooked an arm over the gunwale as the boat sailed past and hauled himself in. By the time the Red Sticks reached the bank, the boat was a quarter mile downstream and increasing speed.

MacDonald grinned as he lay sopping on the thwarts, a fresh scalp dripping riverwater and gore at his waist. "Thankee," he said. "Much obliged."

The sun was now close to the horizon. A cottonmouth moccasin crossed the water in front of them and they gave it a wide berth. The odds that the agile, deadly snake could climb aboard the fast-moving boat were slim, but there was no sense taking chances. Gideon turned to Maria-Anna. "I think we should keep on the river tonight," he said. "Going downstream will be much faster. We can lower the jib, keep to the middle, and let the current do most of the work."

"Very well."

"I'm hungry," MacDonald said.

They had their evening meal, dried meat and biscuit. The setting sun turned the gaffsail red. MacDonald tippled carefully from the whiskey jug—there was little left—and spoke of his encounters. He'd killed an *Ani-Gusa* after he'd parted from Maria-Anna and Gideon, and drawn the enemy in pursuit. A second shot had killed a horse and wounded its rider in the leg. He'd had a hard run until Gideon's shot had drawn them all toward the river. Then MacDonald had quietly returned to the lane to scalp the man he'd killed and carefully returned to the plantation house to look for Jouhaux.

"They killed him in the hallway," MacDonald said, a serious frown creasing his smooth face. "I guess they surprised each other. They killed him, then dragged him into the parlor and scalped him. They got his scalp, musket, pistols, knife—whatever he had with him."

After leaving the plantation house MacDonald returned to the river to discover his employer in her boat waiting for him in midstream. Careful to avoid the Red Sticks patrolling the bank he'd slipped down stream and given them a signal.

"I could of walked home, but I preferred to ride," he said and finished the remaining whiskey. There was another untouched jug, but MacDonald wisely chose not to attempt it just yet.

"That took no little courage," Maria-Anna said. "You're a brave man, Mr. MacDonald." MacDonald hid a grin of pleasure behind his hand.

"Aye," Gideon agreed. "We may thank the Almighty for his courage and our safe deliverance from the enemy."

"Amen," said MacDonald, and took the fresh scalp from his belt in order to admire it.

Gideon took the tiller at nightfall and sheeted the mainsail well in to minimize the danger from any involuntary gybes, an acute possibility on the river at night. They slid down the river into the awakening darkness, the river murmuring beneath the planks, the canoe bobbing astern on the end of its tether. After moonrise Gideon gave up the tiller to MacDonald and went to the bow to sleep. Leaning against the gunwale, he clasped his hands, and as the canvas rattled above him, he prayed for both Jouhaux and the Red Sticks killed that day on the banks of the Tensaw. His last memory before sleep enfolded him in obliterating arms was the great harvest moon above the trees, gleaming on MacDonald's smooth, strong face as the scout quietly chanted a song to keep himself company on the empty river.

15

THE WESTERN BRANCH

Dawn slipped by Gideon unawares; the sun was high in the sky when he opened his eyes. He sat up still seeming to hear MacDonald's soft song, but the Cherokee was asleep, sprawled across a thwart with one hand still clutching his rifle. Maria-Anna was at the tiller.

"Good morning," she mouthed silently, with a smile seeming more wistful than joyful. Gideon smiled as he returned her greeting, but his smile turned awkward, then deliberately grave. He wondered how many years it had been since he'd greeted a woman on opening his eyes. *Too many to ever again feel comfortable at it*, he thought.

They were reaching down the river, the dark water hissing beneath the boat's keel. He glanced over his shoulder at the bank, trying to find a landmark, recognizing a big longleaf pine with its landward branches dead and the rest green and a giant squirrels' nest sixty feet above the clay of the bank. They had made good progress, perhaps twenty river miles since they'd left Jouhaux's landing.

He stood and stepped to the leeward gunwale, facing carefully away from Maria-Anna, and relieved himself over the side. After buttoning he readied the jib and hoisted it, then sat tending the jib sheets until MacDonald awoke.

Following breakfast Gideon took the tiller again; they could make better time if he tended the gaffsail sheet. Soon, after perhaps another ten river miles, they would come to the long, marshy island where they had stranded the three Red Sticks three days before. Gideon hoped the Red Sticks had got off the island, but he would take precautions in any case. When going upriver, they had passed the island on the Alabama's main, eastern branch, the Tensaw; returning, Gideon would keep to the smaller western branch. If any Red Sticks waited for them in the Tensaw, they might be avoided. And if attacked by overwhelming strength, Gideon could run the boat aground on the western bank, and they might be able to escape overland to Mobile, which sat at the mouth of the western branch.

Gideon yawed slightly to avoid another cottonmouth moccasin swimming through the water. Reaching into his pocket, he withdrew himself tobacco and began to chew. The boat followed the river, winding beneath pine-strewn bluffs, between wooded, silent islands; the deserted, smokeless habitations of white men became more common. MacDonald dozed in the bow, his dried-out buckskins stiff, the scalps gathering occasional flies at his belt. The wind, brisk until now, shifted to the west, dropping to a warm breath that sometimes died altogether, causing the sails to flap empty as they passed beneath the wind-shelter of some bluff or stand of trees. Gideon recognized the northern point of the island on which he'd marooned the enemy, and chose the western channel, keeping to the right bank in order to discourage marksmen. It was Maria-Anna who first saw the canoes.

There were four heavy dugouts, carried by a swarm of warriors from their places of concealment among the island's brush to the water's edge. "Red Sticks!" Maria-Anna shouted, and Gideon caught only a glimpse of dark men, bright clothing, the swift, shaped hulls before throwing the tiller hard over. The unexpected gybe threw MacDonald cursing to the planking, and the sweeping lower edge of the gaffsail spilled Gideon's top hat into the water. Hearing the Red Sticks' shouts of triumph as the first wooden keel touched water, Gideon frantically worked the sheet as the boat heeled madly, while MacDonald reached for the jib sheets.

The faint wind was still westerly, and the first long board would be fast, a quick reach across the river to the island—before Gideon would be forced to tack and beat slowly across the river to the western bank. Perhaps, with the wind so westerly, they would actually lose way on the short board as they zigzagged their way upstream.

And the canoes could paddle in a straight line without reference to the light and treacherous wind.

The slow match was lit; the priming of the muskets, rifle, shotgun, and pistols was swiftly assured. A tentative
shot was fired from the bow of a canoe and splashed wide,
the echoing report bringing a flock of blue herons thundering skyward from the shore. Annoyed by the crazed
thumping of his heart at the sound of the shot, Gideon
shifted his sword nearer his hand. It would be a close
thing. The canoes, fresh and only three hundred yards
away as they commenced their pursuit, were gaining even
at the boat's fastest point of sailing.

The parties they had encountered thus far had been plundering parties, as surprised by the presence of whites on the
river as Gideon had been surprised by the Indians. But
this was clearly a war party, assembled for the sole purpose
of ambushing the white party they knew had sailed up the
river only four days before. They had sprung their ambush
a little early, Gideon thought, but even so, they had done
well.

"Ready about!" Gideon called as another musketball
whirred harmlessly past. The gaffsail swept overhead, the
canvas roaring, and Gideon caught an oath on his tongue
as he realized that they were still towing the canoe astern.
Furious at himself, he reached for his clasp knife and cut
the canoe adrift. Two of the lean pursuing craft detoured
toward the helpless prize, hoping for loot.

Between the hampering current and the way the keelless
boat was crabbing sideway, making leeway after it went
onto its new close-hauled tack, Gideon could not tell if the
boat was actually losing ground. He cast a frantic glance
over his shoulder. The paddles still dug tirelessly into the
water, the bright headcloths bobbing in regular rhythm as
the light crafts skimmed over the surface of the water. "Up
onto the starboard side!" Gideon shouted. "Climb up onto
the gunnel!"

Maria-Anna and MacDonald looked at him blankly, uncertain, but did as they were told, balancing high on the
boat's windward side, helping to put the craft on a more
even keel and allowing the flat bottom to increase whatever slender purchase it had on the water. Shots rang out,
and Maria-Anna flinched, going white; standing against the

boat's high side she and MacDonald were in full sight of the enemy marksmen that rode in each Red Stick bow. One shot, twittering like a delirious sparrow, smacked through the mainsail; the others did not come close. Like most inexperienced naval gunners, they were firing high.

Gideon could feel the wind holding steady as the boat passed midstream. Feeling the Red Sticks drawing nearer, hearing their whistling, crackling musketry, he glanced intently toward the northernmost point of the island, at the foam-waisted rocks the boat would have to weather. Trying to concentrate through the shock and horror that was trying to possess his unwilling soul, Gideon forced himself to calculate bowlines. If he could round the northernmost point of the island, he could get the boat back into the main channel of the Tensaw; moving with the current, and if the wind held, he could outrace the canoes once the paddlers tired. It wasn't necessary to go all the way across the river before his next tack, but the precise moment was critical. If he waited too long before tacking, the canoes would catch them; if he tacked too soon he'd fail to weather the point and have to go about twice more, losing the race. *Help us, help us,* he pleaded, his distracted, maddened brain unable to formulate a more coherent entreaty. He watched the foam-ridden rocks, the big flock of herons settling nervously back into their heronry, the bright figures of the Red Sticks against the darkness of the island . . .

"Ready about!" he shouted, seeing MacDonald spring for the jib sheets. *"Helm's a-lee!"* The sailboat, without the weight of the canoe hampering its movements, spun neatly on the water; the mainsail crashed over and filled.

"Back on the weather gunnel!" Gideon shouted as MacDonald sprang for his rifle. The Cherokee stubbornly shook his head. "Look at that," he said, pointing.

Gideon followed the finger, saw that though two Red Stick canoes had been slowed by their investigation of the boat Gideon had cut adrift and another crew seemed to be tiring, the fourth was driving stubbornly on, its path intersecting the sailboat's before it reached the point. MacDonald cocked the lock of his rifle.

"Very well," Gideon acceded. MacDonald was probably better where he was, ducked down in the bow, his rifle leveled at the enemy.

The rifle cracked smoke and fire, and a white feather of spray flew up near the enemy craft. Gideon whiffed gunsmoke as enemy marksmen futilely replied. MacDonald reloaded deliberately, and then the long, rifled barrel tracked the enemy again, the Cherokee taking his time, carefully gauging the movement of the racing craft, the wind, the heel of the sailboat, perhaps even the beating of his own heart and the susurration of his breath. Gideon ducked involuntarily as another hornet punctured the mainsail. Still MacDonald held his fire. Gideon remembered Long Tom Tate, the way the tall black man sighted the barrel of his twelve-pound gun, his slow deliberation and terrible accuracy. Slowly, as the canoe surged forward, the bobbing yellow feather of its bow marksman crossing Gideon's bowline, Gideon realized that the canoe would win the race, and his heart sank.

The rifle cracked. Gideon almost shouted with joy as the Red Stick canoe slewed to starboard, one man slumping back over the next man's paddle, their regular drill spoiled. MacDonald reloaded frantically, too close to move with his accustomed deliberation. The sailboat surged past the canoe's bows at twenty yards, the feathered marksman putting another bullet through the boat's mainsail as it triumphantly weathered the point. The sailboat's bottom ground over gravel for a heart-stopping second and then was free. Gideon felt triumph surge through him. The race had been won . . .

But Gideon's triumph turned to horror as he saw more canoes, with still more Red Sticks howling their triumph. His mind convulsed with admiration for the enemy's tactics even as it accepted the numbing realization that in a very few minutes they would be involved in a deadly battle which they had little hope of winning.

There had not been four canoes; there had been eight. They had known that there was an enemy sailboat up the river, but they hadn't known whether the returning boat would take the main channel or the western branch and so had divided their forces, four on each side of the island.

They had anticipated that the sailboat might be able to escape one group and sail upstream around the island's northern tip, and so the four canoes defending the Tensaw had also spread out and gone upstream, paralleling their comrades chasing the sailboat, to sweep round the point and catch the sailboat between two forces.

Gideon saw Maria-Anna cast an anxious glance at him. He wished in that moment to be able to offer some sort of reassurance, to make a promise that all would be well. But there was nothing else to do. Going upstream, the canoes were faster, for the sailboat had to tack. There was no choice but to run down between the canoes and attempt escape. *For what hath man of all his labors,* he thought, the words coming to his mind with surprising clarity and deadly impact, *and of the vexation of his heart, wherein he hath labored under the sun? For nothing, nothing,* he thought.

"Get yer head down," Gideon said as kindly as he could. The end of the long struggle—here on the dark Alabama, surrounded by canoes and men who cared less for life than for a strip of flesh and hair. Then strangely his heart lightened. He could welcome death if it were the Lord's will that it happen here. It was sad that others had to die as well, but they had come for their own purposes, and Gideon had tried his best to prevent it and could not. He would fight, of course, for Gideon's God would not accept easily a man who surrendered without struggle a life that could have been lived in continued service to the Lord.

Guns flashed, and lead balls whirred overhead. Gideon aimed between two of the canoes and thought for a bright moment that a chance existed of their escaping unscathed. MacDonald's rifle snapped flame, and a Creek paddle whirred lifeless through the air, its owner slumped. The space of dark water between the canoes narrowed. The sails boomed as the wind, perhaps shielded by the island, perhaps simply gusting, died away for the space of two heartbeats. The space of dark water would close. Gideon would have to fight. Calmly he bowed his head and gave thanks for the rightness of his end, then slid off the thwart and crouched down onto the planking, holding the tiller steady with his left hand while his right ducked into his pocket and came out with a pistol.

MacDonald's gun cracked again; no sign that it hit. The scout jumped for the swivel gun in the bows, swung it as bullets tore the air around him, aimed it deliberately at the canoe off to starboard, and put the match to the priming. The brass gun spewed bullets and iron fragments, enveloping the canoe in a sheet of white spray; the spray and smoke obscured for a few seconds the target, but when the canoe was revealed, it was spinning unnaturally, broadside to the current, the triumphant cries of its passengers turned to murdered silence.

It was too late to avoid the larboard canoe: clearly they were going to collide. MacDonald snatched up Jouhaux's shotgun. Reckoning it would be better to collide on the sailboat's terms than on the Red Sticks', Gideon twitched the tiller at the last minute, swinging the bow around, smashing the canoe amidships with the full and stunning weight of the boat. There was crackling fire—pistols, muskets, the deep boom of the shotgun. The canoe scraped down the larboard side, out of control, the occupants of the craft within arms' reach. A tomahawk flashed through the air, tearing its way through the mainsail. Maria-Anna fired a pistol, answering fire from the canoe tearing the air around her, and then she cried out and fell, clutching her hair. Gideon fired his second pistol, brought out his sword, hacked madly at the tomahawk-wielding arms that reached for him. A Red Stick warrior leaped for the boat, his bare feet gaining purchase on the gunwale, was fended off, fell into the waters with a cry. Maria-Anna was up again, firing one of her pistols, and then the canoe was past and spinning in the sailboat's wake.

There was a blessed moment to breathe air free of gunsmoke, to clutch at powder horns and paper cartridges. Maria-Anna, her dark hair spilling free from the comb that had been shot away, her hands busily reloading her pistols, glanced at Gideon. Her eyes danced, and her mouth was set in a spectral, reckless grin. Gideon felt himself returning that gaze of savage assurance, feeling the warm blood gushing through his body as he realized that he wanted desperately to live, that he would fight with all his power if only it meant that he could see another sunset or return another flush-cheeked smile from Maria-Anna.

A third canoe was approaching from starboard, its bow marksman firing a shot that slapped another puncture through the gaffsail. MacDonald worked over the swivel gun, reloading with what Gideon assumed was his usual deliberation until he perceived the scout's painful slowness and saw the spreading red on MacDonald's buckskin shirt.

"Mr. MacDonald, are ye hurt?" Gideon called, alarmed at seeing the crippled arm, the hunched shoulder.

"Go to hell."

MacDonald swung the brass muzzle toward the approaching canoe, filled the touch hole with powder, and sat quietly waiting. Gideon glanced over his shoulder. The fourth canoe was well back, and behind it were the four canoes from the western branch that had finally rounded the northern point of the island; even with the current with them it was plain they would be left well behind. They had but to drive off the one craft ahead . . . and would then be free. The canoe approached the sailboat in a silence broken only by the sighing wind, by the regular splash of paddles, and at the last by a hoarse chant: Gideon realized to his astonishment that MacDonald was singing, a low, murmuring lyric, as the Cherokee raised the slow match and let his breath bring the tip to cherry brightness.

The swivel gun banged the canoe in its swath of metal hail. The Red Stick casualties had come too late to stop the canoe from thudding against the boat's side, and there was another burst of fire as the boat rocked, as gunsmoke concealed the painted features of the enemy, as tomahawks were flung across the gap. Gideon realized with barbaric joy that the sailboat was going too fast for the enemy to board . . . but there was a desperate shout, and suddenly a man was standing precariously on the starboard bulwark, a man with a cocked hat worn athwart his head and dressed in the blue coat of the Continental Army. In his hand was a long knife. Maria-Anna, crouched below him on the planking, raised a hastily loaded pistol and pulled the trigger. Priming powder spurt, and then nothing: a misfire. With desperate speed she flung herself forward over the thwart, knowing the knife was coming. The Red

Stick stepped down into the boat.

Horrified, Gideon reacted more swiftly than he would
have thought possible, slamming the tiller over and gybing.
The gaffsail swung with astonishing force across the boat,
the Red Stick crying out as he saw the heavy canvas rushing toward him faster than he could respond. There was a
thud and another shout as the Red Stick was hurled over
the side, his cocked hat spilling from his head. The gaffsail
crashed as the sheet checked it; Gideon glanced hastily and
saw splashes of daylight through the sail. Swiftly Gideon
sheeted in the gaffsail and gybed again before the Red
Sticks could take advantage of the lost ground, letting the
gaff and canvas sail swing across as Maria-Anna rose wondering from the planks. He shaped his course for Mobile,
right downstream.

"Mr. MacDonald!" Maria-Anna cried from the bow.
The scout was leaning back against the gunwale, one arm
still thrown around the uptilted brass gun. Maria-Anna
scrambled over the thwarts toward the still man in buckskin, reaching out a hand to touch his face, then his throat.
When she turned to face Gideon, he knew from the despair
on her face that MacDonald was dead.

Again Gideon wished he had words of comfort to give,
but again there were none; so he met her eyes solemnly,
acknowledging her grief, and then bent his head for a brief,
muttered prayer. He should be good at praying over
corpses by now, he thought. His path in life had been
strewn with the dead, in obscure battles, in obscure corners
of the globe. But still he felt the same stammered thoughts
and halting phrases as his mind groped for expressions of
praise and sorrow, as he reached so hopelessly for sincer-
ity. There was no getting used to it. And there never
seemed time to mourn.

He stared aghast as he heard a vicious, sudden tearing
and saw Maria-Anna looking aloft in astonishment and
fear. "My God," she said. The gaffsail had torn, spilling air
through a four-foot laceration near the luff.

Why persecutest Thou me? Gideon thought, and his horror at having usurped for himself the words of the Almighty was turned to chilling terror as the rip extended
another twelve inches to the foot of the sail. *The tom-*

ahawks, Gideon thought. The thrown hatchets that had missed the boat's crew but had torn their way through the mainsail combined with all the musket shot the old, patched canvas had absorbed. It had all been too much for the ancient sail; there were no reef lines or battens, nothing to keep the sail's wounds from extending and widening as the breeze spilled through the gap.

"Quick! Take the tiller!" Gideon did not spare himself a look over his shoulder: he knew the Red Sticks would still be falling astern, but at a slower rate. He would have to attempt repairs. Maria-Anna made her way aft. Gideon rummaged through his baggage for his needle and palm. Another rip had opened from the first, and a tattered triangle of flax was flapping in the breeze. The gaffsail was spilling a lot of wind, and as Gideon leaped to make his repairs, a gunshot from astern told him that the enemy had not given up pursuit.

It was hopeless. Once the wind began opening up gaps, new fissures expanded from the old, and another tomahawk-torn gap, higher up where Gideon couldn't reach and right in the luff where the canvas was subject to more strain, began expanding with a deadly inevitablity. Even Gideon's hasty repairs began to tear free. He cast a quick glance astern. The canoes were four or five hundred yards off, but by now they were perceptibly gaining.

Maria-Anna sat in the stern sheets, adamantly refusing to look astern at the pursuers, her mouth set in a grim, stubborn line. Her loose hair spilled across her face in the wind, and she pushed it back with a furious gesture. Gideon felt her anger, her resentment. Their luck had been careening up and down for too long: Jouhaux's death followed by their escape to the boat; the hope of running for Mobile without further incident dashed by the appearance of the first four enemy craft; their evasion of the first set of canoes only to run into the next; the furious battle with the canoes that had raised the hope of ultimate success, only to have their expectation of safety crushed successively by the unnoticed death of Sean MacDonald and the inevitable self-destruction of their means of flight. Each blow had been followed by another blow; each desperate evasion of fate had been succeeded by another of fate's crushing interventions. And now Gideon would have to confirm their latest catastrophe.

"No good," he admitted. "We'll have to put her ashore. I'll take the tiller. You assemble what we need."

Silently she relinquished the tiller and began, with Gideon offering suggestions, assembling what they'd need ashore: dried meat, powder, shot, Gideon's musket, MacDonald's long rifle. They passed the southern tip of the island, where the Tensaw and its western branch merged into a single deep river. The wind increased as the boat passed from the island's shadow, and the mainsail finally blew itself into tattered strips of flax. Gideon looked over his shoulder. The canoes, their paddlers tiring, were still gaining.

"I think we have a good chance," Gideon said, hoping to hearten her. Maria-Anna gazed back at him, sullenly challenging, refusing to accept his words. "They may stop to loot the boat," Gideon insisted. "Their men have paddled four or five miles, and there are wounded to tend." *And a man to scalp,* he thought. "They may decide to take most of our food and drink our whiskey instead of haring off into the woods on another chase." Her gaze was blank, still disbelieving. "We can pray for it," Gideon said. He steered for the western bank.

The boat's balance was bad with the jib still drawing full, but enough of the mainsail was left to keep the boat maneuverable, though it took a lot of rudder. Just before the boat grounded on sandy loam below a tangled thicket of pine and scrub, Maria-Anna threw overboard the weapons they could not take with them: the shotgun, the heavy swivel, the spare ammunition, her heavy, crafted pistols. She stood on a thwart as the case of pistols went into the water, gazing blankly at the box as it filled and sank. Perhaps the last reminders of her husband, Gideon thought. The boat grounded, and she picked up a tomahawk and thrust it through her belt. Then they were splashing through the shallows and into the shade of the trees.

Gideon cast a longing glimpse back before he followed Maria-Anna into the forest at the little twenty-foot boat with its tattered sails, its bullet-marked gunwale, the sprawled figure of MacDonald still lying in the bow, head sunk on his chest, the wind fingering his dark hair. It was not a boat that Gideon had ever loved, not like *General Sullivan* or the old *Abigail*. But it had been fought for and bled for and somehow transformed from an inanimate *it* into a living *her*, and Gideon did not like the idea of letting an enemy have her. For a second a great anger flared in him: he'd turn and fight, a battle as fierce and pointless as those ancient warriors who battled over the armor of Achilles. Or he'd somehow set the boat alight, as he had *General Sullivan*, rather than let the enemy have her. But the anger faded, replaced by sorrow. There was nothing to be done. Gideon turned and fled into the forest.

He let Maria-Anna set the pace, and she set a fast one; within minutes they were crashing through the underbrush like bulls. His own sweat almost blinded him. They ran until they stumbled breathless to the ground; then after gasping air into their desperate lungs they ran again. They came to a creek, splashed upstream for several hundred yards, then staggered out into the trees once more. If there was a pursuit they never saw it. At length, with the afternoon sun beginning to lower into the western sky, they lay against a tree and surrendered to exhaustion. The fitful breeze cooled the sweat on their brows, and they watched cardinals the color of blood flit brightly among the trees.

Twenty miles, Gideon thought. Twenty miles to Mobile. They could walk that in a day if there weren't so much wood, swamp, and brushland with hostile Indians in the way. He looked toward Maria-Anna.

Her face seemed lined and old; she was pale and ill-at-ease, clearly exhausted.

"Can I help you?" he asked. "Is there anything I can do?"

Maria-Anna shook her head. "Just let me rest a bit."

"I think we've done well. They won't find us in this."

She laughed, and he sensed bitterness in it, and some of the brittle hardness of hysteria. "We've been leaving signs everywhere," she said. *"White people are here, white people are here!* We've probably left a trail the Red Sticks can follow in their sleep."

"I don't think so."

She saw no point in argument; instead she lay back and closed her eyes. The color came back to her cheeks, and she breathed easier. "We'd better go on a bit before dark," he said and stood. He took her hand and helped her rise. Their hands remained clasped as they walked south. She seemed to need that kind of reassurance, and so, Gideon realized, did he.

Their supper was dried meat washed down with water from a spring. At night they slept hidden in a little dell; neither kept watch. They awoke in the morning to find themselves swelling with mosquito bites, but refreshed. They ate more meat, drank from the spring, and washed their hands and faces. Maria-Anna's dark hair, freed from the comb that had held it drawn back from her face, was badly tangled, and she tried to comb it with her fingers as they walked.

They hid part of the day from a party of eight Indians on horseback, men dressed partly in buckskin and partly in clothes from the white man's loom. They were painted for war and carried perhaps two firearms for the entire party. They could have been friendly, Lower Creek or Chickasaw, but Maria-Anna and Gideon couldn't be sure and dared not make themselves known.

They crossed the Chickasaw Bayou that day, clinging to a log and kicking their way across the deep, dark water, their weapons and powder balanced precariously atop the log. Alligators watched them from the banks, and cottonmouths from overhanging branches. Reaching the south bank Maria-Anna wrung out her skirts, and they walked again into the forest. Rabbits and wild turkeys sprang leaping from their path, but they didn't dare risk a shot. They walked on, until Maria-Anna's shoulders began to shake and she fell slowly from the path.

"My God, my God," she murmured. She was weeping. "My God, I am a monster." He took her by the shoulders and held her. "I killed them," she said. "Dead. My fault. Oh God." He held her until the spasm passed, finding no triumph, no glory in the discovery of the remorse which days before he had wondered whether she felt at all. He leaned back and closed his eyes, and they slept that way, huddled together like children, until dawn.

The next morning Gideon ran out of tobacco. They walked southward through the trees across creeks and small rivers. Maria-Anna was silent and grave. She had been bronzed by the sun and walked easily through the forest in her tattered skirts. In the afternoon they came to a deserted plantation and washed in its spring; they added watercress to their lunch, and Maria-Anna braided flowers into her tangled hair.

Toward evening they stumbled out onto the Choctaw Pass and saw a little fortified outpost with the Stars and Stripes flying above it just two miles south of them on the riverbank.

They stood gazing at the outpost, knowing the little fort was just north of Mobile and that they had reached the object of their flight. It was the symbol of their safety, but it would take them hours yet to reach it through the swamp. "Let's have supper," Maria-Anna said and knelt in the grass. Gideon, as he knelt beside her, felt the knowledge of their deliverance as an almost physical release. After all the miles through the wilderness, after the loss of their boat, stores, and companions . . . Anything at all seemed possible.

"If you think you can bear it, I'd like to spend another night in the woods," Gideon said as they ate. "I've seen those militia drill, and they're not steady. It will be well after dark by the time we reach the fort, and if we come walking out of the night without the password, they're likely to shoot us dead before they realize we're white."

"I've seen them drill as well," she nodded. "I agree." Her eyes strayed to the grassy bank, then rose to meet his. Gideon remembered the breathless instant on the Jouhaux plantation when he had stood next to her near the rustling corn and had almost taken her in his arms. She was a wildly different sight now, bronzed by the sun, her hair tangled about her head, her face bruised by the bites of mosquitos. The trappings of civilization were gone, the top hat and coat, the cravat that had imprisoned her throat.

Gideon held out his arms and Maria-Anna fell into them. Her scent was of the wildflowers she had woven into her hair. He kissed her lips, her cheek, the bronzed V of her throat where her open collar had allowed the sun to darken her. Gideon felt inspired, suffused with light and intensity, a feeling somehow related to his inspiration on that dark night in Cuba aboard *General Sullivan* with the enemy in possession of the foredeck; there was an ineffable rightness to his actions, and he knew that Maria-Anna felt it, too, though their loving was wordless. They tore off their clothes because it was easier, and he rode atop her small-hipped, agile body, hearing in her murmurs and cries echoes of the waterfowl skimming the waters. When their last shudder was completed, he stayed in her, enraptured beyond words, until his desire rose again and once more they spasmed on the bank. Afterward the mosquitoes became troublesome, and they rolled themselves in their clothes and slept locked in one another's limbs.

16

SILVER IN LAMPLIGHT

Maria-Anna's door closed softly as the liveried Alfred saw them out. Lieutenant Archibald Bullock Blake, his brows closed in a frown, stared at the closed door for a moment and puffed his cigar meditatively. He grimaced in annoyance, took the cigar from his mouth, and looked at it with irritation. The cigar had gone out.

"I can't see how we can do more," Gideon said, cutting himself tobacco. Through the front window he could see Maria-Anna with her guests Charles Jouhaux, Sean MacDonald, and the other planters and farmers connected with her scheme; they spoke animatedly, planning with laughter and wine the next day's ascent on the river.

"I submit, sir, that we must," said Blake, still looking irritatedly at his cigar. They turned and walked down the street, each holding his sword in his left hand so as not to bang the other with his scabbard. Their every attempt to dissuade Maria-Anna and her friends from their attempt on the river had been repulsed, sometimes with laughter, sometimes with annoyance. Furthermore, it had become obvious that the expedition had been badly planned: neither MacDonald nor Jouhaux could claim to be a riverman, let alone a sailor; they knew nothing about boats or stowage, and intended to learn how to handle the newly purchased craft on the river itself.

The oil streetlamp burned softly on the corner ahead, casting a pool of yellow light on the unpaved street below, and onto the gently gleaming leaves of an ancient oak above. Blake paused beneath the lamp to relight his cigar. While Gideon held his cocked hat, Blake stretched up on tiptoe to open the hinged glass door of the lamp, thrust the cigar into the flame, waited for the cigar to be well alight, then brought it down to puff contentedly. Gideon spat tobacco into the gutter. Moths circled furiously about their heads.

Blake took his cocked hat from Gideon and sat it fore-and-aft on his head. The brim cast deep shadows over his face, and his eyes reflected the red dot of his cigar.

"One of us must go along," he said.

Gideon looked uncomfortably toward the house, the door so politely shut.

"I can leave One-Six-Three's repairs in the hands of my midshipman," Blake continued. "We can't let her kill herself."

"Nay. We can't."

Blake fished in his pocket, brought out a dime. "Shall we flip a coin, sir?"

Gideon shook his head. "I'll go."

"That wouldn't be fair, Captain." Blake spoke carefully, studying the coin in the lamplight. "Heads or tails?"

"Tails."

The coin spun in the air, winking silver in the light of the lamp, and landed in Blake's kid glove. He held the glove out to Gideon.

"Tails. My congratulations, sir."

Blake's lively walking stick touched ground every third step as Gideon walked with him to where Gunboat No. 163 sat moored in the Choctaw Pass. Blake hailed his boat, and when it arrived he shook hands gravely, then stepped into the stern sheets.

Gideon remained standing on the muddy bank of the Choctaw Pass, watching the winking tip of Blake's cigar recede toward the bobbing gunboat. He remembered the coin spinning in the light of the lamp, the flash of silver on the kid glove. *These casual gentlemanly games these officers play,* Gideon thought, *pretending that life and death don't matter so long as the game goes on and everyone gets his chance to play.* The river lapped gently at his feet.

Gideon could sense, as the waters rolled past into the bay, that there was a tide rising, rising not just in the bay or the Gulf beyond, but sweeping past into the woods and watersheds of the Creeks, leaving nothing untouched, nothing unchanged. It was the tide of war that had scoured the shingles of Europe, the East Indies, and Egypt, flowing at last to the slumbering, undiscovered woodlands of a vast America. Gideon felt himself drawn with the tide, impelled upriver like a bobbing chip caught in the current to some inevitable meeting beneath the canopy of pine. Gideon shivered; the feeling was awesome, as if he felt the fingers of the Almighty on his neck. The wind was from inland and brought the smoke of distant fires, the scent of sweet gum, a hint of rotting vegetation or some animal putrefaction. The dark river seemed vast; he could almost sense its implacability, and he found within himself a yearning to follow that opaque, watery road where it might take him. He remembered the spinning coin, that trivial wink of silver in lamplight, and he knew that he would not ascend the river because of the chance fall of that coin, but because he found his own internal fitness in it, a rightness which he associated with destiny and with God. For his own reasons, for his own sins, Gideon would sail the river, and in riding the dark waters to the source of their secrets might there discover the warring hands of men and the signature of generating Providence.

17

THE CHOCTAW PASS

Gideon brushed a mosquito from his forehead; he felt the hot sun on his naked eyelids, and before he opened them, he turned his head into shadow. His first sight was of Maria-Anna asleep on her back, her eyes closed, a few sprigs of grass rising through her tangled hair. Her mouth was parted slightly to show an ivory tooth reflecting the sun. Gideon watched her for a moment, content, ineluctably happy, feeling beneath their anonymous clothing the warmth of her legs still tangled with his. He felt the impulse to reach out and tenderly to touch her cheek.

Jupiter! he thought, stunned, as he remembered where and what he was. He drew back his hand and for a moment fought panic, an impulse of terror as strong as any he had battled in war, urging him to flee from the clutches of the monster he'd created back to the unencumbered solitude of the forest.

Lord help me! He remembered that impulse he had felt to touch her cheek, the innocent human warmth of the gesture, the sense of freedom and the utter absense of any knowledge of iniquity. *God preserve her.*

He had almost, with his polluting hand, defiled her once more and had not felt shame. *Forgive me my sin,* he tried to pray, but his insincerity was bitterness to him and ultimately paralyzing. In his memory of the night before, the acts of love performed on the darkening bank, the half-coherent recollection of textures and pleasures and the cries of some distant bird, he could detect no grain of remorse nor any true repentance; instead there was only the lingering reminiscence of the act's unjustifiable fitness. He had sinned, and he was not sorry.

To sin was understandable, and the lot of fallen mankind. Not to repent was hideously wrong.

He closed his eyes and tried furiously to pray, with no success. A few days before, he remembered, he had wondered idly (and viciously, as he now thought) if Maria-Anna possessed a moral sense, if she was capable of feeling remorse for the suffering and death her actions had caused. Now Gideon was demonstrating himself to be a creature apart from humanity, incapable of contrition, condemned to blackness. The utter, devastating irony of it overwhelmed him. Now he knew why he had never truly known his God, despite his prayerful appeals and hypocritical anguish, his outward show of piety: the Almighty had known what Gideon in his presumption had not, that Gideon Markham was not a moral being. Was instead depraved, unnatural. *Damned.* And Gideon knew why God had taken from him his wife and son, the one divine act that Gideon, in his heart of hearts, had not been able to forgive. Gideon understood now that Betsy and Jos had been taken in order that he, Gideon, not corrupt them with his own iniquity; they had to die while still capable of salvation, and they rested in their coffins only because they had chosen to love Gideon.

No! Lord, forgive!

He felt alarmed as Maria-Anna stirred, afraid she would wake while he was still consumed by this sudden despairing vision. But she raised a bare, downy arm and laid the back of her hand across her forehead to shield her eyes from the sun; she smiled in her sleep a brief, almost mischievous smile, then sighed and slept on.

Gideon blinked in the sun. *God help me choose what is best.* He had been right to isolate himself as he had on some vessel's quarterdeck, limiting his capacity to infect humanity by a self-imposed quarantine. But the drowsing woman by his side demanded justice. He had robbed her of her virtue. It scarcely mattered that she had cooperated; he was the man, and furthermore a professed Christian, and he should have been stronger. *God, God help me . . .*

Gideon batted a mosquito away from his ear and imagined Maria-Anna's reaction if he, Gideon, should isolate himself on a ship and never see her again. Her anger, re-

sentment, fury—all understandable, all natural. He had
seen things of the sort before, and deplored the man who
had caused it; a rejected woman becoming bitter and vin-
dictive, flaunting new suitors, new lovers, in the face of convention and decency. It would be Gideon's fault if Maria-
Anna should become such a woman, and his responsibility.
He should do the right thing.

Maria-Anna's eyes opened. There was a strange innocence in her expression, an unfeigned gaze of childlike wonder at the distant blue sky and the white streamers of
clouds; Gideon remembered a similar look one night
aboard *Prinsessa,* when she gazed up at the canopy of stars
and his heart ached. Her eyes turned to him, and she
smiled. She reached out to touch the hair on his temple—
Gideon, anguish throbbing through him, remembered his
own tender impulse to touch—and leaned over to kiss him.

"Is something wrong?" she asked, drawing back, her
brows coming together in a frown.

"Madam, we must speak."

She threw her head back and laughed at the formality;
and Gideon found himself battling an insidious and overwhelming impulse to throw himself forward and kiss that
softly arched, bronzed throat. She lowered her eyes to his
affectionately.

"Very well, sir," she mocked. "Speak on."

He composed his face gravely. "It cannot be said easily,"
he said. "My behavior has been unforgivable. I have taken
advantage of your, your generous nature . . ."

Gideon's uncertain fumbling for words dissolved hopelessly in the face of Maria-Anna's sudden grin. "By Jerusalem," she said. "I wish you'd done it sooner."

He stared at the ground, collecting the thoughts that had
fled like startled birds at the sight of her grin, confused and
embarrassed by the way her laughter, her inviting smile,
had triggered his own arousal, a tumescence which, he
feared, she would soon perceive. Desperately he began
again.

"Madam, I have sullied you. I have allowed myself to
take shameful advantage of your dependence on me." She
frowned, her lips pursing at his words.

"Now we are in the wilderness and in a state of savagery akin to those who live here," he continued, knowing he was being brutal, but knowing also that he was being no less brutal to himself, deliberately wrecking the hope of happiness he had felt hovering over the Choctaw Pass, feeling his heart ache with every word. "Here we may think our behavior has no costs. Soon—today—we will return to civilization, and then we must conduct ourselves as civilized beings. I have ruined you. The social consequences—not to mention the moral ones—will be apparent to you in time. Even if we relate to no one the true story of what has happened here, the knowledge will still exist between us, and there will be rumors which we cannot honestly deny. In consequence of this and because my share of responsibility for what has happened is undeniable, I cannot in conscience refrain from asking for your hand in marriage."

Maria-Anna sat up abruptly, throwing off Gideon's shirt that she had worn as a blanket, and rested her head and arms on her knees. Through the haze of his anguish Gideon perceived the ridges of her supple spine flexing through her smooth skin, the skin that was dappled from lying on the grass; he saw the white swell of her small breasts growing from her shadowed ribs. He turned his eyes away. He must be very, very careful; he must feign, through the years they would spend together, the moral sense that he knew he lacked.

"No," she said. When Maria-Anna turned to him, Gideon was surprised by her fervor and astonished by her undeniable anger.

"I do not need your charity, Captain Markham," she said. "I do not need your compassion. Your offer of marriage, your little chip of mercy, thrown out to a woman you despise because she allowed you, in your sickening phrase, to ruin her. Damn your righteousness! Damn you, damn you!"

She turned her head away and furiously sorted through their mingled garments, snatching at the pantaloons, the shift, the skirt and blouse.

"Ye don't understand! Don't be angry. I'm not good at speech, I must have got it wrong!"

"You got it right, Captain Markham," she said with quiet bitterness. She stood, reaching for her half-boots. "You said just what you damned well meant to say." He thought she might be weeping, but she kept her face turned from him. Half-dressed, she took MacDonald's powder flask and rifle and walked vehemently into the trees. She stood there, a distant, shadowed, disdainful figure, while Gideon dressed, and when he took his musket and followed her, she turned and walked on, keeping the distance between them.

Stunned, unable to understand how he had miscarried or why he had struck her anger, he followed her through the swamp and groves, calling after her from time to time but hearing no answer, until just after noon she walked into the fortified outpost they had seen the previous night and answered the sentry's challenge with a vigorous obscenity.

The commander of the fort, a middle-aged New Orleans haberdasher who had given up all hope of disciplining his men, was kind and restrained his questions; those he could not avoid asking, Gideon answered briefly. The commandant gave them clothes and sent them downstream in a boat. Gideon and Maria-Anna sat in the stern sheets, uncomfortably close to one another, silent, their elbows clashing over the tiller. Maria-Anna's frozen eyes watched the waterfowl. Her hair was tied severely in a handkerchief.

At last the militiamen rowed them around the final bend, and Gideon saw Mobile before them, and anchored before the town in the bay, the low, sleek silhouette of a black privateer schooner, its three masts raked precipitously sternward, its big spars crossed neatly, level with the horizon. For a moment Gideon forgot the woman beside him, forgot his bitterness and ache, and watched instead the big vessel draw nearer, mesmerized by its lines. Lines that he knew well, that he and old Stanhope had carefully labored over before he had ever left New England. The new tern schooner, the Stars and Stripes hanging listlessly over the stern, of which he had dreamed so longingly, and of which he would now have the command!

But the boat took them to Mobile, not to the sleek craft offshore. Maria-Anna stepped stiffly through the shallows, her face frozen, and left it to Gideon to thank the boatmen who had brought them. They in turn thanked him; they would make a round of the grog shops before returning to their lonely outpost, if they ever planned to return at all.

"I'll walk ye home," Gideon insisted, running to catch her striding figure. People stared at them, these ragged figures dressed willy-nilly and carrying weapons.

"You can if you insist. I don't care." Her voice was brisk, businesslike; there was no echo of the loving, wordless murmurs he had heard the night before.

"I don't know what's made you angry, but I'm sorry. I meant well."

Gideon felt the painful inadequacy of his words even as he spoke them, recognized them as an opening for a devastating rebuttal.

"I suppose you did," she said. She did not glance at him, walking with her head held high and her gaze level, staring furiously ahead as she turned the corner that led to her house.

"There may be a future time, Captain Markham, when I am able to look at you without anger," she said. "Perhaps you may address me then. But I do not think it will be any time soon."

There was a shout from farther down the street; Campaspe had been sitting on the porch and had finally spied them. The maidservant flung herself down the street and weeping into Maria-Anna's arms, sobbing incoherent Spanish. Maria-Anna hugged her, stroking the girl's hair, looking down at her absently. For a second her newfound hardness warred with her features, and then it melted. Maria-Anna looked up at Gideon hopelessly.

"Will you come in for some coffee, Captain?" she asked. He knew what she meant: they were again in civilization, there was a witness. Whatever their private feelings they must never be allowed to interfere with the face society demanded. The conventions had won.

"No thankee, ma'am," Gideon said. "Perhaps some other time."

He bowed formally, and she dipped in curtsey. Campaspe, puffy-eyed, gazed at them both, quite obviously seeing something strange in the drama.

Gideon turned away and headed slowly down the street

toward Lieutenant Blake's house, hoping somehow that the formalities would melt away and Maria-Anna would call after him. Instead he heard her bootheels turn away and walk toward her house, slowly, as if she had an arm about Campaspe, or as if she, too, were hoping for a call.

No one called, not even a bird. Gideon walked past the lamppost at the corner and turned away. He could not present himself at the new schooner in his present attire; he would go to Blake's and change his clothes. Soon he would feel the planks of the tern schooner under his feet and live again in the small, ordered, austere world of a ship's cabin, to be tested again by the stern necessities of command and to dwell again in solitude. As he walked, he breathed a prayer that it would all be for the best.

18

OFFICERS AND CREW

As Gideon was rowed by his hired boatmen toward the
new privateer, he saw the schooner was long, almost as
long as the big Humphreys frigates, slightly over two
hundred feet from her overhanging stern to the tip of her
jib boom; she was long and narrow and clipper-built, with
her sternpost drawing more water than her stem. Her foremast and mainmast were raked sixteen degrees aft, and her
short mizzen a preposterous thirty degrees, angling out
over the stern. That she was built for privateering could be
seen by the size of her fighting tops, wide platforms built in
the rigging to hold sharpshooters. Black, very narrow, and
very low, she could furl her wide canvas wings and turn
almost invisible in the night, hiding unnoticed within miles
of an enemy squadron; yet with her big spars she could raise
aloft a monstrous spread of canvas that would speed her
through the waters as fast as a hurtling shark, and more
deadly. The great spars and narrow beam meant she could
spell danger for her own crew as well; a sudden gale could
lay her on her beam ends or carry her gear away unless
the crew were alert to their danger. Yet with the right crew
she was capable of anything. He would have to forge such
a crew, Gideon thought as he dabbed at his chin with his
handkerchief and looked irritatedly at the pinpricks of
blood on the white cloth. He had shaved for the first time
in a week and had scraped himself badly.

Gideon looked up again to admire the sleek tern
schooner, the elegant rake of the masts, the competent
setup of the rigging, the way she rode easily at anchor,
gracefully cutting each wave. Lost in thought, he barely
heard the lookout's hail, Wallace Grimes's bellowed answer, and the sudden trampling on the schooner's deck as

the officers and crew realized their captain was coming aboard.

The boat passed beneath the schooner's bowsprit, and Gideon was surprised to look up and see a figurehead gracing the sleek stem, the effigy looking odd and ungainly on such a clean-lined vessel. It was the weathered form of a Russian horseman, red-bearded, gold in one ear, brandishing a curved saber. A family heirloom, Gideon knew, the original figurehead of the Revolutionary privateer *Cossack*, the ship captained first by his uncle Malachi and then by his loyal lieutenant Andrew Keith, and the ship from whose bulwarks the youthful Gideon in 1794 had speared unsuspecting Englishmen. The figurehead was said to have been carved to resemble Malachi himself, and Gideon could see it had recently been repainted in loving detail.

Gideon's father had taken the figurehead down after peace was declared, and it had been kept in an honored place in his Portsmouth house: Gideon could remember Josiah saying, "It's a figurehead for war, youngster; we won't show that face in peacetime or fly the Rattlesnake from the main."

The boat slipped from beneath the schooner's stem. "Here you are, sir," the boatman said, and Gideon thrust the blood-dappled handkerchief back into a pocket and launched himself nimbly for the entry port, leaving Grimes to pay for the boatman.

He appeared at the entry port without getting his feet wet, catching the schooner unaware. The half-apologetic grin on the deck officer's face faded as Gideon glared at the disorder around him, the on-duty watch running to their stations, the off-duty watch being turned up by the harsh calls and pipe of the boatswain, one elderly, whitewhiskered seaman in a Quaker hat, perched on a twelve-pounder abaft the foremast, calmly mending his white trousers with a yellow patch and puffing absently on a corncob pipe.

"Welcome aboard, Captain. I believe Mr. Martin is below. He'll be up directly."

"You are Mr. Clowes, I believe?" Gideon asked.

"Second Officer, sir."

Gideon knew very well who Michael Clowes was: a tried Portsmouth sailor, officer for many years on New Hampshire schooners and finally, just before the war, his own captain. Gideon wondered why Clowes was not commanding his own ship, either converting it to a privateer or daring the loose, inefficient British blockade of the New England coast to bring profitable commerce into American ports, perhaps sweeping up British merchantmen at the same time with a letter of marque. Possibly Clowes had been unlucky and lost his ship.

"I'll want the names of the lookouts, Mr. Clowes," Gideon said. "They were late in seeing me."

"Ah—aye aye, Captain." Clowes's face froze into a respectful, obedient mask, giving away none of the man's private thoughts. That would do well enough for the present, Gideon thought. Respectful obedience, resentment tempered with civility. Later it might be possible to hope for more.

"Captain Markham!" A familiar voice called from the aft scuttle. Gideon stifled the instinctive distaste with which he had always reacted to the sound of that particular voice and turned toward the dwarfish, leering old man walking toward him.

"I'm happy to welcome ye aboard, Cap'n. Happy as a pig in shit."

Finch Martin. His uncle Malachi's former sailing master aboard *Cassack* and *Royal George*, a sailor of incomparable skills. A small, round-shouldered man, almost a dwarf, his grizzled hair worn in an old-fashioned long queue, Martin had brought home a small fortune from privateering during the Revolution and spent it all in dissipation. He had not been young then and must be in his seventies by now. Gideon had never liked him, if for no other reason than the man's language was always blasphemous and frequently obscene.

"Mr. Martin, I'm glad to be aboard," he said formally, swallowing his distaste and suddenly distracted by the sight of the tall man rising from the scuttle behind Martin: Lieutenant Archibald Bulloch Blake, smiling quietly, puffing cigar smoke from the shadows of his cocked hat.

"Captain Markham, we were plotting your rescue," Blake said, offering his hand. Gideon took it. "We were going to take some of One-Six-Three's men up the river in your privateer's boats along with a hundred of your Yankees."

"Aye, Cap'n," Martin agreed. "Them Indian buggers wouldn't have stood a chance."

"It was your first officer's plan," Blake said, nodding at Martin.

"Sir, I am honored by your concern," Gideon said.

"Mrs. Marquez is well?"

Gideon's heart leaped at the name, and he spoke quickly to cover any reaction he may have betrayed. "I believe so, all things considered. Mr. MacDonald and Mr. Jouhaux were killed, and the boat lost. We walked the last twenty miles through the swamp."

Blake's look of astonishment was only gradually replaced by well-bred surprise. "I am amazed, sir," he said.

"I believe more Creeks were killed than whites. We may consider it a victory, sir, which God has seen fit to grant us."

"Ah—yes." Blake clamped his eager questions within him as he saw Gideon's uncompromising, formal stare. *Victory,* Gideon thought. It had not felt like a victory, that flight through the wilderness. Yet his declaration had seemed the best way to silence questions in advance. Let what happened on Alabama's branches be between Maria-Anna, Gideon, and the witnessing God.

Gideon turned to Martin, who had been watching them with disturbed surprise.

"My father is well?"

"Aye, Cap'n. I spoke to him myself before we weighed; a healthy gentleman he remains, sir."

"And my family?"

Gideon detected a careful hesitation in Martin's answer, a certain discreet calculation behind his weathered eyes. "I have letters from them all, Cap'n. In yer cabin."

Gideon saw from the corner of his eye that the crew had assembled forward of the mainmast, the officers in a line on the quarterdeck, ready for their first view of the new captain. "Introduce me to my officers if you please, Mr. Martin," Gideon said.

"Aye aye, Cap'n. Second Officer Clowes. Third Officer Allen is ashore."

"That would be Edmund Allen?"

"Nay, Cap'n. His brother Francis. As well as being third officer, Mr. Allen commands the gentleman volunteers, sir."

"I see." He knew Edmund Allen well, knew him to be a steady seaman of good parts; the brother he knew less well. Francis Allen, according to New Hampshire gossip, was a bit wild; he had been seen drunk on a Sunday, and there had been a story about a well-brought-up neighbor girl who had to be sent away suddenly to relatives. The "gentleman volunteers" were what served on Markham privateers for marines; they were alleged to be marksmen, fought with a musket in battle, usually from the fighting tops, and were dressed rather extravagantly, as Gideon saw, in green coats.

"The bosun, Kit M'Coy," Martin went on.

"Mr. M'Coy." Christopher M'Coy was a man of about fifty who, while a youngster, had served in the Continental Navy under John Paul Jones on *Ranger,* and later in the more profitable privateers. Gideon was glad to have him.

"Dr. Rivette, the surgeon, is in town."

"That would be James Rivette, the French Vermonter? The papist?"

"I believe he is, aye," Martin said. "Physician and surgeon both, he is."

"I can't understand how such a man was allowed into Harvard. I will have no Romish propaganda aboard this vessel, Mr. Martin," Gideon said, fixing the first officer with a frozen eye. "You will tell that to Dr. Rivette."

Finch Martin accepted his eccentric fate resignedly. "I'll tell 'im, Cap'n. Any Catholic plotting from him and I'll kick his arse up past his windpipe."

Gideon met the rest of the officers, returning formal bow for formal bow: the carpenter, gunner, clerk, cook, the mates, yeomen, and prizemasters; all were New Hampshiremen, and some had sailed with Gideon before in merchant ships. A solid enough crew. With care and discipline perhaps they could become a great one, as fine as the schooner on which they sailed.

He heard a gust of salt-scented ocean breeze shriek briefly through the rigging, felt the schooner surge beneath his feet in response, heard the gridiron flag at the peak snap out; quite suddenly he realized that he didn't know what to call the graceful, deadly thing beneath his feet.

"What's her name, Mr. Martin?" Gideon asked. Finch Martin looked blank. "The schooner, I mean," Gideon added impatiently.

Comprehension flooded into Martin's expression. "I'll be a louse's bastard if I know, Cap'n. We thought ye would name her. She's just been called Number Six after th' way in Portsmouth where they built her."

"I see."

"Cap'n Markham, yer father gave us the figurehead, the one from *Cossack*," Finch Martin began awkwardly. For a startled, disbelieving second Gideon thought Martin's eyes might be bright with sudden tears; but there was no possible credit to pay to the notion that the old cynic might have fallen prey to the sentimentality that inhabited lesser sailors—it was a trick of the light, Gideon decided, or rheum.

"That bein' Captain Malachi's image," Martin went on, "we thought—we hoped perhaps it might inspire ye with a name, like." His conclusion was defiant, his jaw jutting, as if daring Gideon to oppose his idea.

"Thankee, Mr. Martin," Gideon said; against his will, for although he grudged the very idea of Finch Martin's ideas having an effect on him, he found himself touched by Martin's loyalty to his old captain. "I'll try to think of something appropriate."

"We'd appreciate it, sir," Martin said. Gideon wondered who that *we* contained and found himself wondering for a fraction of a second if perhaps the word held not only Finch Martin and the Markham family, but somewhere the spirit of the absent Malachi.

Gideon glanced at the crew again, seeing them still standing forward of the mainmast, one group standing on the main hatch and therefore a head taller than the rest—

mostly an anonymous group of shellbacks, dressed in the universal short jackets and tarred hats, with here and there a familiar weatherbeaten set of features that Gideon remembered from another ship, or had glimpsed in a new Hampshire lane, or glanced at sidelong in Congregational pews. Worn men of the sea for the most part, with here and there the smooth face of a landsman. They would not only have to prove themselves to him, Gideon knew, but he would have to prove himself to them, in leadership and discipline, in seamanship and navigation, in pursuit and in flight, and if necessary in the red heat of battle. A sailor's trust was the easiest to gain of any man's, but once lost it was lost forever. Captain Addams of the *Prinsessa* had lost his men's trust and lost his profession as well, for *Prinsessa*, crewless, still lay at anchor half a mile away, and would lie there until she rotted, or until Captain Addams left her decks forever.

The men waited, quietly watching, quietly judging. Gideon had just come aboard for the first time and he ought to speak. He moved by the wheel, just forward of the mizzenmast, and as he did so he realized that the unprotected wheel might cause trouble later; for the tern schooner's deck was flush, in the American pattern, running unbroken from stem to taffrail, the tern's fine lines uncluttered with the usual poop deck beneath which the wheel sheltered in battle. But that was for later.

He turned to face his crew, seeing again the practiced eyes watching him from out of the weathered faces, the "gentleman volunteers" in their green coats, muskets shouldered and hats cocked defiantly over their eyes, the officers lined on the quarterdeck with their tall hats and dark coats. Gideon clasped his hands behind his back.

"Men of New England!" he began. "The Caribbean is an enemy lake, but we will make it ours, together with its riches. Brave men have gone before us, some from my own family, and always they have brought home enemy ships in triumph. Obey orders, and obey God, and ye shall all be rich men! Ye may return to yer duties."

As he unclasped his hands and walked toward Finch Martin and Lieutenant Blake, he was startled to hear a cheer from the hands—not a great cheer, but certainly more than he'd expected. *We'll see if they cheer tonight,* he thought, *after I've seen them at gun drill.*

"Mr. Martin, I'd like to see my cabin," Gideon said. "By the entry port is Mr. Grimes, my steward, with my dunnage."

"Aye, Cap'n. The cabin's been ready for ye since we entered port."

Gideon turned to Blake. "Mr. Blake, I am sorry not to be able to spend more time with ye, but my duties are many."

"I understand, sir."

"Ye may have the freedom of the vessel if ye wish it," Gideon said. "I will not vouch for what Grimes is able to produce on such short notice, but if ye will be pleased to join me for a late supper tonight, I will consider it an honor."

"The honor is mine, sir," Blake said with a bow.

"Mr. Martin, if ye will lead the way?"

Martin led Gideon and Grimes down the aft scuttle, down a narrow, well-lit corridor lined with the private, boxlike cabins of the officers, past the great rudder post and tiller, to Gideon's cabin on the overhanging stern. It was spacious for a seaman's cabin, and bright with sun entering the two broad stern windows; it was a single room with bed, table, chairs, desk, a wardrobe and thwartships settee, and a door leading to a private lavatory and bathroom. Gideon seemed to remember the wardrobe once sitting in his brother Jeremiah's house, and perhaps the table and chairs had lingered for a number of years in his father's attic; New England thrift proclaimed itself here.

"Yer correspondence is in the top desk drawer, Cap'n," Martin reported.

"Thankee, Mr. Martin. Grimes, ye can unpack later. Show Grimes his cabin on the way out—oh, Mr. Martin."

"Sir?"

"I will require ye to moderate yer language in the future. I tell ye now rather than reprimand ye in front of the men."

Martin looked forlornly at him for a stricken moment, then gave a great sigh and accepted his fate manfully. "I'll—I'll give it a try, sir," he gulped.

"Do yer best, Martin. I'd like to see ye in an hour."

"In an hour, sir, aye aye."

For a moment, as Gideon turned toward the desk, he sensed again a moment of hesitation on the part of the dwarfish first officer, as if he were trying to say something just before he closed the door behind the bustling Wallace Grimes, and had then decided against it. For a moment Gideon had an intuition that the hesitation was somehow compassionate, and that Martin had just stopped short of offering him some unlikely sort of sympathy, but had then decided to allow his captain to endure whatever needed to be endured in the solitude that was a commander's privilege and his penance. The door closed. Gideon shrugged off the feeling as foolishness.

He walked to the settee beneath the open stern windows, feeling the hot breeze on the back of his neck as he sat down, too weary for the moment to read his letters. He closed his eyes, remembering that just that morning he had awakened on a grassy bank with Maria-Anna by his side and that for a moment he had been blessedly happy. Gone, of course, that prelapsarian contentment, in his sudden awakening to his duties; and Maria-Anna was gone from his life as well, leaving a throbbing emptiness . . .

With a start he opened his eyes. Perhaps he had drowsed for a minute or two, overcome with weariness and remembrance. There was no time for such indulgence now, and he forced himself to his feet and toward his desk. The key to the desk drawer was in the lock. He turned it, opened the drawer. The envelopes, perhaps a score of them and all thick, lay neatly tied with twine in a slippery seaman's knot. He sighed as he plucked at the knot, untied the twine. There would be no rest for him, no time for memories or might-have-beens, until after he had taken the tern schooner from the sheltering bay and sailed it on its canvas wings against the enemy.

19

NEWS FROM HOME

Dear Brother:

The latest news from Boston is almost too burdensome to relate, and were it not for the possibility that you might hear the tale from other, less charitable men, I would refrain from writing of it altogether and leave you without its burden as you face our Country's enemies. But as the story may come back to you in some alien land, and in a manner calculated to injure either yourself or your safe prospects, I feel that I must endeavor to unfold for you the unhappy narrative of what has disgraced our Family.

You know, of course, that the Family has always opposed war with England at this time, altho' we have not been of such vehement sentiment as many who also espouse the cause of Peace. As you know, I traveled to Washington City during the war debate, bearing a Petition for Peace signed by many New Hampshiremen. Cousin Lafayette has also spoken out against the war early this year at Federalist meetings in this state, and at a Federalist congress in Connecticut. But Lafayette returned dismayed by the calibre of men he met there, and has not since exerted himself on behalf of the Peace faction.

Though many of those who work for Peace are sincere and honest men, their ranks have also been joined by men whose motives may be less than pure. There are those absolutely political men, whose devotion to any cause may be measured by the opportunities for power that may be discerned in any national sentiment; there are those New England partisans whose interests do not extend beyond those of section, and whose rhetoric has not stopped short of calls for separation; and there are those, vicious, unscrupulous, or bought men, whose opinions stop not at treason, or at reunification with the British crown. Our brother David, whose undiscerning and reckless nature made him a thorough Partisan of any political principle he could be persuaded to adopt, was a natural tool for these last, and in the end became their victim.

As you know, David's last employment was as an agent of various shipping interests, and we had considerable hope that he would at last cease his wayward behavior and accept the life of a sober and industrious citizen. This hope, for some years, showed prospect of being fulfilled: David's business prospered, and he became involved in politics. He worked, more than any member of the Family, in promoting the cause of Peace, and once war began spoke out loudly against it, and was most intemperate in his expressions.

Early this year we began to receive, through our business connexions, disturbing rumours of what corners of the world were harboring David's goods. It seems clear now that he was trading with the enemy. As you know, Wellington's armies in the Spanish Peninsula, prior to declaration of war, depended for their grain supply on American merchants. David's employers were heavily involved in this trade. It seems they continued this trade after the commencement of hostilities, sending American grain to British armies, shipping in American hulls equipt with special licenses from Admiral Warren at Bermuda, whence the grain was trans-shipped. It appears that some hundreds of American ships were, and are still, involved in this trade, and to the shame of our nation this commerce is considered respectable in some quarters. To such disgrace as this has the policies of Jefferson and his ilk forced us.

Our David's ventures were mired in trouble when the

British, too greedy for their own good, seized two of his employers' vessels in Lisbon, claiming their licenses were out of order, or that they were enemies. The owners' names were never published, because the papers were unclear (deliberately so), but the name of their principal American agent was proclaimed in official British pronouncements, and that agent was David Markham. David felt obliged to leave New Hampshire, for certain Federal officers were becoming inquisitive, and thereafter David made his residence in Boston. There he seemed to settle again to his business and prosper. His letters spoke to us diligently and entertainingly of society in Boston, and from Boston newspapers we would occasionally hear of his political activities. He became one of the most energetic young Federalists in the State, and as such was regularly vilified by the Boston *Patriot*, and praised by the *Columbian Sentinel*. His calamity in Portugal served to decrease, rather than enhance, his discretion, and he became one of the great fire-eaters of the Peace faction, and apparently he fell under the influence of men wiser and more unscrupulous than he.

On June 21 of this year David was seen hiring a pilot-boat in Charleston, and was observed the next morning to return. Upon landing, he and the Captain of the pilot-boat was seized by Federal officers and carried to Fort Independence, where a search revealed that he was carrying correspondence from the British Commodore to men of the peace party ashore. These last have not been named; it is possible the letters were in cypher, or the correspondents may be in positions so prominent as to be immune to such evidence as was procured.

Our Brother's trial was accomplished very quickly, on July 1. We of his Family was not informed until days before the event, and arrived in Boston too late to aid in his defence. The trial was swift; the Captain of the pilot-boat, a mere hireling, expressed all innocence for himself, and for David gave evidence most damning.

Certain of the letters was produced, enough to indicate their treasonable content. David did not appear on his own behalf, for to do so would mean having to face, under oath, the Prosecutor's questions concerning the names of his Confederates in this venture. The Attorney for the defence, Ezekiel Hawkesworth, an excellent man, tried his best to attack the evidence and the character of those who claimed to have found it in David's possession, but he could cast but little doubt on it, and our brother was found guilty of Treason. He was hanged on the Fifteenth of July, in Fort Independence. I was a witness to the unhappy event and can declare that David presented a brave and cheerful face to the world in his last hours; he took the Lord's Supper in his cell, asked forgiveness of those he had wronged in his lifetime, and spoke movingly of his hopes of the life to come. About his confederates he remained scrupulously silent, and thus kept far better faith with them than they ever kept with him, this despite hints on the part of the Authorities that they would be willing to forego hanging if David would merely name his accomplices.

Father is much distraught over this, as he had entertained great hopes for David, and he has not been well. He will doubtless write to you in his own time, but for the moment has delegated this sad responsibility to me. He has also bade me send you the enclosed, in the hopes that you will make use of it and that the British will never have cause to forget of its existence. New England is greatly upset about the hanging, for commerce with the English is not considered a great crime here, and Madison and the Republicans are much denounced, with charges of Illuminism being revived. It may serve some good for you to know that the Authorities will never dare to put such another dupe on trial, or spring such another trap, until they can gain greater support for this foolish war. In the meantime we wish you the best. We know this news will add to the burdens of your difficult task, but rest assured that we will do what we can to support you.

A member of our Family cannot help but win honor
in any fight with the English.
God bless you.

Your loyal brother,
Jeremiah Markham

Gideon gazed blankly out the stern window into the
westering sunlight. His youngest brother David, dead at
the age of twenty-three. *Treason.* He could imagine some
Republican official watching the swaying and lifeless body
in its ring of soldiers, thinking, satisfied, *Now these damn'
stubborn Yankees will know they're at war!* And from such
news as the letter contained, and from Jeremiah's wording
in the last paragraph, Gideon knew that the family suspected what they had not quite dared to write—that David's confederates were not named at the trial because they
were Federal agents, tools of the government, *agents provo-
cateurs,* men who would not be paid unless they occasionally created a traitor to feed to their masters. Perhaps not
simply agents of the government, but of the Illuminati, desperate to bring American aid to the Revolution they had
created in France.

As the tern schooner bobbed in Mobile's little tide, Gideon felt despair swell in him. He now wondered if leaving
New England, in spite of the greater profits here, had been
a mistake. He knew his father needed him in Portsmouth,
back at the old home near the churchyard where his
mother was buried, and where David, if the military had
been persuaded to let him go, would now lie in the earth.

Gideon saw the shoreline of Mobile Bay through the
window, the strip of sand, dark trees, herons gliding, and
all at once felt a great hatred for the South rise in him, a
hatred of its manners and its pretension; hatred because he
had lost so much here—his family, his hopes, the illusions
that he was other than what he was, an outcast from God's
grace; hatred because the place was so alien in temperament and inclination. Here fortunes were easy to make: a
few slaves worked to death could outline a plantation; a
few cash crops sold to Europe could provide money to pur-

chase pirate goods in New Orleans, or slaves smuggled free of tariff by Lafitte's pirates, with which to set up new plantations or enrich the old. In New England a man struggled, whether with the implacable sea or with the stony soil; a Yankee fought endlessly with the elements and knew himself well as a result; he drew his impelling God from between the rocks of the world or dripping from the foaming brine. In the South life came easily for those who had slaves, and those who were not planters did not matter; these Southrons did not know themselves, and in their little cathedrals met a comfortable Providence who bore no resemblance to the awesome divinity New Englanders wrested from the elements.

Gideon should not have come. Maria-Anna had shown him that: they could not speak without misunderstanding and could not misunderstand without anger. He had risked his profits, and those of his backers, on a two- or three-year expedition to the West Indies, and if overtaken by misfortune, all would lose. The plan had worked for his father and uncles in 1776, the outfitting of large privateers heavily armed to cruise foreign waters for years at a time, but the world had been larger then, and the Markham brothers had had few responsibilities dragging them home. If *General Sullivan* had been lost early in its career, everyone concerned would have lost his investment. The tern schooner's backers had invested less money than they had invested in *Sullivan*; most of the money in the craft was Gideon's, but the profit would be shared fairly, and the investors would have to be paid for their wait.

The story may come back to you in some alien land, and in a manner calculated to injure either yourself or your safe prospects. Gideon should never have left for long, not even before the war when he saw David's problems beginning. When David and his younger sister Jemimah were growing, their father had been ill much of the time, and their elder brothers had been concerned with their own affairs. David had had too much of his own way, and when brought to book for his escapades, had often as not charmed his way out of difficulty. He'd been the only one of Josiah's sons who could have been called handsome;

with his unaffected grin and an infectious sparkle in his
blue eyes, it was said he could charm the Devil out of hell.
He'd been sent to Yale, as had Obadiah and Micah, but
had been expelled in his first term for running what was in
essence a gambling saloon in his rented rooms. Somehow
he'd kept it from the family for over eight months, and
when an enraged Josiah finally learned what his money
had been paying for, David gaily paid the old man back
with interest and still had enough profit from his friends
and victims to buy part interest in a tavern in York. The
magistrates had taken an interest in that tavern, and David
had sold out in a hurry, but still at a profit.

Tavernkeeping had ceased to interest him, and David
next set himself up as a gentleman farmer. But the farm
had failed, and David found new employment as a clerk;
clerking had not charmed him, and other occupations followed. All were either not to his interest, or he tired of
them quickly. He had been reported by gossip to be engaged to half a dozen girls, but he never married. No one
suggested his going to sea: that had been tried when he
was fifteen, following in the family tradition, the youngest
of five brothers all of whom had been to sea in their time
and one of whom had followed it as a profession. David
had deserted his ship—a Markham ship—two weeks out of
Portsmouth, not finding the discipline to his taste. That
had been forgiven him, as had so much else.

When Gideon left New England, it seemed David had
settled down to a steady job as an agent for merchant interests, and had good-naturedly backed Gideon's enterprise
with two hundred unexpected dollars, the money coming at
a particularly welcome time. Although the family had
never honestly expected David to turn into a sober,
staunch, pious Yankee, they'd hoped that perhaps some
stability had at last entered his life. And now this, an inglo-
rious hanging at the age of twenty-three, dying to protect
the unscrupulous men who had lured him into treason.

If he had been in New Hampshire more often when
David was growing, Gideon thought, perhaps he could
have somehow foreseen the grief to come, acted in some
measure to prevent it or at least blunt its impact. If he
could have spoken to him more often and encouraged his

better qualities, then perhaps David would not have met such a chilling end. . . .

But no. Gideon had forgotten. He could help no one; he was outcast, and better off in some distant ocean where he could no longer contaminate his family with his own encompassing iniquity. His lack of prosperity should have been a clue: the Reverend Gill, a Yale man and his father's one-legged chaplain until, late in life, he'd run off with a woman from Rhode Island and was last heard of managing a bawdy house in Providence, had always insisted that only the godly were permitted to profit in the world, and that wealth was a sign of God's favor. Gideon had always lived in poverty, or near it.

God help my family, he thought, but he knew there would be no answer and that he was exiled from the grace of heaven.

He reached into the drawer and brought out a paper-wrapped bundle, the "enclosed" that his father had insisted on sending. He tore off the wrapper and found a red cloth bundle, wrapped tightly, and heavy in his hand. "The viper banner," he breathed, recognizing it as Malachi Markham's invention, the long pendant flown from the maintops of the Revolution's Markham privateers, a golden rattlesnake on a scarlet background, fangs bared . . . "So the enemy will know us and fear us," Malachi had explained. Josiah had wanted him to fly the flag, a family tradition. Hoping he would not be ashamed to declare himself a Markham. . . .

Gideon jumped as there was a knock on the door. He carefully folded the letter, replacing it in the drawer atop the piles of unread correspondence; he let the viper banner fall in the drawer and closed it. It was time to don his public face.

"Who is it?"

"Finch Martin, sir. You said come in an hour."

An hour had passed, then, since he'd opened the desk drawer and extracted its news, the letter placed so carefully upon the pile. He had not even got to the official correspondence, nor the schooner's log or manifests.

"Come in, Mr. Martin."

Martin entered and stood respectfully in the center of

the room. Gideon rose and clasped his hands behind his back. There was work to be done, work that left no time for indulgence, even in despair. There was always work; that was an eternal lesson taught most thoroughly by the sea.

"I'm sorry about th' news, sir," Martin said. "I felt it would be best not to tell ye on deck, like. I thought th' letters would tell it best."

"You were right, Mr. Martin." He felt an overwhelming gratitude for Martin's entirely unexpected tact, that he had not been told on deck while in view of the crew or even privately in his cabin, but had been allowed the chance to absorb the news quietly, alone, before meeting others.

"Mr. Martin, ye've heard that the Lord has taken *General Sullivan*?"

"Aye. I'm sorry, Cap'n. Mr. Blake told me."

"You were to be master of her after I took this vessel. I'm sorry I have no command to give."

"Aye, sir." Martin's weathered, leathery face, its normal leer subdued, carefully gave nothing away; the eyes were neutral. It occurred to Gideon how restrained they both were, as if there were two automatons in the schooner's cabin, exchanging formalities while their operators stood at a distance. Both had received shocks: Gideon knew that Martin was disappointed, perhaps bitterly, over the loss of his command; and Martin must be equally aware that Gideon, after barely surviving a trek through the wilderness, was mourning the loss of a brother. Both were careful to keep their own sorrows from intruding upon the other's grief and spoke with the restraint of two gentlemen, barely acquainted, encountering one another on the street in the course of a busy day.

"The remaining crew of the *Sullivan* are marooned on Cuba. We must sail there as soon as possible and rescue them."

"Aye aye, Cap'n." Martin's slitted eyes still gave away nothing.

"Mr. Harris, my first on *General Sullivan*, was killed in battle with the British," Gideon went on. "Although I cannot offer you your own vessel, unless perhaps we manage to capture a suitable ship from the enemy, I would be honored, Mr. Martin, if you would stay aboard as my first officer here, or in any such capacity as you feel suits yer abilities."

Relief was apparent in Finch Martin's scarred face; he must have known that Gideon might understandably prefer to continue with the officers he had known aboard *Sullivan,* and that he might demote Martin or dismiss him altogether.

"Thankee, sir," he said "I'd like to stay on as first if I may."

"Your second will be George Willard from the *Sullivan,*" Gideon said. "He is an able and experienced man. I shall see Mr. Clowes and Mr. Allen formally tomorrow, but perhaps in the meantime it would be best to tell them privately they may expect to be demoted and allow them to leave the vessel if they wish."

"George Willard, Cap'n?" Martin asked. "He's a good man, but—some aboard might not want to take orders from anyone who's, ah, who ain't white."

"Which men might those be, Mr. Martin?" Gideon scowled.

"Perhaps I'd best not say, Cap'n," Martin said. Gideon hesitated, then decided not to press; it would be best to let anyone who objected speak for himself, and not force Martin to report his fellow officers' opinions.

"If they are not willing to serve under the officers I appoint, and obey without question, then perhaps they would be happier on another vessel," he said. "You may also tell the officers *that,* if ye please."

"Aye, sir. I'll do it."

"Ye have been drilling the men at the great guns?"

"Aye, Cap'n. We keep Captain Malachi's schedule of drill: gun drill after breakfast through the forenoon watch, then gun or sail drill after dinner through the afternoon watch. We ain't had much sail drill—th' men know their business there."

"That is a comfort. Have ye had live-powder exercise?"

Martin bit his lip. "We didn't know whether ye would wish the powder used that way, Cap'n. A few days we were becalmed off th' Bermudas we hove casks overboard and fired at 'em. But we was after a quick passage and we didn't want to spend the time maneuverin' for exercises; our instructions was to get here as quick as possible."

"Aye. Very good, Mr. Martin. Now let us go on deck and put the men through their paces. Two hours' gun drill directly they finish supper."

"Er—aye aye. They have drilled some hours this mornin', sir."

"Then they shall drill again," said Gideon. "The crew— have they shown themselves good hands?"

"Oh, aye," Martin said. "No trouble the officers couldn't handle on their own. There was one we put ashore here. He was a bumfiddler, preferred the windward passage."

"A what?" asked Gideon, puzzled.

"A buttfucker, sir," Martin said, exasperated with the niceties Gideon had demanded but couldn't comprehend. Gideon decided to overlook the lapse; he knew it was remarkable to have avoided obscenity from Martin this long.

"The word 'sodomite' will suffice, Mr. Martin," he said. "You were right to get him off the schooner. Now let us see how the men handle their drill."

The hands performed well, albeit a bit grudgingly, and Gideon was not ashamed to display them before Lieutenant Blake. Some of the crews seemed consistently sloppy, and Gideon marked them, intending to replace some of their less-efficient men with more practiced hands from the other guns. Their speed was good for four weeks' practice, although it was not so much speed as accuracy that Gideon preached. There were nine short twelve-pounders on each broadside, plus the eighteen-pound pivot gun amidships; Gideon would divide the twelve-pounders into divisions of three and train the crews to fire either singly, by division, or by full broadside at a target. Firing by divisions—it was a system pioneered by Gideon's cousin Favian aboard the *United States,* where it had done wonders; Gideon expected it to do well here. The long eighteen would always fire singly, and once Long Tom Tate became its captain, Gideon had no fear for its accuracy.

As well as the crew, Gideon watched the officers. Finch Martin worked well with the men, always vigorous, even at his age never afraid to handle a line himself in order to show another his duty, willing to praise as well as curse.

Clowes, the second, in charge of the starboard guns, was more reserved; he spoke sparingly, offering suggestions or encouragement, and Gideon noted that the hands listened to him respectfully, sensing his competence. Gideon took that as an encouraging sign.

Francis Allen, the third officer, commanded the larboard guns, and was obviously well-liked by the men who served under him. A slender, handsome young man— Gideon with a stab of pain recognized David Markham in his grace and laughing blue eyes—Allen mixed with the crew, encouraging them, slapping backs and making jokes. Yet he seemed too familiar, and the men seemed to like him too well. Allen was perhaps too fond of company and of approval. Being ship's officer was a difficult task and required a man to endure loneliness. On a ship a man could socialize only with his equals; the hands bunked and messed together, but the officers were more isolated. The captain, should he need some form of elementary human companionship, could talk to his steward; the first officer could make friends with the sailmaker or the cook. The second and third officers had no one, not even one another—for one was superior in rank, and that, unless the men were unusual, would affect the relationship for the worse. An officer, particularly a second or third officer, would live alone: they would eat alone, as they kept separate watches; they would give orders knowing they could be superseded by others, assume the blame of the crew for policies made by their superiors, and bear alone the responsibility for their own orders and their own mistakes.

Gideon suspected that perhaps Francis Allen craved not only companionship, but approval. An officer so dependent on his men's good opinion could be a bad one if his men sensed the weakness and made use of it. Gideon would keep his own counsel and watch.

"My compliments, Captain," Lieutenant Blake said as he obligingly timed with his watch the larboard guns while Gideon timed the starboard. "Your officers have drilled these men well."

"Thankee. The Lord willing, they'll do better."

"Your Finch Martin is an astonishing fellow," Blake said. "He told me stories of the Revolution—he was in the

West Indies then with your uncle. He has great respect for your family."

"I wish he were less profane."

"He *is* vulgar, but it's a wonderful kind of vulgarity, just marvelous," Blake enthused. "A link with the past, to some kind of primeval American sailor, the way our men of the sea were before the Revolution, before anything."

Gideon listened wryly; he refrained from pointing out that Blake's own father, and Gideon's too, were links with this primeval American past, that anyone over the age of forty could remember the Revolution.

"His description of your uncle," Blake said. "It was—how can I put it?—almost reverent."

Gideon looked at Blake over his watch. "Malachi Markham was a blasphemer and an adulterer," he said. "He was also a great captain, the finest in my family. His talents as a seaman were God-given, and I wish I had them; but his sins were cultivated ones that he encouraged. I pray for him often."

"You sound as if you've made a study of his life."

Gideon did not answer; he knew Blake was right. There had been something in Malachi's wayward life that had called to him, particularly in his youth. Gideon supposed that any young man, feeling the constraints placed upon him by society and religion—*for his own good,* Gideon thought, *of course*—could envy Malachi his career, the meteoric, heedless brilliant dash through the era of the Revolution. Or perhaps, Gideon thought more darkly, it was from Malachi that he had somehow inherited his own perversity, his own unnatural nature, and that explained why Malachi's froward example called to him down the generations.

The last gun captain in the starboard battery raised his fist to indicate his gun was run out and ready after its mock-loading.

"Very good," Blake admired. "Your starboard side wins again."

"But only by a few seconds. Mr. Martin, have them do it again."

Martin bawled out an order followed by a furious obscenity, then, with a glance back at Gideon, modified his language suddenly and with an obvious effort. "Dad-*blast* ye sons of . . . of *termites!* I'll work yet *bottoms* off, ye . . . *ye unnatural fellows!*"

Blake burst out laughing at Martin's restrained language, and Martin cast a resentful look over his shoulder. "You'll turn him into an angel, Captain Markham!" Blake said merrily.

"I will settle for a less perfect being," Gideon said with perfect seriousness.

Blake looked at him in surprise, but Gideon was watching the hands' drill, his watch in his hand.

The larboard gun crews won, and Gideon set the hands to mock-loading and running-out once more. The starboard crews won by a clean twenty seconds. They had won seven times out of ten; in punishment for their failure the larboard crews were forced to carry the starboard crews on their backs for a twenty-lap run around the main hatch. Gideon remembered being told of the punishment when young by old Andrew Keith: it had been one of Malachi's ideas, both to encourage the competition between the gun crews and to build up the hands' wind, which despite the hard work on a sailing ship, was often lost from lack of running or walking long distances ashore. Gideon remembered being amazed by the exercise's economy, simplicity, and effectiveness, all combined in a single neat package. He had applied the method in *General Sullivan,* and it had worked well; in the new schooner there was no reason to despair of success.

Gideon called to Martin as the panting crewmen sweated their way about the deck, their piggyback passengers shouting encouragement. Martin, a leering grin on his features, came to stand by the wheel, nodded, and said, "I'm glad ye think well of that old trick, Cap'n. I'd thought of usin' it on the voyage out, but I didn't know whether ye'd approve of this brand of foolery."

" 'Tis *useful* foolery, Mr. Martin," Gideon said. His next question drove the grin from Martin's face.

"Is there liquor aboard, Mr. Martin?" he asked.

Martin turned pale, perhaps remembering for the first

time that not only was Gideon a blue-light captain, who
passed out tracts and preached to the hands on Sundays, but
that he was a temperance captain as well.

"Aye, Cap'n. We've the usual store of rum. And th'
wardroom mess has wine."

"I will have it all off this vessel by tomorrow noon. Take
a reliable man to smash the casks with an axe, let it run
into the bilge, and pump it out. Search the crew's quarters
and get rid of any private stores. If I see a man tipsy after
tomorrow noon, I'll hold you responsible."

Martin's face was desperate. "Must it all go to waste,
Cap'n? It's good rum, not bob smith, and we paid New
England prices for it. Perhaps we can sell it ashore."

"It would hardly be worth the effort. The chief crop
around here is sugar; rum is cheap and plentiful, both a
glut on the market and a bad influence on the community's
morals. But if ye insist, Mr. Martin, ye can sell, if ye can
find a buyer before noon. At eight bells it all goes off this
vessel one way or another."

"And the officers' stores, Cap'n? They aren't schooner's
stores, they were bought by the officers themselves."

"I'll have 'em off the ship as well. We can't have the
officers drinking and the men not."

"But Cap'n!"

"Any man or officer who does not like the arrangement
may feel free to leave this vessel. That offer is continually
open."

"Captain Markham, perhaps I can interject . . ." Blake
began smoothly. Gideon turned to face him. "If the officers
would not care to dispose of their liquor or, God forbid,
heave it overboard, they may keep it in my cellar as long
as they wish, and drink it ashore whenever your schooner is
in port."

"Very well," said Gideon, hoping Blake realized he was
offering to host a debauch in his house every time the privateer touched land. "I'm sure we owe ye our thanks. Mr.
Martin, ye officers shall have until noon tomorrow."

"Ah, thankee, sir. Thankee, Lieutenant Blake."

"Mr. Martin," Gideon began, "perhaps I may be testing
the patience of the wardroom by making this request so
soon after giving my last order, but will the wardroom

mess be so good as to sell me a bottle of champagne if they have it? I have a mind to christen the schooner."

"Champagne?" Martin said, taken aback. "Aye, we have a case. For special occasions, like."

"I will just need the one bottle, thankee, Mr. Martin. Please bring it; ye may charge it to the captain."

"Charge ye, Cap'n?" Martin said hastily. "Nay, for th' christening ye may have the champagne and welcome."

"Thankee, Mr. Martin. I appreciate yer kindness. Please fetch it now; I'll christen the vessel as soon as the hands have had their fun, and then ye may give them their supper and their rum—their *last* rum."

"Aye aye, Cap'n."

Martin, muttering to himself about the infernal eccentricities of blue-light captains, withdrew. Gideon, hands clasped behind his back, watched while the last of the larboard gun crews staggered through their paces, coming to a panting halt to fling themselves on the deck, those that had breath enough to harbor resentment gazing aft with indignation, an indignation enhanced by the merriment of the starboard men, not all of whom had been gentle riders. Gideon bore their ire placidly; it was not an officer's task to care about the petty irritations of the hands unless they interfered with the running of the schooner—and the new privateer was not near that stage yet. The hands had seen their new captain come aboard; they had felt his presence immediately in an unexpected drill; they knew he intended to be master and that he would tolerate no slackness under his eye. That was as it should be. Gideon was content enough.

Martin came up from below with the bottle of champagne. "Lieutenant Blake, if ye will honor us with yer presence?" Gideon asked. He walked with Blake and Martin through the panting crew, past the mainmast into the domain of the ordinary shellback and out to the schooner's graceful, jutting bowsprit. The hands' eyes followed them; perhaps they wondered what manner of new drill Gideon would now torment them with.

Gideon walked out along the bowsprit, balancing carefully until he could see the garish, furious figurehead mounted below; he turned and faced the crew. He could see them clustered well forward, watching him carefully, not knowing yet what to make of him, wondering why he had broken caste and come forward of the mainmast.

"Men of New England!" Gideon roared, raising his voice to a hurricane shout. "Ye men have sailed on a nameless vessel to this place to find her a captain. I do not know whether it is fitting that this is so. I do know, and I appreciate, the honor conferred upon me in being the one nominated to christen her."

The men stood quietly without a murmur. Gideon doubted they were enthralled. They had probably heard such speeches before.

"I have searched in my mind for a name," Gideon continued, "and I believe I have found one. It has been shown me by this noble carving below me, the figurehead of an old and glorious Yankee privateer, said to be an image of my uncle's face; it has been shown me by the willing conduct of the officers and men, who have thus far shown themselves true Yankees; it has been shown me by the conduct of privateers and of the navy in this war, who have done so well against great odds, and who have shown themselves to be true descendants of the heroes of the last war."

He raised the bottle of champagne on high, preparing to bring it down and anoint the glaring figurehead. The crew craned their necks to get a clear view; a few climbed the shrouds.

"In the name of God Almighty," Gideon shrieked, his voice carrying over the still waters of the bay, reaching the oystermen in their boats, who straightened from their work and gazed at the schooner in surprised contemplation of the bobbing brown figure on its bowsprit, *"and in the name of the brave men of New England, I give thee thy name— I christen thee* Malachi's Revenge!"

With all his strength Gideon brought the bottle down and saw it shatter into winking shards and gushing foam on the figurehead's broad back. Martin's voice rang out, leading three cheers, and the crew raced up the shrouds as they answered, the harbor ringing with their hurrahs, the oystermen shadowing their eyes with their hands as they tried to discover what in tarnation that privateer was mak-

ing such a fuss over. Gideon returned to the deck, and
Finch Martin wrung his hand. Gideon was astonished to
see the dissipated, leering face of the first officer streaked
with tears.

"It's a good name, God bless it," Martin said *"Malachi's
Revenge*! Captain Malachi would be proud."

"I'm happy ye're pleased, Mr. Martin," Gideon said,
amazed at this not-altogether-unheralded example of Martin's surprising sentimentality. The crusty old sinner had a
weakness, and that weakness was the past. It was his own
weakness too, Gideon thought darkly.

"I have yet to thank ye properly, Mr. Martin," Gideon
said, knowing it might as well be said now, giving Martin a
chance to recover before facing the men, "for yer plan to
come up the river and find me. It is a thing many first
officers would not consider, for they would know that
they'd have their own command if their captains were
never found. For this I thank ye. I can do nothing else
now, but I will remember."

"Thankee, Cap'n, but I never—it wasn't—thankee . . ."
Martin murmured, still clutching Gideon's hand, trying
with obvious effort to reassemble his wonted, cynical exte-
rior.

"Ye may send the hands to supper, Mr. Martin," Gideon
said. "In the morning we shall work out watch and quarter
bills."

"Aye aye," Martin said, suddenly turning into the efficient, misanthropic, round-shouldered man of the sea he
had always been in Gideon's imagination. "Thankee,
Cap'n."

20

THE FRANKLIN

The supper with Blake was not a success: Gideon was too
weary to be a good host, and Blake took compassion upon
his red-rimmed eyes and haggard, sunburnt face, and left
early. Gideon collapsed into his bunk, promising himself to
finish reading his correspondence first thing in the morning,
and to answer it immediately. His sleep was dreamless and
obliterating. He did not rise until noon.

Furious at himself for giving in to sloth, and touched
with a kind of guilt that his sleep had been so all-
encompassing, that his dreams had been nonexistent and
not burdened with David or Maria-Anna or his own iniquity, he commenced his business. There was much more
than his correspondence to be read and answered: watch
and quarter bills had to be reworked and approved, and
arrangements had to be made ashore to provide enough
coffee and cocoa to replace the hands' liquor ration. Gideon knew that temperance captains were often hated, less
because most seamen considered liquor on a ship to be no
less a right than chewing tobacco, than because thrifty merchants all too often used the cause of temperance as an
excuse to save the cost of rum, and save also the cost of a
substitute. Gideon felt firmly that any privilege taken away
from the hands should be compensated for by adding another privilege, and felt that coffee twice each day and cocoa on Sundays was more than a fair exchange. The coffee
and cocoa cost more than double the cost of the rum; but
Gideon's principles warred with his thriftiness only briefly.
There would be no liquor on his schooner, and his men
would be cared for, and justly.

Martin reported by midafternoon that all the rum was

off *Malachi's Revenge*. It had been purchased, to Gideon's surprise, by the United States Navy, in the form of Lieutenant Archibald Bulloch Blake, for the use of the crew of Gunboat No. 163. He'd doubtless got a bargain price on it.

Martin also reported that during the morning's drill Clowes's starboard gun crews had shaved fifteen seconds off their previous best time, and again had been carried by the larboard crews twenty laps around the main hatch.

Gideon ate dinner as he worked. Francis Allen and the surgeon, Dr. Rivette, were sent ashore to arrange for coffee and cocoa to be brought aboard in sufficient quality and quantity. Clowes was sent ashore with the mail. Writing to his father, Gideon had been at a loss for words, knowing Josiah Markham's deep love for all his children, and knowing that Josiah would be blaming himself for not being able to prevent the series of events leading to David's hanging. Gideon's letter had been short; he knew that loquacity could not better express what needed to be said than a few heartfelt words, but still he agonized over whether the words were adequate. He wrote that he had heard the news from Jeremiah, that words could not express his sorrow, that Josiah must not blame himself, and that he was confident that David was with God. He wrote that he had named the tern schooner *Malachi's Revenge* and that they were about to leave port, heading for Cuba to rescue *Sullivan*'s crew, and that he would write later. Gideon's earlier letters from both Cuba and Mobile had detailed *General Sullivan*'s loss; it was not necessary to go into those melancholy details. He tormented himself, knowing the insufficiency of his words, and in the end, when time ran short, he sealed the letter and gave it to Grimes to post it before he changed his mind and reworked it.

He wanted to raise *Revenge*'s anchors and get out of Mobile Bay before nightfall. It was September, the time of year when hurricanes beat against the Gulf Coast, and he wanted to get clear of the land and put miles of sea room under his lee. In the Leeward Islands, he knew, the great storms were fewer; they rarely hit there with the force with which they regularly pummeled Florida, the Gulf Coast, and Cuba.

He went on deck to hear that three crewmen, unable to live the life of a sailor without their twice-daily tots of rum, had gone ashore voluntarily, without pay, and that the cocoa and coffee had been stowed properly along with the fresh water with which the beverages would be brewed. Gideon knew that the fresh water would soon be green, teeming with squirming animals; but it would be boiled and the animals killed, and the inconvenience was a small price to pay for a sober vessel.

The sun neared the western horizon. The crew seemed bewildered by the rush of events: a new captain come aboard, their liquor vanished, the schooner named, gun crews running with others piggyback, and now the privateer preparing to leave harbor, all in less than thirty hours. The new captain was a fire-eater, they all agreed.

Gideon heard the schooner hailed by a boat as he was preparing to send men to the aft capstan to bring in one of the two bowers, and as he stepped to the entry port, he was surprised to see Captain Addams of the *Prinsessa* propelling his twisted frame through the port.

"Captain Markham, I see ye're preparin' to leave port," he said, glancing about the deck, his eyes shining with undisguised admiration for the tern schooner's lines. "I'll not delay ye, but I'd be obliged if I could speak with ye privately."

"Aye," Gideon said, overcoming his own reluctance. So close to leaving the shore behind, he did not want to be reminded of *Prinsessa* or anyone who had ever been aboard her. Gideon told Finch Martin to get one anchor up and heave the other short, and then showed Addams to his cabin. He did not offer refreshment.

"I've thrown in the towel, Captain Markham," Addams said as soon as they were alone. His voice was too weary to show any great bitterness. "I've resigned as master of the *Prinsessa*. We couldn't sign on any hands, not with those Goddamn mutineers bad-mouthin' me through the town without fear of the noose. Franco can take the ship to Havana if he can get any crew. Heaven help any who sign on under that brute."

"I'm sorry," Gideon said, knowing very well what Addams would come to next.

"I'll be frank with ye, Captain," Addams said, rubbing his jaw. "I've come to look for a job."

"We have no places for officers. We have too many as it is with a new consignment entering in Cuba. Petty officers as well."

"I'd come on as able seaman," Addams said. Gideon could see hurt and desperation mingled in the man's eyes. "I can hand, reef, and steer as well as anyone, blast it!" he said defiantly. "The sea's my life, and I can't throw it away. Not after the t'gallant halliards parted and the yard fell from aloft to leave me with a crooked back for life! Not with this and these!" He showed the livid scars on his cheek, mementoes of the mutiny, and held up his hand. The nails of three fingers were missing, torn out by the roots long ago. It was a common enough seaman's injury; Gideon knew it had happened while Addams was high aloft, trying to fist ironbound canvas from the claws of an angry gale.

"Very well," Gideon said. "You may sign on. You will be treated no differently from the others."

"I wouldn't wish to be."

It seemed to Gideon that Addams was relieved, as if a great burden had been lifted from him. At first it seemed strange, for Addams was starting over, at the age of fifty, in a position he had probably last held in his teens. A penance, perhaps, for his sins, for the man he had flogged to death, and the other killed in the mutiny. But then Gideon knew that Addams was grateful for the chance to breathe a new life in the fo'c'sle, happy to be relieved from the burden of command that had tormented and broken him.

"One other thing," Gideon said. "There is no liquor aboard this vessel. Not a drop."

Addams' eyes were fired with a fierce pride. "I haven't touched liquor since the mutiny, Captain. I swear to heaven it's true."

"Very well. Have ye yer dunnage in the boat? Very good. Bring it aboard; ye can stow it later. We stand watch-and-watch aboard *Revenge*."

He brought Addams on deck and called for Clowes.

"This is Addams," he said. "He'll be in your watch."

Gideon thought he saw Addams stiffen at the mention of

his name: it had been years since he'd been anything other
than "Captain Addams," and he'd been "Mister Addams"
before that. Now the courtesies were over; he was plain
Addams, able seaman, living below decks with others who
were too busy and too low to be addressed by anything
civil.

But Addams slumped, acquiescing in his demotion, and
after that seemed not to miss the titles he had once disgraced.

The square sails were set, and the anchors hauled dripping from the bottom of the bay. Gunboat No. 163 raised
its flags and gave three cheers that were answered by privateers manning the shrouds. *Malachi's Revenge* turned its
fierce Cossack figurehead toward the sea, and as the tern
schooner set its big fore-and-aft sails and turned proudly
from the land, the setting sun dyed the sails the color of
blood. Gideon, standing by the wheel, forced himself not to
look back.

The privateer did not exit Mobile Bay that night. It was
dark before they neared Fort Bowyer, guarding from its
sandspit the main entrance to the bay, and the tide had
turned. The Spanish pilot refused to take them out; he
claimed it was dangerous and that he'd been working for
two days without a rest, but Gideon suspected the man
wanted another free supper and breakfast at the privateer's
expense. *Malachi's Revenge* lay anchored off Mobile Point,
and the pilot messed with the crew, blithely ignoring another vessel, half-seen in the dark, hove-to on the other
side of the point, madly firing guns and lighting false fires
to attract the attention of a pilot. Eventually the other vessel, whatever it was, gave up its attempt and anchored as
well.

Gideon, glorying in the smell of the sea, cut himself
chewing tobacco and paced along the deck, postponing for
the moment his supper. The short journey by water had
been exhilarating; the tern schooner had ridden beautifully
through the water, cutting it neatly, leaving less than a
ship's length of wake behind her. A large, foaming wake,
however impressive it might look to landsmen, was the
sign of a bad sailer and an inefficient hull; and Gideon was

rightly proud of the ease with which *Revenge* had passed through its element.

He knew that he belonged here, living in monastic isolation aboard a Yankee vessel, and not on the land with its complications and ambiguities, with its sophisticated inhabitants, miserable slaves, its politics, falsehoods, and backwater wars. Only the sea could provide what he craved and what he knew was right for him: the cherished seclusion, the longed-for solitude, the calculated loneliness.

A boat had pulled out from Fort Bowyer and now lay off the entry port, calling for the captain. Fort Bowyer's commandant, Captain Lockwood, requested the pleasure of Gideon and his officers at supper. The captain of the privateer *Fränklin*, anchored while waiting for a pilot on the seaward side of the bar, was also invited.

So there was another privateer operating within the Gulf, carrying newspapers, perhaps mail, from home. Refusing Lockwood's invitation would be discourteous, particularly since Fort Bowyer had provided assistance during the *Prinsessa* mutiny, and perhaps still had the mutineers enrolled in the garrison's ranks. But Gideon had no wish to step ashore; it would be torture to leave the schooner for a second. Resolving not to stay long, Gideon fetched his sword and good coat, and lowered himself into the pitching boat. In the stern sheets, feeling Martin and Clowes jostling against him with the pitch of the boat, he cast a look back at *Revenge* and found her beautiful, pitching slowly on the quiet, dark sea, her rigging gleaming silver in the moonlight.

The fort was an old Spanish construction, little more than an earthen dugout, armed with twenty ancient, small Spanish guns. Captain Lockwood was a lean, tall man of about sixty, with a weathered face like a scarred tomahawk and with surprisingly merry eyes. He set a good table and was visibly disappointed that Gideon declined to drink his wine. Less than twelve hours after he'd had the hands' liquor off *Malachi's Revenge,* Gideon was not going to appear on her decks with wine on his breath.

The officers of the *Franklin* were a surprise: Gideon had assumed from the name that the ship was American, perhaps from Pennsylvania, but found to his surprise that she was French. French privateers had occasionally called at American ports during the European war and had tried to dispose of prizes there; but they had drawn the unwelcome attentions of the Royal Navy, and the practice had been discouraged until Congress declared war. Now American and French privateers shared one another's harbors regularly.

Franklin's captain, Julien Fontenoy, was very young, perhaps twenty-five. He spoke English well, carried himself dashingly, and clearly could be most charming when he wanted to; but Gideon considered himself immune from such practice. Fontenoy did not carry a sword. Rather, dangling from his belt were a series of steel rods connected by chain, an old seaman's weapon he called a *fléau brisé*, or broken flail; Gideon had seen specimens in New England called "fighting irons."

According to Fontenoy his father had been a merchant on the island of Mauritius in the Indian Ocean. His family had long been involved in privateering, harassing British ships of the East India trade. Fontenoy had been at sea all his life. When the British had taken Mauritius a few years before, Fontenoy had been held prisoner for three years, and was then exchanged and returned to France. His father had died in the meantime, leaving him with a little money which he invested in a privateer snow of ten guns, the *Franklin*.

Gideon had his doubts about Fontenoy's story: the man was too handsome to have been at sea all those years; Gideon knew well how the hard life would cut into a man's looks.

Fontenoy's lieutenant, a scowling, dark-browed man addressed as Aristide, spoke to no one, glared at everyone, and drank much wine. Gideon suspected it was Aristide, rather than Fontenoy, who had provided the expertise necessary to manage a successful privateer.

Franklin had until recently sailed from the Chesapeake, since all the French West Indian islands had been taken by the enemy. Fontenoy's news was uniformly gloomy, of Napoleon's indecisive battles in Germany and of Austria's entering the war against France, of American campaigns against Canada that went nowhere, of a British blockade tightening on southern American ports, and of an administration in Washington hopelessly entangled in well-intentioned, ill-managed schemes for victory. *Franklin* had slipped out of the Chesapeake two weeks before, certain that any further privateering from the Southern ports would be dangerous, and that if the privateer wasn't caught, then its prizes almost certainly would be.

Gideon secretly rejoiced at the news of Napoleon's disappointments. He had been betrayed by the French authorities once, and lost his wife and child; and he felt that the United States had no business interfering in what was essentially a European war between two indistinguishable tyrannies. Now another score had been laid to the war's account: the loss of his headstrong brother, hanged for his beliefs. The war was foolish, but Gideon would fight it, practicing his trade and sailing upon the breast of the rolling sea the sweetest tern schooner ever built. His heart warmed as he thought of *Malachi's Revenge*. The war was evil, but his privateer was exquisite; and Gideon knew that when the time came to fight, he would be fighting for the schooner and for his family, not for James Madison and his bungled policies.

Gideon finished his supper without speaking to the Frenchmen except for the obligatory polite civilities, toasts to one another's health, to the president, and to the emperor. Gideon received the distinct understanding from the carelessness with which Fontenoy received the latter toast that the Frenchman didn't care a brass button for Bonaparte or his entire family.

After supper Gideon excused himself on the grounds of unfinished work aboard *Revenge*; he urged his officers to stay as long as they wished. Lockwood was reluctant to see him go, but cheered at the thought that Gideon would probably return with prizes, complete with British crews that might somehow be persuaded to join his garrison rather than rot in a malaria-ridden gaol.

Fontenoy, surrounded by infantry officers, preceded Gideon out of the mess; the Frenchman had been persuaded to demonstrate the uses of the *fléau brisé* and Lockwood had announced that Gideon would not be allowed to return to his vessel unless he'd first seen Fontenoy's exhibition. Gideon, grudging the Frenchman every minute spent away from *Malachi's Revenge,* watched disapproving from a distance as Fontenoy stripped off his coat and shook the flail out to its full length.

In New England the fighting irons were considered antiques; they had been a shipboard weapon at one time, and a few Revolutionary privateers boasted of wielding them, but their use had died out. It was still a fearsome thing, however. Fontenoy's version consisted of four short rods of steel strung together with short lengths of steel chain, and was perhaps three feet long altogether.

The army officers had never seen such a thing or ever heard of it. Fontenoy, who claimed to have learned the art of its use in Mauritius from an old, respected merchant who had once been a Red Sea pirate, was cheerfully willing to demonstrate. He put the iron through its paces: swinging it, *en garde,* in a figure-eight pattern in front of him, then swiftly bringing the flail in whistling circles from in front to over his head and behind his back, dealing with half a dozen imaginary enemies at once. Gideon knew that the velocity of that ultimate piece of steel at the end of the weapon was horrifying—it could split a man's head as easily as a child could crush a grape. In spite of himself Gideon was impressed by the young Frenchman's dexterity. Yet he could see why the use of the weapon had declined. Shipboard fighting required agility to move among the tangle of rigging, between the guns, pumps, training tackles, bodies, and other impedimenta that crowded the decks. Close-packed mobs of men would rush into one another, smashing mercilessly with cutlass and pike. A man waving a *fléau brisé* carelessly in a boarding melee could easily do as much damage to his own side as to the enemy; he could even hit himself or get his weapon tangled in the rigging, leaving himself helpless.

His audience applauded as Fontenoy concluded his demonstration, and a few officers, with their commandant's permission, began stripping off their blue dress coats in order to practice with the fearsome thing. The French lieutenant, Aristide, was nowhere to be seen: presumably he had remained in the mess with his wine bottle. Gideon made his farewells to Captain Lockwood and to Fontenoy, bowing when he caught the Frenchman's eye.

"One moment, Captain Markham, please," Fontenoy called after him. Gideon waited for the French privateer, impatient to be aboard his tern schooner.

"I have a proposition, sir, in which you might be interested," Fontenoy said. His English was polished and bore the upper-class accents of Britain. Clearly his imprisonment had been no hardship.

"We are both privateers working against the English," Fontenoy said. "Perhaps we could cruise together and gather more ships."

Gideon had expected the offer. No doubt *Franklin* would enjoy working in partnership with *Malachi's Revenge,* a better, faster, and more heavily armed vessel: the Yankee schooner would do most of the work, and *Franklin* receive fifty percent of the profits.

"I'm leaving harbor tomorrow morning," Gideon said. "I can't wait."

"If you could delay another twenty-four hours while *Franklin* takes on water and stores. We gentlemen of fortune must stick together."

Gentleman of fortune: the old code words for pirate. Gideon felt a weary distaste rise within him. "I would not delay another minute," he said. "If the pilot had not refused to take us out, we would be on the seas tonight. We must rescue some American sailors marooned in the Caribbean."

"Yes?" Fontenoy asked in surprise. "Where?"

Gideon faced him. Fontenoy's expression was too eager, too ingenuous.

"Tortuga," he lied.

"Perhaps we could rendezvous at sea. Where do you expect to cruise?"

"Guiana, down the coast to the River Plate," Gideon said, another lie.

"Perhaps I shall see you there."

"Good night, sir. I shall send the pilot aboard as soon as we have done with him."

"Thank you, Captain Markham. Your servant."

"Servant, sir."

The stern cabin of the tern schooner glowed invitingly through its windows. *Home,* Gideon thought as he stepped aboard. In spite of himself he glanced toward Mobile, only twenty-five miles to the north, and could see nothing there, dark water only, not even the lights of the town reflecting on the bellies of clouds.

Gideon descended the companionway. Tomorrow he would be at sea, he thought, and gratefully leave the land far behind.

21

1810

Gideon, in blackest mourning, stood facing the sea, the wind gusting in his face; below him he could hear the Atlantic crashing against the cliff, but he stood back from the edge and couldn't see the gray swell breaking into foam. "I'm buying a farm," David Markham said. "Jeconiah Gilbert's old place, a hundred twenty acres. I'm going to call it Redlands."

The laughter of their nephews and nieces floated up toward them from the meadow behind. Gideon turned, saw David standing behind him in his shirt, a straw in his teeth; beyond David were the rest of the family, their father Josiah, Josiah's children Obadiah, Jeremiah, Abigail, and Jemimah—all but Micah in New York—all their assorted spouses and children, enjoying the last hour of their daylong summer outing.

"Does father know?" Gideon asked.

David plucked the straw from between his teeth and tossed it casually into the air, letting the wind take it, spinning, briefly airborne . . . "I haven't told him yet," he said.

"Jeconiah hasn't made a success of the place," Gideon said and turned to face the sea. "I'd think twice."

"Jeconiah's old. There's nothing wrong at Redlands that a young master won't cure."

"Think a third time, Davey." *Redlands,* he thought. *He's named the place. That's a bad sign. David doesn't have it in him to be that brand of farmer. . . .*

"I will."

The surf boomed far below. Far out to sea, twenty miles at least, a fleck of white on the horizon showed a distant ship making its landfall.

"You're leaving next week, Gideon?"

"Aye. I'm taking the new *General Sullivan* to the Chesapeake, then to Spain with a cargo of wheat."

They turned as they heard a voice calling David's name. It was their youngest sister Jemimah, a slim, laughing girl of sixteen, four years younger than David. She ran barefoot to join them, taking David's hand.

"Will you raise horses at Redlands, like Uncle Jehu?" she asked. David's amused blue eyes crossed with Gideon's solemn gaze.

"You've made up your mind, haven't ye, Davey?" Gideon asked.

David laughed, a joyous, infectious sound. Jemimah looked at her brother worshipfully.

"I've signed the papers," David said. "Redlands is mine. Jemmie, let's go look at the rocks yonder."

Gideon watched as David and Jemimah walked to the edge of the cliff, peering down sixty feet into the breaking, foaming sea. "Come on, Jemmie. Let's run and see if we fall." David turned and began to run along the cliff edge, his booted feet coming perilously close to the brink; Jemimah, laughing, followed after, her skirts swishing in the wind. They dared oblivion as they ran, brave and surefooted children, their profiles sharp against the blue eternity behind them.

Davey, don't break Father's heart, Gideon almost called out after him; but he knew how it would sound, and could see already the good-humored, quizzical, uncomprehending smile on David's face and hear the dismissing laugh. *Me? You must be joking, Gideon*. And Jemimah would grow angry in defense of her brother, and there would be a fight.

Gideon kept silent, sweltering in his mourning clothes, hearing his siblings' laughter intermingled, seeing them dance on the cliff edge, dizzy with the sun and summer. *Keep them happy*, Gideon prayed. *Keep them charmed. Let them never stop laughing*. Heartsick, he turned from the sight of the sea and walked, a black, solemn shadow, back to his family.

22

RETURN TO CUBA

"Oh leave her, Johnny! Leave her!
"Two hundred men, hand, reef, and steer!
"Leave her, Johnny! Leave her!
"Aboard our schooner privateer!
"Leave her, Johnny! Leave her!"

The chantyman sang out in a clear tenor, and the hands bellowed the choruses, coordinating their muscles into two hauls that brought the fore-topsail yard up from its lifts. Gideon watched contentedly from the quarterdeck. The loosed canvas roared. Black-eyed George Willard, the Gay Head Indian, supervised the hauling line of men, nodding his head to the choruses.

Don Esteban de Velasco y Anaquito bowed farewell to Gideon, then descended to his slave-manned scow through the entry port. Gideon watched the short Spaniard go with a kind of affection. For over a month Velasco had kept *General Sullivan*'s survivors hidden on his plantation grounds; he had fed them and worked them like dogs building a new stable and a cane mill; he had bribed the authorities to look the other way, and when a return of the British squadron had brought a landing party of marines to search the neighborhood, Velasco had kept the privateers well hidden, and eventually convinced an angry Irish peer that his quarry had sailed away to Havana in boats. Gideon had paid for these services, but he had found the price reasonable.

Malachi's Revenge had shaped up well during its five-day passage to Cuba; while there had been no enemies sighted, the crew had been drilled incessantly, mainly at the guns, and, after a few changes in personnel had been made, had improved daily. Their sail drill had been excellent from the start—over two thirds of the crew were prime seamen—and could stand little improvement. Now, with the addition of *General Sullivan*'s forty-plus survivors, the percentage of experienced hands would be increased. Given enough sea-room Gideon wouldn't hesitate to take *Revenge* against any British sloop of war, or even a small frigate.

> "Oh leave her, Johnny! Leave her!
> *"Our captain, he's so full of fun!*
> "Leave her, Johnny! Leave her!
> *"Gives us coffee to drink, but never rum*!
> "Oh leave her, Johnny! Leave her!"

Gideon looked sharply at the chantyman on that verse, but the man had turned his head away, though there seemed, to Gideon's eye, to be a grin even on the back of it. Gideon cleared his throat and turned to watch Velasco being rowed to shore. The improvised lyrics of the chanties were traditionally a way of letting the hands express their resentments, and as long as no outright mutinous thought was put forward, Gideon was willing to consider it healthy. He tried to smile, to show his lack of displeasure, but the smile felt as artificial as the good humor it was meant to express, and he gave it up.

"Anchor's hove short, Cap'n."

"Weigh anchor, Mr. Martin."

"Weigh anchor, aye aye."

Malachi's Revenge lurched as the anchor broke free from the bay's bottom. Gideon would have preferred to have hosted Velasco on board for a good supper and a concert by the schooner's band, but he had lost a vessel in that bay once and had no intention of lingering in so vulnerable a location again. The first tentative touch of the land breeze was filling the square topsails, and the tide had already turned. There should be enough water over the bar to bring the schooner out safely.

Tomorrow there would be a live-powder exercise, the guns firing by division at bobbing targets, a ten-dollar prize to be split by the gun crew that first demolished the floating cask. Gideon was anxious to see what difference the new flint gunlocks would make. The privateer would no longer have to set off its cannon with smouldering slow matches held in the teeth of the linstocks, but instead with a sharp jerk on a lanyard: the improvement was said to make it far more likely that a gun would go off when it was supposed to. The innovation was one that, as yet, was not even used by the American Navy; though the British had been using flint gunlocks at least since the latter days of the Revolution.

Long Tom Tate, now amidships, caressing his long eighteen-pounder with delighted hands, would pick and choose his own targets: probably, to judge from past practice, the aiming points would be bits of scrap wood from carpenter's stores, targets most of the crew would be lucky to see, let alone hit. Tate would hit them regularly, perhaps one time in three once he knew his gun well enough, and the rest of the time would come close.

Malachi's Revenge made its way into the gathering dark, sliding effortlessly over the bar. From a standing start, all sails furled, *Revenge* had got both anchors up, set all six square sails, jib, and spanker, and crossed the bar, all in something less than thirty-three minutes by Gideon's pocket watch. With the reinforcements from ashore there were in excess of two hundred fifty men aboard, enough to man both capstans while men aloft threw the gaskets off the sails; and while those men descended the shrouds, yet others manned the halliards and raised the yards to fill the canvas. The huge crew, rather more than would be needed even in combat, made for crowding below, but fortunately they were cruising the tropics and the off-duty watch could sleep on deck if necessary. *Malachi's Revenge* was standing watch-and-watch, alternating four hours on and four off, even though the schooner had enough men to work three watches—all simply because there was not enough room below for two thirds of the crew to swing a hammock.

Soon, when Gideon was among the Virgin Islands, he

hoped to decrease that overcrowding by assigning prize crews to his captures. Until then, the hands would have to get used to living in close quarters.

As the tern schooner began to pitch on the ocean swell, and the fore-and-aft sails were set to heel her lee rail nearer to the spray and foam, Gideon cast a somber look back into the bay: *General Sullivan's* forlorn topmasts were still visible above the water, flying tatters of flags, the last remnants of her defiance. *Let them fly until she rots,* Gideon thought, *and the sea take her proud bones. She died well and with honor. Let her rest in peace in her element until perhaps the Lord raises her, and all other lost ships as well as the men who sailed them, on the final Day.*

For three days the winds baffled them, blowing light and contrary from all points of the compass; the sea itself was choppy and confused. The days were spent in drills, Gideon teaching the gunners to fire in three-gun sections. Francis Allen, the fourth officer, remained convivial. He seemed to thoroughly enjoy his work and the companionship, but his gun consistently lagged behind the performance of Clowes's starboard battery. Switching personnel from one gun to the other did not seem to improve the performance of the battery as a whole. Gideon watched, made his judgements, and kept them to himself.

The gunnery was good for all that. Soon floating targets were consistently demolished, at least after Thomas Tate showed the hands a few of his tricks. Timing was a major part of Tate's secret. To fire high, in order to hit masts and spars, gunners had traditionally been taught to fire "on the up roll," when the surge of the sea tilted the guns upward; likewise, in order to shoot low into enemy hulls the gunners had been taught to wait until the schooner was rolling into a trough and the guns angled downward. This was not the best option, Tate thought, particularly for firing into hulls. The gun captains should wait until the schooner was just beginning its slide downward, while it was still hovering on the edge of a crest: it was then that the hull was at its most stable and the shot most likely to go where is was aimed. The new flint gunlocks themselves improved accuracy, making it much more likely a gun would go off when it was supposed to, and Tate, who had never used them, was enthusiastic. But Gideon, nevertheless, kept slow matches burning in the sand tubs during practice to use in case the flint locks missed fire.

On the third night the barometer began an alarming slide, and a tall, gray swell appeared from the east, rampaging over the confused waves raised by the continually baffling winds. Gideon set as much sail as he dared, doubled the lookouts, and used every contrary gust to claw eastward. Haiti, with its blood feuds and pirate picaroons ready to row their galleys out against the vessels of any nation, was under his lee, and he wanted to get as much sea-room as possible, knowing the picaroons would kill any man spared by the merciless coast. The stars were dimmed by clouds and soon vanished; scud whipped over the bulwarks. Gideon doubled the helmsmen, rigged safety lines, and furled the square sails. The big square foreyard was lowered on its jackstay, and the other square yards brought down and lashed with the foreyard securely on deck. The barometer continued to plummet. The light winds continued, gusting from all points of the compass, but Gideon knew they would not last long. When the eastern horizon was suddenly lit with lightning, revealing the dark descending storm, Gideon reefed down the fore-and-aft sails and prepared to take *Malachi's Revenge* into the teeth of a September hurricane.

The storm had formed a week or so before within the curve of the Windward Islands, at fifteen degrees north latitude. Heading northwest at a steady rate of fifteen miles per hour, the cyclonic whirl expanded from a fifty-mile diameter to a diameter of more than a hundred thirty miles with an interior velocity of ninety miles per hour and greater. The storm had crossed Latitude Eighteen Degrees the day before, dumping ten inches of rain on the Virgin Islands and taking a backhand swipe at the eastern coastline of Puerto Rico. The hurricane continued on course, a little of its force dissipated by its brush with the islands, heading for the Bahamas and Florida. *Malachi's Revenge* would not actually endure the full force of the storm; the hurricane's center would pass fifty miles to the north. But cyclonic winds of greater than fifty miles per hour would

strike the tern schooner head-on, endeavoring to drive the
vessel onto Haiti's shore, where the inhabitants had always
proved more deadly than its shoals.

Gideon knew it would be dangerous; any storm was, for
the oversparred schooner was built for speed, not strength,
was top-heavy in high winds, and would perhaps be in danger of rolling onto her beam-ends even after Gideon had
sent down most of her yards. The hurricane at first came
gently, a mile breath of wind from the east, steadying the
schooner on the starboard tack; and then with a wail and a
shivering clap of lightning that outlined the schooner's
dark masts against a swirling mass of cloud, the storm
shrieked through the rigging while a small mountain of water, pushed before the storm by the great winds, smashed
itself into foam against *Revenge*'s bow. The flush deck
filled with water; the helmsmen, waist-deep, fought the unsheltered wheel. Gideon clung to his mooring lines and
gasped for air. And though the schooner's head rose to
each swelling wave, and though the lee rail was submerged
by the great weight of wind pushing her over, she still rode
well, and her rudder answered.

They fought the storm through dawn, which simply
brought more sea and wind. The helmsmen worked half-
hour turns at the wheel, unsheltered, battered by the unbroken sea. They ended their duty exhausted, their palms
dripping blood. One helmsman was sent below with a shattered arm, caught in the wheel like the limb of one of the
Inquisition's heretics; and Gideon sent men below to the relieving tackles, hoping to ease in some measure the helmsmen's burden. At one point through the spray and foam
Gideon thought he saw the twisted form of Addams, late
ship's captain, taking his turn at the wheel and bravely fighting the sea. The watches came and went, but Gideon stayed
on deck, his body wet and numbed, his hands gashed whitely,
bloodlessly, as they clung to the safety lines. He fought the
sea with his schooner, watching the water break over the
bravely rising stem and sweep aft to smash against the
double-lashed cannon in their rows and the four helmsmen
clinging to the spokes of the wheel. The winds began to
moderate late in the day, and Finch Martin, bringing Gideon a cup of coffee more than two thirds emptied by the

howling wind, shouted into Gideon's ear that the barometer, although still low, had begun to rise.

Enough. There was room enough under the schooner's lee, so Gideon sent men out along the bowsprit, almost drowning themselves as they brought in the storm jib; the foresail was furled snugly, and the *Revenge* hove to to ride out the storm. She came smartly head-to-wind, her lee rail, pouring water, rising from the sea; the sickening, cork-screw lurch of the close-hauled schooner changed to a manic pitch as she rode each advancing wave. Gideon tried to untie himself from his safety lines but found his hands incapable; his helpless gestures brought one of the watch to fumble helplessly with the knots and then in frustration to bring out his knife and cut them. Gideon staggered down the aft scuttle, seawater spilling from his boots, the sea spilling down the scuttle after him, a last pursuit down the neck of his sou'wester, until he shut the scuttle and staggered for his cabin.

His cabin was strangely untouched; it pitched like the rocker-arm of a Trevethick engine, but it was perhaps the driest place on board. His sodden sou'wester was pitched into a closet—no point in trying to dry it—along with his wet clothes. Grimes brought him a miraculous cup of cocoa and was gone before Gideon could take note that it was laced with rum and scold him, or even wonder how Grimes had kept the officer's galley fires alight to make the cocoa. Too tired to pursue the matter, Gideon drank it off and then, on his knees by his bunk, breathed a heartfelt prayer of thanksgiving for the schooner's deliverance and for Stanhope's genius in building a Yankee schooner that resisted being flung on its beam-ends in a high wind. The bed was cold, but warmed swiftly

There was a sunrise the next morning, rising clear and without the red stain that might mean another storm. The wind was backing to north by east and, though brisk, was no longer a threat. The galley fires were relit; sodden hammocks were strung from the shrouds to dry. After a hot breakfast Gideon had no sooner set foot upon the storm-battered deck than the lookout announced a sail to the south. Upon investigation it proved to be a British brig—and *Revenge*'s first prize.

23

CONVOY IN SIGHT

In the next two days *Malachi's Revenge* swept through the Virgin Islands like the vengeful ghost of the hurricane that had already laid much of the islands to waste. The Danish Virgins had been captured by the British during the course of the long European war, as had every other West Indian island belonging to Napoleon or his continental allies; and as Gideon swept up coasters with Danish as well as British crews, and put his own men aboard, or burned them, or emptied their holds into his own and returned the hollow vessels to the enemy along with his prisoners, he felt confident he was doing harm to the British cause, even if the immediate sight was of some poor black man weeping as his coaster, his only means of income, was set alight by stern Yankee torches.

Twelve vessels were taken, but only four were worth sending home; the rest were burned or sent to Road Town as cartels, manned by released prisoners. The little fleet of four prizes was sent to Mobile under command of fourth officer Francis Allen, who was delighted to command a set of coasting craft on the short, glorious run to port, and who forsook his duties with the larboard battery without regret. George Willard took his place at the guns, and within two days, during which the tern schooner swept from the Virgins toward the Windward Islands, Willard had whipped them into shape, and any sadness felt by the hands at the loss of a sympathetic officer was soon assuaged by the joyful and unaccustomed experience of being carried piggyback around the main hatch by the disgruntled starboard gun crews.

There were somewhere over two hundred crewmen left, and the black privateer scudded onward over the seas. Flying fish sped before *Malachi's Revenge* as she broad-reached through the trade winds; and other, bigger fish, albacore and bonito, pursued the flying fish and were caught by the old seaman's expedient of hanging on the bowsprit and dangling above the water a stout hook baited with an old white rag. Gideon fussed with the canvas wind sails set up over the companionways, designed to funnel the breeze below to the berth deck; Gideon intended to have a healthy schooner or know the reason why.

Here on the decks of his privateer Gideon felt vigorous and confident as he watched his men drill at the guns and the sails, and occupied himself keeping *Revenge* dry, scrubbed down, ventilated, and healthy. He had brought her safely through a hurricane; he had cut a terrifying swath through an enemy archipelago and vanished out to sea again, and there would be no advance warning when he appeared among the Windward Islands, cutting out craft from Martinique and St. Vincent and the Grenadines, and then vanishing over the horizon to strike again at unwarned enemy vessels. The confusions that had beset him on land were almost forgotten here at sea, where he could feel the Almighty's creation heaving the schooner under his feet and blowing fresh into his face. What did the pitiful landsmen know of the great Jehovah, whose terrors and mercies were married so conspicuously on the face of the deep?

Here Gideon knew he was best employed, at sea, where he could find constant occupation working with drills and canvas ventilators, bringing *Revenge* up to the finest pitch of efficiency, its crew skillful, its rigging taut and cared for, its officers knowing their business. He knew that he himself was perverse and wayward, but here it mattered little so long as he drove himself to perform his daily tasks and strove to hide his pernicious iniquity. Perhaps he could hope for the mercy of his God, if the Lord judged by results and not by innate corruption. He felt he must strive to overcome, work to better himself; Gideon still prayed daily though he knew it was a futile hope that his entreaties would ever touch the ear of God. These were functions that must be performed if he hoped to preserve the essence of his own personality against the strength of the sudden revelation of his own nature.

When he thought of Maria-Anna a shadow of the old turmoil returned: he knew not what to think. She had rejected his offer to correct the moral imbalance between them, and he still found himself baffled by that inconceivable response. Was she as depraved as he, corrupted by living in the slave-ruined South; or had she perhaps recognized his own deranged nature, and rejected him for that reason? But still through his bafflement he remembered her on *Prinsessa*'s deck, carrying her pistol; or hatless in the cane field, her cheek smeared with resin, her eyes glowing. He remembered that shot on the riverbank that had perhaps saved his life and her gallant insistence that they remain for MacDonald when their own escape was assured. Most of all he remembered her that final night, the feeling of her arms pinioning his body to hers as she cried in wild joy beneath the glowing stars. He could not repent that act and so had forfeited his place among the elect. Perhaps one day repentance would come. Until then Gideon would do his daily tasks and hope to serve the Lord as a privateer.

The tern schooner heeled with the wind; flying fish soared ahead of the fierce Cossack figurehead. The men had been sent to their noon meal, grouped about the common pots, fishing for boiled meat and vegetables with their knives. Gideon paced the deck, sipping his coffee. He would eat when the hands were done.

"*Sail ho!*" shrieked a lookout. "Dead to wind'ard! No, bejesus, three sail! Three sail!"

Gideon looked aloft in surprise, feeling coffee dribbling down his chin. Annoyed, he dabbed with his handkerchief, threw the contents of the coffee cup to leeward, and snatched a glass from the rack. No sign of any sail from the deck, but that was not surprising. On a clear day a sharp-eyed lookout from his vantage point could see well over twenty miles.

"Haul yer wind," Gideon told the helmsman. "Put her on the larboard tack. Hands to braces and sheets!"

Revenge rocked as she came into the wind, the breeze lifting her square sails. George Willard was sent aloft with a glass to report on the sighting as the hands returned to their dinner, and Gideon requested another cup of coffee.

Willard's report was not shouted down from the masthead; he slung the telescope over his shoulder by its strap and rode down to the deck on a backstay, a swifter journey than was possible via the shrouds.

"It's a convoy, Captain, bearing a little north of east," Willard reported, his black eyes fixed unblinkingly on Gideon's face. "At least fifteen sail, but they're straggled out and there might be more over the horizon."

"Praise God," Gideon breathed, feeling exultation rise in him. British merchant vessels, if wise, traveled in convoy for fear of privateers, and were escorted by warships. But *Malachi's Revenge* could run rings around any British warship built. And to Gideon convoys simply meant a lot of targets together, where he could snap them up at once instead of having to catch them one at a time.

"Call Mr. Martin, and inform him," Gideon told Willard. "We'll have gun drill normally after dinner."

Gideon felt anticipation rushing through him: *a British convoy*. It would be an auspicious start to the new privateer's career; with the Almighty's help he'd have ten prizes at least.

The mess tables were slung up on the beams and the crew came up on deck, curious, peering toward the windward horizon with their hands shading their brows. They were set to gun drill, preserving the normal routine; from the deck there was no sign of the enemy. The lookout had been sharp and had earned himself a ten-dollar bonus.

Finch Martin and Michael Clowes came on deck from the wardroom; each took a glass from the rack and peered to windward. "Poxed if I can see it," Martin growled.

"Stations for gun drill, gentlemen," Gideon reminded them, and with looks of resignation they returned their telescopes to the rack. As the seamen sweated in the sun, Gideon turned his mind to the convoy, his mind churning with calculation. The trade wind at the moment was a brisk northeast by north as far as he could tell, and the convoy was heading, by Willard's estimation, a little north of east. They were close-hauled on the larboard tack, heading—most likely—for Antigua. Antigua held the British Leeward Islands Station: they would be able to meet other convoys there, acquire larger escort, and form into one of the big transatlantic convoys heading for the chops of the

Channel. It was late in the season for homeward-bound convoys—most got out of the Caribbean by June at the latest, to avoid the late summer hurricanes—but perhaps they had been delayed in their port of origin—probably Port Royal in Jamaica—by bad weather, rumors of American privateers, or perhaps by lack of escort.

The British had systematized their escort routine: they would have at least two escorts with a convoy this size. Usually they'd form their convoys in line ahead, one ship behind the other. One escort—the "van ship," in the jargon—would lead, keeping station at the head of the line and setting the pace, signalling any changes of course to the vessels following and keeping a sharp lookout for trouble ahead. A second escort—the "bulldog"—stayed near the rear of the convoy, nagging the slower ships to keep station, even towing the duller sailers if necessary. Other escorts, if there were more than two, might be anywhere. It was heartbreaking work, Gideon knew; British merchant masters were notoriously independent, kept bad station and worse lookout, and since the press kept them from having efficient crews, they were always ready to blame the navy if things went wrong. The possibility of American privateers, or even the sudden appearance of the giant Humphreys frigates like *Constitution* or *President*, would not make the job any easier.

Gideon intended to make the escorts' job downright impossible.

As the men toiled at the guns, their sweat dotting the deck, white flecks gradually appeared above the horizon—enemy topsails. *Revenge* tacked, and Gideon peered at them through his spyglass. One of the enemy ships seemed too smart to be a merchant vessel; its yards were trimmed and fanned expertly, its topsails cut to a *t*: a ship-rigged vessel, a sloop of war or small frigate. Even as he watched, signal flags ran up the halliards, colorful dots against the blue of the sky and the yellowing sails. From upwind came the rumble of signal guns, fired to call attention to the escort's signals. Gideon lowered his telescope, feeling satisfaction spreading through him, a kind of anticipation of triumph to come. Soon he would see the enemy's full strength, and then he would know how to act.

Malachi's Revenge tacked again. More topsails rose above the horizon. The lookouts counted nineteen altogether. They seemed thoroughly alarmed, and attempted to straggle into some kind of formation. There was no need for the raising of flags or any necessity for the formalities of identification: *Revenge*'s lean hull, its awesome spread of canvas, its precipitously raked masts could only be those of an American privateer.

Another escort—another ship-rigged vessel, sloop of war or small frigate—had been at the head of the enemy line, but had worn out of position and now hastened downwind to reinforce the bulldog at the tail of the line, where Gideon was most likely to strike. More signals, more guns. Straining through his glass, Gideon could not discern more than two escorts.

Gideon watched the blue spaces between the bulldog's masts shorten, then disappear. She was wearing ship, coming down the wind to pursue the privateer. Plans flickered through Gideon's mind. . . . He heard the rumble of gun carriages as the train tackles were hauled in, followed by the commands of a simulated broadside.

"Belay there!" Gideon decided. "Halliards and braces! Stand by the sheets! We're going to wear her!"

The hands leaped to their stations, clearly curious, and Finch Martin looked at Gideon appraisingly: there was no reason to wear the schooner unless they intended to run. Gideon approached Martin, aware of the eyes of the helmsman.

"We're going to let 'em see an uncontrolled gybe, Mr. Martin," Gideon said. "I want the helm put up very fast, as if we've just seen the enemy heading for us. The men on the sheets will have to be faster. The booms will have to swing quickly enough so they can be seen from the enemy ship, and then we're going to send men running aloft as if they're checking for damage. While this is going on, I want a Spanish reef taken in the tops'ls and t'garns'ls."

A slow, comprehending leer spread over Martin's weathered features. "Aye, Cap'n," he grinned. "I'll see it done. Mr. Clowes! Mr. Willard!"

The officers stood by the fore- and mainsheets, supervising the work. Forward Gideon could see Oliver Browne,

Sullivan's bosun, and Kit M'Coy—who since the appearance of Browne had been grudgingly assigned the title of "second bosun"—standing by the square sails' braces.

"Ready to wear!" Gideon shouted, his eyes sweeping the schooner fore and aft, seeing no one out of place and comprehension in every man's eyes. *"Wear-oh!"* he roared. The spanker was brailed in. Gideon turned to the helmsman. "Put the helm up—smartly, now! Braces!"

The wheel spun as the helm went a-weather, the tern schooner heeling suddenly, lurching as its course abruptly altered. The fore and main square sails were squared to the wind, helping to bring the bow over.

"Heads'l sheets!"

Malachi's Revenge rolled as the waves struck her broadside. Gideon could hear the voices of the officers at the sheets, chanting, "Handsomely, handsomely . . . well done . . . handsomely . . ." as the great booms were drawn in.

Gideon felt the wind shifting from his left ear to his right, and then the crewmen were hauling like mad on the sheets as the wind took the big fore- and mainsails from the other side, swinging the giant booms with sweeping violence across the deck, to be checked gradually by the skillful men tending the sheets.

"Good!" Gideon exclaimed. "Meet her!" To the British sloop it might well have looked like an uncontrolled gybe, the booms swinging with ungoverned force until stopped short by the sheets, possibly wrecking themselves with their own weight and momentum, the sort of accident that would befall clumsy or amateurish sailors.

"Men aloft now! Set the spanker, but let the peak outhaul jam for a few minutes, and send someone up the mizzen to look at it!"

With a roar of delight the men began tearing aloft, waving fists and shouting, looking like a badly handled crew raving up the shrouds to look for damage. While they busied themselves, Gideon made certain no men were on the yards, then had a "Spanish reef" put in the square sails, the yards lowered to their lifts and the sheets let fly, billowing the sail out and spilling most of its wind.

Gideon seized a glass and looked astern. The sloop, or frigate, or whatever it might be, was racing down on them with the wind on its quarter, the fastest point of sailing. It was still at least four miles off.

The men were sent down from aloft as if the officers were gradually reestablishing control over an ill-disciplined crew; the imaginary jam on the spanker peak outhaul was cleared, and the big sail set. The schooner and its enemy were on parallel courses, the enemy at its fastest point of sailing, the privateer at one of its worst. Gideon intended to encourage the enemy bulldog to pursue *Malachi's Revenge*, and in order to do so he needed to give the British reason to expect they might win. The schooner, even at this angle to the wind, was much faster, but the British could not be expected to know that. *Revenge* had to look to the British like a craft that was trying desperately, if ineptly, to run away; and the schooner had to run slowly enough that the British would think there was hope of a successful pursuit.

So Gideon had staged a display of sloppy seamanship, consisting of effects calculated to convince the bulldog that the schooner's master had suddenly realized he was in danger, then panicked and gybed before the crew were ready. The Spanish reefs slowed the schooner down and might not be seen, or, if seen, they might be interpreted as sloppy handling or a deliberate attempt to avoid strain on topmasts sprung by the uncontrolled gybe.

At this point of sailing Gideon would normally have sheeted the fore-and-aft sails well out at their most efficient angle; instead he kept them close in, where they contributed less to the schooner's speed. The schooner was slowed, and the British, again, might not notice: through the single lens of a telescope perspective was nonexistent, and the British might not be able to perceive that the sails were not well deployed. Even if they did, they might assume incompetent seamanship on the part of the privateersmen; or that the Yankee captain, being caught in an uncontrolled gybe once, was not about to risk another; or that the schooner was being forced not to overstrain its masts; or even that the schooner was getting a wind from

an entirely different quarter . . . Gideon could rattle off
half a dozen reasons to himself without even trying, ration-
alizations for his own behavior that he hoped the British
would reach before the true one: that *Revenge* was shamming.

Malachi's Revenge bucketed along, pitching, its timbers
complaining of their ill treatment. The waves smashing
against the rudder necessitated Gideon's sending men below to man the relieving tackles, easing the work of the
helmsmen. Whatever its other virtues Gideon was beginning to realize *Revenge* was a difficult vessel to steer.

The log was hove every fifteen minutes to keep an accurate record of their average speed, for Gideon would need
it later. The enemy sloop continued its chase into the waning afternoon, overhauling *Revenge* slightly as Gideon intended; the bulldog's every sail was set, a bone of foam
curling from its stem. The trick had worked; or perhaps
the British had reasons of their own for the pursuit. One by
one the convoy's topsails dropped from sight over the horizon as the sun began to settle in the west and the British
bulldog came ever nearer. Gideon counted the gunports
carefully: she was a large sloop of war of perhaps twenty-
four guns; most would be carronades.

His heart surged as he considered, for a brief, enticing
moment, turning on the sloop and engaging her now that
he'd drawn her away from all hope of support. The bulldog
would be shot to bits at long range without her short-range
carronades being able to fire a shot; it could be done almost at leisure. It was what Gideon's uncle Malachi would
have done . . . but no. Gideon was not Malachi, and *Malachi's Revenge* was not in the business of fighting men-of-
war. Night was coming on, and that would mean the fight
would have to be at close range, where the enemy carronades might reach; and then there was the possibility that
the schooner's masts might be damaged and prevent her
from reaching the convoy. The convoy was the target:
once that was in Gideon's hands, then perhaps *Revenge*
could live up to her name and exact retribution for the loss
of *General Sullivan*.

As the sun began to fall, the bulldog, which had closed
to within two miles, was permitted to observe the crew of

the schooner, seemingly desperate, heaving empty casks overboard as if to lighten ship, along with scraps from carpenter's stores. This last bit of deception was soon obscured by the growing night, and under cover of darkness sails were sheeted out, the yards hoisted, the square sails sheeted home and trimmed to the wind. *Revenge* raised her head and sped forward, the sea hissing beneath her keel. The change was exhilarating; Gideon grinned in spite of himself, knowing the distance between the schooner and the sloop of war was increasing and that the pursuers might not know it. The moon would not rise for another three hours, and by that time Gideon intended to be well rid of the British bulldog. They increased their lead for another hour, until the bulldog astern became nothing more than a distant shadow on the dark sea even when seen through the night-glass.

"Halliards and sheets! Hands aloft to furl t'gallants and tops'ls!"

The square sails vanished, furled up to the yards by trained hands working swiftly in the dark. The men came down from the masts, standing at their new stations.

"Ease the outhauls! Haul away on the inhauls and brails! Tend the vangs and flag halliards. Haul away on the sheet!"

Malachi's Revenge slowed as if her stem had struck a sea of quicksilver, its great wings vanishing from the masts. Within seconds every remaining sail on the tern schooner had gone from sight, brailed up to the masts. The black hull rode uneasily on the sea, slowly turning broadside to the waves, rolling from crest to trough, the movement uncontrolled by wind pressure on the sails and sickening.

Gideon smiled. There were nothing but bare poles silhouetted against the stars to give *Malachi's Revenge* away, nothing but sticks and a dark hull so low in the water, it was as good as invisible. The chasing bulldog might pass within two hundred yards and not see her.

The hands were sent to supper, and Gideon went down to his cabin, drawing the dark curtains over the stern windows before he lit the lantern. Leaving his supper untouched he worked with pen and dividers. The convoy, close-hauled, would be lucky if it made four knots; its

course was east by north or thereabouts. *Revenge*'s course
had been south by east, and Gideon had hove the log regularly to gain an estimate of her speed.

It was simple triangulation, but Gideon knew he had no
head for figures and worked it out twice, then a third time
for good measure. Well enough. He ate a few bites, then
pocketed some biscuits and chewing tobacco, doused the
lantern, and returned to the deck with his cup of coffee.

Finch Martin had kept the bulldog in sight through the
night-glass; it was plowing onward, all sail still set, still on
its unaltered course. Gideon wondered if there might have
been an easier way to do this, if he could somehow have
outmaneuvered both escorts without the need for this deception. Probably not, he decided: he could have taken
Malachi's Revenge into the convoy without trouble and got
out again, but any prizes he captured might well have been
retaken by the escort.

Gideon cut himself chewing tobacco. The bulldog approached. She, too, might be shamming; the enemy might
have been able, by some prodigious feat of night vision, to
keep the schooner in sight and suddenly alter course to
descend on them. Gideon called the hands from their supper and had them standing by, silent shadows clumped on
the rolling deck, their whispers drowned by the hissing sea.

The schooner's rolling made it difficult to keep the bulldog in sight, but as the enemy grew larger, its phosphores-
cent wake streaming faintly behind, the hands' whispering
died without the need to silence it. Soon Gideon could see,
even without the aid of the glass, the shape of its sails
against the stars and a gleam of tallow-colored light in a
quarter window. Gideon breathed a small prayer and held
his breath.

The dark shadow passed, leaving only a fading phospho-
rescence. Gideon felt his heart lighten; he spat his tobacco
overboard and began to chew a biscuit, and he heard the
men stir. The bulldog would most likely not return to the
convoy, but head straight to Antigua or the convoy's destination: she would not be a factor in the next day's events.
Gideon sent the hands to finish their interrupted meal and
waited another half hour until the enemy horizon was all
blackness before setting the tern schooner in motion.

"Haul away on the topping lift. Ease the sheet. Belay. Tend the vangs and flag halliards. Ease the peak and foot inhauls and brails. Haul away on the peak and foot outhauls."

The orders were given quietly, as if the enemy were still within listening distance. At first with a rustle and then a roar the schooner's flaxen wings rose from their beds, and *Malachi's Revenge* surged into life.

"Steer east nor'east. Hold her steady."

Gideon stood by the wheel, legs braced well apart, sipping another cup of coffee. His eyes glowed in the light of the binnacle, and those of his men who saw him looked uneasy, uncomfortable with this uncompromising glare of single-minded determination. If Gideon's mathematics were right, the convoy would be his on the morrow. The proud ships, the mean ships, all would be within his net, and nothing but a dispensation from the Almighty Providence could prevent it.

The sea surged past; the bell rang forward, and the watches changed. *Malachi's Revenge* held steadily on the larboard tack. At three bells the wind veered a point, and Gideon fretted beneath the stars. Had the wind veered for the convoy? If it had they would have had to change course, either sailing more easterly or tacking. Could the convoy tack at night? One vessel behind the other in orderly procession? Almost certainly not. They would have altered course, heading east or east by south, perhaps a bit more straggled out than they had been.

"Helmsman, make your course east by north."

"East by nor', aye aye."

Was a point enough? *Malachi's Revenge* might pass them in the night and be out of sight by morning. And if they'd tacked, he'd miss them altogether. East by north was best, Gideon decided. A good compromise. Choose a good course and stick to it. No one could fault him if he had chosen wrongly. God's will if they'd tacked. Nothing he could do about it.

And then at six bells there were dark shapes around them, and ships' bells clanged the hour. Gideon felt his heart blaze, a smile of unholy triumph tearing at his face. He wondered if the first Gideon had felt such vaunting exultation, when he saw the campfires of the Midianites spread before him and knew the hand of the Lord was with him? He mastered his feral grin, but his men still saw the deadly glow in his eyes and were thankful Gideon was not a British captain.

The hands were called up; Finch Martin, in the rumpled coat he'd slept in, stood at Gideon's elbow, and Gideon saw across Martin's face the same triumphant leer he'd felt on his own. No privateer could help but rejoice, seeing the dark forms of the enemy around him, unaware of the stalker in their midst and helpless. The privateers armed themselves with pistols, muskets, and pikes; the guns were loaded but not run out, and all firearms were unprimed to prevent accidents.

The first prize was an hermaphrodite brig from Bristol; they ran aboard her from leeward, and the silent privateers were over her rail like a dark sea before her sleepy lookouts were aware of their existence. Ten men and a prizemaster were sent aboard, and the vessels parted.

The second prize was a big ship, a former Danish West Indiaman of four hundred tons armed with twelve honeycombed cannon, again overwhelmed with a rush of boarders before any alarm could be given. George Willard and fifty men were sent aboard: he was instructed to keep twenty to work the valuable prize and dispose of the other thirty by boarding three other vessels during the night and carrying them off.

Another brig, another ship, a coasting topsail schooner. The captain of the latter, an alert Antiguan black man, shouted through a speaking trumpet for *Revenge* to keep off, thinking a foolish or sleepy helmsman was steering a collision course; but the privateers overwhelmed him and his watch, and he was made prisoner without a shot. His had been the only shout, and no one had heard his cries of alarm but the privateers.

The eastern horizon, above the tern schooner's larboard bow, began to whiten with the approaching dawn, and pale topsails began appearing around them, reflecting the dim light. The privateers hastened. Another brig, another laden schooner. Astern and to leeward Willard had snapped up two ships and was taking them away. Sun glinted from the topsails of the British escort; signal flags ran up its halliards, and guns fired. The middle third of the convoy seemed to be well out of formation; it had to be harried back into place. The privateers, in command of the straggling line of prizes, watched the incomprehensible signals with amusement. It was not until the black-hulled schooner laid itself alongside a smart snow that managed to fire a signal before it was boarded and taken, that the escort noticed the low craft within the middle of its flock. More signal flags, more guns. The xebec to windward of *Malachi's Revenge* paid no attention, and then its surly captain, who thought it too early to obey orders from any jumped-up captain with a commission from the king, was struck dumb with amazement as privateers with pikes tumbled over his lee rail and made his jutting poop their own.

The others paid proper attention to their plight, but for many it was too late. *Revenge* caught another as it ran downwind toward the floundering escort that was desperately trying to reach them on the larboard tack, every staysail set and flags flying. Gideon knew there was no longer any point in anonymity; he sent the boy to rattle his drum and raised the Stars and Stripes to the mizzen peak, the FREE TRADE AND SAILORS' RIGHTS flag to the fore, and on the main the great viper banner of the Markham family, the golden rattlesnake writhing across a pennon of scarlet, that had flown in the last war from the flagstaffs of Malachi, Josiah, and Jehu, and vaunted over prizes from the Caribbean to the North Sea.

Malachi's Revenge had cut the line about two thirds of the distance from its head and had worked its way upwind away from the ship-sloop. Gideon took a glass from the rack and studied the enemy with its familiar outline: a ship-sloop, eleven or twelve gunports per side, slower and less weatherly than the privateer schooner, but heavily gunned and dangerous up close. It had replaced the bulldog at the tail of the British line, harrying the slower ships to keep up with the van. Gideon knew he had seen the lines of that enemy warship before. She was perhaps a sister-ship to the one that had destroyed *General Sullivan.*

Gideon had taken ten prizes; Willard, with the captured
West Indiaman, another two. Eight or so ships were running for their escort to be hidden under its lee, but the
three craft at the very head of the British line were unable
to run for the ship-sloop; the privateer was between them
and safety. There was time enough to deal with the sloop
of war; it was barely dawn. Still there were three vessels to
windward that might get away.

Gideon hauled his wind and set after the trio. Obedient
to signals from the escort, they scattered. At the head of
the line, they were probably the fleetest vessels in the convoy—a ship, a barque, a barquentine. But after a three-
hour chase under the tropical sun the three British flags
were hauled down without defense. Men of the *Revenge*
put aboard the prizes and were sent to make their own
way.

The sloop of war had tried to follow, but as hopelessly as
a terrier barking after a darting swallow. Even before the
barquentine had been cast free of its grapples, Gideon
watched the enemy closely, standing in the lee mizzen
shrouds, telescope in hand. There would be carronades on
the enemy's broadside, thirty-two pounders, with long sixes
or nines as chasers, and perhaps a few nines on the broadside. Gideon felt again the wolvish grin tug at his features.
He meant to have the convoy, every ship, every ounce of
cargo, every seaman and officer prisoner by nightfall. And
perhaps that total would include a British sloop of war.

The helmsmen looked at Gideon expectantly as he clam-
bered down from the rigging; Gideon could sense Finch
Martin's intense anticipation, and the sidelong glances
given him by the men standing on deck. To throw up the
helm now would mean committing *Malachi's Revenge* to
battle with one hundred sixty of its two hundred fifty crewmen off manning prizes, unable to contribute the overwhelming strength of numbers upon which privateers relied
for victory.

The tern schooner and its latest prizes separated, wind
filling the privateer's sails as the prize ceased to shadow
her. Gideon returned his glass to the rack and stood near
the wheel, his hands clasped behind his back.

"Up with the helm," Gideon said quietly, and his eyes

shone fire. Finch Martin snatched off his top hat and flung it wildly to the breeze.

"Jesus rollin' in shit!" he shrieked at the top of his lungs, dancing a strange, demented jig forward of the wheel. "It's a man-o'-war we'll take, just like old times!"

"Language, Mr. Martin!" Gideon glared, but his words were buried by the hands' cheers. Gideon was surprised at the sound, at the men who joined Martin's dance, most of them comparative strangers, who were so eager that he lead them into battle at such foolish odds.

"The British'll bleed!" Martin whooped, his wild white hair streaming in the wind. "Three cheers for Cap'n Markham!"

Gideon let them have their celebration, too surprised to restore order. There was affection in the hands' smiles, affection for the blue-light captain who had stopped their grog, made them sweat daily over the great guns, preached to them on Sundays, and who was now about to bring them against a sloop of war armed with carronades that could tear open *Revenge*'s hull in ten minutes should the schooner be foolish enough to close with the enemy. What had he done to deserve popularity? Gideon wondered. He loathed "popular" captains who let discipline and order slide to curry favor with the hands; Gideon's recollection of his own conduct was that he had demanded nothing from his men but instant obedience and respect.

He shook his head. The thoughts and affections of sailors were incomprehensible, and changeable as the tide. Tomorrow they would once again be cursing his strictness.

"That's enough, Mr. Martin," Gideon said quietly. "Clew up all the squares'ls and send the men to their station. For the moment I want the larboard side manned."

It was perhaps ten in the morning. The hands were without breakfast and would probably go without for the rest of the day, for it would be a long battle. The sloop of war was armed principally with thirty-two pound carronades, stubby, short-ranged weapons capable of ferocious execution at close ranges; the schooner was armed with short twelve-pounders and a single long eighteen, guns capable of firing at medium to long ranges. The difference between cannon and carronades, Gideon thought, was like that be-

tween claws and teeth. The privateer would have to stay at
a distance, sparring, scratching the ship-sloop's face with
her claws, while the British would try to close the range so
their carronades would be effective, grappling the schooner
so they could rend the privateer's throat with their teeth.

Gideon would have to stay away from those teeth, from
those weapons that could tear his fragile bulwarks asunder.
He would have to keep his long guns in action constantly,
firing at medium to long ranges, picking the ship-sloop to
bits. It was good that there were twelve more hours of daylight; he would need every bit of it, first to defeat the enemy warship and then to snatch up the prizes the enemy
guarded.

He returned to the mizzen shrouds with his glass, studying the enemy, the battle-flags and the White Ensign, the
bone in the sloop's teeth and her yellowing sails. The
warming, surging anticipation of triumph rose in him
again, glowing, as he saw the sloop bucking the waves
close-hauled, and he fought it. It was too like madness, this
intuition of his own invincibility—he would have to fight
this battle rationally, coolly, and not with impetuous rage.
It would be a delicate business, this judging of ranges and
taking care that he not fire from too close nor too far, and
he could not afford to be headstrong.

But still the glow remained. He had the enemy where he
wanted them, and had the livelong day to pick them to
pieces. He had come from Cuba a defeated man—for no
matter how many men he had cost the British in that bay
and on that river, how was a captain to be judged but by
whether he had lost his ship or kept it?—and he had come
down the Choctaw Pass without half those he had set out
with, defeated and hunted. Both times he had been beaten,
to his sorrow, but now Gideon had come into his own,
standing on the deck of a schooner that had been his
dream for years, with a crew devoted and loyal and trained
under his eye. *Revenge.* It was not a pleasant word, but it
lingered in the back of Gideon's mind and had first come
forth in his naming of the privateer. The mud-streaked,
baffled man, come out of the West Florida swamps after
his humiliation on the river, could take this day an exem-

plary requital upon the flag of the enemy. *Revenge*. And not simply Gideon's account might be squared, but that of others: that terrified seaman, whose name Gideon could not even remember, whose head had been smashed by a cutlass at Jérémie years ago; Alexander Harris, *General Sullivan*'s first officer, buried in Cuba; Charles Jouhaux and Sean MacDonald, dead and scalped, unburied perhaps up the dark Alabama . . . *Revenge*. Other names, other faces, flitted before Gideon's imagination: David Markham, hanged in Boston to the family's disgrace, seduced by cynical, hardened men; others, anonymous, their faces shadows, their voices whispers, men ruined, slain, scalped in the world's far corners, victims of cynical British policy and British greed. *Revenge*.

Gideon was not simply bringing ninety privateers to battle; he felt behind him a host of vengeful ghosts whose distant spirits filled him, and whose voices sang through the rigging. He was glad, as he saw the British enemy over *Revenge*'s pitching bulwarks, that first into the fight would be the effigy of Malachi, glaring through fiery eyes from beneath the bowsprit, waving his curved saber in encouragement, the finest sea-fighter of the family.

Eight hundred yards separated *Malachi's Revenge* from the enemy. Not yet.

Gideon came down from the rigging, replaced the glass, stood by the wheel. He felt the weight of his sword hanging at his belt and the wind tickling the hairs of his neck. The chorus of ghosts faded. It was not Malachi who stood on the schooner's deck but Gideon, and the battle would have to be fought Gideon's way. From Malachi the crew might expect dash, impetuosity, brilliance. From Gideon they would get merely his best. He prayed it would be enough.

Seven hundred yards. "Larboard battery load and run out! Roundshot!" His voice seemed small in the silence, in the faces of the barefoot men who stood by the guns already hot with the Caribbean sun, soon to be scorching with the heat of iron thunders. The men bent to their work, to the cartridges and rammers. This was the battery that had so consistently lagged behind the other at drill, the one that Willard had worked so hard to bring up to standard. Gideon had no fear to use these guns now, and he wished the Gay Head Indian could have been on board to witness at first hand the fruits of his labors.

The deck rumbled to the sound of the nine iron guns thrusting from the ports, and the schooner heeled even further to leeward as the weight of the guns shifted.

Five hundred yards. Close enough.

"Down helm! Larboard guns, fire as ye bear! Mr. Martin, Mr. Clowes, give 'em help. Tate, ye may fire when ye wish."

"No firin' into the drink, ye sodomites!" Martin barked, his face flushed with pleasure as he walked along the row of guns, a man happy in his element, reliving the most intense moments of his youth. "Fire as ye hang over the trough, like ye were learned!"

Gideon saw Tate's intense face peering over the barrel of the long tom, the lanyard in his hand. It was the same concentration he had seen on the faces of certain boxers or wrestlers—the superior ones—before a competition; he had seen it on the faces of preachers during the pause before bursting into eloquence, and on Sean MacDonald's face as he touched the trigger of his rifle.

The long tom, swung round on its pivot, fired over the larboard bows before the other guns bore, the gunsmoke gushing out downwind, hiding from Tate's shaded eyes the destruction he may have wrought. Gideon could see him standing on tiptoe, craning to spot the fall of shot even as his well-drilled crew sponged and wormed the gun. Eventually Tate's shoulders fell, and he shook his head disgustedly. A miss.

Gideon's view of the enemy was temporarily obscured as the mainsail swung out to leeward on its boom. Briefly he considered brailing up the fore-and-aft sail and fighting under square sail alone, but that would require revising his plan, based as it was on the superiority of fore-and-aft canvas over square sail on the upwind tack. He rejected the idea almost before it was formed.

"Meet her," he called to the helmsman. "Good. Starboard yer helm a bit, give 'em time to aim."

The schooner's turn slowed, the deck rocking as the

waves took her broadside. The enemy sloop would move slowly across the broadside arc, allowing the gun captains a chance to anticipate the moment of decision. Gideon found himself holding his breath, anticipating the moment when the number one larboard gun captain would pull the lanyard that was wrapped around his fist as he crouched behind his gun on the deck, peering over the iron barrel at the enemy. . . .

The black line stretching from the gun captain's fist to the gunlock went taut and the gun roared inward on its tackles, spewing smoke. The second gun fired, and the third, and on down the line. Gideon, feeling his blood race at the sound but still blinded by the mainsail, could only imagine the enemy sloop of war surrounded by white feathers leaping from the sea.

"Stop yer vents! Sponge out!" The chorus of gun captains' orders came down the line in the same order as the firing of their guns.

"Down helm!" Gideon shouted. "Put her on the starboard tack. Sheets!"

Martin, Clowes, and Browne detailed men to sheet in the big sails as *Malachi's Revenge* swung its bow upwind, paralleling the course of the enemy sloop. Gideon walked the distance to the weather rail, carefully controlling his own insistent impulse to run, and gazed astern at the enemy. There was a rent in the foresail, no other visible damage.

Well. More broadsides would come.

Malachi's Revenge sailed on, increasing the range, keeping carefully upwind, using the fore-and-aft sails' advantages to their maximum. Close-hauled, the schooner was certain to be more weatherly and faster.

The iron guns ran out, the gun captains' fists came up, showing their readiness.

"Helm up. Handsomely, now. We'll wear and cross their bows."

The tern schooner fell from the wind slowly, the gun captains crouching and ready. . . . The aftermost gun fired first this time, startling Gideon with its noise, and the others followed, Tate's chaser banging out with the rest.

The mainsail was sheeted in this time for sailing close-hauled, and Gideon could see the enemy, the splashes surrounding the sloop's bows, the tear appearing in the fore-topsail, before the smoke streaming downwind shrouded it with its pall.

"Helm down. Put her on the starboard tack again."

They played the trick once more, running upwind to increase the distance and give the guns time to reload, then wearing to send a broadside howling toward the enemy, before they received the first enemy fire. First one, then another gun flowered smoke from the enemy stem, and gunshot skipped over the waves, wide and too high. The American gunners jeered, but Gideon knew the enemy shooting would get better. Having painfully learned the fact that the privateer schooner was not going to sail up close and be obligingly mauled by carronade fire, the British had cleared away their two forward-firing chasers, or hauled up two broadside guns to act as chasers. The two guns fired from right forward over the stem where the sloop's close-hauled pitching would badly affect their gunnery (Tate's long gun conquered that problem by being placed just forward of the mainmast, as near the center of the deck as possible, where it would be least affected by the schooner's motion), but sooner or later the British would get the hang of firing under such awkward conditions, and then Gideon could expect deadly shot smashing aboard his schooner every few minutes.

Another broadside from the schooner, another futile two rounds of chaser fire from the sloop of war. Gideon knew that at least some of the Yankee shot was striking home, hammering through the stout construction of the enemy's bows, crashing through to the crew. Even though the ship-sloop's bows were a small target, any shot that hit would rake the enemy, passing through her fore-and-aft, doing extensive damage.

The enemy chasers cracked out again, and the sky moaned as an iron solid soared overhead, tearing through the spanker with a wet slap, passing on harmlessly. Gideon felt furious at himself for ducking and planted his feet firmly on the deck, swearing not to move unless it was utterly necessary.

Malachi's Revenge wore again and fired another broad-side; chasers barked in reply. Gideon found himself fretting about those chasers: most of the time they had a clean shot at *Revenge*'s stern and flush deck, built cleanly without bulkheads or other impedimenta, which would allow a shot to crash the length of the schooner, perhaps smashing the open, unprotected wheel. There was nothing to be done about it; Gideon could only hope no such disaster would happen.

"Helm up! Larboard guns, fire as ye bear!"

The larboard guns, one by one, roared inboard like machines possessed, rampaging iron beasts held in check only by their tackles. There was a crash somewhere below, and the schooner trembled: the enemy chasers had waited for a broadside target, and at least one of them had struck home.

"Helm down! Put her on the starboard tack!"

Gideon gazed abaft at the enemy, the sloop of war that still seemed in fine trim, its yellow sails bearing a few scars, its pitching hull showing no sign of any twelve-pound shot crashing home. As Gideon watched, the enemy stem hesitated, then swung as the headsails spilled wind.

"She's going about, by thunder," Gideon murmured, seeing the sloop of war bowling up into the wind, her yards swinging. Gideon's fist pounded into his palm: if he'd fired that last broadside while the sloop was tacking, he might have been able to knock a spar away or otherwise interfere with its maneuver, and perhaps keep the enemy in irons, drifting helplessly backward while *Malachi's Revenge* poured in raking broadside after raking broadside.

His mind calculated swiftly as he glanced up at the masthead pendants, showing the wind holding steady. Perhaps the British were going onto the other tack as part of an effort to weather him, perhaps just to get their larboard broadside into action.

Gideon's response was swift and automatic. Unless he wanted to run away, there was only one possible answer.

"Ready about! Mr. Martin, Mr. Clowes, send the men not needed at the sheets to the starboard guns, load, and run out!"

He watched the crew as the impact of his orders registered on them, then as they scrambled to their stations. He nodded to the helmsmen. *Malachi's Revenge* would tack as well.

"Helm's a-lee!"

Gideon wondered, as the booms swung with the wind and the big fore-and-aft sail roared from luff to leech, whether the privateer's crewmen would yarn about this battle in the future, in front of warm fires in seamen's taverns, and whether they would subject his tactics to analysis, whether his tacking in response to the enemy would be seen as a brilliant master stroke, the operation of genius. . . . It was, rather, a straightforward decision to keep to windward of the enemy, to keep his distance and enable the guns to stay in action without risking the tearing destruction of enemy carronades. Gideon had read in books of tactics about this maneuver or that, some act of genius or some other celebrated, egregious blunder, subjected either to praise or withering scorn by those who had never realized how such decisions had to be made. Most were simple responses to simple moves from the enemy, or obedience to the dictates of a long-laid plan, the result of long seamanlike experience.

Gideon's tactics thus far had neither been daring nor original. He was making the best use of his long-range guns and trying to deny the enemy the full effect of his short-range smashers. He hoped that Providence would protect him from disaster. But if disaster should fall, he would do his best to work his way out of it, dealing with each problem in turn, and hope that the Almighty would look with favor upon his endeavors and not condemn him to a superabundance of ill luck.

Gideon did not intend for this to be a battle in which inspiration or genius could take part; he meant to pick the enemy to bits slowly over a period of hours, using nothing more inspiring than his own experience and his vessel's superiority.

His musings were cut short as enemy guns roared and smoke blanketed the ship-sloop's windward side. Roundshot shrieked overhead, and Gideon caught an echo of the startled expression on his own face upon the faces of a dozen seamen. Parted ropes fell from aloft, canvas shook and tore, the deck rang hollow as a spent thirty-two pound shot crashed amidships, bounced from the planking, thudded into the weather bulwark, and fell harmlessly to the deck, having scarred it, but accomplishing little else. The tang of salt moisture hung briefly in the air, the foam of near misses.

Gideon tried to bring his frantic breathing under control, to sternly silence his thundering heart. He forced a ghastly grin onto his features. They were at the limit of the British carronades' range: the enemy shot might simply bounce off.

"If that's the best they can do, lads, they'll have to go back to gunnery school!" he shouted, and at his words he saw faint grins on the faces of the men.

"Them British sodomites can't hit a slab-sided hooker from five paces with a rock!" Gideon heard Finch Martin's voice proclaim. "Tend to yer guns snow, and we'll give 'em a Yankee Doodle serenade twixt wind an' water!"

There was a faint cheer. For all the enemy broadside's fury it had been a poor effort. The carronades had been elevated so high that their accuracy was all but ruined, and the one ball that had actually struck *Revenge*'s deck had failed even to penetrate the deck timbers. Rigging had been cut, of course, and there were new rents in the sails for the sailmaker to patch, but not a man had been struck, not a single deadly splinter raised. Gideon breathed easier.

"Fire as ye bear lads and knock their ship down about their arses!" Martin was shouting. "Steady now—fire!"

The starboard battery cracked out, guns belching fire and smoke, leaping inboard on their tackles, hurling iron at the enemy.

"Independent fire!" Gideon shouted. "Helmsman, starboard a point!"

The two warships sailed parallel to one another at two and a half cables' distance, guns cracking as fast as they could be loaded and run out. A twin crash that made the schooner leap signalled that the enemy had at least two long guns on their broadside. Gideon caught swift glimpses of the fight, glimpses as brief as those of the enemy shipsloop seen from around the edges of sails between blurring billows of gunsmoke. Tate, with sweat streaking the gunpowder caked over his intent face, bent over his gun. Martin, capering on the deck, laughed at each good shot, his speech rife with obscenity and imagination, irrepressible. Addams stood bent with twisted back over a gun as he worked with sponge and rammer. Enemy shot roared and plunged, wailing through the rigging, thudding, spent, against the schooner's bulwarks, and glancing off into the sea. The blackened gunners worked like demons in the red light of the guns, their sweat evaporating from the hot decks.

Gideon stood by the helm, calling minute course corrections, letting his officers supervise the gunnery. Above the fight he could still see the privateer's flags, the red viper banner with its serpent of gold, the fifteen bright stripes of the American ensign. Guns leaped and roared, crashing inward with a furious rush, running out with a low rumble as the men strained at the side-tackles.

"She running!" a voice called, almost overwhelmed by the deadly work on the deck. "She running away!" Tate leaped up onto the breech of his gun, dancing barefoot on the hot metal, one arm outflung. *"She running!"*

Gideon leaped for the main channel, swung himself into the shrouds. Glimpsed through the pall of gunsmoke, the enemy sails were turning, the gaps of bright blue between the masts disappearing. She was turning downwind, out of the fight.

" 'Vast firing, broadside guns!" Gideon bawled, jumping recklessly to the deck. "Tate, keep yer gun in action! Keep killing Englishmen! I don't want 'em to have a minute's rest!"

Tate jumped gleefully to his task, the big eighteen-pounder rolling on its pivot. The wind keened through the rigging, carrying away the soup of obscuring gunsmoke, revealing the ship-sloop's stern quarter as she turned away, heading downwind.

Gideon restrained his feeling of leaping triumph, cut himself chewing tobacco, and considered what the enemy were up to. It was possible, of course, that Tate was right, that they were running away. It was more likely they were retiring temporarily from the fight in order to repair damage, or possibly they considered they were cruising too far from the convoy they were supposed to be guarding, and were intent on rejoining. Gideon could not know.

Tate's long gun roared out; the fall of shot was not seen. Probably a hit. Gideon called for Finch Martin.

"Mr. Martin, I'll want ye to rearrange the gun crews. Transfer the second sponger and the second loader of each gun to the larboard side. The first sponger and first loader will remain even if the gun captains and the bulk of the crews are switched to the larboard side. As long as the enemy's running, I'm going to keep gybing off her stern, using each battery alternately."

"Aye, Cap'n," Finch Martin said, his craggy face opening in a twisted, appreciative smile. "A thought worthy of Cap'n Malachi, if ye don't mind the observation."

"Nay, Mr. Martin, I'm pleased, but all credit for this thought, or any other, must go to the Almighty," Gideon said. "And I will be even more pleased if ye'd restrain yer intemperate language."

Martin's face fell. "I *have* been mindin' it, sir. I hoped ye'd noticed."

"It has not escaped my attention, Mr. Martin; I know you're trying," Gideon said as encouragingly as he could. "But the current excitement seems to have, er, got the better of yer resolutions."

"I'll do my best, sir."

"I can't ask more than that," Gideon said. "Now I'd be obliged if ye'd see to the matter of the second loaders and spongers."

"Aye aye. Right away, Cap'n."

Tate's gun roared again. Gideon turned to the helmsmen. "Put up the helm. Wear-oh! Sheets!"

The tern schooner's low black hull turned downwind, the glaring Cossack figurehead turning his fierce Markham eyes toward the enemy. *Revenge* pitched as the seas swept up beneath her scooped stern, her canvas wings roaring to leeward as she gybed.

"Larboard guns, run out! Fire as ye bear! Helmsmen, bring her into the wind!"

Malachi's Revenge hovered off the enemy stern at a distance of less than two cables, coming into the wind slowly.

The number one larboard gun spoke, shrieking flame and iron at the enemy transom, and the others followed suit as they bore, each roaring inward until checked by its tackles, each bellowing iron vengeance for Americans pressed, blockaded, imprisoned, scalped.

"Helm up! Wear-oh! Loaders and spongers, reload! The rest of ye, man the starboard guns!"

The men ran to starboard, the big fore-and-aft sails slatting, then swinging across as the schooner gybed. For a second the name of the ship-sloop was visible, picked out on the transom before it vanished into howling gunsmoke: *Alastor*.

"*Alastor*, Cap'n," Michael Clowes reported as they gybed again and the gun crews ran to the larboard guns and hauled at the side-tackles. "Rated at twenty guns, probably carrying twenty-two or -four. Alastor, that would be a Greek god of revenge, companion to Nemesis . . ."

"Thank you, Mr. Clowes, but we may discuss pagan mythology on a later occasion," Gideon scowled. "Kindly see to yer work."

The larboard guns cracked out, the gunners' outlines highlighted in the red that reflected off the dense banks of smoke. Perhaps the British were running away after all. Why else would they stand this punishment, this endless raking? The men ran to the starboard guns. Gideon spat tobacco to leeward and mopped the sweat from his forehead.

The schooner's guns roared twice more before *Alastor* swung to windward, replying with its starboard battery. And then it was as before, the two warships running parallel with broadsides flaming out, the roundshot shrieking overhead or thudding into timbers. One nine-pound shot, fired from some accurate enemy long gun, smashed home among the starboard number three gun, the gun's crew flung heedlessly like dolls before the hungry iron, seemingly enveloped in a weird mist that was in reality a humming cloud of splinters. Two dead men were flung overboard, three wounded carried below. Other wounded, bleeding from splinter wounds, insisted on remaining, on doing their share. Gideon breathed a short prayer for the dead and wounded, then ran to the number three gun and seized a side-tackle, helping to replace the lost men, trying to keep up the schooner's rate of fire. No other job called him; there was no longer any maneuvering, just this broadside pounding on the larboard tack.

"Look ye, the jibboom! We've shortened her, sweet Jesus!" Martin's gleeful voice pealed above the din. Gideon stepped back from the gun, waited for a breeze to clear the smoke away, and saw the ship-sloop's jibboom trailing broken in the water mixed with torn shreds of flax that had once been the headsails. The jibboom was the foremost anchor for the complex maze of rigging that supported the masts. Stays connected the jib with the fore-topmast and topgallant mast, supporting them, and even as Gideon watched, the fore-topmast trembled, lurched, and went by the board, falling seamen leaping like grasshoppers for the backstays in desperate effort to save themselves. *Alastor* hung in the wind, hesitated, then turned to starboard, off the wind. The helmsmen's fight to keep the ship from flying up helplessly into the wind had been won, probably with the aid of the fallen topmast that would tend to drag the ship to leeward.

"Helm up! Wear-oh!"

Like a falcon stooping to its prey *Malachi's Revenge* swung downwind, the crew leaping to the starboard guns, blasting another broadside into *Alastor*'s stern. For the first time Gideon saw the damage his guns had been wreaking: the torn stern galleries, the gaping windows, the pockmarked gingerbread . . . and then the whole vanished in smoke and splinters. The tern schooner lurched as it crashed into *Alastor*'s fallen, drifting topmast, and then the privateer swung into the wind again.

Alastor was helpless; the loss of the jibs and foresails had crippled her, and she could no longer maneuver. Gideon dared to bring *Revenge* into range of the carronades, hanging off the stern and pouring in raking broadsides, knowing the British could not turn their ship fast enough to bring their guns to bear.

Musketry crackled, lead balls slapping the schooner's deck. Marines were seen on the enemy stern and quarter galleries, their red coats bright against the broken timber, making targets of themselves to reply to the deadly rakes in the only way possible.

"Brave men, Captain," Clowes murmured, standing near Gideon, his sword in his hand, his hat gone. A man nearby spun to the deck as a musket ball clipped his shoulder.

"I do not want them admired. I want them dead," Gideon said. "Load the next broadside with grape on top of roundshot."

Clowes gazed at Gideon's hard, unforgiving face, his glowing eyes, then turned on his heel and obeyed. The green-coated men that served as *Revenge*'s sharpshooters were all either manning prizes or the guns and could not serve to suppress the enemy. But the grape worked well enough, sweeping the marines away as if they had never been there, scarlet coats staining the water like blood. The effigy of Malachi Markham, perched over the schooner's foaming forefoot, swept past the bodies, indifferent to their fate.

Another raking broadside brought the enemy's mizzen-mast into the drink, the White Ensign draping the sloop's stern quarter like a shroud until the next broadside blew it away and the schooner ground it under.

"Their flag's down. D'ye think they've struck?" Finch Martin asked. "They can't fight any more, that's certain."

"They still have a flag at the maintop, Mr. Martin. Load and run out!"

Alastor's rudder was shot away, and she ran free before the wind, her sole remaining mast gathering wind into its tattered sails until it, too, crashed over the side.

"Helm down! Bring her onto the larboard tack."

The ship-sloop, a smashed ruin, slowed and turned broadside to the wind, wallowing in the trough of each wave, a hulk. Men swarmed aloft onto the foremast, trying to get the forecourse set, the only sail remaining. Gideon brought the privateer schooner on a wide course around the enemy's stern, avoiding the arc of fire of those deadly guns, until he approached the wallowing *Alastor* from downwind. Marines in red coats swarmed over her stern galleries, musketry cracked out, puffs of smoke from the stern galleries hovered in the wind and were swept away.

"Ease the sheets. Handsomely. Overhaul the weather jib sheet. Good." Gideon gave his orders through the speaking trumpet, trying to ignore the popping musketry, the whizzing bullets that dropped another man as he stood by his gun. Fifty yards.

"Down helm! Douse the jib and foresail! Aft the main and spanker sheets!"

The schooner slowed and hove to, pointing right into the wind a hundred yards off the enemy stern. Her guns thundered united into the enemy hulk, sending the surviving marines scampering for the fo'c'sle and safety as iron and grape traveled through the enemy ship, gutting her. The guns crashed again and again, until the men trying to set the forecourse were scattered or dead and the foreyard canted at an odd angle. Clowes looked at Gideon questioningly. *Not yet,* Gideon thought. Gideon would not risk losing a man due to some misplaced humanity. Better all the British should die. God help them all. Let them taste iron again and again. Until they themselves acknowledged their defeat, their humiliation by one of Brother Jonathan's privateers.

The Yankee broadside was working slowly now, the men tired, almost fainting in the heat. Still roundshot spat from the hot barrels, smashing into the Bristish transom. At last the British ended it, flying a white flag of surrender over their smashed taffrail, putting an end to the slaughter.

" 'Vast firing, there! 'Vast firing!"

Gideon picked up his speaking trumpet, spat out his tobacco, tried to clear his throat of smoke. "Ye have surrendered yer ship, as I take it!" he shouted, his voice cracking as it tried, dry-mouthed, to carry over the water.

"Sir, we are displaying a white flag!" The voice sounded harsh, stubborn.

"Then ye have surrendered, have ye not?" Gideon insisted. There was no reply. "My men are willing and able to continue the engagement!" Gideon shouted, losing patience. He had no time for this gentlemanly bantering. "Have ye surrendered or not?"

There was a moment of mulish silence, then a gruff acknowledgment. "Aye. We've struck," that still avoided the hated word *surrender.*

"Prepare to receive boarders! We will be expecting your swords!" Gideon turned to his crew, standing by the gun-tackles, relieved, expectant, smiles spreading over their features as the realization of victory triumphed over weariness.

"Set the jib. Jib sheets to starboard. Set the foresail."

As the backed jib helped the schooner fall from the wind's eye and the sea hissed beneath the privateer's hull, Gideon's men were ordered to snatch up pikes and cutlasses and stand by on the lee bulwarks. *Revenge* weathered the wallowing enemy, then doused sail and drifted gently down to her stern quarter, the Yankee seamen cheering as they swept over the unresisting enemy bulwarks, cheers that dampened quickly as they stepped aboard the charnel house their gunnery had created. Men lay in heaps, the planks stained red beneath them; guns were overturned, yards lay smashed along the decks, rigging was tangled in madman's knots.

They stepped along subdued as more men tumbled over the side, leaping between the British starboard carronades. The aftermost carronade, hidden behind its closed port, had been loaded but never fired; its crew had packed it with a thirty-two pound roundshot and a tin bucket of musket-balls; they had cocked the lock and prepared to run it out, but the order had never been given, and many of the carronade's crew now lay below in the orlop, awaiting the surgeon's saw. The cro'jack yard had fallen over the gun, and the lanyard now lay in a spider's web of torn rigging that lay partly over the carronade, partly over the smashed remnants of the yard.

The boarders came over the bulwarks between the aftermost gun and the next gun forward, jumping down onto the tangle of rigging, kicking to free their bare feet from the clutches of the tangled shrouds, the coiled, torn line . . . the lanyard jerked.

Sparks leaped from the lock onto the priming; the carronade barked, flinging itself back on its slide. The thirty-two-pound ball smashed through *Revenge*'s bulwarks amidships, driving before it a humming chorus of splinters, and then shrieked on and out to sea. The musketballs dropped one of the schooner's helmsmen dead as stone and nipped

the tip of a little finger from the other helmsman. One of
the musketballs, flattened by the impact of breaking out of
the tin bucket, entered Gideon's left arm above the elbow
and snapped the bone like a dry twig. Another musketball
entered his left side, traveled across his back, and exited
without doing major damage. Two of the long splinters
from the bulwark punctured Gideon's coat and drove into
his back, while a third flung itself against his head, spilling
his top hat from his head and knocking the Yankee privateer unconscious to the blood-stained deck.

24

UNDER THE KNIFE

Gideon lay gasping on the deck, feeling the hot, smooth planking beneath his cheek, the wet kiss of the hot tar. "Jesus shit a sausage!" he heard Finch Martin bellow from somewhere far away. "Fetch Doctor Rivette!" Bare feet thundered on the deck.

"Language, Mr. Martin," Gideon said, but somehow he was not heard. He could feel warmth soaking the clothes on his back, warmth that turned cold as it spread. *Blood,* he thought. The British have treacherously attacked. Must rally the men.

"Give 'em grape," he roared, and at this he was heard. He felt a hand touch his shoulder.

"That's all right, sir." It was Finch Martin's voice. "The damn British have surrendered. One of their guns went off by mistake."

"Treachery . . ." Gideon began to feel the pain throbbing in his arm and back. He could taste gunpowder in his mouth.

"If it is, I'll find out. Don't ye worry. Here's the doctor."

Other hands touched him, practiced hands. They lifted the coat, examined the arm.

"Captain, your arm is broken." The voice of the surgeon still betrayed a touch of his Vermont-French origins. "Please do not move. You might accidentally sever an artery with the edge of the broken bone."

"Have the other wounded been attended to?" Gideon gasped. The pain waxed, running up his arm, an increasing agony. "I must insist the others are treated first."

"There were only four wounded, Captain," said the surgeon. "They have long since been taken care of. I must congratulate you on conducting a most economical battle."

Confident hands began to work on his arm. Gideon shuddered with the pain, tried to hold in a scream of agony, and was relieved to discover that he did not have the strength to scream. His attenuated, gasping moan was muffled by the planking.

"I have placed a tourniquet on your arm, Captain. I will make a sling, and then we will move you to the cockpit."

A sling was fitted beneath his arm. There was no litter on the schooner, so he was lifted from the deck by the rough, willing hands of the crew and carried down the after companionway. The pain was of paralyzing intensity, so extreme that Gideon could not give voice to the scream he felt bubbling inside him. Another companionway, a short passage. They were below the water line. He felt the splinters wrench in his wounds; the broken bone grated. At last he was deposited on a bed made up of the officers' chests. Gideon could smell old blood. The cockpit was lit with candles, reminding Gideon of a church. A Romish church.

"I shall have to cut away your coat in order to examine the wounds in your back. I will ask you to drink this opiate. It may serve to alleviate the pain." A cup was placed to Gideon's lips. He could smell rum, neat, and the narcotic tang of the anodyne.

"I will not," he gasped.

"What? Drink it, man."

"Doctor," Gideon said through clenched teeth. "Is there a possibility I will not survive these operations?" He could feel the pain lying in wait, gnawing on the broken bone of his arm like a small animal, ready to bite with needlelike teeth if he was moved again.

Rivette hesitated, then spoke. "There is always the chance, yes," he said. The candles flickered with the roll of the schooner. Their light reflected off pale faces, wounded drained of blood.

"Then I will not drink the narcotic," Gideon stated. "If I am to meet my maker, I will do so with a clear head."

"Good God! Drink it, Captain!"

"Do yer duty, Dr. Rivette!" Gideon croaked harshly, the pain leaping in him. "I will have no papist preaching about how easy it is to be a Christian!"

There was a moment of offended silence. "Very well, Captain. I must ask you to bite this piece of leather. Hold his legs, there."

He could feel with his tongue the impressions of other men's teeth in the leather. Hands grasped his shins, his wrist, his left shoulder above the wound. The knife pared away his clothing. He could feel the blood run coldly down his naked back. "Thy will be done," Gideon tried to say through the leather, through the pain, and then the knife, heated to lessen the pain, sliced through his flesh. . . .

The splinters were eight and twelve inches long respectively, barbed, with half their lengths imbedded in Gideon's flesh. They had to be cut out, the wounds searched for fragments of wood and clothing, then sewn shut. Gideon soon lost the will to scream and consciousness of anything but the knife, the probe, the deft needle. He tried to speak to his God but could not form conscious phrases, could not know anything but the agony and the desire for it to stop.

The last stitch was taken. Gideon collapsed sweating into the hands of Rivette's assistants.

"I should examine the arm, Captain, but you are weak." Rivette's voice was remorseless, unending. Just when Gideon wanted to sleep. "I must prescribe you a stimulant if you are to face this. Rum."

"No opiate," he said through the leather. Rivette seemed to understand.

"Just rum, Captain. I won't try to trick you."

The leather was taken from his mouth. He felt the cool rim of the cup against his lips and drank. The neat rum seared his throat. The cup was taken away, and he fell back to the table. Rest . . .

"Very good." Rivette's voice droned through the haze of pain. "Your pulse has risen. I must tend to the arm now."

Drearily Gideon nodded. *Go away, ye papist,* he thought.

"Captain, you must understand." Rivette's voice was merciless, prodding. "There is a possibility I will have to remove the arm. If this is so, do you wish me to take it off now or after you've rested a bit? You may be stronger later."

He gasped, shook his head. "Now." The rum warmed him. "Do it now. Don't bother me again."

Again the agony commenced, the ritual of knife and probe. Dimly, through the throb of anguish, he heard the ring of the bullet dropped into the surgeon's dish. There was an enormous wrench, a racking torment that threatened to tear his bones asunder. After that the stitches were easy to bear. The splints and bandages were placed.

"Let him rest a bit. We can carry him to his cabin later and put him more at ease. Then another stimulant. I would suggest coffee if the fires have been relit, otherwise rum again." Rivette's voice came dimly through Gideon's consciousness. "You still have your arm, Captain. D'you understand?"

Gideon spat out the leather strap, nodded. The candles swayed, perceived as if through fog, a long distance away. He remembered the streetlamp in Mobile, the ascending cloud of Blake's cigar smoke, stars, and the scent of honeysuckle. His arm was safe.

"Here, Captain." It was Martin's voice. Something cold was put into his hand. He strained to see it in the light of the streetlamp. There was gilt, the figure of a lion, things that sparkled. Diamonds.

"The British captain's sword, sir," Martin said. "He wouldn't give it up, said he'd thrown it overboard, but I searched his cabin. A presentation sword from the Patriotic Fund. Yours, sir. Congratulations."

"Thank you, Mr. Martin," Gideon whispered. His voice was surprisingly clear to him. He could feel the pain receding, retreating dully into his arm and back, alert to return but for the moment content to wait.

"We have the officers' swords as well," Martin continued. "We're chasin' them last convoy ships, sir. Don't worry, Cap'n, we'll have 'em all soon enough."

The presentation sword lay heavy in Gideon's hand. The hilt felt smooth, well-worn, the scabbard tended. Diamonds glittered cleanly in the light of the candles.

"Thanks be to the Lord," he whispered.

"That sloop of war's goin' to sink, sir," Martin said. "Too many holes twixt wind and water, but she's got twelve or more hours left. Enough for us to take the rest of th' convoy. They had Americans aboard, prisoners from Port Royal to Bermuda."

"Very well, Mr. Martin. Thank you . . ." He could feel his voice failing. "Thank you . . . for your . . . inestimable service."

Martin's figure briefly blocked the candlelight as he walked toward the companionway. "Don't ye worry, Cap'n. We'll complete yer victory for ye."

Victory. *Betsy, I've won a victory!* he thought madly. At long last a victory. His. The sword, the enemy sloop of war, the convoy. His fingers closed possessively about the hilt of the presentation sword, receiving it. His.

25

INCIDENTS

The British captain was about fifty, stout, with a reddish, broken-veined face that could have been the outcome either of a hard life among the merciless elements or prolonged indulgence in drink. His voice was loud and coarse, his accent outlandish, his manner a mixture of bluster and prejudice. He had done something brave once in his life, and he'd been posted and given a hundred-guinea sword. Gideon could not imagine that the promotion could possibly have come about from anything but naked courage, for the man clearly possessed not an ounce of imagination, tact, or courtesy; and his social qualifications and "interest," by which promotion was usually obtained in the more civilized European navies, seemed at first and subsequent glances to be nil.

Gideon, pale and in pain, propped on the cushions of his thwartships settee and twisted at an uncomfortable angle, with pillows beneath his ribs placed so they would not afflict his stitches, stared at the British captain with dull eyes. He had been brought up from the cockpit only five hours before and had taken Dr. Rivette's recommended stimulus. The pain was steady but subdued, only flaring into teeth-clenching agony if he forgot to move slowly. It was best if he did what work he could and kept his mind off his injuries.

The British captain, Martin, and a seaman standing behind him ready to remove him if he overtaxed Gideon's slim strength, glared at Gideon as though he were an offending insect. An insect, Gideon reminded himself, who had taken from him what was probably the only command he had ever had or could hope to receive.

"You had Americans among your crew, Captain Trevannion, I believe," Gideon said.

"Aye, we did."

"You forced them to fight against their countrymen," Gideon continued. He knew his voice was harsh and weary, probably rude. He could still taste the strip of leather in his mouth.

"You made them fight even after a deputation from among them had requested ye to allow them other duty."

Trevannion turned a deeper shade of red. His voice was loud and rough when it came, as if he were shouting aloft to a careless topman. "Any Americans we had were volunteers. I kept 'em at their duty. Disobedience I do not tolerate. Nor insolence. Nor slackers. Can't let one man keep from his duty. Then none of 'em will fight."

"We have your muster books, Captain," Gideon said. His arm ached in its sling; his fingers felt numb as he moved the book across his table. He opened it at random, turning the leather jacket and the heavy, mildewed pages. "Joseph Allison and Israel Penvennen, pressed from the brig *Eva Mae*, Baltimore, twenty-third of February, Eighteen-Oh-eight."

Trevannion snorted. "Penvennen! I know a Cornish accent when I hear one!"

"Roger Coucy, pressed from the American schooner *Ulysses*, July fourteenth, Seventeen Ninety-four," Gideon said. "He was aboard your ship for almost twenty years. He was flogged twice for attempted desertion. You have kept him from his country, from all news of his family. He was killed in the fight. You might have condemned him to death by hanging; it would have been more merciful."

"I did not press that man," Trevannion stated. "That was Captain Jones, years ago. I have only commanded *Alastor* for eight years."

"These men had protections signed by American magistrates."

"Forgeries!" Trevannion snorted. "I know a forgery when I see one. Besides, they volunteered."

"They enlisted as volunteers after it was explained the pay was greater," Gideon said. "Two weeks ago you captured the American privateer *Pride of Baltimore*. Its crew has complained of ill treatment. Is it not true that you have kept them ironed in the hold without allowing them proper food or exercise?"

"What was I supposed to do with 'em?" the British captain said, barely controlling his rage. "They scuttled their damn' pilot boat, there was no place to put 'em. I kept them safe from mischief in the hold."

"Seven died."

"They had a doctor with 'em!" Trevannion roared. "If he was incompetent, they should have found another one. It's not my business to coddle pirates, liars, and traitors to their country."

Trevannion's blustering roar broke against Gideon's glare of ice and receded. For the first time Trevannion looked uncertain, as if he knew he'd overstepped.

"Put him in irons and throw him in the hold," Gideon directed Martin. "He may live on bread and bilgewater. We can turn him over to the authorities in Mobile if he lives; and they can exchange him. If the British will want him back, which I doubt."

Trevannion was stunned into silence by the ferocity of the sentence, his eyes bulging in surprise, but when Martin put a hand on his arm to lead him out, he found his tongue. "Damned insolence! You're all a pack of thieves! Picaroons, no better than niggers! No gentlemen!" he bawled as the grinning first officer hauled him from the cabin.

Pirate. Gideon had known the charge would arise sooner or later. It was a label that all privateers subjected themselves to, the more so because it was often substantially true. Privateers waged a private war for their own gain, albeit a private war licensed by their government and sanctioned by the laws of nations. The trade of privateer frequently attracted men who used their letters of marque as licenses to practice piracy, the most prominent local example being the Lafitte brothers of the Barataria colony near New Orleans, who, while ostensibly serving the renegade Republic of Cartagena, an odd political entity at war both with Spain and the other South American rebels under Bolivar, helped themselves and the unscrupulous merchants of New Orleans to any Spanish or Bolivarist vessels that

came their way. Some said they did not confine themselves
entirely to ships not American. Gideon himself had committed acts technically piratical: the attempt to sell his
prizes to Velasco without the intermediary of a prize court
being the prominent example. Still, he considered his behavior scarcely criminal.

But Gideon also knew that privateering was America's
only hope for victory in the war she had so foolishly
declared, and he knew that the more legitimate naval services could scarcely declare for themselves a monopoly on
upright and gentlemanly behavior. The British captain who
had blustered and stormed as he was hauled out of Gideon's cabin had brutally pressed men of other nations,
flogged them when they objected, and thrown his captives,
manacled, into the bilges to rot. He considered them rebellious colonials rather than representatives of a new republic, not worthy of the consideration granted a more legitimate foe. Such would be the fate of American citizens,
Gideon knew, all over the fallen world until American
strength could be projected over the globe to persuade the
world's renegades to leave its citizens alone. A start had
been made with John Adams's navy, but under Jefferson
and the Republicans the navy had been starved and almost
done away with; and the contempt of America and American power engendered by such policy had brought on the
war, and brought to Gideon Markham more than his life's
share of despair and sorrow.

Captain Trevannion had no right to call anyone *pirate*,
but still the charge disturbed Gideon. He knew he had confirmed Trevannion's charge when he'd thrown the man
manacled into the hold, and he knew no good would come
of it. Trevannion would eventually be released and exchanged back to England, where his tale of American brutality would be circulated throughout the naval community
and would probably bring on more reprisals. The tale, of
course, would be shorn of Trevannion's own casual brutality to his American prisoners. It was altogether a pity that
Trevannion had not died with so many of his men. Conflict
roiled in Gideon's mind. Surrendered men had every right
to expect good treatment: why else surrender? Yet the
thought of that ignorant, vicious man on parole, walking

about the schooner's decks, was intolerable. Gideon shook his head. Let the man rot for another twenty-four hours; then he'd be paroled, put into one of the prizes converted into a prisoner cartel, and sent home. Let it be a short lesson. Even so, Gideon doubted whether Trevannion was capable of learning such lessons.

There was a knock on his cabin door. Gideon passed his hands over his eyes. Weariness warred with pain in his body, but pain was yet uppermost. No point in trying to sleep until weariness overcame pain and dragged him down.

"Come in."

It was Finch Martin, accompanied by one of the Americans released from *Alastor*, one who had served for years as a British seaman. The man was about thirty, short, well-muscled, and brown from exposure to the elements. Gideon saw intelligence in his eyes and in the way he carefully looked about the cabin, acquiring his bearings, while Martin spoke with Gideon.

"Th' British officers have all insisted on being put in the hold with their captain," Martin reported. "Unless you say otherwise, we're ready to oblige 'em."

"They give him more loyalty than he deserves."

"Aye. I reckon that's right."

"Put 'em in the hold, but don't iron them. Let Trevannion be the only one so served."

"Aye, Cap'n." He indicated the seaman standing a respectful pace behind him. "This is Joseph Alison, Cap'n. He was pressed aboard *Alastor* years ago and has told me something ye may wish to hear."

"Very well."

Alison looked momentarily startled that he was not given a less brusque reception, but then stepped forward. His hand came up to his brow in the Royal Navy's habit of knuckling one's forehead to one's superior, but then he hesitated and lowered his hand again. Gideon felt, to his own surprise, a surge of savage gratification at this reassertion of republican principles.

"*Alastor*'s convoy was late in the season, Captain," he began. "Waited in harbor from June through August from lack of escort. That was because *Alastor* and *Musqueto-*

bite, th' sloop of war you saw yesterday, were delayed for some weeks in Pensacola in Spanish Florida."

"When was this, Alison?"

"We dropped anchor in Pensacola, ah—that would be four weeks ago this last Tuesday. We stayed for three days while Captain Trevannion conferred with the Spanish governor, and then we picked up a cargo of Indians and sailed to Port Royal Sound."

"Indians?" Gideon could not keep the surprise from his voice. "You say that ye sailed with Indians? What sort of Indians?"

"We were told they were Creek warriors, sir," Alison said. "They were all men in the prime of life, no women or children. They couldn't have been refugees. On our return to Jamaica the royal governor made the *miccos*—the chiefs, that is—welcome."

"How many Indians were there?" Gideon asked carefully, his face creased by a frown.

"Some four hundred, sir. They were sick as dogs for most of the voyage."

"That I can well believe."

"Some had scalps, sir," Alison volunteered. "White scalps often as not."

"Thankee, Alison. If that's all, you may leave."

"Er—thank you, Captain." He turned to leave, then hesitated and turned back. "I didn't want to fight other Americans, sir," he said. "I asked the captain not to. He said I should be flogged after the fight for disobedience."

"Thankee, Alison. I've spoken with Captain Trevannion, and I understand. I shall write a report to the authorities in Mobile when we return." A thought struck him. "Alison, can ye read and write?"

"Aye, sir. I'm a Connecticut man."

"You might commit this news to paper. In yer own words. My clerk will give ye pen and paper."

"Thank you, Captain." The seaman turned to leave, his pace brisk.

"He'll be a good man, Cap'n," Martin offered as Alison left the cabin. "Above the common lot, I'd say."

"That may be so."

"Our prizes all seem to be within sight, hove to. They're carryin' lanterns."

After the victory over the enemy sloop of war and the swift capture of the remaining merchantmen, Martin had made the flag signal to recall all the vessels taken from the enemy, allowing the privateers to form their own convoy under *Revenge*'s protection as they made their slow way to Mobile. The dismasted sloop of war had been abandoned and then, after Martin had relieved it of its stores and small arms, was set afire. Her sixty dead, lying slaughtered on her bloody decks, had been granted a Viking funeral, the flames reaching up into the gathering darkness before the magazines took fire and *Alastor* blew itself to smithereens.

Gideon felt the dull pain throbbing in his arm and his back. There was a persistent ache behind his eyes.

"Why, Cap'n, would th' British be takin' Indians to Jamaica?" Martin wondered.

"For training, Mr. Martin," Gideon said. "To be given arms and training."

"I can't see them Red Sticks acceptin' trainin', Cap'n," Martin said, his face twisted into a frown. "But I'm buggered if I can think of any other reason. It seems like th' British'd do better to just ship the arms through Pensacola. The Red Sticks'd know what to do with muskets."

"Perhaps they intend to transport the Red Sticks elsewhere," Gideon said. "The British can land them on our coast." *Mobile!* he thought, and his heart lurched. "They can land them at Mobile with a British squadron in support."

Martin's expression turned from one of surprise to one of calculation. "Aye," he said slowly. "That would make sense."

"It makes the only sense, Mr. Martin. New Orleans is too strong to attempt with but four hundred men. Mobile is defended only by Fort Bowyer, a few regulars, a score of old Spanish guns, and a disorganized militia. Those four hundred Indians might well outnumber the fort's garrison, and they could be stiffened with marines."

"Aye," Martin said excitedly. "By God, they could take all West Florida!"

Gideon's dull eyes flickered, then turned away. "We can do nothing about it, Mr. Martin, except to inform the authorities when we return. We may have upset their timetable by taking *Alastor*: perhaps their plan will require their awaiting reinforcement. British naval strength in the Caribbean is not great. I think I shall try to rest now."

"Very well, Cap'n. You get a good rest and don't worry yerself."

"See the men get a good breakfast. They've missed enough meals today."

"Aye aye."

Wallace Grimes entered the cabin, arranged the pillows on Gideon's bunk, and handed him a cup of cocoa. He drank, rose from the settee, and almost fell back, submerged beneath the sudden wave of pain. Grimacing, he leaned on Grimes's arm to make his way to his bunk, where he lay down on his side so as not to disturb his wounds. He hated this feeling of helplessness, the enforced lack of activity when there was so much to do on deck. Overhead the watch paced, and somewhere a wounded man—prisoner probably—screamed incoherently in his delirium. Hove-to, the tern schooner pitched on the sea, awaiting the dawn.

Most of the next morning was spent transferring cargo from one captured vessel to another, burning the empty ones, and transforming the captured xebec into a cartel for prisoners. *Alastor*'s officers, after a night amid the rats and cockroaches of the schooner's hold, readily pledged their parole not to fight against the United States until exchanged with an officer of equal rank, then set sail with their captain in the cartel.

The skirmish with the convoy had left the crew of *Malachi's Revenge* even larger than before: forty American prisoners from the *Pride of Baltimore* had volunteered, along with their surviving officers, and thirteen of the survivors from *Alastor*'s crew, all of them claiming to be Americans or foreigners pressed into the British service. *Revenge*'s crew, once taken off the prizes, was too large to accept all these additions, but Gideon supposed a few of the crew would leave in Mobile to spend their prize money, and the new men could take up the slack. Any left over would have to simply be released in Mobile in hopes they could somewhere find employment.

By noon the tern schooner and a convoy of thirteen well-laden vessels straggled into a familiar-looking line and began the voyage to Mobile. The weather held; no longer beating against the wind, the convoy made good time. Dr. Rivette pronounced himself satisfied with the state of Gideon's injuries; there was no sign of infection. By the second day Gideon began to take short spells on deck. His heart leaped as he saw the line of captured vessels, each carrying an American ensign over the British flag, or flying their old British colors below a white signal of surrender. His men cheered him repeatedly as he took his tours of the deck, and though he told them to offer their praises instead to God, the hands continued to cheer. Gideon's eyes blazed at the sound, at the tribute to his skill and victory, and he found himself stepping on deck more often.

For two days they were becalmed in the Gulf, the convoy with all sail set and hanging lifeless from the yards, drifting above their own perfect reflections on the flat sea; and then the easterly winds rose again, bringing brief, non-threatening squalls that might have been all that remained of another seasonal hurricane breaking up over Florida or the islands. The Yucatan Channel, a place of dangerous currents and treacherous winds, was crossed in a day without danger, and the convoy reached northward toward Mobile.

The day after the last sliver of Cuba had settled below the southern horizon, dawn brought the sight of a distant sail, and while Gideon paced nervously on the deck, annoyed at his inability to go aloft with his arm in a sling, Finch Martin was sent up the shrouds with a long glass. "A brig, carryin' no flag," he reported. "I think she's stalkin' us."

Gideon frowned at the news. He was now in the same position as the British had been when he'd sighted them the morning of the battle: a single vessel guarding a long convoy, the latter slow and vulnerable. *Malachi's Revenge* was swifter than the British cruiser had been, and deadlier, but was even more undercrewed than she had been the day of the fight: with substantial reductions for the prize crews there were less than sixty souls aboard—even the additions from *Pride Of Baltimore* had gone to make up larger prize crews.

"Put down yer helm," Gideon told the helmsman. "We'll pay the brig a visit."

As he impatiently paced the deck, a telescope tucked under his splinted arm, and the masts of the brig rose above the horizon, Gideon began to perceive a certain familiarity to the cut of those sails. Could they be, he wondered, the sails of the unidentified brig that had chased *Prinsessa* through the Gulf? "Beat to quarters," he told his drummer, and as the snare rattled out, Gideon looked for Addams, who might have been able to confirm his suspicions, but then remembered that he had sent the ex-merchant-master on board one of the prizes.

The painfully reduced crew manned the guns and crouched waiting behind the ports; as the schooner approached, the brig wore swiftly and tried to race by, but Gideon tacked without hesitation and brought *Revenge* in closer. The American ensign was raised over the quarterdeck, the rattlesnake streamer to the maintop. The brig's course twisted as it tried to shake its pursuer, but *Malachi's Revenge* steadily closed the distance, and eventually the brig backed a topsail as a signal for a parley and raised the flag of the Republic of Cartagena.

Baratarians, Gideon thought, grimly confirming his apprehensions. The Yucatan Channel would have been a good place to cruise for Spaniards. Gideon hove his schooner to off the enemy quarter at the range of a cable.

Through his glass Gideon saw the enemy standing by their guns, their boarding nets triced up, chain slings supporting the yards . . . all customary precautions for battle. He picked up his speaking trumpet in his good hand and raised it to this mouth. In a minute there might well be bloodshed; he could hope that the Baratarians would hesitate before engaging an American ship of war. Their usual prey were helpless Spanish slavers and merchantmen; he hoped they would think twice before firing on the flag that offered them shelter, or on a schooner that proposed to fire back.

"We are the American privateer *Malachi's Revenge!*" Gideon bellowed, his voice resounding from the speaking trumpet. "We are traveling with a convoy of prizes to United States waters! I am Captain Markham. What do ye Cartagenians wish of me?"

The voice that drifted toward Gideon spoke English with some indefinable accent, probably French rather than Spanish. At this distance Gideon saw a lean, dark figure on the enemy poop, dressed elegantly in yellow. "We are the Cartagenian privateer *General Bolivar,* twenty-four guns. I am Commodore Mortier. We wish to search your convoy for Spanish ships."

"There are no Spanish ships in my convoy, sir!" Gideon shouted. "They are British and all my prizes. You will keep your distance, sir!"

There was a moment's hesitation from the brig, a moment filled only by the sound of wind keening through the rigging, the flap of the privateers' flags.

"We wish to see the cargo manifests!" the brig's captain called. "We will see if any of the cargo is Spanish property. We will take your prizes to the prize court at Barataria Bay, and any ship not carrying Spanish property will be released to you."

"That ye shall not do!" Gideon roared. "If ye sail any closer to this convoy, ye shall be fired upon!" He turned to the men crouched by the guns and gave a signal. The gun ports rose, the heavy iron vibrating the deck as they slid out, every man aboard the schooner hauling on the side-tackles and aiming to sweep the enemy quarter.

The figures aboard the enemy poop appeared to be conferring. Gideon intended to give them no time to work out a plan or plot treachery. "What is yer answer?" he demanded. There was a brief flurry of action on the brig's quarterdeck, fists flying, a man led away by his friends. "Commodore" Mortier turned back to Gideon.

"We will withdraw," he announced through his trumpet, "on your word of honor as a gentleman that there are no Spanish ships in the convoy."

"You have my word, sir," Gideon answered instantly. The demand for his word of honor was recognized for what it was: an attempt by Mortier to maintain his pres-

tige among the members of his crew, furnishing him with
a reason for backing down. If the pirates were willing to
leave, Gideon was willing to provide them an excuse.

"Stand by," Gideon whispered to his gun crew, fearing
some last-minute treachery; but the pirates set their sails
and began to beat away from the convoy. Gideon kept
Malachi's Revenge between the brig and his prizes, carefully guarding his flock, until the brig's topsails vanished
from sight early in the afternoon.

Gideon hastened back to his place at the head of the line
and altered the convoy's course to the westward, hoping to
avoid having played on him the same trick he had played
on the British convoy, running during the day and plotting
a course to intercept during the night.

The Cartagenian brig was never seen again. Gideon had
stayed on deck all that night, drowsing fitfully in a hammock chair, but the horizon was clear the next morning
and stayed clear. Gideon's wounds were healing; Dr. Rivette continued to pronounce them free of infection. His
tours of the deck grew longer; eventually he relieved Martin
and the other overworked officers by standing two four-
hour watches each day.

He would return to Mobile in triumph, with thirteen captures bulging with cargo to join the four he had sent
ahead from the Virgin Islands. He could not expect the merchants of Mobile to be able to buy so much condemned
cargo at a still-profitable rate; he would have to take at
least half the prizes to New Orleans and risk further con-
tact with the Baratarians. But that was in the future.

The convoy sailed on, Gideon and Martin learning first-
hand the frustrations of convoy escort, of watches that were
not kept, signals not obeyed, collisions that should have
been avoided. And throughout Gideon was aware of the approach of land, knowing that soon *Malachi's Revenge*
would be sailing up the wide bay to Mobile. He found himself vaguely apprehensive. Isolated on the schooner's quarterdeck he had found a kind of peace for himself; he had
fought a battle his way, and when he'd been wounded, he'd
chosen his own way of going under the knife. But Mobile
was a part of the great world, and there his course would

intersect that of others whose concerns extended beyond the bulwarks of the schooner *Revenge*.

And there was Maria-Anna. He found her image in his mind unexpectedly, memories of the forthright way she had walked over *Prinsessa*'s decks, the touch of her muslin gown against the back of his hand, the high-colored, determined expression on her face as she had raised her pistol against the Red Stick warrior balanced on her boat's starboard gunwale, the pistol that was to misfire and almost leave her dead on a thwart. Gideon would try not to see her again. She had made it clear he was not welcome. *Two are better than one,* his mind cadenced, the verses coming unbidden, *for if they fall, the one will lift up his fellow: but woe to him that is alone when he falleth . . . if two lie together, then they have heat: but how can one be warm alone? And if one prevail against him, two shall withstand him; and a threefold cord is not quickly broken . . .*

Gideon shook his head. No. It was not for him; he was cursed. He grimaced as his wounds stabbed him, reminding him there was no gain without loss, that joy was made joyful only by the presence of pain. Let him do what he knew best. The convoy needed his care, and he would be a good shepherd.

The convoy was within a hundred miles of Mobile the next morning. The breeze, which had backed westerly in the night, brought occasional scents of magnolia and sweet gum, and land birds to perch on the spars. It also brought, low and far away, the rumbling, percussive sound of gunfire, carried down by the breeze. Martin, a little hard of hearing in his old age, conferred with others to make certian his ears weren't playing tricks, and then ran down the after scuttle to bring the news to Gideon. On deck in an instant Gideon swept the horizon with his glass; even the lookouts reported nothing, no sails in any direction. Gideon made swift decisions: the convoy would sail onward for the safe harbor. *Malachi's Revenge* would investigate the firing, and if it proved to be a strong enemy, Gideon would try to lead them away from the convoy out into the Gulf.

The tern schooner forged ahead onto its new tack, close-
hauled, the helmsmen doubled and the crew called up.
Gideon could see Thomas Tate standing by his long gun,
one arm resting almost affectionately on the breech; and he
remembered the first time he'd seen Tate on the wharf at
New Orleans, striding up toward *General Sullivan* with a
cutlass thrust through a purple sash, bare feet stuck out of
ragged trousers, and his head wrapped in a red bandanna.
He had just left the Baratarians, he'd told Gideon, and
wanted a job with honest men. Gideon had told him that
Sullivan already had a cook. "I'm not a goddam cook,
sah," Tate had said. "I'm the best gunner in the Gulf. Give
me a gun and I can prove it." He'd proven it over and
over, and most convincingly in the fight with *Alastor*; Gideon had heard from Martin and Clowes about the number
of eighteen-pound shot that had crashed into the enemy
sloop, upending carronades, tearing chunks from the masts
below decks, and leaving limbless men scattered over the
red-stained planks.

Land began to rise dark above the horizon, the low
marsh of the Mississippi Delta. Gunfire still came downwind, scattered: single shots, as if a chase were under way
and only bow or stern chasers were being fired.

Malachi's Revenge forged past Pass à l'Outre to larboard, then Robinson's point, and as the broad, shallow
Bay Honde opened to Gideon's sight, gunfire again broke
out, an entire broadside this time, and the men of the
schooner saw the combatants wreathed in gray smoke,
their flags flying above the melee.

"Ready about!" Gideon roared, and the men sprang to
their stations, the Stars and Stripes soaring up the halliards. Three masts stood above the fight, two flying British
colors, the other, above a pockmarked trysail with the
French tricolor fluttering tattered from its peak. Two vessels interwoven, connected by writhing smoke and wreckage, one with a mast down. The roar of cannon gradually
turned to the shouts of boarders and the clash of metal on
metal.

A Frenchman, Gideon thought sourly. America's co-bel-
ligerents, as usual in need of rescue. Crewman stood by their
guns, the gun captains uncoiling the lanyard, readying

them to pass alongside the stationary British schooner, spitting at biscuit's throw a raging iron salute.

But swiftly the clatter of arms ceased, and the two vessels drifted apart, the British schooner's wings filling with the breeze, a bone slowly appearing in her teeth as she gained way. Gideon felt his heart lifting: the enemy were running, there would be no fight, no need to risk his skeleton crew to rescue a foolish Frenchman who had got himself trapped against the swampy shore of the Delta. *Malachi's Revenge* would not pursue. The enemy was running away from the convoy, off toward the Isle au Breton Sound, and Gideon wanted them to run. He would encourage it. "Tate, give 'em a roundshot!" he barked, and Tate grinned as he swung his long gun toward the enemy.

The French snow, its remaining mainmast and stumpy trysail mast supported precariously by a few unsevered shrouds, looked very familiar, even with its bulwarks broken by enemy carronades and its stump of a foremast cocked at an unlikely angle. *Franklin*, Gideon thought, Captain Julian Fontenoy, that irritatingly handsome Frenchman he'd dined with at Fort Bowyer.

A handful of ragged crewmen lined *Franklin*'s side to cheer as *Malachi's Revenge* swept up on her quarter and hove to in the quiet waters of the bay. The clanking sound of pumps carried from the Frenchman. Gideon had a boat lowered, and he and Dr. Rivette were rowed to the French schooner's side, Gideon managing to climb the shattered side with only one arm, gritting his teeth, the doctor coming easily behind.

"Wonderful, sir! A thousand thanks!" Fontenoy stood at the broken entry port, his dark face creased by a white smile, his coat nicked and bloody.

"Thank the Almighty, sir, who backed the wind during the night to bring us the sound of gunfire," Gideon said. Fontenoy clasped his hand, then apologized because of the blood running down his wrist. He'd been wounded more than once in the boarding fight.

Fontenoy explained that *Franklin* had chased a British merchantman toward Isle au Breton Sound, probably a smuggler, but it was a trap or a British schooner happened to be cruising there. *Franklin*'s foremast had sprung during the chase, carrying too much sail. After that there was no choice but to turn and fight, to lay alongside and hope to carry by boarding. The foremast had been shot clean away on the approach, but they'd managed to get alongside in any case. The boarding battle had been bloody until Gideon and his crew had forced the British to flee.

Gideon glanced over the decks as Fontenoy talked: dead men lay in heaps, blood spattered about as if by a mad housepainter, guns and tackle overturned . . . He recognized the corpse of Aristide, Fontenoy's first officer, lying almost in two pieces, cut by a cannon ball. Two seamen worked doggedly at the bilge pump. Most of those walking had been wounded at least once. The *fléau brisé*, Fontenoy's strange weapon, hung from his left hand, and the lower links were bloody. The French captain had obviously been in the thick of the fighting.

Rivette approached and addressed Fontenoy in French. The privateer responded cheerfully and allowed the wound on his arm to be examined and stanched.

"Captain Fontenoy," Gideon said, "I will have my other boats lowered, and ye may transfer yer men and their property to my schooner. Dr. Rivette can give them aide in the cockpit."

Fontenoy looked up in surprise from his bandaging. "Leave *Franklin*, *Capitaine*? No, impossible. I shall take us back to Mobile."

Gideon found a certain admiration for Fontenoy's bravery creeping in with his impatience. "Sir, I have a convoy of prizes to escort," he explained. "With that British schooner on the loose I cannot afford to leave them for long, otherwise I'd offer ye a tow to Mobile. Ye've lost a mast, and the other stick will rock out in any kind of sea. Ye're badly holed and taking on water, and there is an enemy vessel sharing with ye a very narrow stretch of water. We can't protect you once ye're out of sight."

Fontenoy shrugged. "*Franklin* is my livelihood. Mobile is not far. I will take the chance."

Gideon shook his head.

"Sir, it is a very small chance."

"We will do our best."

Rivette turned to Gideon, his soft eyes impatient. "I must stay aboard, Captain. There are many wounded here."

"Aye, Doctor, I understand. But I wish you would remonstrate with Captain Fontenoy, here. With jury masts up *Franklin* will rock terribly. It would be mad to subject the wounded to that."

Rivette turned to Fontenoy. "I agree with Captain Markham," he said. "The rocking will be bad for the wounded, and it won't make my job any easier, either."

"My men will stay with me," Fontenoy assured them. "The boat will rock a little, but they will stay."

Rivette sighed. "Very well," he said. "Where may I work?"

Fontenoy called for one of his men to show Rivette the half-orlop below. Gideon frowned at Fontenoy's casual, aristocratic assumption that his men were willing to risk their lives in the leaky, shattered *Franklin* in order that their captain conserve what remained of his fortune, but he could say nothing: a captain's authority must be upheld. His eyes swept the deck once more, seeing the overturned guns, the huddled, mutilated corpses. Brave men to keep the fight going so long. It was not what he'd heard of French sailors.

"It's not a risk I would take, Captain," Gideon said. "I'll pray that ye succeed." He saw the figure of a boy come from the after scuttle of the French privateer, carrying a cartridge case—boys were usually used to carry powder cartridges from the magazine during a fight, and now this one was presumably carrying the extras back. The boy, his face smeared with powder, barefoot and in a short sailor's jacket, a bandanna wrapped round his head to keep him from being deafened by gunfire, looked listlessly over the decks in search of loose cartridges, then saw Gideon, his mouth dropping in astonishment. The leather cartridge case fell to the deck. "*Gideon!*" he shouted in a voice that was somehow familiar, and ran toward him with arms outstretched, being brought up short as Fontenoy seized his collar.

"Do you know this one?" the Frenchman asked. "Stowed away in Mobile with two other boys and an old whore. Calls himself Juan."

Gideon searched the powder-smeared countenance, found he knew the eyes from somewhere, but not the rest. "I don't believe I've seen him before," he said slowly.

The boy wrenched himself free from Fontenoy's grip, tore the knotted bandanna from his head, revealing straggling short brown hair. "*Capitán* Markham, I am Campaspe!"

"Thunderation!" He knew her now, the gawky body disguised by a jacket and ragged trousers, the dazzling, impudent, entirely familiar smile bursting from the dirty face as soon as she saw his recognition. She had cut off most of her hair, chopped it off to the brushy style fashionable among men and women since the Directory, revealing the unfamiliar lines of her scalp and a pair of reddened ears.

Gideon looked at Fontenoy in amazement. "This is a— she's a lady's maid from Mobile," he said. Fontenoy's eyebrows rose as he examined Campaspe more closely. "She's run away from her mistress," Gideon went on. "I'll take her back with me. I know the lady."

"She makes an uglier girl than she does a boy," Fontenoy observed. "You can have her, I suppose. I wouldn't trust my crew with her once they found out she's female, and there's no point in having her aboard if she can't work alongside the others."

"I can find work for her," Gideon said grimly, and looked down at Campaspe with a frown that brought hesitation to her impudent smile.

The following afternoon the convoy huddled off Fort Bowyer, awaiting the pilot, while the amazed officers of the fort came aboard *Revenge* to offer their congratulations. An oversized Stars and Stripes, a battle-flag, floated over the fort: the garrison had assumed the convoy was a hostile fleet, and the water battery of a few ancient Spanish twelve-pounders had been hastily manned by regulars who knew that if the fourteen ships on the horizon were enemies, their task was futile from the start.

"General Claiborne has an army in Mobile," Captain Lockwood announced, pacing with Gideon over the tern schooner's quarterdeck. "A thousand militia drawn from the Mississippi, the Third U.S. Infantry under Gil Russel,

and scouts from the Cherokee and the friendly Creeks."
Lockwood's eyes glowed as he anticipated the battle to
come. "The Red Stick menace to Mobile is over, Captain
Markham. Weatherford will be crushed, and then we can
deal with the real enemy, the Tories and British agents in
Pensacola." He grinned ruefully. "I won't be going, blast it.
I'm to stay in command of the fort."

"Aye, but ye may have to face the enemy earlier than ye
suspect," Gideon said. "Four hundred Red Sticks have
been transported from Pensacola to Jamaica. We've captured the evidence. The only possible conclusion I can
draw is that there will be an attempt on Mobile."

Lockwood frowned and scratched his jutting jaw. "I'd inform General Claiborne, if I were you, before he leaves.
He may want to reinforce me."

"I intend to. I'll send another report to Commodore Patterson in New Orleans."

"You won't have to. He's in Mobile, came with the *Carolina* schooner to see Claiborne. Good heavens!" Lockwood had seen Campaspe, in a homemade canvas skirt,
laboring with needle and palm on the schooner's foredeck.
"D'you have a seamstress aboard?" Campaspe looked up at
Lockwood resentfully.

"A stowaway, Captain," Gideon said. "We've put her to
work assisting the sailmaker in stitching up a spare mainsail. Between the two of them it should take another three
months."

"But a young girl, here on a ship full of men," Lockwood objected. "Won't there be danger of, er—"

Gideon took Lockwood's arm and turned aft toward the
quarterdeck. "We've installed her in the chart room and
forbidden her to enter the fo'c'sle or converse with the
crew," he said. "That will minimize the chance of, ah, con-
tamination. I think she will be happy to return to the
household in Mobile she ran away from."

"Ah. I see." Lockwood permitted a smile to crease his
rugged features. "I think you may have handled it well."

But Gideon remained unsmiling. Campaspe's presence
aboard *Malachi's Revenge* added to the anxiety he felt
about again approaching land. The girl's presence had
crystallized the phantoms inhabiting Gideon's mind, re-

minding him that Maria-Anna and everything else that had happened to him when he'd last set foot in West Florida were not visions or distant memories, but concrete events he'd shared with others, and with whose perplexing reality he would once again be forced to grapple once his schooner slid with its convoy across the wide, embracing bay . . .

He shook his head. He would face his memories at the right time, but not now. "Captain Lockwood," he said. "Have ye ever seen a thirty-two pound carronade solid? We have one aboard, a souvenir of our battle."

"I'd be delighted, Captain," Lockwood said. Gideon showed Lockwood to the companionway and ordered from Grimes a cup of cocoa for his guest.

26

THE DELIVERY

The memory was tender, but no longer raw . . . It could be faced, he hoped, without pain. It would be faced, in any case. There was no other civilized choice. . . .

Gideon marched down the street, one hand firmly on Campaspe's shoulder. Maria-Anna's house was as he remembered it with its imposing front door and brass knocker. His knock sounded angry. The woman who opened the door was formidable and Spanish, and although her English was barely comprehensible, Gideon gathered that Señora Marquez had rented her house to a family of refugees and had taken up residence elsewhere. There followed a trek to another part of town, Campaspe in the lead, having obtained directions in Spanish. All about them bustled the business of war: men drilling on the town plaza, rows of tents on the town's outskirts, couriers galloping on obscure errands, platoons of the Third Infantry in neat if worn uniforms, marching under the rigid discipline of their sergeants. Gideon saw few drunken soldiers, and mentally congratulated Claiborne on overcoming the militia's chief vice.

Maria-Anna's new house was a modest, two-story brick residence, probably built under the influence of American architectural styles. Gideon's knock was firm and in unexpected rhythm with the undesired and entirely frustrating thudding of his heart. The door was opened by Alfred, still in livery; his formal, stern butler's visage melted at once as he saw Gideon. "Welcome back, Cap'n Markham!" he smiled. "Who's this? Oh, Lord . . ." With a cry of frustration at her inability to be recognized Campaspe had flung herself at his midsection.

"I reckon I know her now," the butler said indulgently.

"She ran away to sea," Gideon said. "I've brought her back."

"Please step into the parlor. I fetch this girl to her mistress."

Gideon took off his hat and stepped into the hallway and the parlor, tugging uncomfortably at his neckcloth. There was no way, he supposed, to avoid this: to appear mysteriously at the door, deliver Campaspe, and vanish, would be to cause gossip among the servants, and any sort of speculation at all affecting Maria-Anna's reputation was to be avoided. That, at least, was Gideon's duty. He and Maria-Anna would have a civil conversation in the parlor, and he would take his leave.

He waited an uncomfortable length of time, standing upright, feeling clumsy in his splints and bandages, while Maria-Anna presumably dealt with her renegade maidservant. When Maria-Anna entered, it was quietly through a side door. Her voice seemed ragged; she was trying very hard to keep the tone conversational, under firm control of the proprieties.

"Captain Markham, it seems I am once again in your debt."

"Madam," Gideon said and bowed. Her face, still tanned from her journey up the Tensaw, showed dark against the white of her high-waisted gown, but otherwise no trace remained of the uncombed, half-barbaric woman he had loved. Her hair was drawn back and fixed with a comb, not hanging wildly over her shoulders; she wore a gown and slippers, not a tattered skirt and muddied boots. He tried to read her eyes and sensed a kind of pain there, perhaps a reflection of his own, perhaps an anticipation of hurt to come.

"You've been wounded!" she exclaimed, and for a moment bright concern showed in her eyes, and the proprieties hung dangling by a thread; Gideon felt a mad impulse to step forward into her embrace and felt in her a similar trembling hesitation . . . but she suppressed it, her eyes dulled. The moment was lost.

"I'm mending well enough, thankee," Gideon said. "God saw fit to grant us victory."

"Please sit down."

"Thankee, ma'am."

He hitched the hundred-guinea sword out of the way and sat, perched on the forward lap of a straight-backed chair, aware of the stiff fool he was acting, unable to avoid it.

"I don't understand—" she began.

"I beg your pardon?" The phrase seemed to leap from him awkwardly; he had somehow not been paying attention.

"I don't understand how Campaspe came aboard your ship," she said. "She didn't run away until after you had left."

"It's a schooner, ma'am, not a ship," Gideon said, flinging this hopeless pedanticism out in the face of their bleak awkwardness, knowing it wasn't improving the atmosphere, but unable to stop himself.

"She ran away onto *Franklin*, the French privateer. *Franklin* was attacked by a British schooner and we managed to drive the enemy off. When I came aboard she recognized me. She'd been serving as a powder monkey."

"I see."

"She was disguised as a boy. I don't think anyone knew."

"Captain Fontenoy visited me several times. Perhaps she conceived a sentiment for him."

"Fontenoy didn't know of her deception, I'm certain," Gideon said weakly. He could feel their conversation winding down as if it were a coiled spring: Campaspe's escapade was the only safe subject for conversation. Anything else might somehow wound, even if inadvertently. *There may be a future time,* she had said, *when I am able to look at you without anger.* Gideon sensed the time had not come.

There was a long silence. Gideon groped futilely for a topic of conversation. He stood, the sword clattering about his knees. It seemed very loud, louder than any of their words.

"I should leave, ma'am. I have business in town."

She escorted him to the door. "It was kind of you to bring her back," she said. "I won't forget. I haven't forgotten anything, Captain Markham."

Gideon stood on the street and heard the door close behind him. He looked down at the hat in his hand with a surprised expression, then put it on his head. He would go to Lieutenant Blake's.

He stepped down the street, feeling Maria-Anna's eyes on him from the parlor window, forcing himself not to turn and meet them. Their mutual gaze could speak of more than any parlor conversation, and somehow Gideon was afraid of such mute speech, afraid that it might start what neither of them could properly end. Disturbed by this vague feeling, one he could not explain, he walked down the street, scabbard in his hand, and set his countenance in its usual public scowl.

27

IN THE PARLOR

"You will be at the ball tomorrow night?"

"Oh, yes. I'm going with Mr. and Mrs. Morehouse."

"Supporting the American and not the Spanish faction, Señora?"

Archibald Bulloch Blake, his cocked hat on his knee, lit a new cigar from the old one and leaned back in Maria-Anna's straightbacked chair.

"I'm from South Carolina, you know," she said placidly.

"Of course." The coffee trembled in her cup, reflecting the white light of the window, the furniture of her parlor, an inverted, twisted Blake sending smoke into the air. "Over twenty ships altogether," he said. "Only kept seventeen, though, and burned the rest. Thirteen of them brought in at once two days ago."

"Thirteen," she repeated. Carefully she raised the cup to her lips and saw the trembling world dissolve.

"My God!" Blake muttered. "What thirteen prizes would do for my career! I'd be promoted captain on the spot, even without having sunk a blasted sloop of war."

He smiled at her a bit ruefully and sipped his coffee. He was a regular visitor to her house, civilized and a good companion; she suspected that in some subtle way he had been courting her, waiting for a hint that his attentions were welcome. She was scrupulous not to give the hint, though she had reserved herself the opportunity. At the moment she badly wanted a friend, not a complication.

Blake sighed. "Well, I'm in gunboats, and there's nothing to do about it but accept it. I'm not one of Preble's boys, after all."

"Your time will come, sir," Maria-Anna said. There was a pause, a sip of coffee to disguise an awkwardness created by the reassurance he was too intelligent to accept at face value, but too polite to refuse. "Captain Markham was here yesterday to return Campaspe. She'd run off aboard the *Franklin*, you understand, and—"

"He told me about it; he was my guest at dinner, yesterday afternoon," Blake said. "I wondered—" He hesitated, frowning.

"Yes."

"Nothing. It was the same Gideon. Few words, pious ejaculations, plain talk, plain clothes, and seventeen prizes. No airs about it. You'd never think it to see him on the street, just an ordinary merchant master, chews tobacco, a bit of a bluestocking . . . But seventeen prizes! God."

She lowered the coffee cup into her lap, trying to still its reflected universe, the miniature that might so easily shatter. "I know," she said, seeing Gideon clearly, the brown coat, tall hat, the habitual, puritanical frown. "You haven't seen him in action as I have," she said. "Aboard *Prinsessa* I thought him a prig, quite above it all, and suddenly there was a mutiny and he was the only man aboard who saw it coming. You should have seen him, his eyes lighting up, taking charge, cleaning up other people's messes. In action he's a different person. And on the river. The river . . ." She felt her vision blurring as she remembered images of Gideon, standing in his coat by *Prinsessa*'s wheel, calling out the names of cards; she saw him striking out with his sword at a Red Stick canoe alongside her boat, recognizing the flame in his grim glance as kindred to her own ineradicable fierceness. "The river," she repeated, clinging to the last phrase, seeing the miniature universe in her coffee cup dissolve and spill over the brim onto her gown. She was amazed to find herself weeping as she carefully placed the cup and saucer on the table, and through her tears she saw Blake springing to her aid . . .

28

IN CELEBRATION

The ballroom sweltered, the very walls sweating, scented candles managing to hold at bay the scent of perspiring humanity. There was nothing to indicate that Mobile was, officially at least, still a Spanish possession. Bunting in American colors hung limply from the fixtures, and officers in their tall shakoes strolled on the veranda with local girls on their arms. The band assembled and began to tune their instruments. Beneath an oversized American flag—this one had thirteen stripes and fifteen stars, Gideon noticed, probably stitched together by local Spanish seamstresses with inadequate instruction, or who had perhaps gleefully sabotaged the project—stood the guests of honor: General Ferdinand Leigh Claiborne, brother of the governor of New Orleans and Louisiana; Commodore Daniel Todd Patterson, who commanded the navy's New Orleans Station, consisting of two schooners and a dozen gunboats, one of them Lieutenant Blake's, and who though granted the courtesy title of "commodore," hadn't even a captain's rank; Colonel Gilbert C. Russel, commanding the Third Infantry. The three men wielded all American military power in the Gulf, and commanded the only organized force standing between the British and control of the Mississippi.

Gideon had come as Blake's guest. He sweated stolidly beneath his neckcloth as he was introduced to his hosts, making his way through the throng to the senior military officers. He had only come at Blake's vehement insistence that tonight would be a chance to meet Claiborne and Patterson informally, to speak to them privately of the four hundred Red Sticks transported to Jamaica from Pensacola.

"Beg pardon," Gideon muttered as he clashed scabbards with a scowling dragoon officer in his green-trimmed jacket.

"Watch it, you."

Gideon felt Blake's restraining hand on his arm, but he knew he didn't need it; he hadn't felt anger, just a weary sadness at the other's rudeness. Nerves. In a few weeks that dragoon would be trying to ride his horse through Alabama swamps in pursuit of enemies who were masters of hiding in the foliage, and brilliant at the art of ambush. Nerves. The unremitting heat in the ballroom didn't help.

"There will be half a dozen duels begun tonight," Blake murmured in an undertone. "I don't envy Claiborne and Patterson trying to straighten it all out tomorrow."

They edged their way through the crowd, the regulars in their neat blue uniforms, the militia officers accoutered with a kind of barbarian panache, partly in uniform, partly with homely additions: the tails of animals hanging from hats as plumes, the occasional bear claw necklace, swords beaten out of farm implements. Everywhere there was a certain nervousness, a knowledge that this was the last grand occasion before the American host marched north to meet William Weatherford and the Creek nation.

They stood in the crowd among the senior officers, waiting for a pause. It came.

"Commodore Patterson, may I present Captain Markham, of the privateer *Malachi's Revenge*. Colonel Russel, Captain Markham. General Claiborne, Captain Markham."

"Markham. Is that the New Hampshire Markhams?" Claiborne asked suddenly. The general's middle-aged, long-nosed, aristocratic face was red with heat or drink, beads of sweat standing on his temples. Gideon sensed an edge in Claiborne's voice, as if a sword had sprung half out of its scabbard.

"Aye," Gideon said. "I am of that family."

"I see." The sword was out now. What ancient grudge was Claiborne a party to? Gideon wondered. He searched his memory for any dealings his family may have had with the Claibornes, any relationships on the part of their numerous kin. The general's brother, William, had been the

congressman whose vote broke the tie between Jefferson
and Aaron Burr to make the former president, and had been
rewarded with the governorship of New Orleans and Louisiana; Ferdinand Claiborne had presumably been given
command of the American forces on the grounds of his
brother's accomplishment rather than his own, but . . .
Gideon saw no place in his family's history where they
might have crossed paths with anyone named Claiborne.
He plunged on.

"General Claiborne, I've a man aboard my schooner.
One we took from the British. He tells me that the British
sent two warships to Pensacola and—"

"Sorry, Markham. Can't talk now. Colonel Russel, I was
speaking to you earlier about this matter of proper side-
arms for the scouts, and . . ." The general turned, took
Russel's arm, and walked away, leaving Gideon with his
words still spilling foolishly from his mouth. He felt Blake's
hand on his shoulder.

"I'm so sorry, Gideon," Blake murmured. "It must be
that matter about your brother." Gideon felt the words
burning from his memory, filling with anger the hollow he
felt in his chest: *the story may come back to you in some
alien land, and in a manner calculated to injure you or
your prospects* . . . General Claiborne would not be seen
speaking to the brother of a convicted traitor, even about a
matter touching the security of his own command.

Gideon slowly recovered himself, seeing to his vexation
that Commodore Patterson was still standing by him, the
naval officer slim and rather young for his post, his face
well-formed but too acutely intelligent to be called handsome, the insignia of a master-commandant on his bullion
epaulette.

"You must try to forgive the general, Captain Markham," Patterson said gravely. "He has many burdens now.
I don't think he would have given you this rude reception
if he knew it was you who so bravely captured the British
convoy or that your injury was sustained honorably in battle."

"I don't think it would matter to him."

"Perhaps not," Patterson conceded. "Come, have some punch. I'd like to speak with you of your action with the convoy." Gideon allowed Patterson to steer him toward the punch bowl. "I've never fought a ship action," Patterson said. "I spent most of my time in Barbary in prison with Bainbridge and the crew of the *Philadelphia*. To be truthful I'm rather jealous."

"There's another matter, Commodore Patterson, that I think may be of importance," Gideon said, allowing Patterson to hand him a cup of punch. "When we took the *Alastor*, we released a number of American crewmen who had been held prisoner, and who reported that four hundred Red Stick warriors were recently transported from Pensacola to Port Royal Sound. Just two months ago." Gideon felt Patterson's eyes on him, coolly assessing the information. "I can't think what it could mean, Commodore," Gideon said, "except Mobile."

Patterson nodded slowly. "I think you're right. But we're not in danger here so long as Claiborne and his men are in the vicinity."

"The militia only serve for three months, Commodore."

"Yes," Patterson said briefly.

"I can send a written report to ye with the details. I can also send the men as witnesses."

"Do that, sir. I shall be obliged."

Gideon was surprised by Patterson and impressed: it had taken much intelligence and willpower to hold his command together on this remote station, unsupported by his government, surrounded by alien intrigue, yet the man had done it. *One of Preble's boys,* he remembered Blake saying about him, and he wondered if Preble had truly been as remarkable as had been said of him, whether he had in fact been the making of Hull, Decatur, Bainbridge, Lawrence, the stars that shone in the American naval ensign.

"There is another matter, sir, that falls perhaps more within your jurisdiction," Gideon reported. "I had a skirmish with a Cartagenian cruiser while attempting to convoy my prizes to Mobile."

Gideon felt Patterson's acute gaze fall on him once more. "Which one?" Patterson asked sharply.

"A brig, the *General Bolivar*. Commanded by a Frenchman calling himself Mortier. He said he had twenty-four guns, but I think he exaggerated. He was cruising in the Yucatan Channel."

Patterson listened intently, then nodded. "That's a new one, I think. Perhaps a member of the Lafitte gang, perhaps not. If he was a Frenchman, I suppose he was."

"He wished to inspect the prizes for Spanish goods. After I ran out my guns, he thought the better of it."

Patterson nodded appreciatively. "You know how to handle them, at any rate."

"Is it known whether they take American ships?"

"You understand I have no good sources of information. But we've found some evidence, and at last we're able to act." Patterson allowed himself a careful smile. "Jean Lafitte's been outlawed," he said with reserved satisfaction. "We've put five thousand dollars on his head, Governor Claiborne and I. It's not a great deal—we don't expect to see him in prison anytime soon—but it's a step. Unfortunately we can't touch Pierre yet—he's still playing the businessman."

"I hope yer efforts succeed, Commodore."

"Thank you. And now, sir, if you'll forgive me, I see an inebriated midshipman I'd best speak to before he gets himself in trouble."

"Of course, sir."

Patterson, carefully setting his face in a calculated expression of grim ferocity, strode off to deal with the unlucky youngster, leaving Gideon and Lieutenant Blake staring at one another.

Blake sighed. "That's *my* midshipman, you know. Just my luck."

Gideon shot a glance at Patterson, seeing the commodore's slim, elegant figure bent over a youngster in uniform. "I'm impressed," Gideon said. "The man knows his business. That's one firm hand out here at least."

"Aye, he runs a taut ship, and that's what's needed."

They glanced about the rapidly filling ballroom. The town's Spanish partisans were maintaining a strict separation from the rest, clustered by one wall, the women's fans aflutter; they could not celebrate the American occupation, but neither could the fashionable families miss the greatest social occasion of the year. They had come to observe, enjoy themselves, and afterward disapprove of the entire proceeding. Blake mopped sweat from his brow with his handkerchief, then stiffened.

"Look! That's Fontenoy, isn't it?"

The French captain had indeed entered the hall, dressed neatly in a yellow coat, a tricolor cockade on one lapel. "Thunderation," Gideon murmured. The man had got *Franklin* back to Mobile under jury sail and with half his crew dead, avoiding both British cruisers and the Baratarians. The Frenchman's eyes slid over the hall, saw Gideon and Blake standing together. He smiled and strode toward them. Gideon noticed that at his waist he was wearing a formal, silver-hilted small-sword instead of his fighting iron.

"Captain Markham. Captain Blake."

"Captain Fontenoy."

"As you see," Fontenoy said gaily, "I got *Franklin* back to Mobile. We arrived under jury rig this afternoon. I have returned your Dr. Rivette to your schooner, sir. He refused a splendid bribe, by the way, in order to stay with you. You have a way of commanding loyalty, Captain Markham. My felicitations."

"Thank you, sir," Gideon said, frowning at Fontenoy's gay manner, his unabashed talk of bribes. "Allow me to offer my own congratulations on yer safe return; it was a remarkable feat of seamanship."

Fontenoy shrugged. "Not so remarkable, perhaps. The winds were favorable." He glanced about the halls again and lowered his voice. "You have heard the news from Europe?" he asked. "Bonaparte has been defeated at a place called Leipzig. He's lost tens of thousands of men. I think he's finished."

Gideon listened curiously, noting Fontenoy's calling the French monarch "Bonaparte," not "Napoleon" or "emperor." Gideon recalled his earlier suspicion, acquired at Fort Bowyer, that the Frenchman didn't like the head of France's regime.

"He may last another few months," Fontenoy went on.

"But I don't think he'll keep the Allies out of Paris. And then—then Wellington's soldiers will come to America."

"Aye," Gideon said, feeling his heart sink, knowing how little prepared the American armies were to battle the victors of Salamanca and Victoria.

"I shall have to arrange my American citizenship if I am to continue my profession, eh?" Fontenoy grinned. "Captain Markham, I have a question to ask you. You have seen my little *Franklin*, how badly it needs repair." Gideon nodded, knowing what was coming.

"You have also seen how *Franklin* can fight," Fontenoy said. "You know we can make a big profit if we can get repairs. But I have no money—it all went into fitting out the privateer in the first place. You have become wealthy with the capture of this convoy. Perhaps, Captain Markham, you would be willing to become one of my backers. With your support we can gain much money, take many British ships. And you will, of course, see a percentage of any vessels taken."

"I'll have to think about it," Gideon said.

"Of course, of course," Fontenoy said. He glanced over the ballroom once more, then said, "The little sailor, she was returned to her lady?"

"Aye. I trust her welcome was warm."

"She belonged to Madame Marquez, *n'est*-ce *pas*? I realized this afterward."

"Her mistress was very worried," Blake interjected. "She feels a responsibility for the girl—Campaspe was orphaned in Mexico when very young, in one of the little wars they're always having. Mrs. Marquez has almost raised her as a daughter."

"Ah, the lady herself," Fontenoy said delightedly.

Maria-Anna had entered the hall, surrounded by a swarm of Morehouses. Gideon knew Neal Morehouse by sight, the merchant who had sold *General Sullivan* stores in times past. But he'd never seen the entire family: the rather formidable-looking Mrs. Morehouse, a brother-in-law, two sons (one in the uniform of an ensign in the militia), five daughters, and a son-in-law. Among the Spanish contingent Gideon saw painted mouths whispering behind fluttering fans, and presumed that the town's old inhabitants recognized Maria-Anna for a traitor, coming to the ball with the family of an American merchant who had the local reputation of a filibustering patriot.

Gideon's eyes crossed awkwardly with Maria-Anna's, and he bowed in her direction. She looked briefly startled, but then curtsied hastily. Blake's scabbard thudded against Gideon's knee as he bowed in turn. As he straightened, Gideon saw Morehouse smilingly advance across the floor, his hand outstretched, and the entire brood following.

"Captain Markham!" Morehouse exclaimed delightedly. "Please let me refill your cup of punch and introduce you to my family."

Marriageable daughters, Gideon thought sourly as he was introduced to Mrs. Morehouse and the children, all in proper order of seniority, receiving practiced bows and blushing curtseys. Morehouse obviously considered Gideon a good risk as a prospective son-in-law. Maria-Anna was introduced—"and of course you know Mrs. Marquez"— and Gideon bowed again. Captain Fontenoy bent to kiss her hand, and Gideon felt a flash of angry resentment as the Misses Morehouse tittered; it was an example of continental familiarity entirely unsuited to the occasion. Gideon knew that he himself was bound to the proprieties, that in public he dared not budge from proper formality lest Maria-Anna's reputation suffer. Carefully he would stay within the boundaries, those that demanded that any serious topic be approached obliquely, so that the inevitable chaperones, these Morehouses, this Blake, and that Fontenoy, would hear nothing to raise their eyebrows.

Gideon knew from looking at Maria-Anna that she was playing by the same rules; her face was friendly but reservedly so, respectful, a formal mask. Gideon wondered if she had been brought as a partner to the eldest son, the unmarried heir presumptive to the business.

"Captain Markham, with respect to your physical condition, might we see you dance tonight?" Morehouse asked heartily, a rather obvious attempt to fill his daughters' cards.

"I am not a dancer, sir," Gideon said. "I shall probably be leaving shortly. I have business aboard my schooner."

His words, following the indirect rules of the civil masque, were a signal to Maria-Anna that soon the social awkwardness would end, that he would soon be away.

"What a shame!" said Mrs. Morehouse. Her eyes turned toward Blake and Fontenoy. "But of course you gentlemen are staying, are you not?"

Blake and Fontenoy, smiling politely, acceded to the inevitable and consented to a dance apiece with each of the daughters. Gideon stood with his hands clasped around his cup of punch, awkward in his splints and sling, feeling distinct tracks of sweat on his nape and scalp.

"I am sorry you are leaving, Captain Markham," Maria-Anna said quietly, almost in his ear, as the Morehouse brood fell upon their prey.

"I, ah—thankee, ma'am," Gideon replied, feeling the room shudder. Flashes of color and sensation penetrated his spinning senses: the gold of Gilbert Russel's bullion epaulettes, the blue of American uniforms, winks of white light from the diamonds on his own hundred-guinea sword . . . Perhaps it was a polite formality; but no, there was no one to overhear or demand the proprieties, and if something was required to break the silence, any polite expression would have done. Her face was still scrupulously polite, still a masque of the civil dance, giving away nothing; not allowing herself the opportunity of acknowledging her public hurt should his reply be other than that which his thundering heart was urging him to make . . .

She opened her mouth to speak again.

"Your attention, everyone!" a voice boomed out. A stout, white-haired man with a puma-skin waistcoat stepped out into the hall, calling out loudly again for the attention he had already gained. Gideon realized that the man was his host, to whom Blake had introduced him earlier in the evening. He also realized that he had no memory whatever of the man's name.

"Ladies and gentlemen," the host bellowed, "before commencin' the entertainment, I should like to introduce our guests of honor!" The band struck up the first few bars of "Liberty Tree."

"Those men to whom our city of Mobile owes its safety and prosperity, those men who keep at bay the swarms of savages and the merciless enemy privateers who haunt our shores . . ." The speech was mercifully brief. Gideon's whirling mind paid no attention; he could feel Maria-Anna's presence by his side, but did not dare to look; he had to plot carefully the possible meanings of her words.

"Brigadier General Ferdinand Leigh Claiborne!" the host shouted. The crowd roared its welcome; the Spanish element applauding with reserved politeness. The red-faced general bowed, his gold epaulettes flapping.

"Colonel Gilbert C. Russel!" Another roar, another bow. The sound broke against Gideon's heedless mind. There was no alternative, he thought frantically: Maria-Anna's words had been an invitation. But an invitation to what? Dance, conversation, a renewal of the reckless relationship that had been broken into fragments on the banks of the Choctaw Pass. . . ?

"Commodore Daniel Todd Patterson!" Their host was following strict protocol, the senior service first, Russel before Patterson, and both before the militia. The applause was reserved: most of the town's merchants made their living at least partially by smuggling, and Patterson's attempts to enforce the revenue laws had not made him popular.

Gideon, feeling his heart thundering louder than the applause, turned in a moment of supreme bravery toward Maria-Anna, saw her for an unguarded moment looking at him without the mask of propriety or ritual, saw in her glance something he had never expected to see in her eyes again, and that brought to his mind the sound of cicadas, the rustle of corn, the flight of crying birds over the water.

"The brave privateer from New Hampshire, who has brought in these last few days the fruits of over twenty enemy vessels to our port, as well as the sword of the captain of the British warship, *Alastor*, whose ship was captured and sunk just weeks ago! Captain Gideon Markham!"

Gideon felt his senses spin as he heard the introduction and the crowd around him parted and burst into wild applause. The faces around him were broken with hysterical, somehow hallucinatory smiles. Maria-Anna's eyes dazzled as she broke into applause. Gideon felt himself flushing and recovered himself sufficiently to bow to the crowd . . . and somehow across the room he caught Commodore Patterson's eye and saw the officer nod. He understood that Patterson must have had a word with their host, that the commodore had been as offended by Claiborne's discourtesy as anyone, and that this public mention was as much a rebuke to the general as a compliment to Gideon. Gideon looked for Clairborne and saw that the general was not pleased, either because Gideon had been publicly complimented or because Claiborne himself was shamed at being so rude without reason. Gideon hoped, with a certain conscious malice, that it was both.

"A guest upon our shores from our ally, the Empire of France, the captain of a privateer named after our own Dr. Franklin, Captain Julian Fontenoy!"

Gideon felt exultation rising in him dangerously as public attention moved from him to Fontenoy; he felt as he had on the quarterdeck of the *Revenge* with the British convoy looming darkly about him; there was a sensation of vaunting triumph and certitude in daring. He turned to Maria-Anna as the crowd burst into another ovation and awkwardly in his good hand gathered her two hands in his.

"Come away with me," he said. "I love you. Marry me."

She found no words to answer him with, but none was needed; he saw her careful mask, her civic pretense, dissolve, and saw the leaping affirmation in her eyes. They fought their way through the crowd, Maria-Anna guarding his injured arm; they paused only to collect his hat and stick, and then made their way into the cooling evening.

Somehow the air held a lingering scent of the sea. On the terrace they embraced, tasted the first incredible kiss. Inside the crowd howled, cheered, stamped. Some popular militia officer was being introduced.

"Gideon, my God." A sigh in his ear. "Your poor arm. How did it happen?"

"Case shot. An accident."

"There will be no more such accidents." Angrily. "Have the man responsible flogged."

"Marry me tonight. It should be right this time."

"Yes, of course. Where?"

"You don't mind losing the Romish faith?"

"I never really had it, I think." Her face looked miraculously youthful in the starlight; she seemed a young girl, starry-eyed, a faint, luxurious smile on her lips.

"There is no Congregational minister in Mobile. A Presbyterian will have to do; it's accepted under the Plan of Union. Did you see Pastor Graves at the ball?"

"No."

"Perhaps he's not going. Let's go to his house."

"Gideon." She rested her cheek against his shoulder. He kissed her hair. "I don't know if I can give you children, Gideon," she said. "I was married for fourteen years, and it never happened."

"That's for the Lord to decide." She raised her face to his, and he kissed her, then took her hand and began walking down the darkening streets.

"You understand we cannot have slaves?" he asked anxiously. "That those you own will have to be emancipated?"

"What?" Her face showed wonder, not offense. His heart eased. "There are forty," she said. "I bought the planters' and then loaned them to the army. Gideon, it can't be done."

"It must. They should be liberated. I will not profit from the labor of a bondsman."

"Gideon, they can't!" she said with finality. "We can't possibly emancipate that many; there are laws to stop us." She went on hastily as he threatened to interrupt. "The laws aren't to keep us from freeing them, not really. It's because if emancipation were easy, unscrupulous planters would free every slave they owned as soon as they grew too old to work. It's for the slaves' protection, so they won't starve in old age."

Gideon absorbed the news with a frown, then spoke. "Very well. We'll do what we can, then; d'ye agree?"

"Oh, if we must. But the plantations I bought will be worthless without slaves to work them."

"You won't lose money."

"No." She smiled. "I won't."

They passed hand in hand through the shadowed streets. Gideon felt a kind of euphoria sweep through him, a knowledge of special bliss that overwhelmed his senses. Captain Trevannion's diamond-hilted sword clattered against his knee; nightbirds flittered over rooftops. It had been easy, so easy.

Pastor Graves had been working late in his study, tidying up a sermon for the morrow. Surprised and a little pleased, he offered to fetch his servants as witnesses to the marriage, but he was concerned over their evident haste and let them into the chapel in the meantime, bidding them pray for wisdom.

Gideon caught Maria-Anna's eye as they slid into the pew. There was a kind of reckless happiness in her face, a knowledge that, like Gideon, she was bidding defiance to the odds. He turned his eyes from her and prayed.

He felt suspended within a shimmering globe of happiness, his mind in a strange but delightful turmoil. A week ago he had known himself outcast, cursed by his God for his own waywardness, but now it seemed as if the sentence had been reversed and he was free again to walk upon the earth without the risk of transferring his particular blight to others. He felt bondless, deliriously free, far more unrestrained than he had ever been aboard *Malachi's Revenge* with its wings of flax and thousands of miles of ocean before it. There was a special grace in all this, he recognized; the Almighty had removed the shackles from his soul and sanctioned his union with Maria-Anna along with granting the act of divine pardon. *Use me as Thou wilt,* he prayed, awed by the feeling of special providence he felt warming him. *No longer damned,* he thought. He looked at Maria-Anna and caught her watching him out of the corner of her eye; they grinned like schoolchildren. As he met her eyes he realized that this grace could have come earlier, that although he had spoken on the Choctaw Pass of morality and the laws of convention, he had unaccountably forgotten in that regretted moment the power of words of love.

The pastor returned with his witnesses. As they rose, Gideon held out his good arm. They walked to the altar.

29

OLD PRIVATEERS

Jehu Markham's estate, some mile inland from Portsmouth on a tributary of the Piscataqua, lay out of sight of the sea; the rolling New Hampshire land, on which old Jehu still bred horses, bore upon it no reminders of Jehu's past. The carriage passed acres of wheat stubble, and the interior of the carriage filled with the smell of new-mown hay. It was September of 1814, and of all the world only America and England were at war.

"Welcome. Good to be seein' you." Jehu hugged his brother as Josiah stepped from the carriage; Anne, still graceful, her face browned by daily riding, kissed his cheek. Josiah's face cracked in an unaccustomed smile. One of the surprising consequences of old age was the warmth and affection Josiah felt for his brother; they had been so dissimilar when young. Josiah had castigated Jehu for a worldly pride akin to that of Lucifer, while Jehu condemned Josiah's Puritan intolerance; but age had united them, smoothed out the very real differences of opinion and temperament if only by contrast to the young who seemed so strange, so foreign. The brothers were survivors of an earlier age, and this united them more than sailing under the privateer flag ever had.

Josiah still wore his white hair in its old-fashioned sailor's queue; his only concession to age was the cane upon which he limped, for the hip broken five years before still bothered him. He was sixty-five; his brother Jehu was four years older. Josiah had often wondered why Jehu chose to live apart from the sea upon which he had spent so much of his life. Josiah's chief exercises were short walks, which he took ostensibly to keep himself in trim, but which all led him seaward to gaze over the surface of the deep and taste the salt in the air. He felt he could not live without it. Yet Jehu, after he and Josiah had turned the Markham & Sons Corporation over to the younger generation on New Year's Day, 1800, had retired inland to live in baronial splendor and raise horses. Josiah supposed it was Jehu's wife, Anne, who made it bearable for him, the loss of the sea. Josiah had never ceased mourning his own wife, Ellen, who had passed away so unexpectedly, so intolerably, ten years before.

"Come sit. Damme if it ain't a pleasure. Will you have some claret? It's too hot for tea or coffee."

Josiah accepted, and sank with gratitude into a comfortable armchair while Anne rang for a servant. Jehu sat in a chair opposite: age had thinned him and turned his hair a distinguished gray, but otherwise he was much the same man. The aristocratic nose, the sardonic, affected accents of a British squire, the richness of his fashionable dress— even at home his cravat was folded just so, his boots were shined, supple calfskin, his demeanor was artificial and studied, carefully controlled. All these traits Jehu had maintained as long as Josiah had know him, these and radical politics, but they had ceased to irritate Josiah; he accepted them as something known and familiar, an element of stability in a world rapidly losing its equilibrium.

"Did you bring any news?" Jehu asked, taking a cup of claret from the servant's tray. "The last war news we heard was a week old."

"General Brown is still besieged at Fort Erie. Prevost is still halted before Plattsburgh. Did ye hear what Prevost is calling us? 'Damned Yankees.' It's in all his proclamations: 'Damned Yankees.' " Josiah smiled. "There will be a battle on Lake Champlain any day. Perhaps it is already fought."

"And at sea?" Josiah detected a flash of impatience in the question, and inwardly he smiled. Jehu, too, realized that the important battles of the war would be fought at sea or on land within gunshot of the sea.

"Cockburn and Ross are still in the Chesapeake, burning and plundering like the British did in the last war. They may attack Baltimore or Washington City. *Constitution* is still blockaded in Boston. Captain Snow and *Yankee* have brought four prizes into Providence, worth at least half a million dollars. Boyle and *Chasseur* are still in the Channel."

Jehu nodded over his claret. "It's the Snows and the Boyles that will bring the British to the peace table," he said. "They, and men like your son Gideon. How is he?"

"Married, as ye know from my letters," Josiah said. "Eleven months ago in Mobile. The Caribbean has been rich for him, as it was for us." Jehu nodded, smiling faintly in remembrance, recalling like Josiah the warm blue waters, the cloud-topped island peaks, the shoals of whirring flying fish driven before the stems of cruising privateers.

"He's sent a snow into Portsmouth, the *Franklin*," Josiah reported with distaste. "Commanded by some Frenchman, Fontenoy or something. Gideon's bought a part interest in the Frenchman's venture. The man's become an American citizen now that Napoleon's been exiled. Impudent fellow, I think, but charming enough at it. I came to visit ye to get rid of him. He brought bills of exchange and some silver, though. Gideon's transferring some of his funds to New England. A wise decision."

Jehu smiled. "Favian is in New London, supervising the building of a fast corvette he's to have the command of. *Shark*, it's to be called."

Josiah nodded. Favian was Jehu's youngest son, a captain in the new navy, one of the rising crop of heroes who had seen their baptism of fire off Tripoli and gone on to a series of amazing victories against the British. *Preble's boys*, they called themselves, honoring the memory of the commodore who had made them.

"I think he is unhappy," Jehu continued, his eyes saddening. "He's inherited the darker strain of the family, I think, as our father had. And Malachi."

Anne came gracefully into the room in a hiss of skirts, reached out to take Jehu's hand. The Honourable Anne, Jehu called her, his English, titled wife. Had she ever looked back, Josiah wondered, to the land where she was born and raised, to the hall of her ancestors; or had she turned her back on it as Jehu had turned his back on the sea?

"The dueling, you mean?" Josiah asked.

Jehu shook his head. "That's not it. His duels are—
they're expected in a naval officer, almost required. He
couldn't have avoided them, and he's done better than
many in keeping out of quarrels. But he's bitter. I wish I
could help."

Anne squeezed her husband's hand. "He should never
have been sent to sea," she said quietly. "He hasn't got the
temperament for it. But we couldn't have known. It was
the natural thing to do in our family."

Our family. Josiah's head jerked up at the words. The
Honourable Anne had made her choice, he thought with
fierce pride, to throw in with us Markhams. The connec-
tion with Britain had gone for her as it had for the rest of
the country; she had thrown it off in her own act of rebellion, as daring as any taken by the Minutemen of Concord,
when in 1779 she'd arranged to break Jehu out of the British prison in which he'd been held since his capture the
year before. She hadn't looked back; none of them had.
They had all become Americans now; the little differences,
the accents and fashions and residences, were insignificant
in the light of that single overwhelming fact.

"You haven't touched your claret, Jo. Would you prefer
hock, or perhaps coffee?"

Josiah started from his musings. "Why, no, thankee,
Anne. I was just lost in thought."

That night as he lowered himself stiffly on his knees to
say his prayers, Josiah found an image of Gideon entering
his mind. The only one of the family to carry on the family
trade, the only privateer left. Gideon's brothers and cousins
had all invested in privateers, and Favian Markham served
in the navy, but Gideon was the only one who still walked
his own decks, who still dared the British in personal combat. Gideon had been often in Josiah's thoughts—more so,
in fact, than Gideon's brothers, whom Josiah saw almost
daily. Josiah prayed that Gideon was happy with his new
wife, that his son's luck had finally turned. Mobile was
now safe from the Indians, he knew: Ferdinand Leigh
Claiborne had defeated the Red Sticks on the Holy
Ground, and Andrew Jackson of Tennessee had crushed
the last of the Red Stick movement at the Battle of Horseshoe Bend, and accepted William Weatherford's surrender.

But Josiah could read maps, and if the British could read maps as well as Josiah, they knew that Mobile was located on a broad bay that would make a perfect base for an attack on New Orleans. Gideon might be putting his head into the British lion's mouth if he remained.

Josiah finished his prayers and rose, gritting his teeth as his hip stabbed him with a knife-jab of pain, a *memento mori* he no longer resented. He had never expected to live this long, surviving his wife and his son David, both of whom he loved beyond his capacity to express it. He knew he could not last much longer, that one night he might close his eyes and never open them again. The possibility did not alarm him. But he wished to know, before the end, that his son Gideon was well and at peace. All his other surviving children, three sons and two daughters, had made lives of their own, even Micah, who had married a New York heiress and lived on Manhattan, attending the Anglican Church with his family—all but Gideon were settled. Josiah hoped Gideon was happy and safe and that there would be children. *A man needs a family about him,* Josiah thought, *when he's old.*

His brother's sheets were warm; a summer breeze whispered through the curtains. *This part of America is at peace,* he thought. Before he slipped into sleep, his final, pleasantly vague thought was that wars should not be allowed to trouble the dreams of old men.

30

THE PRESENTIMENT

The room, in early morning, was filled with gray light, the objects occupying it seen as if through a gauze curtain, colors muted, perspective uncertain. A mockingbird outside the window repeated a call several times, then began to add variations.

Gideon awoke early these days, the heritage of years of being on deck at dawn; he would lie awake in the bed, enjoying the stillness of Maria-Anne's house, the slow awakening of the town and the household. There was no work for him, no log to cast or squalls to observe. Instead a kind of slow delight filled him, lying in the deep bed, hearing Maria-Anna's slow breathing, feeling the warmth of her hip against his leg. He had been eleven months married. At least half that time he'd been at sea: he had just come into port two days before after a voyage of nine weeks that had brought in four prizes, one of them very rich. He had found Maria-Anna gone upcountry to visit her plantations; she had come into Mobile late the previous afternoon, unexpectedly finding Gideon waiting for her, the reverse of their usual routine. And she had brought news.

A child. Maria-Anna was with child; she was three months gone, had not been certain of her condition when he'd left, but was now. Gideon lay in the bed, an unaccustomed emotion sweeping him, one that with some astonishment he recognized as happiness. The mockingbird called again; below in the street a horse clopped by. Gideon was bemused by the unlikeliness of it: Gideon Markham, so far from the forbidding coast of Puritan New Hampshire, made happy by an unlikely life on the American Gulf Coast, in this strange and ungodly town with its mixture of

New World frontier and Old World corruption, its slave-
holding aristocracy and buckskinned half-breeds . . .
None of that really mattered, he supposed; the source of his
happiness was Maria-Anna and the child to be. *A child.*

Maria-Anna had been flushed and pleased when she'd
told him; but Gideon had sensed a current of nervousness,
and he understood. She was thirty-one now, had never carried children, and her hips were narrow; but she was
strong and healthy, and the doctors—she had consulted
more than one—assured her that she would be perfectly
fine. It was not the rigors of Maria-Anna's pregnancy that
worried him.

But Gideon had returned to astonishing and ominous
news: a British squadron, presumably with the connivance
of the Spanish governor, Manrique, had in July occupied
the forts, bay, and town of Spanish Pensacola, raising
the British flag not sixty miles from Gideon's bed in Mobile. Proclamations had been issued to the beaten remnants
of the Red Stick rebellion, to the Louisianians and Ken-
tuckians, urging them to enter British service. There were
reports of Indians in red coats, drilling in the Pensacola
sun; the four hundred he'd discovered almost a year ago
had finally appeared and were gathering recruits. The British would not have captured Pensacola for its own sake; it
was a prelude to another move, a base for an attack on
Mobile or New Orleans.

It was probably time to leave the Gulf, Gideon decided.
Mobile had served its purpose. He had to think of the
safety of his family, his child-to-be. Mobile was dangerously unprotected. Ferdinand Claiborne's replacement,
General Andrew Jackson, had been in Mobile in August,
after hearing the news from Pensacola, and tried to provide
for the town's defense. There was nothing that could be
done, nothing but ride again to New Orleans and try to
reassemble the scattered forces that had triumphed at the
Holy Ground and Horseshoe Bend. Until a new army was
mobilized, the city would have to depend on the few regulars in Fort Bowyer supported by the local militia. It was
too dangerous.

But it was not the possibility of British attack that ultimately disturbed Gideon; there had begun in these last

months a nagging intuition in his mind, the shadow of a doubt. . . . It seemed impossible that his happiness should be so complete, yet so scatheless. The suspicion had begun to arise as to whether this extraordinary example of God's grace and mercy, giving him a new life and renewing his faith, should not be preparatory to something else. Perhaps, he had begun to wonder, he would soon be called to his God; perhaps this glimpse of earthly bliss was only to fortify his faith so that he would have a chance of salvation when his end came; perhaps it was to prepare him for further hardship, as his life with Betsy had been a prelude to his years of misery. He had known people to feel such intuitions; he had seen it in battle, for a man to seemingly become aware of his own impending death; and Gideon knew it for a gift of God, so that a man could make his peace with the Almighty before his end. Gideon was beginning to feel such an intuition of doom stalking him, and the news of the British occupation of Pensacola had served to sanction rather than dispel it.

But in the light of his own overwhelming felicity the niggling worry seemed peevish, the reflex of a man accustomed through bitter experience to assume the worst. Its petulance seemed particularly obvious now, as Maria-Anna turned to him in her sleep, stretching her arms, her lips twitching in the mischievous, half-conscious smile he knew to be a prelude to her awakening. Her eyes opened, and the smile turned to one of languorous, drowsy pleasure. Gideon kissed the smile, slid a hand over Maria-Anna's warm, rounding belly, alert to sign of the slumbering child within.

"Good morning," Maria-Anna whispered, her eyes bright, and she slid her arms round him, kissing him tenderly, trying comically not to grimace at the scrape of his morning's whiskers. For a moment Gideon, his doubts suddenly rushing in on him, felt death hovering in the room, an almost palpable presence on soft night-wings. *Lord, do with me what Thou wilt, but keep this woman and the child safe,* he thought fervently, and suddenly the presence was gone, replaced with the voice of the mockingbird, and the room was filled with nothing but sunlight. "Is something wrong?" Maria-Anna asked, feeling his tension.

"Nothing," said Gideon. "I felt a little cold for a moment, that's all."

There was a quiet knock on the door, and Campaspe entered with a tray, coffee, three kinds of bread, and jam. She set the tray on a small table, then maneuvered the table near the bed. Campaspe had changed rather startlingly in the last months, Gideon thought; she had grown inches, her figure had ripened, the way she carried herself—her entire public demeanor—had modified. Occasionally there was still the news of some escapade, a prank played on a neighbor or an unexplained absense from her duties, but Campaspe, for the most part, had inexplicably matured. Her behavior was discreet and proper, she carried herself with dignity, and Gideon suspected her of affecting, in private, genteel mannerisms. Returning home late one night, he'd seen her walking alone in the garden, wrapped in a curtain that was worn in imitation of a gown, mimicking the bearing and ostentation of a great lady. Gideon hadn't mentioned it to her; he supposed that, kept in perspective, ambition was not a harmful thing.

Gideon attempted with mixed success to keep crumbs from the bed as he ate a piece of bread and drank his coffee. Then he stepped out for a wash and shave while Campaspe helped Maria-Anna dress. There was going to be a celebration: the officers of Fort Bowyer were throwing a daylong party—"picnic" was their word—for their families, friends, and admirers, and Captain and Mrs. Markham had been invited, along with the officers of the privateer *Malachi's Revenge*. *Revenge* would incidentally be used to transport the guests from town to the fort, which in Gideon's mind helped explain the privateers' invitation in the first place. Gideon untypically found himself looking forward to the occasion; he would be able to see Lieutenant Blake, whose now permanent duty involved guarding, with his pathetic gunboat, the entrance of Mobile Bay from the anticipated attack of the entire British squadron at Pensacola.

Gideon dressed, tied on his neckcloth and cravat, and returned to find Maria-Anna, dressed in her formal gown and slippers, selecting a straw bonnet. With bonnet on and outstretched arms Maria-Anna modeled the gown. "Will this satisfy the society bitches?" she asked. "They demand a person wear the latest from Europe before they speak to her without condescension—well, I'm wearing it, except for the corsets. I'm not wearing stays in this weather."

"You are lovely," Gideon said, kissing her. "But I wish you wouldn't pay attention to what those ladies say."

"I must if I'm to be accepted," she said pragmatically, "and I must be accepted in order to sell the plantations at the price they deserve. After we've got their money, we can say adieu to their notions."

Gideon kissed her again and sighed; it had been explained to him several times that someone selling off perfectly workable land would be assumed to be bankrupt and would scarcely be offered more than Maria-Anna had paid for the plantations in the first place. A show of wealth was necessary: Maria-Anna wore the most expensive clothes available, gave exclusive parties in which fashionable Mobile was served off silver plate—a privateering acquisition—by servants in livery, while Gideon had been presuaded, as his sole concession, to exchange his linen cravat for one of silk.

"I'll do the books before we leave," Gideon said. "We've another two hours before we have to be aboard."

"Are you sure? Don't you think it will wait?" Her resistance was unusual; ordinarily Maria-Anna was happy to demonstrate to him her economies of household management. He had married a hard-nosed businesswoman and was thankful for it; but still the remark was odd.

"I'll see them," he said, and she shrugged and led him to the study. The books were bound in leather, massive and weighty, yet with few columns filled. Their marriage, here reflected as entries for candles, plate, furnishings, stores, all carefully noted as those of any business partnership, occupied the first few dozen pages of each volume. Yet the "expenses" column for the first month of Gideon's absence was swollen with items ambiguously marked "plantation equipment," while the subsequent months showed an inordinate increase in items marked "foodstuffs," as if whole crews of men had to be fed. Only one explanation offered itself to Gideon's stunned brain.

"Thunderation!"

Maria-Anna, her face a wry acknowledgement of the inevitability of Gideon's discovery, perched carefully on the desk and said calmly, "I've put the plantations under cultivation. If we don't show a profit we won't be able to realize their worth."

"Ye've bought slaves! After I've forbidden it!" He thrust back his chair and stood, his astonishment turning to inevitable, grim fury. The issue of slavery had been their only real difference of opinion. He had refused to allow the purchase of slaves even if, as Maria-Anna said, they and the plantations could be sold together after a single productive year: he was not willing to show tolerance for the system of bondage or compromise with its enormous evil in any way. *This is what comes of concession,* he thought bitterly. His father Josiah had been right that to stray from the path of righteousness at any point was to open oneself to infiltration by evil.

"I haven't," Maria-Anna insisted. "I haven't bought anyone." Her mouth tautened in a grim line, her own fury rising.

"Then how d'ye explain—"

"I *rented* 'em, damn it!" she answered, almost shouting. Gideon stood thunderstruck, stunned by her vehemence. "Thirty-five niggers I've rented for the season, to return to their owners after the harvest—and all at a dead loss! If I'd been allowed to buy 'em, we'd at least have got their value back next year!"

"I—"

"That's how I've accommodated your scruples, and if that's not good enough, I wish you'd explain them better, because I don't understand!" Tears stood out bright in her eyes, her fists were clenched. Gideon seized her, crushed her against him, heard her gasp out, "I don't understand!" again and then break into sobs.

"Never mind." Gideon was baffled by the mixture of steel and sudden vulnerability. *In much wisdom is grief; he that increaseth knowledge increaseth sorrow,* he thought. She had been raised in Charleston, probably within walking distance of the slave markets; she saw nothing wrong with the practice, understood none of the horror Gideon felt when he saw the naked blacks, shackled at the neck and ankles, shuffling in their chains from the ships. She was genuinely baffled by his reservations. It was Mobile that had caused this, Mobile with its aristocracy of planters and underbody of accepted brutality.

"We'll leave Mobile as soon as we can provision the schooner," Gideon said. "Sail for New England, leave some agent to manage the plantations and sell them after the harvest."

She looked up at him, still showing a flash of anger. "And leave all we've—everything?" she demanded.

"Everything, aye," he said calmly. "We're no longer safe here, not with the British in Pensacola. We'll take what we can to New Hampshire. We can live well there on what I've brought in. This doesn't matter."

She allowed herself to be persuaded, but he sensed a core of resistance, which he thought he understood. Most of their money was his contribution, the result of his privateering, but the plantations were *hers*, the offspring of her own industry. She had risked her life for them alongside Gideon, and it was natural to want them to prosper, to make a contribution to their material well-being, and perhaps there was in her resistance a desire to justify, in some measure, the deaths of Jouhaux and MacDonald. Her talents for managing money complemented Gideon's well, and he knew she was ambitious. But it might well be folly to stay; aside from any danger from the British Gideon was not prepared to face any more compromises with the way of life here, with the mode of existence that united wealth with human chattel.

They walked to the water's edge, a proper couple walking arm in arm, the man with his stick and diamond-hilted sword, the woman with her parasol. George Willard brought the launch to meet them; Gideon helped Maria-Anna into the stern sheets and then took the tiller himself. Their welcome aboard *Malachi's Revenge* was performed in proper military style: Gideon, senior in the boat, came up to the twitter of pipes, and Maria-Anna, scorning the offer of a bosun's chair, climbed the schooner's side nimbly in her slippers and was handed aboard.

"Welcome aboard, Cap'n. Ma'am." Finch Martin, grinning in his usual leering way, stood in a line of officers: Martin, Michael Clowes, Francis Allen, Browne, Rivette . . . with Willard in the boat; they were the same men Gideon had first sailed with. They worked well together now, free from their initial awkwardnesses and rivalries. Francis Allen had at first shown open resentment toward George Willard when, after the taking of *Alastor,* Willard had appeared in command of the larboard guns; but Gideon had left Allen command of the "gentleman volunteers," a job to which Allen's cheerful informality had seemed more suited, and after Allen had consoled himself by buying an extravagantly red uniform coat and a new sword, he'd apparently buried his grudge and was at least civil to Willard thereafter, whatever resentments he may have maintained in private.

"Reeve a whip from the yardarm and put a bowline in it," Gideon ordered, intending to prepare a bosun's chair for his lady guests. "Mr. Martin, dismiss the hands. Mr. Willard, take the launch back to shore and wait for our guests."

Gideon showed Maria-Anna to his cabin, where refreshments had been readied by Grimes. She hadn't been aboard *Revenge* since the first few weeks of their marriage, when Gideon had taken ten of his prizes to New Orleans to sell them there. She browsed through his logbooks while they waited for their guests, the first group of whom arrived an hour later.

Hoping Martin would remember to control his language in front of the ladies, Gideon walked with Maria-Anna to the deck. The boat was full of Morehouses, father, mother, and marriageable daughters. They had long since forgiven Maria-Anna for dashing unannounced from the midst of the party, given the romantic circumstances, and were now part of the Fort Bowyer party. Morehouse had to be desperate for sons-in-law, Gideon thought, if he was willing to contemplate the officers of the Fort Bowyer garrison.

Mrs. Morehouse slipped the two loops of the bosun's chair over her lace-ornamented bonnet, positioned them on her body, and waved her readiness to those waiting on the deck. "Ready, thar!" Martin shouted. "Heave away, handsomely!"

There was a shriek and a splash, and then Mrs. Morehouse, soaked to the lace on her bonnet, was hauled dripping above the bulwark, gasping for breath, her body curiously horizontal in the loops of the bosun's chair, which seemed to have constricted tightly about her, cutting into her flesh. "Swing her in!" Gideon bellowed. "Lower her handsomely. Mrs. Morehouse, are ye hurt?"

The lady choked on her reply, unable to breathe. Maria-Anna rushed to her aid as Gideon eased the loops from around her. They had tightened unexpectedly, crushing the breath from her as they'd ducked her into the water, and a single look at the knot in the line told Gideon why.

"Who tied this?" Gideon demanded, holding up the damning evidence. Martin looked at the knot and flushed beet red.

"Don't know, sir," he said. "I'll discover the hamhanded lubber's bastard who did, and—"

"Rogers, sir," Clowes volunteered. "I saw Alan Rogers going aloft to reeve the whip through the yardarm. It must have been—"

"Rogers!" Gideon and Finch Martin's bellows were almost simultaneous.

The seaman in question was a tall, thin man with reddish hair and a face that couldn't quite disguise his amusement.

"Who told ye to tie a bowline on a bight?" Gideon demanded. "I wanted a French bowline!"

"You didn't say what kind of bowline you wanted, Cap'n," Rogers said. "I rove a bowline on a bight because I thought you'd be bringin' up the passengers' dunnage, sir."

"Are ye drunk, Rogers?" Finch Martin demanded. "Blasted if it ain't rum on yer breath!"

"Just came from ashore, sir."

"Aye, and ye were ashore bringin' aboard the supplies for the picnic, and ye'd been at the rum!"

Gideon glared, the incriminating knot still dangling from his hand. The French bowline was the knot most often used for bosun's chairs; it left two long loops dangling, one of which could be sat on, the other capable of going under the subject's arms to help keep him upright. Both loops were adjustable. A bowline on a bight also left two loops and superficially looked similar, but if the knot wasn't properly set, it would run when any weight was placed in the loops, constricting like a hangman's noose—fine for swaying up baggage, which would not fall out of the tightened loops, but dangerous for Mrs. Morehouse. When her weight closed the loops, she'd first been dropped into Mobile Bay and then caught round the middle by a double lariat that was ever tightened by her own weight.

"Even if ye thought a bowline on a bight was correct, ye didn't set the knot properly," Gideon said. He pointed his finger up the length of the mainmast. "I want ye at the masthead, Rogers," he said. "Ye're our lookout—without meals—until I tell ye to come down. And I'm telling ye now that I plan to forget about ye for weeks if possible."

"Aye aye, Cap'n." Rogers, accepting his fate without visible dismay, leaped for the main shrouds.

"What happened? How is my wife?" Mr. Morehouse, mopping his brow, his face bright red, came storming through the entry port and ran for where his wife was spluttering on the deck.

"My apologies, sir," said Gideon. "It was an unfortunate mistake. The man responsible will be punished."

"Flogging, I hope," said Morehouse. "I've never seen a flogging."

"Shall we help Mrs. Morehouse below?" Maria-Anna asked.

She and Mr. Morehouse helped the lady rise to her feet, then half-carried her below to Gideon's cabin, where she was outfitted with blankets and given hot cocoa. Gideon stayed on deck, supervising the knotting of a proper French bowline, and saw the remainder of the party's ladies swayed up on deck without incident.

There were two more boatloads—friends, wives, sweethearts and their chaperones, plus an amazing amount of baggage for a single day's outing. The capstans were manned, the anchors brought up, and *Malachi's Revenge* got under way. Gideon kept the schooner under foresail, topsails, and spanker, using the mainsail boom to stretch an awning for the passengers. Maria-Anna came on deck just after the anchors were catted, taking Gideon's arm. "The crisis is passed," she whispered. "We're drying her clothes, and Mrs. Morehouse is clumping about the cabin in your heavy-weather gear. I'm letting her drive Grimes to distraction. Better him than me."

"I'm glad she's well."

"Gideon, I was planning to use your cabin for a game of *poque*, but that's impossible with the Morehouses there. Do you think we could persuade the officers to offer the wardroom?"

"Ah—it's their last refuge from the passengers," Gideon said. "I can't ask them for it."

"I expect I can," Maria-Anna smiled. "Don't worry, I'll be tactful. Which one of your officers is the more gallant? Oh, I know. Mr. Allen!"

Gideon watched Maria-Anna approach Allen, who had been impressing some of the ladies with his red coat and dashing manner, and knew without a doubt she would succeed in her object. He glanced over the passengers crowded under the awning amidships. They seemed happy enough even without the use of spirits, which Gideon had been careful to explain could not be drunk on board, even though he was transporting rum and whiskey for use once they arrived at the fort.

"Captain Markham!" It was one of the Misses Morehouse, the youngest, offhand and charming, and, Gideon guessed, rather careless as well.

"I was wondering about some nautical language I heard one of your men use—that man there," said Miss Morehouse, indicating Finch Martin, who with a party of men was setting the jib.

"I'll do my best, Miss."

Maria-Anna, a smile of triumph on her face, returned and linked her arm through Gideon's.

"He was calling them 'soft-handed, dog-buffing buggers,'" Miss Morehouse said smilingly. "I know what a dog-buffer is, but what's a bugger?"

While Gideon stood paralyzed, Maria-Anna stepped tactfully in. "It's a tribe of Indians, British allies," she said.

"Mr. Martin was saying they were no better sailors than Choctaws. He meant it only figuratively, of course. *Malachi's Revenge* has the best sailors in the Gulf."

"Oh, I see." She laughed gaily. "How amusing."

"That reminds me, Miss," Gideon said grimly. "I should speak to our Mr. Martin. If ye'll excuse me?"

Gideon delivered a brief, vigorous lecture to Finch Martin, and the rest of the journey continued without incident. Mrs. Morehouse appeared on deck toward the end, her clothes tolerably dry and her dignity intact. *Malachi's Revenge* anchored off Mobile Point. Maria-Anna came up from her game of *poque* having won two hundred dollars from the local merchants, and the privateer, the fort, and Blake's gunboat exchanged salutes.

Malachi's Revenge, instead of furling her sails, let all her sheets fly, letting her billowing "laundry" signal a celebration. The officers of the garrison, in full dress, clustered expectantly on the sand. A boat was manned and rowed out, and the guests transferred to shore, Gideon himself tying the French bowline in the whip. Mrs. Morehouse manifested little trepidation after other ladies were shown to make the journey successfully.

"Shore party! Assemble at the entry port!" The schooner's shore party consisted principally of musicians, the two chantymen, and some of the more spirited dancers, all to provide entertainment on shore.

"Sail ho! Suth'ard of us! Three sail—no, four!"

Gideon looked in annoyance up the masthead, wondering if Rogers had managed to stay drunk and was looking for more attention, or whether there genuinely were ships on the horizon.

"Deck thar! Five sail, five!"

Gideon fixed George Willard with an impatient eye. "Go aloft, Mr. Willard. Take a glass and see if ye can make sense out of it."

The long glass over his shoulder, the Gay Head Indian nimbly went up the shrouds to the maintop, fixed the glass to his eye, and swept the horizon.

"Rogers is right, Captain," came the response. "I make seven sail with the glass: three ships, two brigs, two schooners. I'd say they're British."

Gideon saw Maria-Anna staring at him, her expression questioning, awaiting his decision. "Hands aloft to furl sail!" he shouted. "Mr. Martin, I want spring cables bent to our anchors and the best bower broken out and made ready! Clear that awning away!"

The hands sprang into action, the shore party dissolving as they ran aloft to furl the canvas that would give away *Revenge*'s size before the enemy were close enough to achieve the knowledge by careful observation. The commander of the fort had to be informed, Gideon thought, and the civilians cleared out somehow.

"What's happening, Gideon?" asked Maria-Anna quietly. "Are we going to be attacked?"

"It seems that way, my love," Gideon said, knowing that she had spoken not because she was uncertain, but because it comforted her in some measure to hear her certainties confirmed by the familiar sound of his voice. He reached out, took her hand.

"I'll have to go ashore. You'll be safe here for the present."

"It's not *my* safety I'm concerned for," she said and gave his hand a squeeze.

He nodded, seeing the tenderness in her eyes, and then walked to the entry port, stepping down into the boat sent out from shore. Lieutenant Blake met him at the water's edge, his browned face splitting in a wide white smile as he held out his hand. Gideon jumped from the launch and shook it, and saw Blake's smile fade as he perceived Gideon's sober expression.

"What's wrong?"

"A British squadron sou'east of here. Seven sail, heading for us."

"My God."

"I must speak to the garrison."

Blake nodded. "So you must. This way."

They walked across the sand, following the tracks of the celebrants, the men and women who had come to join their friends, husbands, and lovers, and might instead soon be privileged to watch them all fall in battle, and perhaps themselves die, victims to the enemy.

Two hours later Gideon stood forward of the fort's entrenchments with Lieutenant Blake and officers of the garrison, including Captain Lockwood, and various members of the excursion from shore, the latter still in a festive mood. Lockwood no longer commanded Fort Bowyer; he'd been superseded by one of Andrew Jackson's favorites, Major William Lawrence. They watched the British squadron cautiously nose its way toward the shore, a leadsman in the chains of each vessel, and then begin disembarking men in red coats. Apparently the British had no intention of attacking in the afternoon, instead being content to observe the Americans with the same morbid intensity with which the Americans observed them. The boatloads of redcoats came ashore in the surf, the heavily uniformed men struggling through the waves while holding their weapons high; their very presence on the sandy spit upon which the fort had been constructed cut Fort Bowyer off from any possible retreat save by water.

"Keep a tally here, Sergeant," Lockwood said, peering through his glass at the boats in the surf. The sergeant nodded, his pencil scratching on a pad of paper as Lockwood chanted aloud his estimates of the men disembarking. "One hundred forty Royal Marines," Lockwood said, watching the men on the landing ground fall into formation, sweeping efficiently across the sand to take a position guarding the rest of the men coming ashore. "The marines are the ones with the white facings on the uniforms. What the devil are those others?"

"Hundreds of them, whatever they are," Blake said. "Some kind of militia regiment from Jamaica? They're not very well disciplined."

The soldiers in question clustered on the beach until hurried into ranks by their officers, moving themselves into position. Gideon watched them in their ill-fitting red coats, seeing the loping strides more suitable to scouts in forests than soldiers on parade, the dark faces below the felt shakoes, here and there a knife thrust through a pipe-clayed belt . . .

"Indians, by thunder!" Gideon said. "They're landing Indians!"

"Really? Do you think they're Buggers?" asked the delighted voice of Miss Morehouse. The officers stared, and the sergeant dropped his pencil.

"They are Red Stick warriors, Miss," Lockwood said evenly. "I think you should retire behind the ramparts; they may send out sharpshooters." Miss Morehouse withdrew, annoyed that by calling attention to herself she was no longer allowed to watch.

Gideon and Blake exchanged uneasy glances. The presence of the Red Sticks made the officers' decisions all that much more difficult. England's Indian allies had rarely managed to restrain themselves, even under British officers, from any opportunity for pillage or massacre. No one had forgotten Fort Mims, the five hundred whites, men, women, and unresisting children, killed and scalped just over a year before. Now, the Red Sticks' presence made surrender impossible. They would have to fight to the end, and they could expect no mercy.

"I'll tell Major Lawrence," Lockwood said, his face grim. "I've counted three hundred so far, and there's another wave embarking."

Gideon looked about him as he stood forward of the rampart: Fort Bowyer had twenty guns, all old and of Spanish manufacture, some perhaps unsafe to fire. The British vessels, if they were typical, would total perhaps a hundred guns.

The guns of *Malachi's Revenge* and Gunboat 163 were critical in evening the odds; they would double the defenders' available force. The twenty-four pounders in Blake's gunboat would be of particular use, Gideon thought; they were heavier than anything the British were likely to have aboard their squadron, and in proper hands were deadly. Yet Blake could not risk bringing his frail gunboat properly into a fight; its fragile scantlings could be crushed even by a spent ball, and No. 163 might roll so heavily in any case that the twenty-four pounders might not even be successfully aimed. It was entirely a pity that 163's guns weren't mounted on land . . .

"Lieutenant Blake," Gideon began, an idea striking him. "D'ye think it might be possible to transfer yer twenty-four pound guns to the fort's water battery? They might be bet-

ter protected there—the British aren't going to sink Mobile
Point—and yer gunboats could take the civilians back to
the town."

"Another hundred at least," Blake murmured, still
watching the Red Sticks disembark. He turned to Gideon,
then looked toward the fort's water battery with its tired
Spanish twelve-pounders, seeing the masts of the dandy-
rigged gunboat bobbing beyond in the ship channel.

"We can move the guns tonight," he said. His speech
was brisk, professional; he appeared to have made up his
mind instantly. "The British won't attack with an entire
squadron in unfamiliar waters in the dark." He sighed. "I'll
have to put myself under army command, of course. Let's
hope they don't bungle it like they have everything else in
this war. I'll go to Lawrence and make the offer."

Gideon turned his eyes again to the enemy, watching
more Red Sticks descend into the boats, saw them rowed
to the edge of the sand, descend into the crashing surf,
form up on the beach. He shivered, knowing now what he
had felt that morning, the strange hovering presence of
death that had filled him. It was a warning, a sign. . . .
There would be battle on land and sea, and whatever its
outcome Gideon would not survive it. He felt empty, a hollow filled only by the wind and by the certain preknowl-
edge of his own end; there was no fear, no apprehension,
only resignation and a gratitude for the grace that had let
him live for a few months in happiness. There was no task
left but to make certain of the safety of his wife and child,
and then go as well as he could to his ordained ending. He
turned and walked toward the ramparts.

As the sun touched the western horizon Gideon returned
to the privateer schooner. Maria-Anna saw his sober face
as he climbed aboard, and silently led him to his cabin for a
meal.

"I've offered Major Lawrence my services," Gideon said.
"He's called a council of his officers, and they've voted to
fight to the end. They won't surrender."

"Their chances?" Maria-Anna's face was calm. He saw
on it a surprising version of the same acceptance that he
felt himself, a readiness for whatever fate might offer.

"Not good. There are six hundred Red Sticks, drilled and equipped by British officers, and a hundred forty Royal Marines to stiffen 'em. No artillery, but they won't need guns. The guns on the ships will do the job. The defenders have just a hundred thirty men. Outnumbered almost six to one."

She put out a hand, clasped his. "And we?" she asked.

"We're to help cover the entrances to the channel. It's very narrow and we can probably block it. If any enemy make for the western approaches, we'll head 'em off, but that's not expected."

He had consulted with a pilot that afternoon, a man who had volunteered to join the privateer's crew. Aside from the main, narrow ship channel past Fort Bowyer there were three shallow entrances to Mobile Bay from the west, beyond Dauphin Island: Passe aux Huitres, crowded close to the mainland at Cedar Point; Grant's Pass, centered between Cedar Point and Dauphin Island; and Passe Maronne, between Grant's Pass and Dauphin Island. The western approaches were narrow and shallow, difficult for anything as large as warships to navigate; but they were in common use by the coasting craft that navigated the Mississippi Sound, and perhaps the British had been able to acquire a coasting skipper as a pilot. Although an unlikely possibility, it was still an alternate entrance to the bay, a back door, and had to be covered.

"Lieutenant Blake is taking the guns from his boat and putting them in the water battery. There are only two of them; the third gun burst during exercises last week. That's Blake's luck all over. But the civilians will be moved to town later tonight. Do you have your things packed?"

Maria-Anna smiled slowly, and squeezed his hand. "Darling, I shall not go," she said softly. "I'll stay with you, as you stayed with me on the river."

Gideon wondered as she spoke if she, too, had been granted a presentiment of the future and knew, as he did, that the battle would result in his death. And then he thought, for a moment of horror, that perhaps his warning had not only been for his death, but for her own as well. *No!* he thought and shook his head.

"There's no need," he said. "On the river *I* could help *you*. Here, you're not needed."

"I shall do what I can," she said firmly. "I'm not going to wait in Mobile for the news of the battle and for the Red Sticks to begin their massacres if they win. I'm safer here. If the battle's lost, we might escape. To New England."

Gideon still shook his head, but said nothing. There was no answer to her arguments; Maria-Anna was probably correct in stating she was safer aboard *Malachi's Revenge* than on land, as long as there were Red Sticks about. What could he say to oppose her: that he'd heard the whisper of death's wings above him, that he wanted to know her safe? There was no assurance of safety, not as long as they were in the Gulf.

"We'll meet it together, whatever it is," she said.

"It's in God's hands," he said, and it was decided. "You can assist Dr. Rivette in the cockpit if you think you can stand it. It will be ugly."

She nodded. "If that's the best place."

It was the safest as well, though Gideon didn't mention it. He hoped his own end would be swift, that he would not lie once again under Rivette's knife while Maria-Anna was forced to watch. He thought, with the same intuition that gave him the knowledge of his death, that when it came it would be swift. He prayed it would be so.

"I'll speak to the officers and inform them of my decisions," Gideon said, "so that each of them can prepare themselves in their own way."

31

ASSAULT ON MOBILE

The tern schooner rode out the night unmolested. Gunboat No. 163, minus most of its crew and armament, passed astern during the night with its cargo of noncombatants. Blake had cut himself off on Mobile Point with no way of retreat, and would share the fate of his army colleagues.

Malachi's Revenge was made ready, anchored with spring cables fore and aft, able to train its guns on the narrow opening between Mobile Point and Dauphin Island, guarded against surprise by the boarding nets triced up, overhanging the decks like a great spider's web. There was no need for precautions: the British did not move, and the smoke from their campfires overhung the point.

The morning showed the sea breeze westerly and freshening. Gideon served his men a hot meal at noon.

At one, after dinner, signal flags went up the masts of one of the British ships, and in response sails blossomed onto the yards of a ship-sloop and a schooner, both of which began a long tack out to sea, heading southwesterly.

The western approaches after all, Gideon thought, somehow without surprise. The two enemy would try to enter Mobile Bay by its back door, through the Mississippi Sound, and attack the fort from the rear as the rest of the squadron attacked it frontally. The water battery, the two twenty-four pound guns with their navy crews, would not be able to meet both attacks.

The tern schooner would have to keep the fort from being outflanked, thereby giving up its superb position in the main channel. Somewhere just north of Dauphin Island in the Mississippi Sound *Malachi's Revenge* would have to battle the enemy. *Teeth and claws, long guns and carronades again,* Gideon thought, but this battle would be different from the fight with *Alastor*. It would be a close-quarters fight, fought in constricted waters where the enemy carronades would be able to bring the privateers within range of their crushing jaws. He remembered what the enemy carronades had done to *General Sullivan,* the way they had methodically torn the little schooner to bits in the Cuban bay. He would have to face that again.

"Cut the taffrail away," he ordered. "Have two of the twelve-pounders, carriages and tackles, shifted to fire aft. Man the capstans. Let's get the anchors up."

He sensed Maria-Anna's eyes on him and he turned to meet them. She stood inconspicuously by the weather rail, one hand on a pinrail as if she needed balance, one hand pressed over her abdomen as if protecting the unborn child. He walked to her, feeling his sword banging foolishly against his knee with every step.

There was expectation in her face mingled with resignation, and a peace Gideon envied: she had made her choices; she could live with them. He hoped he would be able to accept as well as she the consequences of his own decisions.

"It will be some hours yet," Gideon said. "We'll be defending the western approaches after all."

"Dr. Rivette has shown me my duties," she said. "It sounds grim. I hope I'll be able to . . ." She shook her head, left the thought dangling.

"You'll do well," Gideon said.

The anchors were brought from the bay bottom, and under jib and spanker only, and with the volunteer pilot calling minute corrections to the helmsman, *Malachi's Revenge* beat to the west, moving slowly to avoid running aground on shifting banks of sand and mud. Two leadsmen stood in the chains, chanting off the alarmingly shallow depths as the schooner progressed over the bay.

Offshore the two British vessels tacked, heading toward the Mississippi Sound. *Malachi's Revenge* slipped neatly through Passe Maronne into the Sound, Little Dauphin Island sliding astern, and as they reached the western point of Dauphin Island, Gideon dropped his stern anchor and used the spring to bring the schooner squarely athwart the channel, placing himself as a floating battery past which any enemy attack would have to come.

The enemy vessels were still four or five miles offshore, coming toward the land under easy sail. It occurred to Gideon that perhaps the most intelligent thing for the British to do was for the two detached vessels not to attack at all. When *Malachi's Revenge* had moved from its position near the fort, the defenders had been deprived of almost half their strength. The five vessels of the large squadron could attack the fort without fear of Gideon's interference if the other two simply *threatened* to attack through the Mississippi Sound; they would fix Gideon in place without risking his fire or chancing going aground in the narrow channel.

But that wasn't the British way: ever since Nelson succeeded with an apparently reckless attack at Trafalgar, the Royal Navy's policy was one of aggressive, often heedless onset.

God make them attack too heedlessly, Gideon thought.

As he watched the enemy, he saw flags rise on their masts, Union flags on the masthead, the White Ensign at the peak. The British would attack; probably even now the British captains were assembling their men forward of their quarterdecks, haranguing them about king and country, hearts of oak, and upstart Brother Jonathan. Gideon glanced over his men: they stood easily by their guns, their movements unhurried and exact, their heads professionally wrapped in scarves to lessen the chance of their being deafened by their own gunfire. Their voices were a low murmuring occasionally drowned out by the monotonous scrape of the schooner's grindstone putting a new edge on pikes and cutlasses. Gideon knew these men wouldn't need his speeches. They had seen British craft beaten and humiliated before, and wouldn't need to be reminded of it.

"Deck thar! Signals from th' enemy flagship! She's makin' sail!"

Gideon snatched up a glass and trained it on the enemy, but he could see from the deck only flag-becked mastheads over the silhouette of Dauphin Island, and the edges of yellowed canvas as the flagship led the other four British vessels into the main channel—timing their attack to commence just before their two comrades entered the Mississippi Sound. With Dauphin Island in the way Gideon could see nothing of Fort Bowyer except the big fifteen-striped battle flag tugging at its halliards in the freshening breeze.

Gideon turned his glass to the two vessels that would be his opponents in the coming fight, seeing colored rectangles running up their signal halliards as they replied to the flagship. The ship-sloop had shortened sail to topsails and foresail and fallen behind; evidently the captain of the sloop of war intended to let the shallower-draft schooner precede him into the Sound and run the initial risk of going aground.

He lowered his telescope. One of those vessels would be his death. He returned the telescope to the rack.

Maria-Anna stood near him by the mizzenmast, trying to stay out of the way of the privateers as they went about their unhurried tasks. Her face reflected annoyance, her fingers nervously plucked at the hem of her sleeves; she was still dressed in the fashionable, high-waisted gown she had planned to wear to the fort's picnic. Gideon touched her arm encouragingly.

"I feel so blasted useless," she said, trying to smile. "Is there anything I can do, anything at all, instead of standing about like some piece of clutter the men are too polite to heave overboard?"

"Ye can fetch some tobacco from my cabin, enough to fill my pockets."

She nodded wryly, as if she knew that even Grimes the steward had better things to do at a time like this than fetch his captain tobacco. She brought the tobacco, and as Gideon stowed it and thanked her, there were two distinct reports—gunshots, echoing over Little Dauphin Island from the fort. Gideon watched Maria-Anna turn pale, felt her hands reaching out blindly to take his hand.

"That's Blake's twenty-four pounders," Gideon said, trying to keep his tone light. "They'll be doing a lot of work today." He reached for his pocketknife and began to cut himself tobacco.

"Gideon, I want to kiss you before you start chewing

that awful stuff. And then I'll go below before your crew sees me trembling."

As her arms went around him, Gideon sensed the nearby crewmen turning away, trying absurdly to give their captain and his lady a minimum of privacy on the crowded deck. They kissed, and then their arms tightened, her cheek resting on his shoulder.

Blake's long guns cracked out again, and he felt her jump. She took a deep breath, then backed off, holding him at arm's length, her manner brisk and businesslike. He knew it was an act, one for his benefit, intended to keep him from worrying about her during the fight; and understanding this, he felt love for her rising in him.

"Keep yourself safe," she said. "I'll see you afterward."

He nodded, finding it impossible to speak. He watched her as she walked down the companionway, trying to give a brave smile as she vanished from sight. And he tried to fix the smile in his memory, knowing it would be his last sight of her.

The sound of Fort Bowyer's water battery came again, the sound rushing over the low sandy islands. Chewing his tobacco, Gideon walked the decks, nodding to the men, confirming with his own eyes that everything was in its place—the shot garlands full, the slow matches burning in their tubs, and fresh flints in the gunlocks. Two of the twelve-pounders and their tackle were shifted aft to fire directly astern. The two enemy were less than two miles off, the schooner still in the lead.

Gideon passed by Tate's long gun on its swivelling carriage and nodded to Tate, who, with his bandanna wrapped around his head and a red sash wound around his waist, looked like the pirate he had once been.

"Fire when ye're ready, Tate," Gideon said. "Don't wait for my signal."

"Aye aye, Cap'n."

Martin, Willard, and Clowes were clustered together near the wheel, conversing in low tones, each with his sword clipped to his belt. "Gentlemen," Gideon said as he approached. "Let's raise our colors."

The Stars and Stripes rose up the peak halliards and at the fore, the FREE TRADE AND SAILORS' RIGHTS

flag at the head of the mizzen; from the main flew the long
red-and-gold rattlesnake of the Markham family, the pen-
nant that had witnessed the greatest triumphs of Gideon's
family since the Revolution. Gideon wondered if today the
flag would witness a defeat, not only his own death but the
death of all his hopes, *Malachi's Revenge* a broken hulk on
a sandbar, Maria-Anna alone and with child. He prayed it
would not happen, and as his lips moved in prayer the
sound of gunfire rose from Fort Bowyer, gun after gun
roaring out, the overwhelming broadsides of the British
squadron lashing out against the earthen bulwarks of the
fort. The drumroll seemed to last forever, one gun after the
next; and then Tate's long tom spat out an iron-lunged answer, the receding shot tearing through the wind.

The enemy schooner had weathered Dauphin Island and
rounded its western tip to enter the Mississippi Sound. The
enemy had shortened sail, coming slowly toward them under square topsails alone, men in the chains casting the
lead. The westerly wind blew the smoke back into the gunners' faces, blinding them to the fall of the shot, but Tate
and his men seemed confident and cheerful; they loaded
the eighteen-pounder and fired again, then a third time.
Gideon knew the little two-masted schooner, no larger
than *General Sullivan*, was not built to take the kind of
punishment the eighteen-pound shot could give, the heavy
iron balls that could pierce the schooner through and
through. Gideon was thoroughly glad he had not num-
bered such a man as Tate among his enemies when he'd
commanded *Sullivan*.

Tate's fourth shot smashed the schooner's sprit, leaving
it dangling in a tangle of lines and stays; his fifth shot
brought the foremast down, breaking it off somewhere near
the deck, tumbling it over the schooner's larboard side in
splintering ruin. The drag of the wreckage swung the
schooner's head to larboard, and as it swung out of the
channel, Gideon could picture the frustration of its captain,
the helmsman trying futilely to check the swing, the fury of
the crew as the schooner slid onto a sandbank and stuck
fast, its starboard gunports almost under water, the guns at
a useless angle.

"Out of th' channel and out o' luck!" Gideon heard
Finch Martin shout, and the hands broke out in a frenzy of
cheering at the swift, efficient way they'd driven their first
opponent out of the fight before it had fired so much as a
single shot.

"Silence, there!" Gideon shouted. It was too early to celebrate. He had expected to drive the schooner out early,
from the first or second broadside if not from Tate's careful
sharpshooting. The sloop of war would be quite another
matter; the ship-sloop, its flags staining the sky, weathered
Dauphin Island even as the hands' cheering died away.

"Tate, bring ye that ship under fire!" Gideon shouted.
Tate nodded coolly and swung the gun on its pivot.

"Deck thar!" the lookout howled. "The fort's struck its
flag!"

Gideon, his blood sinking, ran for his telescope. It was
true. Amidst drifting clouds of gunsmoke Fort Bowyer's
flagpole stood naked, the fifteen-striped battle-flag no
longer waving above the battle. Much of the firing seemed
to have died away. With the fort unable to block the enemy's path, the British squadron of five vessels could enter
the bay unopposed and attack *Malachi's Revenge* from the
east while the ship-sloop attacked from the west. Tate's gun
barked, furious gouts of smoke shooting out into the wind.
Gideon thought furiously: he'd have to fight the sloop
quickly, drive it out of the channel or out of the fight, then
make his escape to seaward while the British were celebrating their triumph over Fort Bowyer. The tern schooner
wasn't provisioned for a journey to New England, but
could stop for supplies in New Orleans or hope to capture
provisions from a prize. . . . What could have happened
to Lawrence that he would surrender so quickly?

More gunshots came from the direction of the fort, then
a regular fusillade. Gideon strained through his telescope:
new clouds of gunsmoke were rising, but the flag was still
down. Strange, it didn't sound as if the fort had struck.
And then Gideon realized what had happened.

"The flag halliards must have been shot away!" he
shouted loudly enough for his men to hear. "The fort's
guns are still in action!" He returned the glass to the rack,

seeing the men around him grinning with relief at their not having to face the British squadron alone. Tate's gun cracked out. The ship-sloop was still about four cables distant, cautiously approaching through the channel under closely reefed topsails, its outlines obscured by the haze of Tate's gunsmoke.

"Mr. Martin!" Gideon called. The dwarfish, twisted old man came forward, his determined eyes showing the dangerous battle-light that Gideon recognized and knew so well—hadn't he felt his own light, just under a year ago, in the fight with the *Alastor*? He felt no such inspiration now, no certainty, only the complete assurance of his own death, and a stubborn determination that if he should die, it would be in victory.

"Detail a party of men to cut the stern cable on my signal," Gideon said. "Have men standing by the jib halliards and sheets and the spanker gear."

"Aye aye, Cap'n," Martin said and turned to give the necessary orders.

"I'm going to precede the ship-sloop down the Passe Maronne and engage them with our stern battery," Gideon added unnecessarily. "We can hope to drive them out of the channel."

"Aye aye, sir. Thankee, sir."

Tate's gun spat out again, and Gideon saw the dark blur of the shot outlined against the sky before it fell toward the enemy. Martin and Browne were assembling details fore and aft. Gideon spat tobacco over the lee rail and frowned. He had never told the officers his plans before; it had seemed enough that they'd obeyed orders. But Gideon had no foreknowledge, today, of when he might fall: it seemed only sensible that he give his first officer his plans. It chilled him, the thought not of death, but of his dying while the issue was still in doubt; how much better, Gideon thought, to die like his cousin Favian's particular friend Lieutenant Burrows of the *Enterprise*, knowing that the *Boxer* had struck and with his enemy's sword clutched in his hands.

The disabled enemy schooner gave three cheers as the sloop of war passed.

"Men from the larboard broadside, man the capstan!" Gideon called. "Starboard broadside, stand by yer guns!"

Tate's eighteen-pounder barked, the capstan pawls clattered, and *Malachi's Revenge* was hauled round on its spring, the entire broadside bearing on the enemy.

"Starboard guns, run out and aim! Every shot to strike home! Fire on my command!"

The deck rumbled as the starboard guns thrust from their ports, the seamen's bare feet gripping the deck as they hauled on the side tackles. Tate's long gun amidships swung minutely as Tate corrected its aim. Fists began to rise along the line of guns as captains signalled their readiness.

"Gun captains make ready to fire! Ready, men . . . *Fire!*" The eight guns of the starboard broadside, along with Tate's long tom, roared in unison, smoke and flame spitting to windward, masking the effects of the keening shot. Gideon would have preferred to let them aim and fire individually, not as a broadside. But anchored and to leeward of the enemy, the smoke from the first guns would spoil the aim of the others; a broadside would have to do.

"Stop yer vent! Worm out! Sponge out!" The cadence of the gun captains seemed subdued in the unnatural hush following the thundering broadside. Gideon raised his handkerchief to his mouth and nose, coughing in the smoke.

Gideon peered anxiously at the enemy as the ship-sloop gradually became visible through the gray pall of dissolving gunsmoke; he was somewhat relieved by a pockmarked fore-topsail and a spritsail yard that seemed to have been knocked cockabill, most of its gear trailing in the water.

"Deck thar! The enemy ship's aground!" Gideon glanced up in annoyance at the maintop, then realized that the lookout had probably been shouting about one of the ships attacking the fort.

"Masthead there! Which ship?" Gideon shouted.

"Sorry, sir! The flagship! The flagship's aground, an' the fort's shot up an attack by redcoats and sent 'em packin'!"

Gideon breathed out relief: Lawrence, Blake, and the others were doing well. He would be able to concentrate on the enemy near him.

"Run out! Take aim! Fire on my signal!"

The ship-sloop was getting close, perhaps a cable and a half. The tern schooner would have to run shortly or face being mauled by carronades.

"Stand by, heads'ls and spanker! Martin, make sure yer axemen are ready. Starboard broadside, ready! Fire!"

The guns roared inward on their tackles, and no sooner had the final twelve-pounder spat fire and thunder than Gideon was bellowing orders to get the schooner under way.

"Cut the stern cable and the spring! Set heads'ls! Set the spanker!"

The stern cable, run out through a rear port of *Malachi*'s cabin, vibrated to the bite of axes, and Gideon watched the imposing masts of the enemy ship-sloop appearing through the gunsmoke, moving stately and slowly as it groped its way through the channel, but threatening deadly retaliation from its thirty-two pound carronades. The cable parted, and the tern schooner jerked as its headsails drew its bow toward the channel leading into Mobile Bay.

"Tend the vangs and flag halliards. Ease the peak and foot inhauls and th' brails. Haul away on th' peak and foot outhauls. Belay."

At Martin's orders the spanker rumbled into life, the jutting boom swinging to larboard as the canvas caught the wind; and the sleek schooner gained way, increasing the distance between herself and the enemy. Gideon felt his blood race, felt a grim smile of triumph growing on his features. He'd escaped enemy vengeance, at least for the moment. He turned to the Spanish pilot.

"See us out through Passe Maronne. Aft twelve-pounders, fire as ye bear. Tate!"

The two short twelves shifted aft earlier in the day spat out their iron right into the enemy bows at the range of a cable, a defiant Parthian shot as the schooner slid out of enemy clutches.

"Aye, Cap'n."

"Mr. Tate, give our stern chasers yer advice. Mr. Martin, stand by the wheel. Mr. Clowes, I'll want our mains'l set as well."

The two stern chasers banged out again, urging the enemy sloop to keep its distance. There was at least a mile to the entrance of the Passe Maronne, and Gideon hoped to be there well ahead of the enemy. He knew the ship-sloop would be watching carefully as *Malachi's Revenge* threaded the channel, and he hoped not to show them the way.

"Mr. Martin."

"Aye, Cap'n." Martin's yellow, craggy teeth were bared in a vicious, triumphant grin. "We've tapped their claret, Cap'n!" he enthused. "Just like we did *Alastor*."

"Mr. Martin, we're going to precede them through the channel. We'll be showing them the way, but we can't help that."

"No, sir."

Gideon took a deep breath. "Mr. Martin, if I fall, I hope ye will do what ye think best," he said. "but it may aid ye to know my plan. It may be the enemy will run aground in the channel—if they do, we'll pound 'em to splinters from long range. If they succeed in getting into the bay, we must keep them from attacking the fort."

"Aye, sir," Martin said, his grin fading. He looked at Gideon curiously, his head cocked. Gideon had never confided in him before, and Gideon could almost follow what the old man was thinking. Martin had fought in two wars, and he'd seen the premonitions men sometimes had of their own fate: Gideon knew that Finch Martin was wondering if he, Gideon, might have had such a presentation.

"We'll have to haul our wind, Mr. Martin, and face their carronades," Gideon said. "We can't hope to beat them at close range with the guns, so we'll have to run the enemy on board and try to take 'em with pike and cutlass. It's almost certain we outnumber them considerably; we may beg the Lord for success with a reasonable chance of our prayers being granted. If we're successful, we can capture the schooner without effort."

"Aye aye, Cap'n," Martin said, still fixing Gideon with his curious, respectful gaze. "I thank ye for yer confidence."

The sound of gunfire echoed from the fort, the gunshots no longer distinct but part of long drawn-out roars, the smoking thunder of battle to which the schooner's stern chasers added distinct claps.

Malachi's Revenge slid easily through the channel, the pilot calling corrections to Martin at the wheel, and then the schooner ran free into the broad, shallow bay. Little could be seen of the fight at the fort. Above the pall of smoke surrounding the battle Gideon could see the bare masts of the British, flags flying. One of the enemy ships seemed to have gone aground right under the fort's main battery and was probably being severely handled, perhaps even raked. But Gideon could see flashes of gunfire through the smoke and knew the issue was still in doubt. The addition of a ship-sloop to the forces bombarding the fort could change the complexion of the fight entirely.

Gideon craned his neck back at the enemy, saw the ship-sloop working its way slowly through the Passe Maronne. It showed signs of the beating it had taken: pockmarked topsails, the spritsail yard now gone altogether, cordage dangling. But it was still far from beaten; if he was to help Major Lawrence at the fort, Gideon would have to make certain the ship-sloop would stay out of the fight.

"Down helm!" he shouted. "Mr. Martin, put her on the larboard tack!"

Malachi's Revenge swung nimbly into the wind, Tate running forward to his eighteen-pounder, swinging it toward the advancing enemy. It looked as if the sloop of war was going to manage the channel successfully.

"I'm going to go about, Mr. Martin, and head for her. We'll either collide or drive 'em aground. Mr. Willard, brail up the boarding nets! We're going to board if we can!"

It seemed to Gideon that quite another person was speaking, watching his orders carried out. He had known, when he spoke, what his orders meant: they would run alongside the enemy, there would be a broadside or two, cannon against deadly carronades, there would be an attempt by the privateers to board . . . Somewhere in the vicious, deadly action Gideon Markham would receive his death wound and fall either in triumph or defeat.

He was not afraid of what he knew was coming, but felt rather a regret, a sorrow that he would not be with Maria-Anna when their child was born; that he would never again hear the rush of water beneath the tern schooner's keel or hear her canvas rumble in the wind. Yet he accepted death and hoped it would do his country and his God some good; and he was thankful for the brief term of happiness he'd been granted before the end.

Tate's long gun spat iron at the enemy, and it was time to think once again of action.

"Both broadsides, doubleshot yer guns! Odd guns add grape for good measure, even guns canister! Run out when loaded." *Revenge* was headed right for the enemy's bows; he didn't know yet if they would collide, or if the enemy flinched, whether the starboard or larboard broadsides would be engaged. He'd have both ready.

"Number one guns, don't fire until ye pass the enemy's mainmast! Men detailed to the grapples, stand by for yer orders! I want all men on the unengaged side to lie down when we pass, then after we're on board, take yer boarding weapons, stand by yer officers, and wait for orders. I don't want any man jumping aboard the enemy ship without orders! Mr. Martin, port yer helm a bit. Very good."

Malachi's Revenge slid once more into the channel, Tate's gun booming a savage salute to the British flag. Gideon saw the enemy sloop of war grow larger, more threatening, as they neared. He held his breath. They would cross bowsprits at this rate unless one of them flinched; and Gideon had no intention of altering course.

The British captain blinked first. Gideon saw the ship-sloop begin a slow turn to larboard, avoiding the collision, and as he saw it, Gideon's heart leaped in warm triumph. He had them, by thunderation!

"Deck thar!" The long-forgotten voice of the lookout. "The enemy flagship's afire! She's being abandoned!"

"By the Eternal!" Gideon roared in frustration. He wouldn't have turned to engage if he'd known the enemy had lost a ship; the fort's situation was much improved, and if the main enemy fleet was defeated, then there was nothing for the ship-sloop to do but head back for the Mississippi Sound.

It was too late. To alter course now would be to run aground or to be raked by the enemy. There was no alternative but to keep on fighting, to try to carry the ship-sloop by boarding and hope to achieve success. The situation seemed to be designed for one thing only, and that was the death of Gideon Markham.

"Port yer helm, Mr. Martin. Let's crowd her."

The schooner edged nearer the sloop of war. Gideon could see Tate's long tom tracking the enemy, ready to fire on order, and the sight gave him an idea. "Mr. Tate," he called, "I'll thank ye to reserve yer fire until just before we board." He saw Tate nod.

"Larboard battery, lie down. Starboard battery, stand ready."

Seconds to go. The sloop of war was painted black, its sides striped yellow in Nelson-fashion, its bows scarred and battered by American shot. Gideon could see the British crews crouching by their guns, at last given a chance to strike back against the impudent privateers that had been battering them half the afternoon. . . . He heard the sound of cheering on the wind as the enemy anticipated victory.

"*Roar, Yankees!*" Gideon bellowed, feeling the blood rise in him, fighting anger clutching at his heart. "Let 'em hear ye shout!" The privateers began a cheer, a long, savage drone that buried the enemy cheers, and then the craft passed bulwark to bulwark and the roar of gunfire buried all shouting.

"Down helm!" Gideon barely had the time to give the final order as the guns thundered, hurling shot and grape across the decks, flame licking at enemy ports. Men were flung across the decks, lying in bright pools of blood; one of the starboard twelves was struck end-on and reared up like an enraged iron bear to topple on its screaming crew. The irregular pop of musketry added its crackle to the din, and in obedience to Gideon's last order *Malachi's Revenge* swung into the wind, losing momentum as its starboard side ground down the enemy's starboard quarter.

"Grapples away!" Finch Martin was shouting. "Grapple the sodomites!"

Gideon stood by the wheel, his breath suspended, his heart pounding. There was nothing he could do but stand and wait for his death, for the musketball to pierce him from above, the piece of wreckage falling from aloft to crush him, or the inevitable charge of grape that would fling him like a rag doll to the deck. He waited, hearing the wooden craft scream as they came together, deafened and blinded by the guns' thunder and smoke, awed by the close-range firepower of the carronades, and knowing that another few minutes of this punishment and *Revenge* would sink without ceremony. But death did not come. In sudden, stunning silence Gideon slowly realized that the sloop of war was aground, and that the tern schooner had come to a halt, *Revenge*'s starboad side against the sloop's starboard quarter, grapples holding them fast.

"Boarders, take yer weapons!" Gideon shouted, realizing that the boarding battle would have to come quickly, before the enemy's quarterdeck carronades tore the privateer to scrap. The hands leaped for the weapons tubs to seize cutlasses, or to the racks for the keen-edged pikes. Musketry crackled; Gideon felt invisible claws plucking at his coat and hat and felt anger filling him, anger for the men dead and maimed on the deck, for all those whose lives had been ruined by the mad conflict, for Maria-Anna below, in the dark, candle-lit cockpit, hearing the gunfire and feeling the collision and fearing for her husband's safety.

The armed privateers stood grouped around their officers, their faces streaked with powder and blood, and alight with feral grins. Above them tracked Tate's long gun, aimed for the enemy taffrail, its shot ready to travel the length of the enemy ship.

"Tate, do yer duty!" Gideon bawled and swept his sword out of its sheath, its diamond hilt glittering. The loud tom spoke, grape and canister blasting the ship-sloop's taffrail to fragments, sweeping the enemy poop and leaving carnage in its wake. "Boarders!" Gideon shouted. *"Boaaarders!"*

With a roar the privateers surged forward, Gideon at their head. He cleared the dangerous distance between the schooner's side and the enemy poop, saw an enemy seaman, tarred hat and ragged trousers, brandishing a cutlass; he brought his sword up to ward off the stroke. The blades grated on one another, and Gideon saw his enemy clearly, his old-fashioned pigtail and a day's growth of beard, his teeth bared. And then one of the privateers came up beneath the man's sword arm with a pike and pierced him through and through.

Gideon rushed on, leaving the man to die on the deck, hearing the privateers roaring around him. He slipped on the bloody planks and went down on one knee, seeing an enemy officer in a cocked hat lying dead on the deck, one gold epaulette on his shoulder. Tate's last shot had killed the enemy commander. Gideon rose, hearing the clash of blades around him, the British falling beneath a whirlwind of steel, and then the poop was theirs, the enemy massing in the well and on the gangways. The privateers paused to catch their breath and gather reinforcements. Gideon saw Addams crouched over a pike, Martin with a homemade weapon that looked something like a cleaver mounted on a three-foot shaft, Tate leaping from the *Revenge* after having armed himself with a pair of cutlasses. Gideon waved his sword and led them forward.

The air filled with the clash of steel, the desperate cries of the combatants, the sickening sound of cutlasses cutting open the bodies of men. Gideon led his boarders down the larboard gangway, hacking at the men who dared to bar his path, trampling on them when they were down, hearing himself shouting meaningless, inarticulate cries. The privateers, gaining strength as they were reinforced from the schooner, overwhelmed their opponents by sheer weight of numbers, pressing them back to the fo'c'sle. Gideon slashed at a man before him, saw him fall, saw the man behind him, eyes staring wide, turn to run. Gideon's sword hacked at his head and the man tumbled off the gangway. He led the rush to the fo'c'sle, a wave of maddened privateers that drove the enemy before them.

And then Gideon saw the British officer, standing less than five paces away. His cocked hat was scarred, his cheek was bloody, and he seemed very young. Yet he didn't seem afraid, and Gideon recognized an acute intelligence in his eyes as the British lieutenant raised a pistol and pointed it toward Gideon's breast.

Gideon lunged forward desperately, knowing himself too slow, too late. His mind was filled not with acceptance but with anger, with the bitter knowledge that despite his earlier resignation he did not now want to die, and would fight death with all the strength at his disposal until oblivion's greater might overwhelmed him. He lunged forward, though he knew it was hopeless, and in the lieutenant's pistol he recognized the instrument and nature of his own death. . . .

He saw the hammer fall, the priming powder spurt, and then the lieutenant let his pistol fall to the deck and raised his hands in surrender.

"Lieutenant Brooks, of His Majesty's sloop of war *Musquetobite*," he said clearly, and then Wallace Grimes reached the man and smashed him in the face with the hilt of his cutlass, dropping him to the deck.

"Let this teach you for playin' that damned scurvy trick!" Grimes bellowed, and he kicked the lieutenant viciously twice in the groin.

A misfire. Gideon saw the British seamen with upraised hands, the privateers capering in glee on the decks of the enemy ship, the White Ensign lowered from its peak to proclaim the capture. The overwhelming fact of his own deliverance swept him—the knowledge that his death had been postponed by some freak of fate, or a special dispensation of Providence. The battle was won, and he was whole.

EXCERPT FROM

THE RAIDER

If you enjoyed *The Yankee*, you'll love *The Raider*, the third volume in Dell's magnificent PRIVATEERS AND GENTLEMEN series by Jon Williams.

In *The Raider*, you'll meet Favian Markham, son of Jehu Markham of *The Privateer* and cousin to Gideon Markham of *The Yankee*. After the famous American victory of the frigate *United States* over the British frigate *Macedonian* in 1812, Favian is assigned to sail the prize and its three hundred prisoners across the Atlantic Ocean to America.

The extraordinary success of this mission, and his two later assignments as Commander of American vessels, mark Favian as a leader of distinction. But as much as his valor it is his experience with women and the death of a close friend that chronicle his growth to manhood.

The following is a brief excerpt from *The Raider*, the rousing third volume of PRIVATEERS AND GENTLEMEN.

Vixen's lieutenant had carried a challenge from every officer aboard to an equal number of Spaniards. The latter had drawn lots for the honor. Armed with pistols, the entire complement of *Vixen's* officers, minus the captain, would meet at dawn in a Spanish orange grove, to fight the first lieutenant of the Spanish frigate and five young *guardiamarinas*. There was excitement in *Vixen*'s wardroom, and considerable bustle as everyone overturned his trunks to discover black collars, blue trousers, dark cravats, and black gloves, so that no one would show white during the combat, and make targets of themselves.

The scent of oranges filled the groves, and Favian felt a strange intensity of sound and color, of feeling and sensation, perceiving as unique and extraordinary even the feel of the turf below his feet. He was not afraid until the moment when the duel's seconds, the xebec-frigate's second officer and *Vixen*'s master, began pacing over the ground, running through the checklist required by ritual and custom: no unfirm ground, the rising sun out of the participants' eyes, the pistols loaded carefully in front of all concerned . . . and then the deadly purpose of it all became clear, striking Favian cold like a handful of snow on his neck: Twelve people were meeting in an open field, following an ancient ritual designed so that neither side should have an unfair advantage as they met for the express purpose of killing one another. *Fairness!* There were no tactics; there was no skill; there was no advantage given intelligence over stupidity. Nothing that Favian had learned in his sixteen years could help him. Two lines of men would fire at one another at the drop of a handkerchief, and it would be purely the gods of chance who would determine who was hit and who was not.

And when Favian found himself opposite his opponent, the outrageous *unfairness* of it all struck him again. The *guardiamarina* was a tall, gawky creature in his midteens, with a nervous tremor in one pustuled cheek and at least the intelligence of an intelligent ox. Every midshipman's berth had a specimen of this sort: willing to learn but somehow unable, a dull-witted creature in whose mind rudiments of navigation swam helplessly in a whirlpool of insensibility, whose arms and legs thrust hairy wrists or perpetually barked shins from outgrown uniforms, a boy who found buttoning his jacket a challenge and wounded himself during sword drill, whose sole redeeming grace was the humor with which he viewed his own ineptitude.

One of these incompetent gecks was standing fifteen paces from Favian, holding a pistol, under orders to kill at the drop of a hankkerchief. Favian felt like throwing down the pistol and screaming in outrage. Why couldn't it have been swords? Favian could have carved his opponent like a slab of mutton. *This lowbrow moron could kill him! Kill him by accident!* And duelling was supposed to be *fair!* That was the ostensible purpose of all the pacing, all the ritual, all the bickering about the position of the sun.

Anything that gave an ox an equal chance with a human being was not in the least fair, Favian's vigorous but unvoiced opinion . . . meanwhile he took his position, and tried to assume the stance of the duellist: right side toward the enemy to narrow the target, left arm dangling behind the body where it couldn't be hit, left leg shadowed by the right. The right arm was bent at a peculiarly uncomfortable angle, bent to shield the body from a shot, a pose which brought the pistol almost to Favian's eye. The scent of the orange grove threatened to smother him. Spaniards were singing somewhere in the distance. He was going to get killed without ever seeing the war he had come to fight.

"Gardez-vous!" The Spanish second lieutenant was calling out the traditional commands in French, the international language. It was all worse than absurd. The Spanish singing was suddenly cut short, as if a band of workers had suddenly seen the peculiar apparition in their orchard, men in neat uniforms preparing to murder one another.

Vixen's sailing master raised the handkerchief. Favian tried to line the neckless figure of his opponent over the unsighted barrel of the pistol. It was absurdly heavy; it seemed to require all of Favian's strength to keep it raised. Favian ran through the checklist in his mind. Elbow cocked. Left arm out of the way. Stomach sucked in to narrow the profile. What had he forgotten?

The handkerchief fell, and the orange grove rang with gunfire. . . .